Brotherly Shackles

To Jennifer, Tracy, Jason

BROTHERLY SHACKLES

Remi Shitu

Illuminating the
Literary World

LUMINAIRE

First Published in Great Britain by Luminaire Publishing in 2012.

This paperback edition published in 2012

by Luminaire Publishing Ltd,

Ground Floor, 2 Woodberry Grove,

North Finchley,

London N12 0DR.

www.luminairepublishing.com

A CIP catalogue record for this book is available from the British Library

ISBN 978-0-9571140-1-2

CONTENTS

Period One

CHAPTER 1

The Standards

Carlos Retfil raised his chin to the rear-view mirror and watched his passengers as they dismounted. Next, he lowered it down enough for the eyes to meet the face of the watch he had on his right wrist. The instrument confirmed he was still on time. "But these two idiots again," he swore silently, "won't they make me loose the time?"

Johnson aided Tonga up the seat and passed over to him the crutch, for the duo to start getting off the bus. As they struggled on, Carlos watched again and silently prayed they would allow him to complete the mission of the day on time. He was hopeful, and determined. He wished something pushed the brothers out of his bus.

"Johnson, do you require some help to get Tonga down?" he asked at last, walking along the aisle to the two brothers.

"Help? What help?" Johnson snarled back scornfully. "No thanks. We can manage."

"Okay then, if you can," responded Carlos, forcing himself to stop and withdraw the hand he already stretched out unwillingly.

With the bus empty, he was on the last lap for the day. His concerns over the time he already lost fired him up enough to keep the acceleration pedal in eccentric depressions. In fifteen minutes, he assured himself to have parked outside Ral Ralgrub's house; in twenty, he would have taken his seat inside Ral's; in another twenty, he would have totally won him over. Oh God, the burning anxiety, the short but long road!

"It's wrong. Very wrong," Ral snapped at him, Carlos, an unappreciated persuader. "Not only that, I have put myself into his position and thought it all over."

Ral had, severally, from when he embarked on the pressure on Ral. If Ral were Chief Daniels he won't take it kindly. How could he? Having worked hard to develop a business in a far-away place, shared the profit with the locals, had the locals developed into partaking in the running of the business, and for the locals to turn on him and demand he, Ral, handed over the business? Sure, that would only happen over his dead body.

"No we can't do that to Chief Daniels. Chief Daniels is a
…"

"Shish-sh," he quickly interrupted his host. "Don't mention any name; we know who we are talking about. You know, the walls may be blind but they have ears."

"But Chief is a nice man," Ral resisted the attempted gag. "And the two of us should be the first to accept that. It won't be a crime to, would it?" Ral added with an upward adjustment of his voice.

He was determined not to allow any argument to develop; it could again eclipse the idea he must sell to Ral. The warning in Ral's ascended voice of loyalty was clear enough for him to recognise.

"Of course it won't be a crime," he quickly agreed. "It is the havoc which the unseen, faceless human transmitters behind the wall could cause that we have to guide against. We both know Chief is a man everybody wants to please.

"Basically, our chief is a simple man; and where we all are united, this proposition is a simple one. Quite simple - like ABC."

He remembered how he could not differentiate between the cool anger and the amusement on Ral's face. Simple as ABC? 'Since when has a task become as simple as ABC to you?' he remembered Ral asking him rudely and arrogantly. Ral was still dwelling in the past, measuring him up with when he was a slower-than-others learner during their joint primary school days; and later when it took him more driving lessons from Ral before he was able to move about the buses.

"Listen to me again Carlos," emphasised Ral, "any sort of unity, proposition or whatever – ought to be about cooperating with Chief Daniels. Have you thought of what our lives would have been without him? The trust he had and has in us; the employment he offered; the buses he loaned us; and now, the kind gesture he has just extended to three more of our local men. Well?

"How should we ever forget we owe him our lives in more than one way? How would I have overcome the problem of maiming Tonga and killing his father in the accident? One should have conscience, Carlos."

Ral rapped on while Carlos watched him with caution, realising that more-than-anticipated job of convincing needed to be done on Ral. Carlos realised counter-rapping must be the least option – the last time it ended in the two of them abandoning the same topic in rage. He must, this time, recognise the limit of Ral's thinking faculty: that of one incapable of bending a straight mould, straightening a bent one, or of getting off a stool he was made to sit on. But despite all these limitations, he fully recognised Ral's leadership role was required for Chief Daniels to favourably consider any suggestion from them, the local bus owners. Smartly, he descended to Ral's level.

"When are you going to understand me?" he pleaded. "When? What I am putting across is love and respect for Chief

3

Daniels and his ideas. Don't you agree he deserves them? I swear he does."

Good mix indeed. One that bamboozled Ral on whether Ral heard his friend right or his friend was simply out of his mind. He had successfully, the suddenness notwithstanding, turned pro-Daniels and implied that Ral of all people didn't want to respect Chief Daniels!

"Hahaha! You are funny today Carlos. Love and respect for Chief Daniels? They are two things you never have."

"That is not so. After you, it's him I most respect – both of you before my family. The chief wouldn't have known me without you; and I wouldn't be in this business without him. This is why my recognition and respect. The proposal I have is how to show him our appreciation and make him feel proud of us."

"And how are you going to achieve those?"

"We, behind your leadership, Ral. By openly enforcing his teachings and rules of business on all of us for him to see, and displaying to our people the type of kindness he displays from time to time to them. In this way he would trust us if we should ask for more sponsorship, or should ask him to leave to us the menial management of passenger transportation and take over the bigger job of giving all of us the technical support."

"Supposing he agrees, would his usual business sense not compel him to pass the care of Tonga over to me? Have you considered that too?"

"No, he won't do that because that's long solved. Didn't he pledge before you and me that because it's his bus you were driving when the accident occurred, that he would take care of Tonga's health forever? Did he not repeat the pledge before Tonga's family? It's two years since then, and no one has got a ground to complain.

"Or, why don't we even take it over from him? He would be more pleased – because it's the type of things he loves and teaches…!"

It all contrasted crystal-clearly in Carlos Retfil's mind and he felt pleased with himself, with the high extraordinariness of his own achievements. It's six years ago since he finally had his, his way, with Ral Ralgrub, and used the triumph therefrom to overpower Chief Daniel Daniels. That particular day of overpowering, only someone adjudged starkly insane would have predicted the kind of today's meeting with Chief Daniels, for which he, Carlos, was about to depart.

* * *

At six feet and one inch, with a round and smooth face accommodating a small mouth, Chief Daniel Daniels clearly passed for a very handsome man. Some called him Danny, short for Daniel; others called him Chief. Personally, he felt on top of the world whenever he was called the latter. It was all he needed to remind himself he had actually arrived, and that he was above his colleagues as well as above the majority of his fellow countrymen.

Daniel was extremely popular and well respected not only in his own town, Togana, but also in far away Regin City and nearer towns like New Angel and Lal Town. He was never short of perfectly acted, broad smiles and hand-wave acknowledgements that were more physical than would have normally been required for the occasion. With these, he encouraged the people to hail him more by the name of 'chief', so that they would not have the chance of substituting his preferred popularity with undue familiarity. The name 'Danny' he therefore, preferably, reserved for the members of his social and business caucus.

"Thank you, folks," he would croak as he lifted off-ground his ever shinning walking stick. At other times, he would say 'yea', or 'God bless', depending on how he felt. With the support of the left hand however, he always maintained that his long black pipe did not drop off his mouth, not even for once, whenever acknowledging the cheers.

It was exactly half past nine in the morning when Daniel's car pulled up in front of Majesty Hotel in the Satellite Acres area of New Angel. Though the meeting was to start by ten, he characteristically arrived thirty minutes earlier, as he used to do with all his meetings and appointments.

Time was a true master of Daniel Daniels. He worshipped it the way the ancient Egyptians worshipped *Ra* and spent it the way *Shylock* spent money. "Man is created to spend his life over a definite period of time," he would say on different occasions, "and the wealth which man is destined to acquire in his life-time is spread over this period – in hours, minutes and seconds," he would add. "You waste a minute of it, you waste a minute of your wealth; you waste an hour of it, you waste an hour of your wealth; you waste a day of it, it's a day's worth of your wealth that you have wasted," he would conclude. He thoroughly loathed latecomers and time-wasters, and would use anything, including serious jokes, to inquire why, if any of his staff did not wear his watch.

Smartie, the driver, had hardly lifted his foot off the brakes at the hotel portico when he dashed out, turned round, and pulled the rear door open to allow his boss out of the car. This was one of his duties at which he would beat any waiter or similar staff whenever on an outing with his boss.

True to name, he, Smartie, was always smart – just like the boss he chauffeured about. Whenever on duty, he was in his boss-provided white poplin suit. Because of the delicacy of both the colour and the weave, provision was made for four sets per year. In return, the generosity in the provision always emboldened Daniel to query Smartie any day the neatness fell short of his expectation. "Wear something neater tomorrow," or "go home and wear something neater," Daniel would order, depending on how serious he viewed the untidiness that time.

The make-up made Smartie's uniform unique. Starting with the trousers, on each of the two outside legs was a green, two-inch wide trimming, running from the lower end of the waist-band and all through down to the ankle width, thereby covering up the central seam all along. In the middle of the trimming was a shinning yellow cord of less than half an inch diameter, and secured by tacking-on. The same green, but this time without the yellow cord, went along the side seams of the jacket, on the collar edge, on the four front pockets as laps, and on the cuff edges.

Most conspicuous on the jacket was the pair of shoulders. Each carried a thick white flap, about two inches wide, and as long as the entire shoulder seam. Each flap wore three bands of green cords, and was sewn down at the arm side and buttoned down on the neck. And though each band represented a year of Smartie's service under Chief Daniels, the chief had always insisted each represented a promotion.

The same jacket carried four golden yellow, mushroom-shaped shank buttons on the front, and two on the shoulders. One might be excused to assume that by the time Smartie, going by the speed at which he got the so-called promotion, had been in Daniel's service for a decade, there would have been a need to sew on much longer shoulder flaps, or use narrower bands of green cords. For now, Smartie and his uniform still had a clear seven years to reach that point.

The cap was of green velour fabric on the top and the side round, while the peak is black trimmed with a golden yellow leaf ornament.

Lightweight white was the inner shirt; and when completed with green tie, Smartie perfectly commandeered the appearance of an actively serving, senior naval officer.

Chief Daniels walked through the corridors and made necessary turns towards the room reserved for the meeting, bypassing those who actually knew who he was, and those who felt strongly that they knew him but were not sure of where they did. While the former hailed "chi-ef," "shi-ef", the latter pondered as if trying to recollect the face of a television newscaster met outside the studio just after being seen casting the news.

Johnson and his mother were among those then at the hotel, who knew and could not forget him. They just supplied some quantity of goat meat from their farm to the hotel when Daniel arrived. "Oh, Chief Daniels," Lais remarked as he alighted, calling the attention of Johnson.

"Chief Daniels?" Johnson asked, "what about Chief Daniels?" he added courtly.

"Over there, just coming out of his car. Do we walk over and say hello to him."

Johnson could not believe his mum. He expected her to know what his answer would be. "To walk across and say hello to him?" he asked. "Oh mum, you mean we walk across and say hell and not hello to him?"

"Come on, dear, Chief Daniels is a good man – whatever has happened between us. He's never like the rest of them."

"Mum, go and shake hands with Daniel if you want to. After all, you are a true wife of your husband – just as dad would pray for him and his fellow transporters every Sabbath before they snatched him away from us."

"Your dad prayed always for everybody."

"But did he not specially bless him and his gang of transporters, including Ral Ralgrub?"

"He blessed everybody – inside and outside his congregation. That's his job, as a good pastor."

"But they did not recognise him as such – as a good pastor who didn't deserve to be killed, and whose son didn't deserve to be crippled. And I know too, that you don't deserve to be widowed and I, to be made semi-orphaned."

"But dear, that's an accident."

"Mum, you know you are in the minority. The majority, old and young, still know it's not. Why should it all happen immediately after he preached against them, against their ungodliness?"

"You also have to remember that the bus involved was Ral Ralgrub's, and not Daniel's."

"But Daniel gave it to him in the first place, didn't he? Why did he do it if he couldn't control it? Why did he aid him to escape the right justice? He should have known they are vengeful bastards."

"Look, Johnson, that is alright," called a shocked Lais. "You are a young lay preacher now and should strive to be like your dad, making him proud of you even in his grave. Remember how he would read Mark eleven, verses twenty-five and twenty-six, from time to time to preach forgiveness."

"Yes, mum – preached forgiveness, until forgiveness killed him, until forgiveness leaves us in this misery. They all deserve to be thra..."

"Sh sh, Johnson," she made a loud whisper and stretched her hand out in a flash to cover her son's mouth. She never dreamt her son still nursed such a scale of animosity. Luckily, Chief Daniels walked past without seeing them, and with Lais too embarrassed by her son to greet Chief Daniels.

At the door to the room of the meeting, Smartie briskly overtook his boss and pulled one half of the door open for him to enter. Chief Daniels entered with a bit of difficulty.

* * *

The convener, Chief Daniels, ensured the meeting was not a round-table one, which he believed was meant for people of equal or near-equal status. His arrangement was u-shaped, to satisfy his belief on how the superior should meet with the inferiors. With the parallel rows arranged to the right and left on entering, the biggest chair showed distinctly at the extreme middle. It was on top of the table to this chair that Smartie put his briefcase and then returned to the car.

"Of course, they knew they had to be here," he muttered as he drew out the big chair he was sure was meant for him. He stared at the pendulum clock hung on the wall between two other framed pictures directly opposite where he was; it was going a quarter to ten. "What could have been holding them? Another gang-up or conspiracy?"

Chief Daniels used the idleness forced on him to gaze at the numerous pictures on the walls. This, he followed up with short paces before he finally returned to the big chair. He leaned his walking stick against the left side of the chair and sat down. Then, he noticed the time was a couple of minutes to ten. "How could they, despite all these lessons, still be this irresponsible?" he asked himself in anger. "Is it a case of 'when the pupil hasn't learnt well, the teacher hasn't taught well'? No, the pupil could be downright stupid," he consoled himself. "And the good teacher only needs to put more efforts at the lessons." He would use the meeting as an opportunity for him to do so. He dipped his right hand inside the left inner pocket of the jacket, took out a tin of tobacco. He was ready for the replenishment of the depleted stock of the pipe's content when Ral, the first of the local transporters to arrive, like a policeman looking out to nick a pickpocket, entered.

"Chief Daniels, good morning, sir," beamed Ral as he rushed to the man he idolised as a superior chief. "Good morning, sir," he repeated with a broader smile and arms fully stretched out in an anticipation of obtaining Daniel's customary warm embrace.

"Good morning Ral. And how are you?" replied Daniel, stretching his hand out for a handshake without lifting himself up.

"How was your journey, sir?"

"Fine. Quite fine, up to the Majesty Hotel when it hit a standstill."

Ral looked round and felt something. "Others are not here?"

"Are you making a statement or really asking me a question?" Daniel asked with a frown of disgust.

"But I think they would have arrived."

"Oh, so you think? Just the way I expected you all to have kept a reasonable time and be here punctually."

Ral got jolted; he turned to take the reading on the wall clock. Twenty minutes past ten o'clock.

The others by coincidence arrived at the portico at ten-thirty and engaged themselves in exchanging unnecessary pleasantries and irrelevances. Among the hilarities being shared was one from Joseph Tolp who, on seeing Smartie, had told his colleagues that money had already dragged out Chief Daniels to the Majesty Hotel.

"Or it could be time that has," derided another transporter. "You know all those bogus appointments he claims he has with the whole world."

"Yes," said Joseph, "money and time are the two masters he serves; and so, how will they not kill him one day?"

"They will, they will…" all roared into laughter as Joseph asked the others to wait for him while he used the reception toilet. Thereafter, at exactly twenty minutes before eleven, he led the file into the room of the meeting, carrying the mouth and tongue riot with them.

"Our chief, welcome, sir," weirdly led Joseph who, like Ral, ran forward to Daniel for an embrace, which Daniel promptly refused him. In the pandemonium that followed, Daniel could neither hear distinctly nor respond adequately to each of the greetings. One customer of the Majesty Hotel, on sensing the scene, alerted a waiter nearby of a fight probably going on at the meeting room. The waiter, in turn, called a security officer to accompany him to the room where, upon opening the door, the claim was instantly dispelled as witnessed by the hysterical smiles on all the faces inside.

"It's eleven now; and won't be right for me to join you to further waste the precious time. So, we take up the first topic I have here," Chief Daniels was rounding up the opening part of his introductory address. At its start, he had expressed his disappointment at their habitual late coming each time he summoned them to a meeting, despite the advantage they had in

11

living nearer to the venue of such meeting which was usually inside NA, New Angel. He wondered if they had passed the bad habit to their bus drivers and conductors. If they had, it would breed a feeling of dissatisfaction among their passengers.

He asked if they knew that every minute released by nature was not for a particular person, but for all the living things of the universe at the same time. If they didn't know, he emphasised, men, forest animals, insects, birds, plants seen or unseen, heard of or unheard of, were among such living things. It therefore became necessary for the wise among the lot to struggle and partake in the share of the single minute. It was only the fool that had excuses for not struggling to take a part of it, though to the advantage of the wise.

"Gentlemen," Chief Daniels continued, "to go straight to the point, I feel bad and disappointed that in the past six months, you were not regular with the repayments of the money you borrowed for the coaches spare parts. This was in spite of the monthly emissaries I sent to you to collect them in the main, or, to remind you in the least.

"Or, to be fair and precise, only two of you are somewhat up-to-date; meaning that others are either 'middle-to-date' or completely 'down-to-date.' For the benefit of doubt, I will read out to you, how every person's account stands as at today."

He opened the appropriate page of the file he earlier transferred out of his brown suitcase onto the table. Then, he noticed a raised hand. "Tolp, do you want to say something?" he inquired.

"Yes sir. It's about the reading out of what we owe. In my own humble opinion, it is unnecessary since none of us is claiming he is not in arrears."

There was a murmur coming from the opposite side of Joseph Tolp who was sitting to the right of Chief Daniels. Daniel acknowledged the mutterer.

"Mr Duarf, it seems you are saying something."

"I just want to correct the last speaker," said Duarf, "and to let him and this sitting know that I, Chief Olu Duarf, am not in arrears in my payment; and that of course, there is equally someone else here who is not in arrears, meaning that two of us are in the clear."

Carlos Retfil did not feel the urge to stand up and recognise himself as that second borrower in the clear. He never was a great talker, but a very attentive listener. An outwardly shy man, he would avoid a crowd as much as possible. Nonetheless, the more he tried to hide himself, the more he's found out and talked about. To the people of NA, he had developed into a 'behind-the-scene' man capable of attaining any height of benevolence as well as any height of sadism. At the transporters' or other meetings that are important to him, he would wear a black or dark grey, well cut suit, which he would match up fibre by fibre from his head to his toes. His quietness notwithstanding, he could be easily recognised – as the only man who would rest his chin on his left palm and appear dozing. Nowadays, he usually spoke last, quietly, firmly and convincingly. His colleagues therefore believed he would talk at a point best for him, be it the end of Daniel's speech, or the closing part of the meeting. For then, he dozed on – seemingly.

"That is why, why I am reading out the list to you all. First, it will remove the doubt any of you might have; and the question of 'is it me?' or 'is it him?' would be out of it. Secondly, each man will know by how much he is in arrears, and how much he owes. Thirdly, those who have done well in their repayments and could qualify for further assistance will also know themselves, and be known.

"And as for you Mr Duarf, I believe your claim is not correct; but we wait till I get to your account."

He removed the sheet from inside the file, closed the file itself, and with the left fingers held the sheet down on top of the closed file. Next, he adjusted himself on the chair, ready to start reading, while the other participants looked on attentively like

13

students listening to the principal for the result of a final examination.

"Mathew Rebbor!"

"Yes sir," Rebbor replied, rising up at the same time.

"Remain seated," Daniel urged him, and then turned to all the others at the meeting. "Everyone, just listen. But where you don't agree with the account, you are at liberty to object before I proceed any further. Clear?

"Mathew Rebbor. Paid: eight thousand and eight hundred; owing to date: two thousand and two hundred; total balance to pay: four thousand and four hundred only. Do you agree?" he turned to Rebbor.

"Yes sir, I will balance up soonest."

"Joseph Tolp. Paid: five thousand and five hundred; owing to date: five thousand and five hundred; total balance to pay: seven thousand and seven hundred only."

"Ike Elfans. Paid: like Joseph, five thousand and five hundred; owing to date: five thousand and five hundred; total balance to pay: seven thousand and seven hundred only."

Daniel paused and traced the list further down with his eyes and fingers, and then continued with the announcement.

"Isa Reduaram. Same category as Joseph and Ike, do you agree?"

"Correct sir, we agree," Joseph Tolp shouted back the reply.

"But Joseph, look," cut in Isa furiously, "always speak for yourself. Since when have you added 'Reduaram' to your name?"

"But our names were read out together."

More anger instantly put Isa on his feet. "If that is your reason, did we take the same spare parts? Are we paying from the same purse? And why had Elfans not risen to speak for the three of us?" He was going angrier particularly because he viewed Joseph Tolp as being intentionally and arrogantly unreasonable. Soon, the argument took the dimension of one normally seen between a learned prosecutor and a learned defender in a case each man wanted to win. Isa Reduaram pointed it out to his fellow participants, how, at the meeting held a few months ago, the same Joseph selfishly defended only himself out of the accusation of poor vehicle maintenance culture which Chief Daniels levelled against him, Rebbor and Tolp. He accused Joseph Tolp of trying to be a 'star transporter' before Chief Daniels.

"That's your headache," Joseph told him unapologetically. "You were alive and physically present at that meeting with your ears functioning but your mouth shut instead of it being opened to convince Chief Daniels you were a 'moon transporter'," he further insulted Reduaram.

Within minutes, the pure business discussion developed into personal accusations and abuses, which then metamorphosed into political brick-brats where other participants started to take sides. Chief Daniels, a veteran of boardroom and business meetings of many years, quickly sensed how this chapter of, if not the entire meeting, could end; and moved to gain control.

"Aaal-right gentlemen. All right!" Chief Daniels yelled out. Now, he was on his feet for the first time since the meeting began. With a repeat command he knocked the table with the smoke pipe like an auctioneer would his table with a hammer. "Quiet, I say!" he yelled severally.

At once, though slowly, this mixture of force and dominance of Daniel's started to work. The fury in those already fistfully on their feet started to take a dive, while those of them on their seats rose as a mark of respect to Daniel.

"Gentlemen," Daniel went on, "I am disappointed for the second time in this meeting. You have allowed a simple discussion to turn into personal quarrels. For the second time today, some of you have disregarded the standing rules and regulations, or have forgotten they are still in existence. You all may take your seats."

Slowly, each participant started to sink.

15

"And, there's a word for Joseph Tolp," he continued. "It's a final warning from me as the first ever, and the day's chairman of the transporters' meeting. He must henceforth stop his habit of claiming to lead and speak for others. You all remember he got the first warning at the first meeting he ever attended with us. We shall have it down that next time he makes a false leadership claim, he stands expelled from the association.

"From now on, we shall apply the full force of our rules and regulations. As mature men, I expect you, whenever there are disagreements – and there will always be – to express yourselves without anger or noise. A statement tinted with anger and noise is easily infected by errors. Besides, no person who is free in his thoughts likes to welcome it.

"Let us now have our tea break; we continue after the break."

The post-tea time session commenced with Daniel's full explanation of how the account of each borrower was basically made up. The total of 90,000 he handed over to them at 10,000 each was not his money; he was only the kind guarantor.

The lender, he claimed, charged an interest of thirty-two percent bringing each man's debt to 13,200, and wanted each man to pay up in six months at 2,200 per month; but that he, Chief Daniels, pleaded with him to agree to twelve monthly instalments of 1,100 each. He told them the lender agreed, but not until after he had pledged a bus as a guarantee from each of them.

He further reminded them how they had voluntarily consented in the signed, sealed and witnessed agreement that one bus automatically stood forfeited after a four months default, and two after eight. Unfortunately, his argument based on 'first time borrower' to persuade the creditor to be flexible, failed.

He said the previous month was allowed for a last adjustment for any of them whose repayment was still in arrears. He hoped he had made himself clear enough for their understanding; in which case if he had, he did not expect any more of the kind of verbal turmoil that ended the first session.

* * *

The second session was in progress by twelve-thirty. That was after the last twenty minutes or thereabout had been spent on tea, coffee, soft drinks, toilets, short walks within, and of course, some private group comments on what went on at the last session. Evidently, the short break managed to restore peace among the transporters, albeit grudgingly. Chief Daniels, feeling happy for the peace, returned to complete the reading out of the list:

"Papah Feiht. Paid: eight thousand and eight hundred; owing to date: two thousand and two hundred; total balance to pay: four thousand and four hundred only.

"Linus Isho. Paid: nine thousand and nine hundred; owing to date: one thousand and one hundred; total balance to pay: three thousand and three hundred only.

"Olu Duarf. Like Isho, paid: nine thousand and nine hundred; owing to date: one thousand and one hundred; total balance to pay: three thousand and three hundred only."

Even though both Isho and Duarf owed and paid equally, Daniel would no more create a loophole for feuds; he read out fully and separately, the lines of their accounts.

"Ral Ralgrub. Paid: eleven thousand; owing to date: nil; total balance to pay: three thousand and three hundred only.

"Last on the list is Mr Carlos Retfil. Paid: eleven thousand; owing to date: nil; balance to pay: two thousand and two hundred only.

"You should note that only the duo of Ralgrub and Retfil are up-to-date in their payments. I am pleased to inform them that because of how healthy their accounts stand presently, if they so wish, they are allowed to take more loans to further improve their services to their people."

17

Up to this point, Chief Daniels was pleased with himself. To him, the only minus so far was the late start to the meeting, which was pleasingly dwarfed by his personal pluses. He was pleased with himself that he whipped through his control of the meeting, and he got away with a pack of lies. Specifically, he saluted his own brilliance and shrewdness for charging a high interest rate and securing a double guarantee for his money.

Having showered some praises on Ral Ralgrub and Carlos Retfil, he thought of extracting more promises of prompt payment from the defaulters. "With all we have discussed so far, I take it as a promise that any person in arrears will balance-up this month-end," he put it to them, expecting a collective yes as an answer.

There's a moment of silence. Joseph Tolp who signified an intention to talk broke it. Daniel nodded him on – again.

"Chairman, sir," he started, standing. For the first time within the premises of the Majesty Hotel, Joseph Tolp displayed the comportment of a man who had just finished a situation-imposed thinking exercise. "I personally will like to thank you for the loan. Everybody here will recollect that I was the first to pick up and return a fully completed loan form as soon as the package was introduced. I intended to be the first to return the loan too. But now, here I am before you, a sad man; not because of the quarrel I had with my good friend Reduaram – that was nothing, long gone and forgotten – but because I am behind in the re-payment. I believe that man, being no more than a mere proposer, can only plan; he cannot be wiser than God who is the real disposer.

"It was as if the problems were waiting for me to take the money. As soon as I took it, my family members started to pass the baton of illness from one member to the other, without stop. And truly, when it comes to the number in the membership, I am not proud of it, mine is on the high side." Others laughed instead of pitying him.

"The second problem has to do with the drivers of other zones coming to pick-up passengers from ours. They are daily increasing in number, and they deprive us of our own home passengers.

"Therefore, sir, I will like to seek a further assistance from you and the creditor. Please, give me up to the end of the second month-end from now to pay up whatever might be due, without losing any of my buses."

Isa Reduaram classed the effort of Joseph as courageous and brave; and the boldness he derived from it suddenly brought out of him, his natural self. He wanted to talk next.

Anywhere Isa was, he was always curious – he easily grew impatient. He remained upright and stiff on the chair until towards the end of Joseph's speech when he started to tap the front parts of his soles on the floor, and at the same time, both palms on the table. As soon as he gauged Joseph was at the end of his speech and was sitting, the swiftness with which he sprang up, coupled with a hand he already raised, gave Daniel no chance of calling any other person but him to talk.

"Please sir, our chairman," Isa commenced talking, "allow me to make these few comments, still on some of the problems we experience as causing delays to the repayments.

"First, I want to add to Mr Tolp's, about not getting enough passengers. I noticed many still shun the advantages offered by our modern and comfortable buses and go on bicycles and animals. The question is: How do we convince them? The effect of the boycott is serious on my takings and repayments.

"The next problem could be attributed to luck. Last month, one of my buses lost four days to a breakdown. Another lost six, and yet, another, eight. All to breakdowns! Returns lost to those days certainly affected my repayments.

"Thirdly is the aspect of the actual performance of the spare parts for which payment we are now being threatened. The more I change them, the less the effects are on the buses. Chief Retfil, I am happy you are here now, and can witness how I once reported the matter to you – that I strongly doubt the quality of these spare parts and that…"

"No, no, no, don't say that Chief Reduaram," Carlos Retfil forcefully interrupted him. "You told me; and I told you that it was impossible that the parts supplied to you would be different from those supplied to the rest of us. I told you too, not only to ensure they were well fixed, but also to see that they were actually fixed. Didn't I?" Carlos wasn't sleeping after all. If he was, he had been woken up by the mention of his name and the resolve to act and save all the defaulters from the likely ugly actions Chief Daniels would have wanted to take as a counter to the unprofessional excuses of Joseph Tolp and the outright silly talks of Isa Reduaram.

"If we are to go by personal problems," Carlos went on, "we will not pay up, because every man has his own. Why hasn't anyone seen the rough state of our roads as a big problem? No other zone in the area has it worse. I have followed the drivers and seen them; and believe me, I can recall hearing the jingling of loose parts, as if they were of a tambourine in use, at some points on the road. Why hasn't anyone begged the chairman to tell us what we could do, especially in the area of training of our maintenance staff?

"Another problem is about taxes. Why has everybody here forgotten the multiple, crippling taxes we pay? Now, there's a new one called Route Identification Tax. Already there is Identification Tax One paid to paint-on a logo or a symbol, and Identification Tax Two to put a name, phrase or motto. Who knows, we could wake up tomorrow to find Identification Tax Three to be paid before hanging the normal number plates! Sir, we shall appreciate the chairman's advice on these killer taxes.

"The last is the weather; I mean the heavy rains of the immediate past months. It had contributed in no small way to low passenger turnout, and caused some late re-payments. But now, the sky is clear, and nobody should have excuses.

"I thank you sir, for allowing my small contribution."

The next minutes of the meeting were complimentary to the immediate last. Another non-defaulting debtor, Ral Ralgrub, took them up. He signified his intention to speak by raising his left hand while at the same time resting its elbow on the table before him. Chief Daniels first hesitated to call him among the three others who raised their arms about the same time. He was being careful not to allow those who were against his policy to hijack the meeting once more, and end it in his personal failure. Daniel looked through the faces as well as the hands of the three, and then x-rayed their minds. The next speaker had to be the only one of them not – and never was – defaulting, Ral Ralgrub. Non-defaulting Carlos Retfil who just spoke against the rebels did so only by luck. And he, Daniel, would be lacking in brains not to uphold and build on the lucky strike. Stamping a diplomatic gag on the silly debtors among them must be his immediate solution.

"Yes, R-ralgrub, let's hear you."

"Thank you sir," Ralgrub began as he was rising up from his chair. "Mine will be brief because time is flying.

"Today's meeting brings me the memory and teaching of *A.F.*, the late principal of my secondary school. May his kind soul rest in peace.

"More than other things, he would stress the goodness in the value of morals to the students at the 'morning assembly' that used to start each school day. He would start by defining the words 'morals' and 'gratitude', to the hearing of the students within the assembly hall's four geographical cardinal points, and end up with the same question: 'When the receiver of a favour says a prompt 'thank you' to the donor, what does he, the receiver, get in return from the donor?'

"At first, that was before we knew and got used to his better answer, we would answer a mixture of 'you are welcome!' and 'with pleasure!' He would then look across our faces with all the possible seriousness he could assemble in his large eyeballs and say 'no, no, no, the answer ai-i-i-s `another fa-ai-vor`…what is it?'

21

'Another fa-ai-vor!' 'And again?' 'Another fa-ai-i-vor.' 'And for the last time?' 'Another-rr fa-ai-ee-vor!' And because a last time never arrived, the students nicknamed him A.F., meaning 'Another Favour', a name he not only carried to his grave, but one that also outlived him by appearing in every yearly obituary done for him since his death."

There was a roaring applause.

"Therefore sir," Ralgrub continued, "I am expressing my very appreciation for this loan and other benefits before it. A few years ago, I was only one of your obedient servants, an ordinary driver in one of your passenger buses. But now, thanks to God and to you that I now have my own four buses, and will soon forfeit the loan on the spare parts. My appeal to you is that as soon as it is fully forfeited, you will surely find at your door, an *Oliver Twist* who you should please not turn back, because his real name would be Ral Ralgrub." He ended his speech with a broad smile that was subconsciously commandeered by the faces of other participants, Chief Daniels' including.

An announcement by Daniel of a one-hour lunch break followed Ralgrub's speech even though Daniel knew clearly Ralgrub was not asking for more food but for more money. Expectedly, the announcement was greeted with hilarious applause.

Observing break times – with tea, lunch and dinner he would personally fund at any of the meetings he summoned – was one thing Chief Daniels always enforced. A seminar he attended as a young chief executive of his last organization convinced him that the advantages derived from such a break outweighed its monetary cost. It proved itself during the last tea break, and would prove itself again during this lunch break. Turning the participants into his personal guests, and having them fully lunched at his expense ensured that one, invitees loved to attend his meetings. Two, while there, they were never in a hurry to leave, but to reach that special item as early as possible. And three, on any day of a meeting with Daniel, their wives spent less time inside their respective kitchens.

Twenty minutes into the break time, Chief Daniels stood up to go somewhere. He took excuses from those nearest to him and disappeared with his file, creating a further opportunity for absolute freedom among the local transport chiefs.

Away from the main reception desk, the Kings Restaurant of Majesty Hotel was about twenty yards to the left, the meeting room being to the right. Though the corridor prevented it from being seen from the reception desk, but a white-painted *lolly* with a red inscription of its name and arrow, and standing in front of the reception, did all the directional jobs. Chief Daniels obeyed its command and landed in the restaurant.

* * *

John Martins was already in the Kings Restaurant awaiting the arrival of Chief Daniels. He was Chief Daniels personal assistant for half a decade. Inside John Martins, his own loyalty to his boss seriously competed with his enviable professional efficiency. He prepared Chief Daniels for, and accompanied him to most meetings, even when he, Martins, was not going to take part in the sittings proper. Because of an important errand Daniel sent him on early in the day, he was unable to accompany his boss down to the Majesty Hotel. Instead, he was arranged to be at its restaurant by noon.

"How is it going? No problems?" asked Martins, as both men jointly pulled out the chair to Martin's right for Chief Daniels to sit on.

"Well, yes, but manageable."

"Did they attempt to create problems?"

"Yes. It was started by one of those dullards, joined by another blockhead, and the whole thing would have reached a brick wall."

"Eh?"

Chief Daniels narrated all that happened at the meeting to John Martins who heard them with astonishment. He was particularly happy Chief Daniels did not entrap himself or get

23

entrapped. Martins resolved that in the next twenty-five minutes, which was all that remained before the resumption of the post-lunch session, he would prepare him fully enough to meet other eventualities.

Both men considered all the issues discussed and yet-to-be-discussed, and agreed on the specific actions Chief Daniels must take. Of utmost importance were the followings: No waiving, alteration or concession should be allowed on the conditions under which the loans were granted. Two: Detailed accounts of income and expenditure of all defaulters, most especially the incorrigible Tolp, Elfans and Duarf, must be called for and be publicly analysed. Three: Each complainer should be asked to be specific on which of his buses always suffered breakdowns, for all the other participants to assess openly, the type of reasons for the breakdowns. Four: Each transporter should make known openly, his number of working days and the maintenance programme per week. And five: Any of them who paid up to date should be guaranteed another loan at a reduced rate of interest.

* * *

After a brief welcome, Chief Daniels got down to business with the transporters.

"Gentlemen," Daniel started again, "you will recall that earlier in the meeting, on the same issue of loan, some of you made some comments while some were about to do so. Those who did covered almost all aspects of the topic so well that further comments from you are not necessary. Let me now comment on what you said, and offer the advice you requested for.

"One issue we can't do anything about now is that of the agreement already signed for the loan. There is no part of the agreement we can change because it involves persons other than us. Above all, most of you are coping well with it; those who are not must critically examine their methods of management. Please, pay up in time so as to avoid self-imposed inconveniences.

24

"On the next issue, the issue of taxes, I, for one, cannot see a reason for your complaints. You know why?" He looked into their faces for an answer. He got three – all useless to him, all very unhelpful to his objective.

"No."

"We don't."

"Why?"

"Then, we shall answer the question together," said Chief Daniels. "Who are these tax payers?"

"Whee!" they answered in a coarse voice.

"Whose government demands and receives the taxes?"

"NA's!" again, they answered him almost in unison.

"Where do they spend the taxes? I mean which town?" yet, he asked.

"NA!"

"Who are the inhabitants of NA?"

"Whee!"

"There we are. If you pay the taxes demanded by NA government, that spends the taxes for you inhabitants of NA, then, you have no justifiable basis for complaining."

"We are not complaining as such," said Joseph Tolp. "What we are saying is that they ought to be reasonable and non-repetitive."

"Most certain, it's only you people here who couldn't see the justification in what you pay; I could," Chief Daniels asserted. "You chose the people in government, and so, you could approach them to review anything you don't agree with. But you have to convince them. 'Convince' is the word. Otherwise, they would successfully convince you that the repairs of your roads are more important, that your lights need restoration, that your motor-parks need facelifts, that NA needs to be properly run to the full benefit of its inhabitants, and that you, as the wealthiest group of men in NA, must never be seen dodging simple civic responsibilities which thousands of poorer citizens patriotically meet.

"I am sorry if what I am saying sounds harsh, but it's the truth – it's time you knew what you should do, and what extra you must do for your own people. Most of you here know neither."

In the moment that followed, everybody and everything in the room was quiet. Definitely, the truth as seen by Chief Daniels, and the bluntness at its dispensation, pushed the wealthy transporters into a corner of shame from where only their repentance and good behaviour could have them rescued. In the immediate moment of quietness that followed, one man tried to raise his hand to say something; but the contrast between the sluggish velocity with which he raised the hand and the fast one with which he brought it down must have told him that a battered image required a time of proper planning to redeem.

"Alright," continued Daniel, "let us now visit the issue of out-of-zone bus operators you alleged to have annexed your area with their own normal zones of operation.

"I am not saying you should not protect your business, but you shouldn't do it in a way that would portray you as being lazy and unsure of your own ability to operate successfully. A piece of Glundales will help you understand what I am talking about. You have all heard about him I suppose."

"What Glundales, the goldsmith shops?" Tolp asked.

"Yes, the pioneer and head of the company itself; do you know what he thinks about competition?"

"No, but what has a goldsmith got to do with competition in a bus transport business?" Tolp replied and asked again.

"Soon, you will find out. I told my PA to make copies that would go round all of you. He would bring them in anytime from now. But remember, in the past when some of you were my drivers, you had no zone restrictions. The same thing continued immediately after some of you were on your own; and it gave you enough money that further qualified you for both the loans and the higher purchase facilities. Correct?"

"Oh yes," Ral Ralgrub took his turn to answer.

"Therefore, if they cross into yours, you too should cross into theirs. But it is important you study what enabled them cross successfully, and that you consolidate on the local operations before going inter-zonal.

"There is a last observation before we leave this issue. I noticed an increase in the number of trekkers within and outside the town. Could this be as a result of an increase in population or, of poverty? Or, is it a protest? It is your duty to find out, in other to help yourselves and your people."

There was a turning starting very slowly from the outside on the knob of the door to the room. When the door was opened, John Martins walked in with some white sheets of paper in his right hand.

"Excuse me please," John apologised to none of them in particular, as he walked to his boss. He whispered something into Daniel's ear, handed over the sheets, and went back.

Chief Daniels counted nine of them in his hands and dropped the remaining two on his table. He passed the pile in his hand to the right. Joseph Tolp, who was nearest to him on that side, slid off the top copy and passed on the pile to the next person on his right. The last copy, like a lone traveller, landed before Olu Duarf sitting first left to Chief Daniels. It was a quotation captioned 'A Tribute to my Competitors', expressing why the author had high regards for them:

> *I pay more attention to my competitors than to my friends.*
> *Nice and loyal, my friends see not my weakness,*
> *While my competitors without mercy search and expose them*
> *With all their intelligence and attention,*
> *Thereby drawing me into further improvements*
> *Which retain the acceptance of my products –*
> *And acknowledge the improvement of my services.*
> *Had it not been for my competitors,*
> *The discipline might have wobbled,*

And the business probably gone the negative.
God bless them, my competitors.

The next topic Daniel introduced dealt with the trio of Tolp, Elfans and Reduaram. Daniel demanded that each of them tabled before the meeting, details of what kept him behind in his repayment so as to enjoy from others, a free advice on what to do to get out of the debts.

"How many of your buses are running now and how many are not?" Daniel asked Isa.

"Could I say eem…two; two are running and two are not."

"Does that mean you are not sure?" Daniel asked.

"Yes, yes, I am sure; the second just started running. There are two buses running and two, not."

"And why are the two not running?"

"One is in need of two tyres, and the other, in need of some body works because it just had an accident where almost all its rear went into bits and twists."

"Since when have they been down?" asked Daniel.

"Two tyres busted four weeks ago, and a driver had an accident three weeks ago."

"In that case," Daniel started to judge, "you ought to have got the one lacking tyres back on the road three weeks ago. You could have temporarily transferred two tyres from the one with the accident."

"But it was towed into custody by the police for two weeks before being released last week."

"Since then, you could have transferred the tyres, and completed the repairs. Anyway, how did the accident happen?"

"I was not there, but those who were said it was the driver's fault – that, that, that he was careless," replied Reduaram, stammering.

"I wasn't anywhere near there too, but the report I had was different. If we may ask you, how many return trips did you mandate your drivers to complete in a day?" the chief asked, and could see Isa Reduaram's shocked by the question.

"Three – between six in the morning and eight in the evening."

"But two is about the normal maximum, isn't it?"

"Yes, but talents differ. Apart from talents, different goals pursue different people, and different people pursue different goals. For example, if I should rely on only two daily trips by each bus, how would I get enough to meet the monthly repayment of the loan?"

"But you are still not meeting them, and you could soon end up without a single bus," Daniel stressed.

"No Sir, God forbid. I don't pray for that."

"Nobody wishes you that either. But without wasting much time, this meeting could now see very clearly what went wrong with you. And you must correct them at once.

"Carelessly, and uneconomically, you have been going on three daily return trips since being in this business. I called you once and cited my own case as an example – how, years ago when I was in similar business here, it was only between one and two daily trips I made between six in the morning and five in the evening, Monday to Saturday only, using the evenings and every Sunday for servicing and cleaning of all my buses. Making too many trips goes with overspeeding, and aids rapid wear and tear. If you have planned for a moderate number of trips, the senseless, excessive speeding that partly caused the accident would have been avoided. If you have made regular servicing and prompt replacement of worn parts a habit, it's unlikely that your tyres would have worn to the state of being busted by their own wires. And do you target an amount of income and savings per day, Mr Reduaram?"

"Me?" asked Isa Reduaram.

"Of course, you."

"Okay, yes; but that is private."

"I don't think so. All of us here are in the same business. OK, suppose we put it this way: What proportion of your revenue goes into savings?"

"That, sir, is not easy to determine. It depends on the states of other things that day – the road, the driver, the passengers, the income itself, and so on."

"Is that all?" asked Daniel semi-mockingly. "Seems you are just trying to avoid an answer. Would it not depend on the degree of your extravagance as well? According to reports, the way you display your wealth at various social gatherings would easily drag and hold any person down," he finally rebuked Reduaram.

Next, as the meeting progressed to the design of Daniel as aided by his PA, the two other major defaulters, Elfans and Tolp were asked questions similar to those asked Reduaram. And, astonishingly too, their answers revealed they were unable to keep up with the repayment due to one recklessness or the other.

It was not that Joseph Tolp spent too much on anyone's illness, but that he was diverting some of his daily takings from his buses to building a big house that he meant to make the talk of NA upon completion.

The same was true of Elfans who, having been inspired by the handsome income from his four buses, engaged himself in the business of money lending. Chief Daniels mocked a sobriquet Elfans who wanted the nickname of 'Elfans, the banker,' currently being whispered among his colleagues, to become a household one in NA. And, if by ill luck, his debtors should give him a dose of his own medicine by lending out some of the money they borrowed from him, his transport business would hit the rocks. Daniel wanted him to take the warning very seriously.

By five o'clock, Chief Daniels had successfully put each of the participants on the defensive by making him accept at least, a principal guilt of mismanagement, however light. Even, Ral Ralgrub and Carlos Retfil were not exempted. The deliberate implication,

Daniel believed, would make all debtors feel the urge to pay him in time.

Chief Daniels, victorious enough, proceeded confidently to the last stage, that of delivering a mixture of instructions and pieces of advice that must all be followed, for him to further render his services in loans, purchase guarantees, insurance and technical advice:

Each transporter must put up a good system of financial control. Every bus must henceforth have its own account to show the daily income and expenses as well as the reserves to be saved in the bank. The account must be accumulated on daily basis and thoroughly analysed every weekend; in this way, each transporter would be able to work towards a self-set target.

Like in the case of having individual accounts, each bus must have its own logbook and job record properly maintained by the driver and the mechanic respectively.

Drivers must be properly trained to sense dangers before they happened to either the passengers or to the vehicles, so as to avoid delays and unnecessary expenses, as well as to guarantee passengers safety. They must not overspeed because the life and health of the passengers were in their care. Overspeeding could prevent the passengers from reaching the desired destinations within the desired times, or, caused them to reach the destinations in bad, physical and emotional states.

Mechanics must be given good enough tools and training to enable them carry out reasonable and honest jobs on the vehicles. They must not turn the buses into travelling morgues.

Each man must put in place straightaway, a weekly work arrangement that would allow the weekend for bus servicing.

Six. All the required key staffs must be carefully selected to complement the jobs of the current staffs. Such other staffs include the conductors, the motor park attendants and the cleaners.

Provision of comfortable, whole-destination trips must be guaranteed. Attraction must be extended to the fares so that those who love to travel by any other means, or in other buses, would be enticed to travel with NA buses.

Nine and finally, Chief Daniels enjoined each of them not to see himself only as an owner, but as a provider of fair packages for the passages of humans and human belongings. He must therefore always ensure the passengers started well, passed well, and landed well.

Period Two

CHAPTER 2

The Ambition

Six months had passed since Chief Daniel Daniels met with the nine local transporters. Carlos Retfil, now the *de facto* leader of local transporters due to his wealth, personally demanded that Emmanuel Titoloujou, his head driver, made a weekend of full Saturday and Sunday work attendance. This was because he, Carlos, had just paid for a new bus; and his private garage needed to prepare for it early on Saturday, before the collection would be made later the same day. Sunday was to ensure none of the other essentials he paid for on it was defective. Where all was certified fine, the bus would start plying the routes from Monday. For the same reason, his head mechanic was also mandated to come. But then, for Emmanuel, the request was a formality.

Emmanuel was very much dedicated to his master and the basic job that connected the two of them. To him, physical job attendance outside the normal Monday to Friday's was primary. Almost every Saturday and Sunday, he would find himself a reason why he should be in Carlos' garage. Saturdays he shared between social functions and the garage; and Sundays, between church activities and the garage.

Emmanuel's self-imposed job on Saturdays included ensuring the mechanics got from him, the compiled list of the repairs required, and carried them out accordingly. He would then return to do a final test-drive on the vehicles on Sunday mornings after attending the church services. Occasionally in addition, he oversaw how the cleaners got on, but would leave the actual cleaning job inspection till late on Sundays. This endeared Emmanuel not only to Carlos, but also to the other drivers he supervised for his boss. They believed Emmanuel would always look after their interests any time, any day, their presence or absence notwithstanding.

"I am off now," Emmanuel said, hurriedly finishing his breakfast and shooting up from his dining chair.

"Off? To where?" asked Minat even though she was prepared to hear the usual weekly answer.

"To the garage. You know those boys – the mechanics and the cleaners – they need being checked, otherwise, they damage Monday for my men. There were many complaints from the drivers this week. And, we need to prepare for a new bus coming in quietly later today."

"But weren't you supposed to have compiled and left a list of what they have to do?"

"Yes, I have; but you know them, how ignorant and uncaring they could be sometimes. You know their attitude towards the new system: hate! And I have to guide them. This weekend, it's busier and more complicated. That's why the boss personally requested me to come."

"But how about today's charity party for the children, aren't we going?"

"Ah, yes. Two problems. So, what do we do?" he asked, and found an answer before Minat would talk. "Yes, yes, I know. Since we have got the gifts all wrapped up, you go with them to the party while I go to the garage. This is another case of two heads being better than one – an advantage of being husband and wife. Trust you would represent us even better."

However, two groups of Carlos Retfil's staff, the cleaners and the mechanics, loathed Emmanuel's style of hard work. For example, on few occasions, the head mechanic had, out of annoyance, handed over the spanner to Emmanuel to carry out the repairs to the buses by himself, because he saw Emmanuel's certain insistences as insulting challenges to the professional competence of the mechanics. The problem this Saturday however, was with a cleaner. It arose when, on noticing a bus seat wasn't clean enough, Emmanuel advised her to re-clean it. The cleaner, already in waiting, took it as an opportunity to put a stop to Emmanuel's incessant and nauseating poke nosing.

"Which one do you complain about: the driver's seat?" she asked, expecting a non-affirmative answer.

"Oh no, not the driver's," Emmanuel answered, "a passenger's, one of those on the third row."

"Could I then ask you, what your concern is, about the seat of a passenger who is neither here nor even known?"

"My concern?" Emmanuel asked with shock. "It is that when he eventually takes the seat on Monday and discovers that his clothes are soiled by it, it is I, the driver," thumbing his chest with the apex of the cone formed by all his fingers of the right hand, "who will be the one to face the music. And who knows if that victim of your dirty seat and of your laziness would not be your oh-own brother."

"My brother?" she angrily picked that out. "What has my brother got to do with this? It is the truth then – that you drivers would always be as rude as ever to anything that is unfortunate enough to come your way?" she snapped. "May the Lord help you."

"It is people like you who really need the prayers, to enable you change for the better," Emmanuel retorted back. "You still expect to do your usual full time of half rest, and half job of full pay? That's a big joke, and I mean it.

"You are making a mistake if you think you would not accept the new rules already being accepted by everybody. Hello, our lady of the past."

Of course, Sammy the Spanner, real name Samuel Dodo, the head mechanic, was nearby, but he pretended not to hear the on-going brawl. Why should he, he resolved, when his own job had been criticised many times previously by the same driver who never tried to remove specks from his own eyes first before pointing to the specks in the other peoples' – a foolish servant who preferred to die doing the jobs of others while leaving his own unattended? Since he had never had the courage to put up a challenge to any of Emmanuel's current meddling, he took what was going on as comparable to the case of a big but weak brother having a brave and strong one as a small brother. Samuel did not mind the escalation, which eventually sent the echoes across the garage into Carlos' house, landing them directly inside the tympanic membrane of Carlos Retfil. Carlos came out to impose a settlement between the two – angrily and firmly.

For the first time, Carlos confirmed his knowledge of some workers kicking against the reasonable instructions of the ever hard-working Emmanuel. He asked the cleaner in a message meant for all his staff, if her disobedience was because Emmanuel, as the head driver, had the same office title as the other headmen, specifically the head mechanic and the head cleaner. It was time, he said, that every worker knew who was who, what was what, where was where, when was when, and why was why. All being well, he said, the following Monday, he would announce and confirm Emmanuel as a 'chief driver'. He concluded the reprimand by awarding the guilt to the cleaner, handing her a final warning against further planting of any act that could grow into pure irresponsibility towards their esteemed passengers. He empowered Emmanuel to dismiss her if at the end of another month she failed to exhibit some positive changes.

As soon as Carlos gave his ruling and walked away, Emmanuel turned to the cleaner to tell her he was sorry that she allowed a small issue to develop to that stage. The head mechanic, still standing near the two combatants, slowly looked at both Emmanuel and the cleaner; and he finally thanked his own star that he did not after all carry out the animosity attack on Emmanuel.

For Emmanuel, it was the first time since the regulation of the new system was spelt out to the organization that he felt he got an open confirmation of his superiority over the drivers and other workers of Carlos'. This went home with him that day, stayed with him throughout the night, and encouragingly kicked him out of the house the following morning, Sunday, a clear hour earlier than usual, for the voluntary inspection of repairs executed by the mechanics on Saturday, and to collect the new bus that the dealer made unavailable for collection the previous day.

For the past six months, the system being used to operate the transport business had taken a turn apparently easier to be adjudged better. In all cases, all the transporters were complying with the directives of Chief Daniels. It was not because they liked to, but because of what they stood to lose should they choose to ignore him. A number of them had even taken another loan for business expansion.

Among the new, six-month old directives was the making of the weekends work-free. To comply with this, the transporters adopted three systems. In the first, Mathew Rebbor, Ike Elfans, Linus Isho and Olu Duarf, operated the buses from Mondays to mid-day Saturdays; and immediately afterwards, carried out the servicing and cleaning jobs. Sundays were left work-free. Thus, this group, comprising of the majority of them, took to Daniel's directive in such a way that Daniel would not feel ignored, and they too would not experience a loss in daily revenue. The buses would be serviced and both staff and buses would still have extra one day, Sunday, to rest.

In the second, operated by Isa Reduaram and Joseph Tolp, work went from Mondays to Saturdays all day, while Sundays were left for servicing and cleaning, on compulsory overtime basis.

What was most important to this second group was the daily taking. Right after the meeting with Daniel, Joseph exposed his feelings to Elfans and Reduaram with the aim of making the two who both owed heavily like himself, share the same arrangements with him. He went round both men rubbishing Chief Daniels' working days formula – that it could never guarantee daily incomes handsome enough to allow them to meet their monthly indebtedness to their families and to Chief Daniels. While Elfans refused to join up, Reduaram readily accepted and joined with Joseph. He, Reduaram, even saw it as being unwise for the business to abandon the streets and garages on Saturdays when people had more time to go out for leisure and shopping. He told Joseph that the withdrawal of their colleagues meant better fortune for them, as they would be able to carry more passengers and make additional trips.

In the third system, adopted by Papah Feiht, Ral Ralgrub and Carlos Retfil, the buses were operated full day Mondays to Fridays, with Saturdays reserved for servicing and cleaning, and Sundays completely work-free for all buses and staff.

The three adopters of the third system had particularly opted to give Chief Daniels' advice a chance, and had swallowed it line, hook and sinker. They believed no wise man rides his horse all day; otherwise both he and his horse would face the repercussion. To them, having seen, or at least heard, how Daniel was a good administrator, then a successful transporter, and now, a well known transport consultant cum financier, they trusted his words must be those of wisdom, and his directives sure path to successful business management.

* * *

The distance from Emmanuel Titoloujou's house in Eddea Hill to Carlos Retfil's in Satellite Acres was about two miles; and by

Emmanuel's walking velocity, one that consumed about thirty minutes of his time every day between five and five-thirty in the morning, and between seven and seven-thirty in the evening. The time bracket exceptions were Saturdays and Sundays when the trekking times came up much later in the mornings and earlier in the evenings.

The walk usually took him through his favourite route. On leaving his house, he would join the nearby NA's main road, the Glass Street, and then went on to the new motor park. Half-way round the motor park, he would turn right into Satellite Street, which directly entered the Satellite Acres, passing under the arch of its main gate. He would then walk straight on and pass the first street called Road One on the right, then Road Two on the left, Road Three on the right, Road Four on the left, and so on. He seldom went beyond Road Seven because Carlos' place, a larger-than-others in the area, and on about an acre of land, was sandwiched between Road Five and Road Seven.

Ironically, none of Carlos' two outer gates faced that main Satellite Street. The first and smaller was along Road Seven, and was at the front of the house. The bigger second was on Road Five, serving as the entrance to Carlos' private bus garage cum workshop at the back of the house.

Also, recently, Carlos' residential premises had attracted, and in fact taken some spending in the names of security to the buses and of peace to the house. First, the original six feet wall fence that surrounded the compound was replaced with another, about eight feet high and carrying coils of barbed wire. Its height successfully prevented a view of the house, the buses, and of all other things within the entire premises by anyone outside it. Within this wall was another. It was unbarb-wired and about five feet high, and used to cut off the house along the back and left sides. Two doors, one to the left side and one to the back of the house, lead to the garage. Therefore, as the outer wall maintained the privacy of both the house and the garage from the public, so did the inner wall maintained the privacy of the household from the workers in the garage yard.

On his arrival at the smaller gate on Road Seven, Emmanuel gave its door his unique four knocks. Though he did not see Zaki, the keeper, he was certain Zaki was on duty, as usual.

"Are you there? It's me Emmanuel," he shouted to the unseen other side.

His belief that the keeper heard him and his knocks as confirmed first, by the keeper's footsteps he heard from behind the gate, followed by the jingling noise the keys were making with the padlock behind the door.

"Just wait a minute, CD," he shouted to the chief driver. "It is the lock. Rust is stiffening it up."

"No problem. Take your time," replied Emmanuel who was already accustomed to the fact that entering his boss' yard at weekends required some patience, as Zaki would always find something wrong with the lock, the latch or the key. These notwithstanding, every staff coming on weekends still had to pass through Zaki's. From there they would proceed into the bus garage proper, through the left gate made in the five feet high wall.

The first thing in Emmanuel's mind was to collect the ignition keys and start the buses one by one. He therefore headed straight to the small office that served him directly, but other drivers indirectly, to collect the keys. A few steps from the office block, he turned as was usual of him and glanced across the buses parked in their spaces on the far right. What he saw forced him to give the spot a keener look. It was the front of a brightly coloured bus with a row of coloured lights across the top front.

"Could it be?" he murmured to himself as he changed course and walked towards the parked buses. "Could this be it?"

Every step Emmanuel put forward added to the positivism of his original thought. He had about a score left to reach the targeted bus when he saw boldly written in its front, the popular phrase, 'God First'. It was what his boss adopted on all his buses.

41

Highly elated, he moved near, dashing and looking around in a manner too fast to note anything specific about it other than that it was a new bus. He broke the cycle and headed back to the gatekeeper.

"When did it arrive – the bus?" Emmanuel asked him.

"Yesterday in the …" Zaki was still giving the answer to a man too impatient and overjoyed to catch the answer.

"When?"

"Listen, CD; I said yesterday. Just as soon as you left."

"Who drove it down?"

"I have never seen him before. I don't know him, and I don't have to know him. Mine was only to go round to Road Five and open the gate to let them in, and lock up after he was let out – as per the boss' instructions."

"Who took the delivery: the boss or the madam?"

"Since none of you was here, I, Zaki, took the delivery," he said with all the pomposity he could pack in his toothless mouth. "I opened the gate, showed him exactly where to park, and collected the keys from him."

"Poor you. But the keys were of no use to you – you can't drive."

"Yes, I know," admitted Zaki, "just the same way you too were useless to the keys at that time of yesterday – you were not here."

Both men burst into laughter so loud that it caught the attention of Carlos Retfil from inside the house. Carlos, still in his pyjamas and dressing gown walked into the garage yard to meet them.

"Good morning you two," he greeted the duo.

"Good morning sir," Emmanuel and Zaki jointly replied.

"And congratulations sir," added Emmanuel.

"Thank you, Titoloujou; thank you very much."

"But sir, I was expecting a vehicle much different because you told me to be ready to collect a smaller bus?"

"Well, Titoloujou, you take what you get – and as you get it."

"Who brought it, I mean, drove it here sir?" Emmanuel still remembered to ask.

"One of the drivers from the other side did."

"And the one happened to deny me the chance of baptizing the new bus. He robbed me the opportunity of being the first to drive it."

"The first to drive it? Don't you know that somebody test-drove it during, and after building? Anyway, here, the keys." Carlos stretched his hand out to Emmanuel, dangling a bunch of three flat keys. "Have them, and go and add your own test-drive – or, baptism, if that is what you prefer to call it. Soon, there would be another, and you would do the baptism right from where it would come from."

Emmanuel took the keys, and strode towards the office, humming along a song that must have been a very joyous one as evidenced by the smile he carried beyond his face to his ears. Carlos returned indoors, and Zaki, to his gate post, leaving Emmanuel alone to it.

Emmanuel Titoloujou was used to respecting his profession and his buses like he would respect a fellow human being. This morning, as was usual with him on occasions like this, he was determined to accord the bus its initial respect by climbing into it for the first time only in his full driver's uniform. He hurried back to his office, removed the clothes he had on, and replaced them with his complete driver's uniform: poplin jacket, trousers, tie, cap and badge. Then, he returned to the new bus – for both inspection and a test drive within, and by luck, outside the garage.

He was at its front when he looked up and read 'God First' again. Instantly, he felt something was either wrong with or missing from the inscription, but he could not think of what it was. It was more important to him to know what the inside of the bus looked and felt like first; he would come back to the inscription later!

The only key-lockable way into the bus was through the exclusive driver's door by the left hand side of the bus. The other two doors, one on the rear right and the other on the front right opposite the driver's, could only be operated from inside, using the hooks and latches; there was no provision for their automatic control on the bus. Emmanuel discovered later that the provision was made, but was ordered removed by Carlos himself. If the two last buses much older in age had the provision, Emmanuel could not understand the reason behind its removal from a new and modern bus like this one.

The first key he tried was the right one. Two steps up, and he was on the floor of the vehicle, and by the driver's seat. Emmanuel threw his buttocks onto the seat and it readily surrendered to his weight, straining itself down the centre from the circumference until it reached the lowest possible depth. He lifted up his bottom and the concealed under-springs instantaneously sent both the man-made fibre web and the leather cover after it. He did this thrice before proceeding to his test number two.

He searched for, found, and operated a lever on the stem of the seat; it caused the seat to rise, gaining about six inches. He operated it again and it sent the seat down from its new height by about twelve inches, meaning the seat could be adjusted six inches up or down from the central level he met it. He did this twice before finally agreeing the seat passed the height test. "Fine, but still, there are more things to be checked on it," he told himself.

Looking down at the chair from the top, one saw the seat as a perfect resemblance of the fifteenth letter of the English alphabet in capital. Just less than half of the arc of its circumference was built up to a height of about a foot and half as its backrest. It was the reclineability of this backrest he wanted to check as his third test.

Emmanuel found another lever under the seat and thought it could be the one he needed. He rested his lower back heavily on the backrest while at the same time was pushing the lever up and down for a result. When the result eventually came, he nearly paid with both his tendon and ligament together with the cervical vertebrae they served. The moment the lever was pushed up, the backrest took a backward flight so sudden that his back he rested on it went all the distance with it – swiftly and violently. Though the backrest went three-quarters of its possible recline-able distance before it stopped, Emmanuel's neck threw back his head even further. Had there been an object of similar height with the seat at the back of the chair, the back of his skull would have certainly crashed against such an object. The resulting painful snap to the neck made him realise that his own anxieties had prevented him from noting that the chair did not have a headrest!

Having recovered from this incident, Emmanuel decided to press on and off the backrest with his hand instead of with his back while manoeuvring the lever to discover other stop positions on it. From the trials, he finally knew it could rest at six positions: a quarter to the front, normal perpendicular, a quarter to the back, half-way to the back, three-quarters to the back and flat back.

Upon a final assessment, he gave the chair a pass mark even though he could not understand why such a beautiful chair with such a good shine, a comfortable seat with backrest fully covered with real leather, could not have a headrest. He opined that if for whatever reason someone had thought the inclusion was unnecessary, why did his boss not correct the person and order its inclusion. After all, nowadays, he claimed he wanted first class comfort not only for passengers, but for his drivers as well.

Emmanuel also remembered how in the last two years, Carlos had repeatedly told them that he belonged to the same family with them as far as the work was concerned. Why then couldn't Carlos start the charity from his own home, the claimed family? Perhaps, he thought further, it could be the case of the wicked acting the benevolent – like a colleague, another chief driver, had twice attempted to convince him about the behaviours of the transporters. The friend believed that they were all the same money-crazy, wicked and exceptionally deceitful lot.

45

The next he wanted to do was to start the engine. He selected the right key and slotted it into the ignition hole that was clearly visible to the right of the steering shaft. He adjusted the seat using the combination of its levers, his back force and his bottom pressure. Satisfied, he put his left hand on the clutch and depressed it while using his right hand to push about the floor-type gear lever: he wanted to ensure the gear was in neutral. He was returning his right hand to the key in the ignition slot when an instinct, habitual of an experienced driver's, made him raise his head and look out right and left to the side mirrors; he remembered they needed separate adjustments. In normal circumstances, it was the duty of the conductor to adjust the right's while his own was to give the order 'up a bit', 'back a bit', 'forward a bit', 'backward a bit', 'too much', and so on; until he would arrive at 'okay, okay like that', 'stop'. Now that the left's was nearer, and the right would require him to leave his seat and go across to reach it, he opted to adjust only the left's for whatever test-drive. At his first and only attempt, his experience assisted him to rest it at a position adequate enough on taking his seat; he was able to see almost all that should appear on the left and the rear. Finally, he lifted up his hand and adjusted the long, rear-view mirror.

Emmanuel turned the key from 'zero' to 'one'.

On few occasions, Emmanuel had been forced by circumstances to boast of his job experience. On any of such occasions, one could forgive him, as the boast would certainly be devoid of pure vanity. At worst, one would be able to attach to it some basis, however rudimentary. He would brag that as a man of many years on the wheel and behind the steering – in fact, fifteen – there was nothing left in driving for him to see; that there was hardly any type of bus ever made that he had not handled personally and perfectly. But the moment the key he turned to 'one' triggered-on both the illumination in the dashboard and a radio not previously turned off to come on, he became convinced that he had more to learn and see in his trade.

The rude, loud noise from the speakers in the passenger area, complemented by the strong flashing of the rainbow colours on the dashboard and rooftop, first gave him a jolt from which he however quickly recovered. This, he believed, must have been caused by a driver too careless or too inexperienced, or both, to know that all gadgets must be switched off before the engine would be turned off. The last driver not only left the radio on at a high volume-setting, he did not turn off the inner, the parking and the roof-top lights, now all flashing orange, red, blue and white.

Emmanuel noticed the position of the radio to the top centre of the dashboard, and he zeroed his eyes on its two black knobs. Eagerly, he stretched out to them to turn off the nuisance. Unfortunately, and unknowingly to Emmanuel, the knob he first touched was the radio tuner; and the touch suddenly changed the chorus into grammar, having moved the dial from a station airing a church service to one where some sort of jokes were going on. Realising his mistake, he quickly went for the second knob.

The stiffness of this second knob forced out of him, a more serious re-look at both knobs. He could see 'on', 'stroke' and 'off' written in capital besides the knob that would not turn. He re-attempted to turn it but met the same negative result. It was at his second attempt that the radio programme reached a point where laughter took over the jokes. Like an imbecile, Emmanuel joined in with a self-deriding laughter, hoping the speakers were not laughing at his own ignorance.

He noticed a drawing of two small blocks of equal width, but with one having a height twice that of the other, placed side by side below the 'on' and 'off'. He pushed himself to a cautious third attempt at the knob, but this time, by pressing it down against the radio before letting off the three middle fingers he sent on the errand. Simultaneously, the speakers went dead. Emmanuel had learnt another thing new.

Now, he had only the flashers to knock out. He tried out three different switches. The nearest he could go was getting the flashing stopped without the lights getting turned off. He stood and wandered off his seat to the bulb positions in the passenger area, to see if they had separate switches. As he saw nothing helpful, Emmanuel faulted his own assumption – that were he to be correct, he would have needed to climb up to the rooftop before he would be able to turn off its lights! Then came to him another hard discovery on the dashboard. It was a penny-size red light clearly marked out with two circles. A further probe of it confirmed that he only needed to depress its centre with the tip of a finger for all the lights he was battling with to go off. It was another lesson he learnt and would never forget easily, if not forever.

In all, Emmanuel was pleased with the instrumentation and control gadgets. He practised using them up to the point he almost turned them into toys. Especially because of those controlled with electronics, he admitted within himself that there would always be more than a numerical count of seventy after sixty. At the temporary end of the first round of his practices, he returned the ignition key to 'zero', removed it and tucked it down his pocket. He was ready for the inspective probe of the passenger area proper.

Visibility in this part of the bus was slight, the lights having been turned off; and more significantly, the curtains on the windows having been fully drawn.

Starting from the window nearest to the front, he drew the curtains one after the other, passing to reach the windows through the space the front's two adjoining seats to his left made with the backs of the two adjoining ones to his right. In order to save him from passing through all similar spaces, he adopted some lean-over actions that enabled him omit some of them.

As he went from one window to the next, the incoming natural light simultaneously captured more of the passenger's area. He completed those on the right, then those at the back, and finished up with those on the left. "Why is this elaborate curtaining?" he asked himself, and headed towards the passenger doors, starting from the one at the front.

He descended a couple of steps to reach the door. It had two sets of latches, one up, the other, down; and he undid both to have the door opened. There was a whirl of in-rushing fresh air. He went to the rear passengers' and did the same; the whirl of air could almost be heard, but certainly, could be felt. In wonderment, he stopped, shook his head; moved a further three steps, and stopped to shake his head again. He was now certain he had more things to learn and understand.

Next, Emmanuel decided to open the windows. He was doing the first when he saw another surprise, this time, of a different kind. It was Samuel Dodo, coming to work on a Sunday for the first time in almost a year! Both relief and a strong urge to speak to someone instantly overpowered Emmanuel.

"Hey man, this is a beautiful lady you are in," Samuel said as he climbed inside to join Emmanuel. He was too carried away to say hello to Emmanuel.

"Yes Sammy, it's indeed a beautiful lady – to keep you busier."

"You mean to keep me less busy."

"More busy – to ensure the beautiful lady doesn't get old fast like the others did."

"Which others?" Samuel asked in disagreement. "Those others got older faster because they were already old mechanically before I started to maintain them. So, don't blame me. I did my best."

"Not all of them were old," said Emmanuel. "Some could have been kept tidier and running better."

"This is not the time for that. Anyway, I agree this is new – the newest ever. I have got the complete workshop manual here with me. Chief just gave it to me. He said he has given you the keys. Have you fired the lady?"

"Fired the lady? No, not yet. I am still carrying out some checks. It is all too wonderful, as you too shall see when you carry out your own checks. Truly, it's a new-age bus, a great coach," Emmanuel said.

They started with the passenger seats. Simultaneously, they selected and felt two with the tips of all the fingers firmly and stiffly lengthened out. They threw their buttocks down on each for a confirmation test that was certainly more meaningful than any form of finger tipping. They inspected the backs, the backrests, the headrests, the seatbelts, and the reclining levers, all with an amazement that was too much for them to describe.

"Why do you think Chief purchased something like this?" Samuel asked.

"I wished I knew. I have asked myself but could not find an answer," Emmanuel replied.

"First, I have never come across seats as comfortable as these. I am yet to see the seats of an aeroplane though, but I doubt if they would be any better. But why?"

"Maybe," Emmanuel started to search for an answer, "maybe it's for night service. In which case, passengers will be able to have nice sleeps and sweet dreams, at the annoying expense of us drivers. That is what came to my mind the moment I saw the curtains."

The remark directed Samuel to take a critical look at the curtains. He noticed the drape; it was beautiful and made more effective by the vertical stripes. He noticed the colour; it was in complete contrasting harmony with the brown leather-covered seats. "Yes, they look perfect," he said, "an alluring recipe for sleep, whether day or night.

"But wait, Emman, could this be an extension to his craze for the so-called modernization? He has refurbished all the buses, purchased more tools and repainted the whole premises. An extension it must be."

"I think I will agree with you," said Emmanuel. "Even though some of his friends have done similar things, they have not gone as far as getting a bus as new and as fashionable as this one."

"But you know your favourite boss. He will always go more than one step ahead of his friends. Do you know I once heard him bragging to his wife that though he outwardly carried the same status as his friends, that in reality, he was superior to all of them?"

The discussion was broken by a resumption of further inspection of the inside. They commented on the two rows of luggage racks – on how they were more luggage accommodating than those in 'God First' number four being used for both day and night services. They commented on the single night-light above every seat, and how a passenger could use it without disturbing the other sitting beside him. They commented on how the seats that were three on a side row inside other buses were only two in this; and how the back row that used to have six seats now had only five – all in order to make passenger comfort a priority.

They commented on the aisle, and how it lacked vertical poles or horizontal rods for standing passengers to hold on to. It dictated compulsory sitting for every passenger.

They noticed the opening on the rooftop with its advantage of good ventilation and the disadvantage of easy break-ins.

They noticed the writings inside the bus and how they were a mixture of advices, warnings and commands to the passengers.

And so, a notice of something by Samuel, followed by a discovery of another by Emmanuel went on in turns and simultaneously as if they would never end, until Samuel broke the trend. With his left hand on the waist, he walked to Emmanuel and asked him, "don't you think so – that this must be more than for modernization or pace-setting? There must be something behind this, typical of your boss and his friends."

Deep down his heart, Emmanuel knew many of the business antics of his boss. More than anything or anybody else, he knew that his boss, if needed be, would always meet business with an approach that went beyond the territory of ruthlessness to that of demoniacism. He knew that the main reason why most people could not see the ugly side of Carlos Retfil was because of Carlos' brilliance at pretending about the pain-to-the-opponent-actions he loved to take, and at soothing the pains from every sting he ordered or personally inflicted. He, Emmanuel, was close to him, or so he thought, so much as his chief driver, that it would be improper for him to speak evil of him before any other worker. In fact, he would not give any chance to anyone to hold him to any bad talk about Carlos. Therefore, instead of answering Samuel in the affirmative sprinkled with some facts he knew so well about their joint boss, he evaded with his own set of fresh questions. "Why? Why would there be something behind it, unless of course, it is something good?"

"I can swear he is doing it for something," Samuel went on. "Your boss will do nothing for nothing. My perception never deceives me, and I always believe it, especially in something like this. I know he is doing it for money – more money. I will not be surprised if he has acquired it for a special class of people, the rich, who he will be able to charge conveniently for every wrinkle on its leather seats."

"But Sammy, even if they are not buying, all these other friends too are renovating. It is not him alone."

"That was why you don't have to go on pretending and dodging. We have both been working with them long enough to know them. They must have got some dubious reasons behind suddenly starting to make the journeys comfortable for helpless passengers like us."

"Oh Sammy, you are classing yourself as a helpless passenger; are you no more a mechanic?"

"What is the difference?" asked Samuel. "When and how will a mechanic not be a passenger? I must start and end journeys, however short, however long, however comfortable or uncomfortable. And so must you, the driver. You are on the driver's seat only at the mercy of the owner, and you cannot be there most of the time. Even when you are there, the owner dictates your destination. Therefore, you must know the fact that the man who gave you the bus to drive and me the bus to maintain is both the owner and the real driver. We are just helpless passengers on a journey we don't really control."

"Okay, if we are, as you said, what about those we carry in the buses?"

"Simple; hopeless passengers. That's what they are!"

"Okay Sammy, Sammy the passenger."

"But you still haven't quite got it. You miss out something, that all-important qualification!"

"Okay, Sammy, the helpless passenger!" Emmanuel corrected himself as both men went into a very long moment of laughter punctuated by mocking interchange of 'helpless driver', 'helpless mechanic', 'helpless Sammy' and 'helpless Emmanuel'. As they wiped off tears from their eyes, they dragged themselves out of the bus to discover what its outside would reveal.

They began from one of the two longer sides, the driver's. It was sprayed with two shades of sky blue, with each of the shades running from the front to the rear. A white, foot wide band, also running centrally in the same direction, separated the two shades and carried in its middle, the popular business motto of Retfil family.

"Fine colour, isn't it?" Samuel asked Emmanuel.

"Yes, fine indeed – and very pleasant too," answered Emmanuel. "I particularly love the colour of the motto; it is very radiant," he added.

"But I can't see any logo. Emman, have you noticed?"

Emmanuel looked and confirmed Samuel's observation. "You are right, Sammy; there is none," he said. It was the first time he would see his boss' motto not supported on either side by a crown. "No wonder, when I first came and read it, I felt something was wrong with the writing even though I could not figure out what it was," he added. He remembered how it was not only Carlos Retfil's' vehicles that used to carry the combination of the motto and how the combination turned into a permanent means of identifying anything Retfil's. They were on his car, on his gates and on every receipt of business transactions that originated from him.

"Emman," Samuel called again, "there is something else missing. Where is the quantity number of the bus? What should it be; eight?"

"No; seven. You should know that. This is the seventh. But, like you asked, why has the number not been put?" Emmanuel wondered.

"That," said Sammy is what I should be asking you, since you always claim you understand and can predict your boss any day. One of those days is here now."

"Anyway, what even is in a number, or in numbering itself?" Emmanuel attempted to dismiss the relevance of the current argument. "The normal mother does not necessarily need names and counting to identify her children."

"Yes, you can say that not to convince me, but to shade yourself from the fact that you know only very little of that man. I don't even believe his wife can claim to know him well enough, talk less of his transport colleagues, or of his poor driver and mechanic like you and me.

"Why is the colour blue instead of the usual orange? Why were there no crowns? Is he tired of being a self-proclaimed transport monarch? Why no number? I am sure that if God allows our hearts to continue pumping, we are likely to see some surprises in no distant future."

The tyres were greatly admired by both men. They were a total of ten. Of the five on each side, the four to the rear were paired while the one at the front was single. In height, each was about half of Samuel's, the shorter of the two. The threading on them was a type none of them had seen before. Ordinarily it looked like a zigzag; but it was in fact, a carefully interlaced herringbone design where the width of every stroke was about half an inch wide, and about the same deep. In the centre of the ten pieces of shining chrome-plated knots that secured both wheel and tyre was a large cup with a bold tri-star embossed on it to distinguish the bus as a Mercedes Benz.

"How do you see these tyres?" Samuel asked another question. He hit the side of the rear tyre they were standing by with the fist of his right hand.

"Oh, beautiful. Beautiful. My men would love them," Emmanuel replied. "The threading is one in town, and so would its tracks. They would also love the hold on the road," he added.

"That is only if you would warn them not to over-speed," Samuel reminded.

"Over- what? You know that is an eradicated behaviour among my men. Since they went on that Drivers Course, their standard of driving has improved. Anyway, only the most experienced would handle it."

"Well, let's hope so."

As they moved to the rear, there was before them a large painted picture of an aeroplane cruising on, in a cloudy sky.

"Let's also hope your boys will not turn it into a flying bus," added Samuel.

The third side, the second of the long, was almost the same as the first long, in construction, colour and inscriptions. The little difference was an additional set of two keyholes, each on top of a small knob that doubled as a handle. The keyholes were midway between the side tyre positions and about two feet up the clearance line. They were the locks on the doors to the larger luggage compartments. When Emmanuel used one of his keys to open the two, they found a large space about two feet high and occupying the whole of the space between the clearance from the ground and the passenger floor.

"Oh God" exclaimed Samuel, "but why should a bus have a space as massive as this just for the luggage?" He bent and rolled himself in. "What does it expect to carry with it – hippos and elephants?"

"Get out Sammy. It is only you who could ask that question or think the compartment is massive," replied Emmanuel. "The experiences we get from some passengers over their luggage are so bad that they don't deserve to be stored in our memories. At times when there are more loads than the available space, the trouble is passed solely onto us. Even if the space is bigger than one for a camel combined with your hippos and elephants, it will not be beyond our use. It would make the journey easier for the passengers and for us."

"For you; not for us. Have you considered other implications – more loading, more offloading, dragging, lifting, and all those?"

"You could be right," agreed Emmanuel, "but even then, that makes a lesser evil. By comparison, it is a better alternative. It could also mean extra reward."

"Reward...what reward?" Samuel was unable to believe his *tympanum membrane*. He laughed loudly. "When has your boss ever given any reward of an ordinary type, talk more of an extra one, to anyone? Never, never, never. Anyone waiting for a good reward or compensation from him might just as well wait to see the crab blink."

"You are perfectly entitled to your opinion. But surely, he is not that bad."

"Well, that too is your own opinion."

Emmanuel was closing the doors to the compartment when Samuel noticed certain objects at its extreme opposite, and he called out to stop Emmanuel.

"Hold it; let's see those things inside there," he was pointing and bending. "I can see a box and what looks like a tyre."

Everything was dragged out. Truly, there was a tyre beautifully fitted on a Benz rim. It bore the size number they could not understand, together with the name of Dunlop which they both knew very well.

The box, on the other hand, was a big metal one, brown with collapsible half-lids and handles. It was the tool box containing among other things, a set of ring spanners, a set of flat spanners, a set of sockets completed with ratchet extension bar, a big hammer, a mallet, a set of Allen keys, a set of drain-plug wrenches, a torque wrench, a set of feeler gauge, a set of flat screw drivers, a set of star screw drivers, a set of spark plug sockets, a set of punch and chisel, a medium-size hack-saw, a steel wire brush, a set of flat and round files with interchangeable handle, a set of thin-nose side-cutter and combination pliers, a piece of cleaning cloth, a circuit tester, and a set of padlock with two keys.

Three other items, a pair of axle stands, a trolley jack and a grease gun, were left outside the box because of their big size. In all, Sammy was pleased with the tools. He was particularly pleased his team would be able to use them on other buses as well.

Next, Emmanuel and Samuel moved to the front for the inspection of the last side. Here, the mechanic naturally took over while the driver looked on and followed round, as would an apprentice of the trade. The 'master' lifted the bonnet, and checked the conditions of water, engine oil, brake fluids, and battery connections. Having satisfied himself with the checks, he was ready for Emmanuel to start the engine. "Now, you can take over," he instructed, and ordered, "go in and start it."

Both men were surprised at the noise that came from the engine. Because the engine was big, they expected a big roar – the type that would catch the decibel on the high side. Instead, what came from the engine was a medium, followed immediately by a smoother noise, the type that would come from a small virgin engine. The soot emission from the exhaust followed the same pattern, coming first in thick, and immediately after, in light clouds.

"Fine, what a nice sound," Samuel said as he climbed up to Emmanuel through the front passenger door. "It sounds smooth, but how does it feel?" he added and started to admire the dashboard before Emmanuel.

"Feels cool, really obedient – at least, up till now," he cautiously replied. He was not going to mention his past experiences with the lights and the radio.

"Then, let's move it around, so that you can feel it better. Or you want me to come to your rescue?"

"Yes; why not? You are welcome," Emmanuel replied jokingly as he pushed the gear lever to the first, and gently let go the hand brake. True to the thrust of mechanical obedience, the bus inched and then rolled off the point it was parked, to the open space in the yard.

Both men took the bus up and down as much as the garage space would allow them. They wished they were allowed out with it on to the streets. As soon as they realised that their common boss would never grant such a wish, they reluctantly returned and parked it. They had enough for the Sunday already, and it was time to go home.

"Gentlemen, how did you find it?" a familiar voice came from the side. It was a male's, Carlos Retfil's; and they were surprised to hear it. Both men turned to its direction and there were Carlos and Evi, his wife, already waiting.

"How did the trial go?" Carlos asked again.

"Good afternoon sir," Samuel greeted. "We don't know you are here."

"Good afternoon madam," Emmanuel added, as if Samuel had committed a sex discriminating sin that he, Emmanuel, must correct.

"Good afternoon to both of you," responded Evi, "and how did you find the bus?"

"Ah madam, it's beautiful, nice and quiet," replied Samuel.

"Did it drive well?" she asked again.

"Yes madam, really well," answered Samuel again.

"Sammy," interrupted Emmanuel, "that question was meant for me. Was it not me who drove it? Was it you?" he asked light heartedly.

"Emman," Samuel countered, "this is a simple matter of doing away with trivialities." He tried to justify the response he gave to Evi. "But we were both here, and on the bus. Weren't we?"

"But I actually felt the real thing – the gears, the throttle, the breaks, pointers, everything."

"Yes, you are correct; but the fact remained that it was me who felt the true comfort of the seats while you drove, and who had the honour of sitting and assessing your overall ability at handling the bus, together with the smoothness of its response to your efforts."

"Okay, gentlemen," intervened, Evi. "I believe you have done very well today; and, that what you need now is some rest to end the Sunday." She opened the small purse she was holding and took out some amount in notes. "Here, take this for your fares," she said as she stretched her hand to Emmanuel.

"Thank you madam," both men acknowledged as Emmanuel received the sum on their behalf. Leaving the Retfils by the bus, they headed for their office to exchange their work clothes and go home.

* * *

Mrs. Retfil felt the body of the bus by slapping it delicately with her right hand; then, she turned to her husband. "But dear, I still don't know why you made this bus blue," she protested. "That colour is near to Mathew Rebbor's."

"Did I make it, or, the makers did? It is much darker than Rebbor's."

"Yes, the makers did, but, on your recommendation and to your specification. You were paying your money, and so, if you didn't like it, it would have been changed for you. After all, there were occasions when they gave you other colours and you promptly made them change such to the usual orange."

"But what is wrong with blue? And what is special about orange, this colour you love so much?"

59

"Blue is duller. And however bright you make it, its brightness will forever line up only behind that of orange. This was why you initially chose orange, wasn't it? And when your friends later saw yours, it was not that they had to make a Hobson's choice, they all went for it, madly adding areas and objects of orange colour to their buses."

Carlos Retfil knew his wife was right, at least as far as that time was concerned. But that was years ago, when only Chief Daniel Daniels' buses dominated the roads of the locality and beyond; and Ral Ralgrub with his only two buses, was the sole prominent local man known to challenge Daniel – most feebly though.

Carlos, perpetually deceitful at watching, and correct at planning, however had specific ideas when he joined the transport business. Among these was making his only bus unique in view and identification. At first, he picked white colour to satisfy this idea, but his wife convinced him that it was a colour very difficult to maintain. He went to blue, then green, but was convinced by her that the number alone of Chief Daniels' buses would easily swallow any of these up. When at last he arrived at orange, his wife swiftly applauded him for arriving at one that would be showy enough, as well as would maintain a basic protective colouration against mud and dusts that took it seasonally in turns to subdue their environment.

"Evi dear, you are quite right," Carlos admitted without hesitation. "But you also should remember it was the correct decision for that time, and that being correct is never everlasting – its lifespan is in the hands of time and environment. That time, we had just one bus among many, and there was need to show it up. This time, there is no need for a show up, or else it is perceived as a show off."

Evi was becoming somewhat puzzled.

60

"But, if that was more important to you, why did you have to add to the number you already got? Are you going to lock it up in the yard so that you would not be showing off?"

"Dear, by tomorrow, the selected driver would get used to its system; and the day after, it would be on the roads. So, there is neither the intention nor the possibility of keeping it locked up.

"And why it was added? Of course it was to allow for more business. Or to be precise, to enable Evi and Carlos to add a little more to their worth. We happen to be born and grown in NA, and there is no running away from that.

"And clearly as far as NA is concerned, money means power; more of it means more or double power; and more of more means triple power. Here, no amount of power is too much. Even, power among the powers is excellent because it means money above money. With such money and power, I shall have absolute control on almost, if not on all the journeys ever made by any living or dead citizen of NA."

As Evi listened to her husband, she became worried that something evil or crazy was behind his current thirst for money and more money, power and more power. Until now, he was a good husband with who she had shared a for-poorer-for-better life. She believed she knew him and could safely predict him any day. With these utterances of his, she was forced to doubt herself if she really knew him, or, if she really knew herself well enough. She wouldn't deny the fact of knowing her husband's love for money, but never the knowledge that the love was already in the neighbourhood of madness or evil. Could it be true that money is the root of all evils? If so, how long had the seed itself been sown, and how deep-rooted had its plant grown in him? Definitely, she knew she had more questions to ask her husband.

"I am afraid, Carlos, dear – really afraid. How can you be sure of how easy that would be in this business you operate among juniors, rivals and superiors? You think they would all fold up their arms and watch you monopolize transporting all the living and the dead, all the young and the old?"

"There is no need to be afraid. I have done it before, though on a smaller scale; and luckily, it landed us where we are now. Is it a bad place? No. I understand fully all the classes you mentioned, and can repeat similar successful deals with them."

Evi was getting more stunned. "How?" she forced herself to ask.

"I make sure my juniors have my respects however feigned, and without getting to the point that will infer a suspicion of flattery; this blocks their grey matters. For my rivals, I make them feel they are my superiors and pretend my utmost cooperation and support; in this way, they under-estimate me. For my superiors – luckily, their number is insignificant now – I have learnt to give them honour that is limited in expiration, only to the time they show me the white of their teeth and call me nearer enough to see all they do; this tells me how next to handle them.

"So, that colour, blue, stays, so that the bus looks as if it belongs to an entirely different line. There is no 'crown' logo in order to dispel arrogance and to show the type of humility they want by all means.

"The last protective insurance is that the bus has not been count-numbered so that neither the rivals nor the superiors would feel choked.

"The wise hen does not count her chicks in the open. We shall get there safely and occupy the seats comfortably long before we announce our arrival."

"Yes, dear," replied Evi, "your plans sound beautiful, and so is the intention. But the important question is: for how long?"

Unable to give her an appropriate answer, Carlos just offered her a difficult smile.

CHAPTER 3

The Growth

Should Chief Daniel Daniels want to get a break from New Angel, it would be difficult for New Angel to do away with him, even for the shortest of periods. Yes, Togana was his home town and the base of his business, but his few years as a senior administrator in NA, another few as a transporter – a pioneering one at that – and the current, as a financier and technical consultant to the new crop of local transporters, all in NA, could not leave him alone to Togana. From time to time, his presence in NA was always required for one thing or the other.

This time, a full year after his meeting with the transporters over debt repayment, it was to a social function organized by some of his former administrative colleagues he was invited; and the venue was the same Majesty Hotel.

By coincidence, and for their own socio-private reasons, both Carlos Retfil and Ral Ralgrub were then at the hotel. Ral Ralgrub was the first to see Daniel Daniels in a group made of John Martins and their hosts, coming towards the table the two of them occupied in the bar. Ral promptly alerted his friend.

"Over there, look," he pointed to the approaching group, "Chief Daniels, coming with John Martins and some others."

Carlos turned to look and Ral resumed the reportage. "I wonder what he is doing here this time. He just wouldn't take a rest."

"I don't even mind that," said Carlos. "The problem is that he won't just let people have a rest. That is the thing."

"Do you think he has seen us?" asked Ral in a display of panic. He was worried-shy that their history, together with their financial standing with Chief Daniels, wouldn't favour them at that place in that particular extravagant table setting.

"I don't know – don't think so. But why should we bother ourselves with that?"

But Ral feared so, and believed both of them ought to be bothered. Even though everything was just like yesterday, their joint long history with Chief Daniels, he believed, demanded that.

Both Ral and Carlos became associates by virtue of being the first drivers to work for Chief Daniel Daniels. At first, Ral was a junior messenger in the office of Daniel, the senior administrator. The co-existence exposed his smartness, productivity and honesty to Daniel who would give his office keys to him to hold whenever he had to go out of office, or whenever his office needed to be tidied up. By the time Daniel had enough money and decided to call it quits with civil service job, for his dream ambition of developing a passenger transport scheme, Daniel had developed so much trust and likeness in Ral that Daniel did not hesitate to invite Ral to his business, offering Ral a better future. That was how he, Ral, an office boy in the first place, became a general assistant to an administrator turned to a private driver of his own small bus.

Daniel Daniels made a fast progress and soon had a second bus, this time, a bigger one. Next, Daniel taught Ral how to drive, and immediately after that, handed to him the key to the first bus. Further progress made Daniel allow him to bring in a trustworthy friend to join them. Ral thought of Carlos Retfil, his friend from the elementary school days, and offered him the invitation to employment. Before long, Ral was permitted to teach Carlos how to drive, and thereafter allocated a bus by Daniel. And since then, Chief Daniels had not only turned the two men into owners of transport businesses, he had also sponsored other people the two men introduced to him. How could Carlos foolishly forget all this? In such a situation, how would Chief Daniels feel seeing them with the table full of lavish assortment of alcohols and king-size dinner plates?

"What does it matter if he should see us?" Carlos asked again. "We do not owe him."

"Do you know what you are saying?" Ral asked. "We owe him a lot. We did then; we do now; and remember, we have just appealed to him to let it continue. It speaks evil to lead a group of debtors and still be found like this, celebrating the birthday of omni-sexual Bacchus," Ral concluded.

"Come on, Ral. The bird would only take to flight with what it has been able to ingest. Here, the right to complain belongs to no one except the management that just served this table – and that is only when we cannot settle his bill."

By the time Chief Daniels looked in the direction of Ral and Carlos, both men had bowed to the reality by tilting and turning their backs and sides to the approaching group. However, after such a multi-conditional acquaintance that spread over a long period of time, it was not surprising that Chief Daniels did not need a second look at the two men sitting lavishly to know who they were. He pulled John Martins and quietly pointed at the men.

"Can I quickly pass by them?" Martins asked.

"No. Just look on," Chief Daniels replied.

The two men were feeling confident of a successful dodge when, suddenly, Daniel took an excuse from his friends, moved his burly body out of the group, and walked towards Carlos and Ral. Again, Ral was the first to see him coming, and the panic sent him to tip his drink.

"Hello, gentlemen," greeted Daniel, stretching out his hand to each of the men for a handshake, and complicating the environment further for the two men. Only Carlos could respond, as Ral was already busy cleaning the mess off his shirt and table. "Having a nice time, and feeding well to work well?" Daniel further joked dryly. "Anyway, I leave you. Our function is about to start in the hall. Enjoy yourselves."

Daniel made a few steps away when he suddenly stopped and returned to the men. "Excuse me gentlemen; just a quick one. I wanted to bring it up at the last meeting but there was no time: that your business has now expanded to the point you all should be thinking of renovating and expanding your bus garage in any way possible. Please, discuss this with your colleagues as soon as you see them, and see what you think of my observation. You can call for my assistance when and if required."

From that moment on, and with the intention of making the transporters shelve foolish for wise spending, started Chief Daniels' calculated and relentless mishmash of force and persuasion that would make the owners favour having a bus station that would be more useful and beneficial to them and to their people.

The eventual result of Daniel's pressure went positively beyond his wildest imagination. It's six months after he diplomatically derided Carlos and Ral at Majesty Hotel; it came to him in the form of an invitation letter to the fund-raising and foundation laying ceremony of a new central motor park, organised by the bus owners. The special delivery of the letter was delegated to Isa Reduaram, the head of its planning committee.

"Lalala-la.Ultra-modern Bus Station? In NA?" exclaimed Chief Daniels. "This is marvellous. Please call in Mr Martins," he begged Isa, even though both men knew Martins, only separated from them by a door that was ajar, could hear all the excitement. "More ears need to share this piece of good initiative."

"What is going on here sir?" Martins asked his boss on entering and seeing the two happy faces.

"Here," Chief Daniels said, handing the letter to his personal assistant. "An ultra-modern bus station for NA!"

"That is great sir. And congratulations to you," remarked John Martins.

"To me? It should be to my men in NA, for their bright ideas," said Chief Daniels.

"Okay sir, should I then say, to you first. Your men there only complemented your persistent efforts of pushing them to do it."

"Yes, that is it – that complement! They need to be congratulated for it. Suppose the complement by them never came?" insisted Chief Daniels.

"Suppose it didn't? Well, it would have spelt doom for their business as well as for their people. Simple. In the long run, they would still have to do it," re-emphasised John Martins.

"It all equalled to the same thing," intervened Isa. "We congratulate Chief for his inspiration and education, and congratulate ourselves that the doom is averted," he added and thus vacuumed the dusts of unnecessary argument out of the room they all were.

"So, what's your plan for the day?" Chief Daniels asked Isa. "Your detailed programme, and what exactly you want me to do for you?"

Isa Reduaram took out a folded piece of paper from his pocket, shook it open and explained all that Chief Daniels wanted to know at that stage, making several visual references to the paper.

Isa talked on how a comprehensive study had been done, what the total estimated cost was to be, and how the townspeople had been so supportive to the extent of donating both the land to be developed and many of the items to be bazaar-ed away among the invitees. Reduaram stated how much they had contributed so far, what anticipated minimum they expected to fund-raise, and how they intended to look for extra money among themselves to complete the project within six months.

Concerning the government officials, Isa said they had approved the construction plan with no amendment, and had promised easier and less taxation.

Chief Daniels was told how dignitaries were invited from far and wide to attend, and how every invitee was expected to give above the widow's mite. As their mentor and adviser, Chief Daniels would double as the chairman and the chief launcher.

"I will try my best to come," Chief Daniels consented at the end of the briefing, "but on one and only one condition." He paused, and picked up again before Reduaram could ask him what the condition was. "That your scheduled starting time of two in the afternoon is two this time."

"Thank you, sir. Definitely, that time shall promptly be; and we are all expecting you," Reduaram replied, and left.

"What do you think about this bus station thing?" Chief Daniels asked John when Isa was out of the door.

"I just wish them well – that they are able to do it," said John Martins, "and that the project doesn't add to the list of the abandoned."

"Oh John, give them a chance for once. You see, this time, I could see some determination and originality in them. They look set to do it – to work towards improving their own lots and those of their passengers."

"Honestly sir," said an unimpressed John Martins, "I see no determination or originality. The project was your idea, and was being done as a bow to your pressure. I still believe they are being dragged into it; and dragging never makes a smooth journey – not for the dragged, not for the dragger, and not for the route."

In the end, the two-man conference agreed to give the bus owners a chance – that, it could well be the start of a genuine change for the better. But then came a snag: Chief Daniels was just discovered by the PA to have got another engagement in Togana on the same day, and almost about the same time. Chief Daniels resolved to attend the Togana's while Martins would go and represent him in NA – with his donation, and of course, his speeches.

* * *

If there was an event that was ever arranged and staged to time in NA by the association of the bus owners, it must have been so far back or too insignificant for any memory to retain. For this one, by 1.45 p.m. when Martin's car pulled up at the venue, a spacious-enough primary school field bordering the current garage and the site acquired for the project, all seats that mattered for the day were already occupied. The few that were not had their allotted occupants already arrived, but busy carrying out other functions.

The unexpected efficiency of the organisers actually prevented John Martins from noticing the drawn faces of the host members who received him at the entrance to the venue. It was Chief Daniels they were expecting.

"Where is Chief?" Carlos Retfil impatiently asked John Martins.

"Sorry, he couldn't make it."

"Oh my God," screamed Isa, with a deep breath.

At this point, Isa looked at Carlos, and Carlos at Isa, and next, simultaneously, both men shifted the visual interchange to the new arrival. It was not that they were worried about the well being of Chief Daniels, but that primarily, the chief's absence could mean a reduction in their takings, and, possibly too, in the image of the gathering.

Trust John Martins' adequate knowledge of psychology; he was at once able to give a correct reading to the faces that were down and drawn, as well as to the minds that triggered them to be so.

"There was an earlier engagement which Chief forgot about when Isa brought the invitation," he told them. "But gentlemen, not to worry, he has made an allowance adequate enough to make your day," he added to calm down the apparent but undeclared mood of the group. Half frowning, half smiling, they walked him to the seat reserved for the chairman cum chief launcher, Chief Daniel Daniels, placed at the centre of the front row reserved for the occasion's VIPs.

The first item on the programme: Introduction of events.

A man walked out from one end of the row occupied by the VIPs. He made a majestic stride to the front of the chairman's table and stopped. Swinging to different directions, and using repeated greetings and subtle requests for their attention, he managed to drown into complete disappearance, all the on-going murmuring and side talks. He was Joseph Tolp.

In few short sentences, he welcomed everyone, gave the reason for the gathering, and announced as the day's master of ceremony, a middle-aged man dressed flamboyantly in local attire. He called him Ecaf Lawrence.

Ecaf, though possessed not a single bus, a tyre or a spoke, was all the same very qualified for the task by the virtue of his being the government official in charge of registration and taxation of all vehicles in NA. Thus, he was familiar with all the bus owners of NA.

As Ecaf walked out to meet Joseph Tolp, Joseph too walked up and met him. Joseph handed over to him the microphone, beckoned his last round of greetings to the crowd, and walked back to his former position amid a round of loud applause. The MC had now fully taken over.

"The one item," commenced the MC, "that always racks my brain whenever I am called upon to perform this kind of duty, is one like the next – the prayer." He was already on the second item of the programme. "'Why?' you may ask. It is because of the good presence in this town, of all religions – Christianity, Islam and our forefathers'. And so, as the true city of God – or, of gods, if you want it pluralized – I always prefer to have the prayers done according to all religions, as it would be this afternoon here. Certainly, it would not be too much; prayer is ever never. Besides, prayer, and not force, is what God loves to appreciate from us, humans. He won't need or appreciate our wealth or worldly possessions because He had them in abundance, and gave them to us in the first place.

"I therefore call on Papah Feiht first, to lead us in Moslem prayer. After him, our dear lady, Lais Dorman, and Linus Isho, will lead us in the Christian and forefathers' respectively," he directed.

Lais who was there with young Johnson, was unperturbed by the last directive. As a pastor's wife, she had been called upon at several gatherings to lead in Christian prayers. She looked at her son's face, clasping her hands in acceptance.

"Glory be to God and unto Holy Prophet Mohammed, His servant; and may peace be unto Him," Papah Feiht repeated thrice. "Let everyone here thank God for His mercies ten times, seek for His forgiveness ten times, and humbly acknowledge He is the Greatest ten times," he sort of commanded.

There were short murmurs, confirming compliance, by a large number of those present.

Papah Feiht thanked God for giving the transporters the wisdom to plan the project, and the good health to see that particular day of the launching. He begged God to direct the day's affairs, bless all who turned up, and guide them safely back to their respective homes. He acknowledged the excellent leadership of Carlos and Ral, and wished them more wisdom with which to continue in their leadership roles. He rounded up by directing everybody to continue saying "amen" while he cited what he announced as *Al Fatiha* followed by a short, beautiful song heartily chorused by other Moslems in the gathering.

One man was so marvelled at Papah's performance that he asked his wife sitting by him if she was ever aware of Papah being in Riyadh at any time for a course in imam-ship. The wife replied she was not aware, and that it was unlikely any of the transporters would take any period off work for anything that would not fetch him some money. If for any reason Papah went to Riyadh, it would be more likely to be for business and moneymaking than for imam-ship training, since Riyadh delicately balanced the best aspects of

71

business and religion. "Many of them are equally good in religion," she stressed, adding, "haven't you heard that our neighbour, Carlos Retfil, is building a private church which he intends to upgrade to a theological seminary? So does a strong rumour have it. People suspect his motive is pure business."

"Well, the people could be right," nodded the husband. "No one hides both himself and his intentions forever anyway."

'Introduction of the guests' followed the prayers, and the MC himself took it, using a booklet containing the data on everyone that mattered in that gathering. The Launching Committee compiled the researched list weeks before the day of the launching.

It was planned that the MC called out the name of each guest and asked him to remain standing for proper recognition. Then, the MC would proceed to read out an index of imagined and exaggerated achievements of each guest, with carefully programmed commas, and hardly full-stops, so as to allow for clapping and cheering.

Particularly, Pa Hassan, an old farmer of NA, got an extended cheering. Ecaf Lawrence was about halfway down the introduction of the standing old man in the front row when he decided to add some descriptions to the man's commendation:

> *The in-submersible papa*
> *The tractor of our plantation*
> *The caterpillar of our agriculture*
> *The grand wizard of farming*
> *The feeder of NA, and*
> *The grandpapa of all farmers!*

The palms clashed and the throats opened up and roared; and Pa Hassan bowed continually in all directions, to thank the ecstatic crowd. He was just returning to erection from the last bow when the tall-crowned, short-brimmed hat on his head flew in the opposite direction. Had his left-hand-held walking stick been a biologically living thing, it would have been believed that the flashy speed with which it rose to meet the falling hat was a result of its own super-sensitive, pull-up reflex action. As it rose, it blocked the hat from plummeting further. At exactly the same time of the rise, and with the speed of a mother eagle after a prey, Pa Hassan's empty right hand dived after the falling headwear. The double ambush worked well as the hat was not only back in his right hand, sandwiched to the stick, but was immediately raised high overhead together with the stick to greet the crowd, as if the incident was a pre-planned circus act. The people were ecstatic, and they responded with a standing ovation to Pa Hassan, appreciating how a man that old could still command and coordinate such a good strength and agility. The aftermath of the incident brought forth the story of how Pa Hassan, during his younger days as a farmer, would chase two goats or two hens, each running in different directions at the same time, and have both smartly caught and returned into their enclosures.

Grandy Ezidie was recognised after Pa Hassan. In age and business type, both Grandy and Daniel stood within the same contemporariness. However, three differences stood between the two men.

The first was in the geographical zone where each of them operated his business. Ezidie controlled the transport business of Zone 4 from Terra, its biggest town southwest of NA. On the other hand, Daniel's influence was strong and supreme in Zones 1 and 3. From the time he shifted to just financing the local transporters of Zone 1, he had his head office in his town, Togana, in Zone 3; but he also maintained a small office in NA. Regin City in Zone 2 was neutral and common to both men, and to other men in the same trade. It was a sophisticated and commercially buoyant city that many people dreamed of visiting for business, pleasure, or just for a piece of the action. To many, its prominence equalled that of the last bus stop on a very important route.

The second difference was in their style of operation. Daniel owned his own business and preferred others to own theirs and take full responsibilities. He refused to form partnerships with the locals he introduced to the trade. Instead, he gave them the financial and technical back-ups and allowed them their freedom. He expected a good businessman to be fair and self-disciplined at all times. Ezidie, on the other hand, ruled over a transport cooperative that was formed with equal contributions of several individuals. Through a smartness of pretence and intrigues, he not only rose to become its managing co-operator, but also allocated to himself the power to choose who served with him in the cooperative executive.

The third was the perception of the two by the public. From his days as a civil servant, driver, and businessman in the localities, Daniel had endeared himself to most of the people with his kindness, humility and social linkages. Around NA in particular, his efforts at checking the excesses of the bus owners and drivers so that the citizens would have safe and smooth journeys, were popular and appreciated. To the citizens, he was beyond any blackmail that could be planted by the bus owners and drivers. He was their man any day even though he came from a town different from theirs.

That Grandy Ezidie, like any mortal, was selfish was never the issue with the public. What they could not understand was why he had to be so, over a business that equally belonged to others. He pretended equality, but his fellow co-operators knew he maintained a standard of living much higher than theirs, and at their expense. Upon these, he loved to be hailed "Double Grandy" by the members of public, who were happy to replace this behind him with "Double Greedy" they deemed more appropriate.

Very rare were occasions that would bring the two men together in a place at the same time. But where there was such an occasion, Ezidie would display cold jealousy to Daniel. Once, Daniel had just given him a warm handshake and hailed him 'Double Grandy' among other pleasantries when Ezidie replied him with 'Daniel, elle...the elle...' he coined from the end of Daniel. Daniel understood the mockery and calmly stopped him, lecturing him that 'elle' was meant to be a reference to a woman or a female, and he, Daniel was neither of these.

Typically, the gathering was eager to know who the day's chairman would be. It followed up with keen interest, Ecaf Lawrence's pronouncements, which were regarded as the countdown to unveiling the chairman. By the time Ecaf Lawrence called Grandy to be recognised, it was clear that the only invited VIP yet to be called was Chief Daniels' representative, his already existing occupation of the chairman's seat notwithstanding.

"When you want the carnival to be remembered longer, round it up with the biggest float," was Ecaf's next pronouncement as he zeroed on the last man he was going to recognise. Then, he observed a short pause. "Our next dignitary to be recognised is always here for whatever we do, and he is also here now, even though, by representation."

Ecaf created another pause he knew would increase the anxiety of the crowd.

"Ordinary words of mouth may not be adequate to describe the success and achievements of this man, but what else can we do other than to try."

He made another pause.

"He remains our constant mentor and guardian since we knew him. He is a 'Venetian grandee' of transport."

The crowd interrupted with appropriate applause, without realising yet, how further the MC would drag them along with him.

"He is a guru of economic and financial matters."

There's another loud hail from the crowd.

"And above all, he is an unadulterated salt of the earth for this and other communities…" Ecaf was still going on, but then the crowd hijacked the rest from him with an impromptu chant, to complement his grammatical gymnastics:

Da-aniel, Da-aniel;
Da-aniel, Da-aniel…!

And in the on-going roar, Ecaf struggled by design to advance. "And his name, ladies and gentlemen? The one and only-y-y Chief Daniel Daniels…ably represented here today by no other person than his two e-y-e-s, Mister-er-er Jo-hn Martins!" His listeners knew Ecaf meant like in the force's 2i/c, a second in command.

Every guest was now on his feet clapping and cheering, while John Martins, the licensed usurper rose to take the scholarship of the honour and applause meant for his boss. It took two minutes for the ovation to lower down enough for him to respond.

"Good day," he started, "our fathers, our mothers, our brothers, our sisters, all dignitaries, ladies and gentlemen – at the front, at the back, right and left. I want to start by thanking you all for the honour done to my boss by giving him such a huge applause even though he is not here with us. His absence was due to certain emergencies, and he sends his sincere apologies and greetings.

"And even though he is not here, he gave me a written and signed message for this important occasion. The message will be delivered at the most appropriate time.

"I have sought when that time would be from the honourable organisers, and they told me it would be at the start of the donations proper.

"Therefore, for now, I would not take more of your time. Once more, I thank you all very much; and let us all sit down and enjoy this function."

The next item was 'introduction of the association members'.

Like the big claws distinguish the soldier ants in a colony, so did dressing distinguish the nine members of the Bus Owners Association of New Angel from all other persons at the occasion. They were uniformly in dark-blue trousers under similarly coloured tuxedos that were all made and fitted by the more experienced tailors of Regin City. The back of each tuxedo was comically longer than usual. Under the tuxedoes they wore white shirts, some figured, some plain. Each suit made a perfect artificial coverage of the wearer's body – whether tall, short, fat, skinny, bent or straight. Shoes were united in blackness, but bow ties went with individual's preference for hue, shape and size. On the whole, when one viewed the group from a short distance, a clear picture of a group of emperor penguins on an Antarctica ice barrier came to the mind. And despite the visible self-display of the members, Ecaf Lawrence still proceeded with the recognition, starting with a wasteful preamble on the necessity to know who these hosts and patriots of NA were, and calling them to come out one by one:

"Biz Olu Duarf, please join me here for recognition." He had coined 'biz' as his own abbreviation for the word, businessman. "Ladies and gentlemen, please give him a round of applause.

"Biz Ike-eeh Elfans. Please join us; and a round of applause for him please."

Preceded by encomiums and succeeded by applauses, all the nine names were called out.

Olu Duarf, Ike Elfans, Papah Feiht,

Linus Isho, Ral Ralgrub, Mathew Rebbor,

Isa Reduaram, Carlos Retfil, Joseph Tolp.

Before Joseph Tolp was called, Ecaf reminded them the calls were being made in alphabetical order; and that it certainly did not mean that the last to be called was the least in importance.

'Refreshment and Entertainment' followed, as the next item. Its cultural aspect was spectacular; *Kids-Kiddy Dance Group* came out to do it.

Two heavily decorated and mounted horses led a file of six boys and six girls all aged between seven and twelve. Two other horses followed after the twelfth kid. They were closely preceded by a band of another six kids playing some instruments to the dancing steps of the horses and the sweet singing of all the eighteen kids.

One of the two leading horses moved to the right and the other, about twenty feet, to the left. Then, both stopped and faced the dignitaries. Behind them, the dozen kids formed three rows of four kids per row. The last two horses stopped at the end corners of the last row.

Two long sofas were set about six metres behind the last two horses. The band occupied them.

When both kids and animals had taken positions, a girl in the group blew a whistle and the group went still – the kids almost to steel-rod stiffness, and the animals as much as their sensibility would allow them and their riders.

The horses were then made to march further out to the sides, then, back to the original positions of departure and bowed to greet the crowd. Next, the kids bowed; and the band, now seated, went into action for the kids to dance. As the acts went on, it became obvious that the kiddies' knowledge of culture was by far greater than their ages.

In the course of the kiddies' performance, a guest sitting behind John Martins recognised two of the kids. He saw them in the novelty football match featuring the kids of between ten and twelve years, that took place that morning to raise fund for the same project. "My God, since the morning. Don't these kids ever rest?" he asked himself, to the unavoidable hearing of John Martins.

"Do you mean they have been dancing all day?" inquired Martins.

"No, not dancing. But those two in the second row were among the kids who featured in the novelty football match this morning."

"You mean there had been a football match today?"

"Yes, a match, put up by the kids. And the gate's taking was handsome, I was told."

"That's serious," said Martins. "I hope the children are not being overworked and exploited already; and that they are going to be adequately compensated."

"One way or the other they would be," the guest believed. "After all, the project is in NA, and it's them it would serve."

"I pray so, that it would be allowed to serve them adequately, that the transporters would realise the importance of their own growing youths, and stop getting deeper into the dungeon of money making."

* * *

The last horse was about disappearing at the end of the kiddies' dance when an announcement came from Ecaf Lawrence. "We have now arrived at our destination," it said, "that is, at the launching and donation proper. This is why we are all here. Therefore ladies and gentlemen, on behalf of the Bus Owners Association of New Angel, I now call on our able chief launcher, Chief Daniel Daniels represented here today by Mr John Martins, to perform this duty. Mr Martins, please."

John Martins rose again and hailed the association members and other guests on behalf of his boss. He reminded them of the earlier deferment of Chief Daniels' message till the appropriate time, which had now come. As he read out the message, he wanted everyone to follow it in its copies already distributed by the MC.

"Members of the Bus Owners Association of New Angel, fellow invited guests, ladies and gentlemen, I greet you in the name of our Lord.

"First, I would like to apologise, especially to the Association, for being unable to be physically present here today. Just as it was never intended, so it was circumstantially unavoidable. My assistant, Mr John Martins, here among you now, would make you forget the saying that many faces can never be equal to the real. He, as my able lieutenant, is designated to give me a full representation at this launching and foundation laying ceremony of your ultra-modern bus station. I have no doubt that the representation would surpass your expectation.

"I have to admit, that the arrangement, up to this laudable stage, took me by surprise. It is neither because NA does not deserve a good project of this sort, nor that nobody has ever discussed a project like this one with the members of the association at one time or the other. It was because when I raised it a long time ago, it was met with very little interest and acceptance. This therefore, to me, is like the resurrection happening after both the burial and the funeral were over. Nothing could be more surprising, nothing could be more gladdening. Members of the Bus Owners Association of NA, please accept my congratulations."

There was applause.

"I was privileged," the message continued, "to see the plan of the station, and this very plan," he raised it, keeping it up, "promises to be a fantastic piece of project. By the time it is completed, I believe it would represent not only a beautiful structure in NA, but also one that all the citizens, the owners including, would trust as the best provider and guarantor of smoothest journeys. Therefore, gentlemen of the association, as you can see, it is by no means a small task that is ahead of you.

"As you officially commence this project today, I will discuss five aspects of it with you. I noticed you gave yourselves six months to complete it. My comments would therefore assist you towards achieving your aspiration without much waste of materials, time, labour or purpose.

"The first is the foundation, the underground work and base that will carry your dream project and provide stability to it over a long time, perhaps, forever. It is the most important aspect of the structure, and as such, the very reason why I choose to be here today – albeit, representational – instead of waiting till the day of commissioning. You cannot be too economical with the foundation, erroneously believing that your structure is only comprised of the standing walls, open spaces and a bit of storey-ed areas. The ability to safely carry whatever load – dead or living – will depend on the foundation. A good one, even where you need to pile or steel-pile it, will save you from the type of initial problems created by Justonian at the Church of Saint Sophia. Yours should not be a bad foundation. Amen.

The Growth

"Two, your structure: This comprises of your floors, columns, walls, braces and other connections that would guarantee stability, and hence, more safety. The materials employed must be excellent in weight, length and durability. Overall material quality is then achieved, and your maintenance is made easier and cheaper. Yours should not be a bad structure. Amen.

"Third; exterior: I mean the walls, roof and whatever is visible from the outside of the project. With the current high spate of development in NA, your project needs to be beautiful and befitting. It should be compelling, not repelling. This is what draws in the passengers and other potential users from who you can derive your profit. Yours should be a loved exterior. Amen.

"The fourth is the interior of your project. Everything there should be functional. Partitioning should not be all rigid because the future could demand for changes. A too-rigid interior makes internal arrangement, re-arrangement and adaptation difficult and expensive – it is purely anti-current, anti-future and anti-development.

"The choice of colour is also very important; bright is suggested, as it radiates life.

"Amenities therein provided should relieve, not aggravate problems. Systems of light, water, conditioning, waste disposal, fire protection and internal transportation or movement should be adequately provided and maintained. It would be unforgivable to deny or starve your passengers and staff any of them. Even, the insulation and soundproofing should be good. All should aid concentration and give a peace of mind; they must not – I repeat, must not – deafen you to the point of isolating you from the knowledge of the world on the outside. Yours should not be a bad interior. Amen.

"The fifth, and last, I would mention are your passengers. The business opportunities the nine of you have now should be those that privilege you to serve them fairly, leaning and adapting yourselves to the basic philosophy of Paul Harris. Please read at your leisure, this philosophy, set out in five paragraphs under the heading 'Object of Rotary' on the second page of this speech.

"Some years back, the rare opportunity did not exist; when it eventually did, it was, shall I say, only to a couple of us. Your aspiration must be to increase the number of your membership and that of the passengers, all significantly. With openness, fairness, hard work and human feelings, you can achieve all. I implore you to give them definite opportunities – like I gave you – to become owners. I also urge you to cooperate fairly with yourselves so that you can record many successes in this all-important business. It is only when you and the passengers benefit from the system that the system would be genuinely defended and further developed. In summary gentlemen, may it not be a regrettable system to you and to your passengers especially. Thank you for your attention, ladies and gentlemen."

There was another round of applause. It was evident that most people followed the speech with very rapt attention.

After John Martins had finished delivering the main message, he still had the rituals of the donation to perform. These he went into, using his own words.

"Now, coming to the subject matter, that is, the launching together with the offering of Chief Daniel Daniels' widow's mite, the MC had informed me that all those building blocks – a hundred of them that I'm pointing to now – together with that beautiful piece of marble, are waiting for a 'buyer' who will be kind enough to buy and donate them to the Association. It is then the Association will use them for the actual foundation of this bus station. I therefore humbly call on the MC, and on the members, to accompany me to these materials for my closer look and proper evaluation."

John Martins was accompanied to the beautifully ribbon-decorated stack of building materials on the field. There, he pretended an inspection, and signalled that his verdict was ready.

"Ladies and gentlemen, every material here, without doubt, is very standard and of very good quality. It means there is every confidence that all others following will equally be of very good quality. Therefore, I will now carry out the purchase instruction of the chief launcher, Chief Daniel Daniels, by paying two thousand and five hundred for each of the hundred blocks; and a hundred thousand for the marble, in the name of our Lord. Amen."

In NA where the amount of a hundred is restrictively rare, a thousand did not therefore come as a commoner. And, when the thousand came in multiples, it became very unimaginable to most people who, at best, found such an amount easier to hear than to actually value. Without any doubt, many of the day's guests and hosts clearly belonged to the category of this 'most people'.

The two-stapled sheets of paper earlier distributed among the guests at the start of the speech became handy now for their recipients. They rose and clapped excitedly for Chief Daniels, many of them turning the sheets into second palms for clapping. Others just waved them to cheer the generosity of a man who, though was only there in spirit, had clearly deposed the intended donations from those present in person to a lesser valued secondariness. The frenzy that accompanied the applause reached high heavens. It continued till the time John Martins laid the foundation.

* * *

The donations started by Chief Daniels' biggest went on among other guests, with Grandy Ezidie's coming a distant second with a cash donation of a hundred thousand. The style was cash until a man was called to make his own. He, in turn, called the MC nearer to himself and told him that he would be donating a thousand, but in promise. The MC told him to put into an envelope, a hand written promissory note of the amount he wished to donate, and hand it over to one of the appointed collectors, just like the real thing. Thereafter, the MC announced his name and the single thousand for the association to note; and then, there was applause. From then on, it was either cash or promised donation, with the number of those doing the latter being very negligible.

Apart from Chief Daniels', another donation was received with a lot of emotions. It came from an unexpected quarter, towards the end of that item of the programme.

A boy of about thirteen, smartly dressed in full referee uniform, and clutching a football with the left hand, and with a whistle chained to the neck, led a file of six kids to the front of the chairman. With the exception of two of them, the kids were in their football playing jerseys, shorts and boots. The two different boys were in the dancing costumes they appeared in with the troupe that earlier performed with the four horses. They all formed two rows of three each, behind the boy in referee uniform.

"Mr Chairman, sir," announced Ecaf Lawrence, "these young men have got something to say through their leader, Master Gerald, the young, smart referee."

Lais and her son, Johnson, already knew Master Gerald. He came from her church. Had it not been for the difference in the age group, Johnson and Tonga, his brother, would have featured in the same match and troupe.

There was a general eagerness to hear him and know what his group had to offer. Were they going to play football – more football? Had the people not testified that they had played in the morning? Were they out to toy with the ball and win some applause? A lot was going on in the minds of the guests and of the chairman. At this point, Ecaf Lawrence nodded-on Master Gerald.

"Fruh uh uh!" went Gerald's whistle. The hoot sent the kids into standing to attention.

"Sir, we represent the children of New Angel," Master Gerald started. "We want to thank you for permitting us to play our match in the morning, and for allowing us to appear here now.

"We, the youth, are delighted that we are going to have a nice bus station because it means that from now on, we are going to have nice starts and finishes to our journeys.

"We are sorry we don't have enough to donate, but we are happy to pledge our free labour for six Saturdays and Sundays when we may be called upon to be on site. We agree to the weekend days because they are not school days.

"Secondly, at today's football match between our two teams, we made fifty thousand, which we hereby donate towards the building of the new station. Thank you sirs, and God bless New Angel."

At the end of his speech, the kid at the centre of the last row made an about-turn and marched along his outer right to reach Gerald in the front. He handed over the big brown envelope in his hand to Gerald and smartly retraced his steps to where he took off from.

As the deliverer was departing to the back row, Gerald simultaneously marched to the chairman, John Martins, to deliver the envelope. From the point of emotional mercerisation, the chairman uplifted himself from his chair and stepped out to meet Master Gerald. He collected the envelope from the junior presenter and, to the delight of the entire gathering, replaced it with a warm handshake and two Russian hugs. He went on to give each of the kids a similar handshake and a 'thank you'.

The same guest sitting behind the chairman felt strongly that the expression of thanks should not be limited to the kid-players alone – that the chairman himself deserved to be thanked. In the world where many had eyes but couldn't see, had ears but couldn't hear, and had brains but couldn't think right, the chairman saw the thoughtfulness and the goodness in the kids and he swiftly recognised all. Therefore, it would not be out of place, he thought to himself, if any or some of the association members had joined the chairman right away, and out there, to praise the kids and shake hands with them. He was disappointed none of the association members did any of these. Could it be that the members thought the stage would be crowded up? But in an occasion like this, did the crowd not improve the pulse of the party? Or, could it be that they wanted to wait till a later time to give the praises? If so, how sure were they, if they would ever be able to re-assemble the same kids for the deserved praises? The guest doubted the ability of any of the members to see, hear or think right!

When John Martins was returning to his chair, and Ecaf Lawrence called for another round of cheers for the kids, the guest seized the opportunity to carry out his resolve to show an appreciation to the chairman.

"Thank you sir, for the beautiful act," he said, stretching out his hand to John Martins for a handshake as the latter finally found his way back to his chair, but before he could occupy it.

The action proved itself influentially timely. No sooner had both men disengaged hands than another guest rose and shook hand with John Martins. By the time the buttocks of John Martins could touch the seat of his chair, his hand had met those of all guests sitting within an arm-, body- and step-stretch from him, and his face, the approving smiles of the same people.

* * *

"Just a minute," Carlos Retfil stopped Isa Reduaram who was walking past him by one side of the crowd. The standing together of both men, even though not lasting for more than two minutes, was reminiscent of old Cassius and Casca's before the strike at Caesar. At its end, Isa, the man at the head of the launching's planning committee walked straight to the MC who was nearby.

"What next?" Isa asked sharply, "Vote of Thanks?"

"No," Lawrence replied, wondering how Isa, a strong partaker in the day's events, could forget or not know the sequence of the programme. "We still have more acts and dancing before the votes."

"And how many of them are we expecting from the children group?"

Mr Lawrence looked through the sheets in his hand. "One – one kids' and two adults' and then, the vote of thanks. Anything wrong?"

"Oh, no, nothing at all. Continue then. It is just that we have had enough of these kids stuff. They need to rest now; they must be tired. Just go straight to the two last adults'. That is the decision." He handed it out with unmistaken clarity.

Strange. Ecaf Lawrence was at loss in those few seconds. He had not noticed any meeting of the planning committee took place anywhere in that gathering. Could it be that Mr Reduaram, as the head of the planning committee, had a veto power, which he now used?

"But why?" the MC asked Isa; he wanted to be sure. "The signal I got from the kids is that they are ready. They have been brilliant. We mustn't stop them now."

"Oh yes, we can," snapped Isa. "We are. We can and we have. I told you we haven't got the time. Call out only the adult groups."

The sharpness of the conversation drew the attention of Johnson who's just returning to his seat by his mum's after easing himself. He slowed down his movement without stopping completely. He was attentive to the incredible orders of Isa and suspected a raw deal had been hatched against one children's group. He returned to his seat and promptly shared his fears with his mother.

Ecaf sensed that what came to him from Isa Reduaram amounted to a final instruction on the matter. As a man of socials, such high handedness was not strange to him. On many occasions, he'd seen this type receiving the full and blind embrace of members who did not know how it was hatched in the first place. From his experience, no good or bad idea is ever started by a large group, but by an individual who would sell it out to anyone and any group who cared to buy it. Unfortunately, where most people felt unconcerned, the individual was always able to sell such an idea selfishly and successfully. He knew this bad one was hatched between Carlos Retfil and Isa Reduaram.

Ecaf wanted to be seen as being neutral, first by the kids who were stopped impromptu; and second, by the guests who, having got their own copies of the programme, were expecting the kids to come out next and perform. Of most importance to him was also this: if the kids did not have a clear perception of why and how they were stopped, they could wrongly label him as its architect and as being anti-kid, anti-growth or both. He quickly found a way out.

"Okay sir," Ecaf said to Isa, "could you please help us sort out the kids in their dressing room while I call on the next adult group? They need to know of the changes." Isa disappeared to go and face the kids while Ecaf Lawrence headed for his microphone.

"Ladies and gentlemen," the MC blared. "Thank you very much. We shall now take on the next item, item number eight, which is a resumption of the entertainment. I have just been reminded that time is very much against us. We shall therefore skip the next group and go to the second group on that item. That is the *Sekere Dancers*.

"For any of us here who doesn't know the group, I love to be bold to say that it is the one and only *gruppo famoso* that had performed so brilliantly and won laurels in and outside NA.

"For this very show, I was reliably told, that among what we should expect are 'the high-up' dance displayed before the king of Regin City, 'the frog jump movement' used to thrill the senior comrades of Terra, and 'the innocent wriggles' that dropped saliva off the lips of the nobles of Togana. Once again ladies and gentlemen, enjoy the *Sekere Dancers*."

It was five minutes into the time of expectation and there were no *Sekere Dancers* on any part of the stage. The void gave the guests enough time to evaluate the past shows, including especially, the last one. In general, they gave a pass mark to every show and expressed great delight at the wonderful contribution of the young ones. Down the extreme left of where the chairman sat, some guests were even seen congratulating Olu Duarf and Ral Ralgrub, the two other members of the planning committee, both for the good show and for the brilliance of the youths. Inside the preparatory room, it was a different scenario. Isa Reduaram managed to convince the kids on the need to cancel their show; and they agreed with helpless reservation. They felt bad that they had wasted their money and sweat on materials and rehearsals for a show that was in the end nullified off-handed.

There was another serious problem inside the preparatory room. Because the *Sekere Dancers* were slated to perform after the now-cancelled kids show, its members were not ready either as individuals or as a group. Two of them were not in the room, having had in mind that they still had thirty minutes or so of the kids' performance time to finalise their own preparations. Five, ten and fifteen minutes afterwards, Isa was still busy trying to get the dancers out of the room, and the effect of the anti-kids plot was just beginning to take its toll.

"Eh, everything has stopped," Grandy Ezidie remarked to Mr Martins. "Are we through then with today's activities?"

"No, I don't think so," replied Mr Martins. He knew Ezidie was only teasing.

"But," observed Ezidie, "but didn't they say they were trying to save time by omitting the kids' play? Wouldn't they, by now have finished with the play, or be at the point of doing so? Simple arithmetic: What they are imposing on us and on themselves is nett time loss!"

"You are correct at both your observation and calculation," John Martins agreed. "It could be they meant to save something else. Besides, eh, when a full moon is used to dress up for a show, one wonders how many quarters the actual performance would take."

Similarly worried was Ecaf Lawrence. A couple of times, he shuttled between the preparatory area where he eagerly gauged what was going on and the outside where he wore a bold face before the people.

At last, twenty clear minutes after his last announcement, the dancers filed out, slowly convoluting towards the centre stage. Not surprisingly, they were without two of their core members. Hurriedly but with relief, Ecaf Lawrence ran ahead of them to the stage to announce their arrival to a gathering that had already seen them arrive. "Please ladies and gentlemen. Please welcome the one and only-y-y *Sekere Dancers*!" he said almost belatedly.

The barometer of the welcome stayed below the impressive – both visibly and audibly. This was not because the gathering itself was not enthusiastic, but because it was already too tired, having spent a lot of energy staying in expectation. The call by the MC for a second round of applause to boost the first low-volume one did only a negligible repair, as evidenced by scattered eyes deeply sunk in sleep.

As the *Sekere Dancers* mounted the stage, so much confusion on their faces betrayed their unpreparedness for the act they worked so hard to put together. This negatively affected the precision of their coordination, to the extent that a few miss-steps glaringly occurred.

Secondly, the two core members eventually returned to the preparatory room, found that their mates were already forced on stage, and joined them to perform their own special roles. It turned out to be an addition of confusion, a multiplication of error, and hence, an enlargement of failure, because perfect and uniform movement could not be achieved. The best of their attention as well as that of the party was over.

By the time the last entertainment was in progress, there were empty chairs in wide scatters. By the time Ral Ralgrub was delivering the vote of thanks, the presence of the remaining guests dotted mainly around the chairman. And by the time the pastor finished saying the Lord's grace, the number of people that remained to respond, apart from the MC and the nine association members, was barely the number of letters in their 'amen' response, tripled.

Grandy Ezidie would not miss the opportunity of berating before Mr Martins, a show that was seen by many to have made a good take-off, fair flight, but a poor landing, especially when he perceived it, wrongly though, to be wholly an instigative brainchild of his rival. "How do you see it, Mr Martins?" he gave John a tactical push.

"It's okay – and over, anyway."

"Yes, okay; but I believe it could be better. It should have been, considering the enormous guidance that came from your side. Don't you agree?"

Mr Martins knew the minimum Mr Ezidie would go, and so, he was determined to terminate the discussion. "Oh, Mr Ezidie, the launching is in the past tense now." He wore a smile that was wrinkle-diluted enough to show his disinterest. "Well, I must go." He stretched out his hand to Mr Ezidie for the last handshake before both men were seen out and off by some members of the association and the MC.

* * *

Back in Togana the morning after the launching, Chief Daniels arrived in the office, anxious to have the full report from his assistant who had already thought and mapped out how he would give them.

"Good morning, the man from NA," Chief Daniels fired the first greetings on meeting John Martins in the office.

"Good morning sir," he rose as a courtesy.

"Sit down. Sit down. Anyway, settle your table first, and come over to my office."

The settlement, up to his arrival in Chief Daniels' office, was accomplished within five minutes.

"So, have your seat and tell me."

John Martins accepted the first order and, knowing what his boss wanted to be told, commenced on the second.

"Well, it wasn't bad, even though there were certain incidents that could be judged as not being good enough. Or, let me say, things that could disappoint you, but which wouldn't surprise me because of my knowledge of our friends in NA. Yes, for the sake of clarity, I will report what happened under three headings: the timing, the takings and the entertainment, starting with the timing."

"Yes, fine," nodded Chief Daniels who was not surprised that his assistant recognised and respected how he, Daniel, pre-eminenced measuring time within incidents, and incidents within time.

"The timing – its keeping – was very good, even by my boss' standard."

There was a relaxing laughter.

"So they also said," he continued, "of the football match that took place earlier in the day, from ten in the morning to midday. The actual launching programme took off at exactly five minutes before the scheduled time of 2 p.m."

"That is interesting. I told you these people are improving. Who says it is not working? Was there really a football match? Between which teams?"

"Between two teams selected from among the children of NA. Even, the referee and his two assistants were kids. We were told the people were well mobilised to attend, that an admission fee was charged, and that the pitch was packed full."

"Oh, that was quite inspiring and original," remarked a delighted Chief Daniels. "I would have loved to see that – to see how those small tummies protruded innocently out of the jerseys, and how one tiny step outran the other in the name of chasing the ball."

"But sir, they were not as small as you probably think. They were between ten and thirteen years old."

"That was equally good. It must have been very amusing. Better to catch them young!"

"The day's total taking was excellent too. Each donation was followed by the latest sub-total until at a point – of about two million – when, for reasons best known to them, the association stopped the MC from making any further public announcement of the sub-total. By my own following, they took another full one million after that."

"That too, was excellent. I am happy for them."

"Your three hundred and fifty thousand was the highest, and the most valued. It was followed by Grandy Ezidie's one hundred thousand as a distant second. The ovation you got was unmatched in length, width and height.

"The kids' fifty thousand stirred high all emotions, because it was least expected. The unsure were the promises and pledges from about a dozen guests."

"Fifty thousand from the kids, did I hear you well? They must have raked-in from their parents!"

"No, no, no. That was the takings from the manned gates during the match. But all of it. Then, they pledged free weekend labour for six weeks."

"Did they return some money to them, or offer them some gifts?"

"No, none whatsoever, as much as we knew. Some of us felt bad at that, and more so when the poor kids were stopped from putting up the other show they already spent their own money to prepare."

"That was unfair," said a depressed Chief Daniels. "It contrasted poorly against all the good stories you already narrated. But why would they do that?"

"We overheard that the members felt the kids' performances were upstaging the Association. So, they quietly ordered that further kids' performances be stopped. That was why the tail end was not as good.

"But they were too clever – they wouldn't do all the nonsense until well after all the donations were in from everybody, including from these same kids."

"You call that clever?" asked an angry Chief Daniels. "No, that was pure shame and heartlessness! Look, if well executed, that project shouldn't take more than half of the donation they already secured. They had enough and should have returned something to each of the kids. Above all, why adding insults to the injuries already inflicted on both the young and the old show groups?

"And Grandy Ezidie, did he say anything?"

"Of course, he clearly did – that the event would have been better than that if you, as their true patron, had tutored them well enough."

"Oh, my God. That political beast!"

CHAPTER 4

The New Tool

It was one Monday eight months after laying the foundation, and two, after the commissioning of the new motor park. About five-fifteen on this dark but dry morning, two buses moving along the road linking Carlos Retfil's home and private garage with the new bus station were disturbing what remained of the nature's balance of peace and quiet. The first of the two was new; it was another just delivered to Carlos Retfil's home garage the previous Saturday, but now making its debut entry into the new station. The driver was Emmanuel Titoloujou. The second bus was Emmanuel's normal, but now being taken to the station by Adnata Ineso, his assistant in Carlos Retfil's employment.

It was not that the combined noise of the two engines involved was abnormal, but because it was the time most people were in their last rounds of night sleep before they would be up for the day, and because the streets were still empty of other noticeable living things, the noise was distinct enough.

Something else that shattered the peace of the hour was the combination of head and rooftop lights of the two buses. The total emission, as they revolved and flashed and moved along with the buses, appeared more aggressive than actual because most of the light bulbs on the poles along the route were burnt out and had not been replaced.

They were at the intersection some five hundred yards away from the station when another bus was noticed coming from the secondary road off the left. Though Emmanuel could see neither its colour nor its registration number, but the similar rooftop revolving lights told him it was another one for the garage. Whose it was in particular however, he wouldn't know.

The lone bus, stopping and giving way to the two buses on the major road before adding its own headlamps behind them, completed the procession. Within five minutes, and in a velocity dictated by Emmanuel's hearse-like, the three buses were at the gate of the bus station. There, they met a light-dark situation that was definitely worse than the one they drove through – instead of the accustomed inter-penetration between these two elements, everything was in total darkness.

"Tuut, tuut, tu-uu-t," Emmanuel depressed the horn thrice in a bid to attract Kresta Ali's attention from whatever part of the station he could be.

Kresta was the chief security officer of the station. A well commended and retired army warrant officer of the second category, he was given the job over six other applicants just six weeks earlier, after a thorough Carlos-led interview panel where he impressed the panel on how he would complement the efforts of the association to maintain good security in and around the station.

Kresta's incredible show of thoroughness – in its crudest form – was two weeks back, which was just four into his new appointment. Determined to stop once and for all, all the seemingly intractable rot of on-duty sleeping of the two but older security officers he was employed to supervise, he quietly set out from the gate house that night's 3 a.m. for the duty posts of his inferiors. One after the other, he met them fast asleep, giving him the opportunity to take away unnoticed, the hourly clocking card from one, and the security officer's cap from the other. It was all he needed to disprove the recent past denials of the two men before he successfully pushed for the men's dismissal at the same time, the very same morning. When, later in the day, the report of the incident together with the actions taken reached Carlos Retfil, he supported Kresta's vigilance but differed on the actions Kresta took. He was of the opinion that for thoroughness to be effective, it must be accompanied with humane politics; and that if there would be sackings, they should have been spaced out to allow for orderly replacements. Carlos, believing that acquiring experience in a hard way was always a good teacher, prevailed on his colleagues to make Kresta combine with his own for two to three weeks, the jobs of the two men he sacked at a time. With the engagement of two new hands scheduled to take effect from the night of that Monday, he was about to end the period of the punishment imposed on him for his supervisory recklessness.

Therefore, Kresta, mindful of the regulation governing the offence of sleeping on duty, ensured he did not commit the same offence. He kept himself busy by making repeated patrols to every section of the station. In-between these, he would return to the gatehouse and engage the companionship of coffee, the reinforcer-friend he trusted to keep him awake all night. Unfortunately, at that early hour when the buses arrived, the friend could not stop him from losing the battle to the superior force of nature. With his head chinned down on both palms, and the elbows resting on the table, Kresta crossed the thin line separating slumbering from sleeping – helplessly into the zone of the latter.

Kresta jumped up, grabbed his long torch and rushed out to shine it at the full lights of the leading bus. The effect was insignificant – he perceived nothing in the ordinary sense, and realised instantly that the sin of sleeping had caused him to act in the foolishness. He pulled back the torch's switch and yelled out a correction: "Who is that?"

"Titoloujou. Good morning."

"Good morning sir. Please, just a minute."

Kresta ran back into his office and returned with the bunch of keys hung on the wall. On it was the operator of the padlock that held down the lighter end of the bar that was rested across the gate. He undid the padlock and dashed across to the other end, the weighted. He was halfway depressing it when he noticed at the front, a new number plate on a strangely non-radiating bus. "Is that you, chief driver, sir?" he stopped to ask again.

"Yes, Ali, it's me I said," re-confirmed Emmanuel. "Can't you recognise my voice?" Emmanuel could see through the beams how Kresta was struggling to wrestle off the state of confusion he was in. "It is a new bus, a new addition to your garage and to your register. The one behind is my usual one."

The clarification pushed Kresta to look further behind the leading bus. He could now see two other sets of dipped lights, signifying the presence of two more buses.

"And which bus is the third, sir?"

"I don't know," replied Emmanuel. "It caught up with us shortly before we got here."

Kresta went to ascertain. In it was Lela Adamu, the chief driver of Isa Reduaram.

Entry formalities completed by both sides, Kresta let in the three buses.

* * *

Under a serious assessment and fair judgement, and as far as other nearby bus stations were concerned, the new, New Angel's was in a distinct class of its own. It was as beautiful as it was functional.

From far away, one could see the inscription, CENTRAL BUS STATION, centrally arched high up across the main entrance gate, and between two, twenty feet high concrete pillars. The two pillars were thirty-six feet apart.

Centrally under the inscription started the arc of another object, a smaller one with a diameter of about eighteen inches. It was a *Smith* clock with all hands and numbers in pitch black. The hands were so bold that the sectors they formed were clearly visible from a far distance.

The front wall by the right of the gate was four hundred feet long, and by its left, a hundred and twenty, thus making the overall position of the gate in relation to the wall to be to the left. Therefore, while one could from the gate, and before one's actual entry, see almost all the inner left, the other side, the right, could not be all seen from the same position.

First within the easily visible portion was the security gatehouse itself; it bordered the left of the main gate. It was about six by ten feet with its longer side along the front wall. One of its windows opened outside to the street, one inside to the station, and the smallest third to the entrance gate itself. The only door into the office was by the right of the third window. All windows, except the third, were partitioned and bridged with iron rods to deter burglary.

From the main gate, one is fascinated by the direct expanse of concreted floor boldly lined out with yellow paints into rows A, B and C. Each row was further sub-lined and numbered 1 to 12 to accommodate twelve buses parked side-by-side but parallel to the front wall. Two lined, wider passages separated the three rows. Each passage ran along the depth of the station, terminating four hundred feet down at the back wall.

The drivers' block was inside at the extreme left corner. As wide as the security gate office, and almost three times as long, it accommodated a small sitting hall, a rest room, a cloakroom, a toilet and a shower room. As far as this side of the station was concerned, it, and the security gatehouse were the only two edifices that were roofed.

On entering the garage, the paint-demarcated longest road ran in both directions along the entire front wall and touching both the bordering right and left sidewalls. As it did so, starting from the left, it went past the three parking rows together with their two accesses, a large low-roofed building, and a single storey building, and then terminated at the right sidewall.

The low-roofed building was mainly the passengers' waiting hall, and as such was provided with long, but beautiful, wooden benches carefully arranged in groups parallel to the front wall. It fully occupied the space between row C and the storey building, and was as deep as each of the rows.

The storey building was fifteen feet wide all through; and it went further than the hall before it went left to form a figure seven over the hall. One external stairwell from each end of the building and an internal one at its middle went up to the iron-railed, open balcony along the entire front of the top floor. The top of the storey building housed the offices of the transporters, the training rooms, and the store for items like trolleys, cleaning materials, the fire fighting equipments and the staff uniforms. The ground floor housed a number of small shops, a snack bar, three mini restaurants, a ticket office and a large luggage department that extended up to the first floor where it handled cases of lost and found items.

Two major agreements were among those reached at the pre-commissioning meeting: how to meet the cost of site maintenance, and how to share the thirty-six parking spaces available among the transporters. Reaching an agreement on the first was relatively easier than on the second.

To fund the maintenance, they agreed there was no need to levy themselves any further – that they had done more than was expected of them in providing the station in the first place. "It is the duty of the ingestion to complement the kindness of the throat," Carlos Retfil told them. Therefore, they would rely on both the indirect taxation of the passengers, and on the rents collected from the shopping outlets, to maintain the garage. The taxation would come in the form of extras put on every fare, and would vary with the route distance.

For the space allocation, direct balloting was first agreed upon. On thirty-six papers, each two inches square, were handcrafted A1 to A12, B1 to B12 and C1 to C12, to represent all the available parking spaces. They were individually folded and thoroughly shuffled in a bucket; and then picked one by one, and in turn, by the nine transporters. The result of the exercise was far from interesting to everyone of them.

Olu Duarf's A7, A10, C1 and C5 banished him entirely from row B; while Isa Reduaram's A10, B10, B11, and C10 put him in an area more obscure than peaceful. As for Carlos Retfil's pick of A8, B4, B6 and C11, they spread him out in an un-mathematical fashion.

It was Carlos Retfil who instantly directed towards a solution, the internal protests that followed the balloting. "Where everybody is unlucky," angrily observed Carlos Retfil, "then, something must be wrong with luck itself," he charged. "The unlucky should exercise his right to seize luck and veto its direction. And thank God it has no mouth with which it can protest, isn't it?" he concluded in a pointedly suggestive manner.

Without any further extension to the debate, the local tycoons arrived at these resolutions: one, any bus could occupy any space not already occupied by another bus; two, spaces specifically reserved for buses departing for and arriving from certain destinations and clearly displayed by station officials should be strictly used for that purpose; and three, where two or more buses were for the same route and destination, the bus that arrived first at the station would load first. The new resolution sent Emmanuel in the new bus to A12, the most extreme space near the drivers' block, while at the same time directed his other driver, Ineso Adnata, to stop at B1 already marked for New Angel – Fali Point – Gemmo – Regin City. Lela Adamu, on the other hand, positioned his on A1, ready to load for the same Regin City, but via Togana.

* * *

As at that time of the morning, Lela Adamu still had an hour before he would start checking in his passengers. He decided to go and satisfy the curiosity aroused in him by the sight of the new blue bus.

"Good morning," Lela addressed Adnata Ineso, his colleague of lesser grade, "and congratulations."

"Good morning, Lela, but I don't have to be congratulated for anything," responded Ineso.

"Yes, you do. What is that new bus for then?"

"Well, I believe if anyone has to be congratulated, that one has to be its owner, and not a mere driver of Ineso's category."

"Okay, if you say so. But which route will it ply?"

"I am sorry; that, I don't know either. Probably one of those long ones, because it is new and so, mechanically more sound. Only the boss and the driver who brought it here could be definite on that arrangement. I just guessed."

Up to this point, Lela felt he had derived nothing from the neutrality, if not the negativity, of Ineso's responses. He terminated the disappointments and walked to Emmanuel himself.

"Morning, Emman," he greeted. "Your new bird is beautiful. I am here for my own bottle of wine."

"Thanks, Lela, I see. You are going to wait a long time for it; you could even wait forever!"

"Why? Why should that be?"

"Because the person who should provide that bottle is the owner, Carlos Retfil himself; and he is not here now."

"But he is your boss. And you are his chief driver."

"Exactly. Lela, you are right," cut in Ineso conspiratorially in support of Lela. "Before we left home this morning, I asked our boss the same question, and he referred me to Emmanuel; he said my immediate boss will provide it."

"It still does not make it right," said Emmanuel, "and you both could repeat the request as many times as you wish. I expect you to know that there is a difference between the depositor and the banker; a good banker does not wait until the depositor comes for a withdrawal before he realises the fact that he is only a keeper.

Besides, may I ask you two: Who should do the house warming – the buyer of the property or his tenant? The way you have to wait is the way I am waiting too. The boss promised to mark it, but said I too should wait."

"Only that by the time he answers you, you won't call any of us. It would just be between you and him," joked Lela.

"Well, sir," said Ineso, "which child calls his friend to his own pot of honey?"

"Why wouldn't I call you? Don't worry, I will. You both know I am not greedy when talking of anything for sharing. 'Live and let live' is my policy," Emmanuel said, laughing. "Unlike you two."

"That's mere saying; it doesn't confirm that policy you claim. Okay, we just wait and see," said Lela. He did not want to over-flog the issue to the detrimental omission of the next thing he wanted to know from Emmanuel. "But which route would it ply? Ineso said it would be a long one, to Regin City; true?"

"Ah, I-n-e-s-o!" Emmanuel shouted in amazement. "How do you know that? Anyway, I have forgotten you even surpassed your boss in the ability to x-ray solid objects with naked eyes. Well, maybe you will tell us more of what we don't know."

"But," Ineso started to simplify the reasons to the two men, "which route would be more appropriate for a bus this new and this lavishly decorated? Which one? No special skill is required to know that."

"You may both have your points," intervened Lela, "but with this type of people we serve, I don't expect anything to be that straightforward. In all my years of experience with my own boss, I cannot boast of knowing him well enough beyond being able to predict his constancy at funny inconsistencies. Normally, he works against general beliefs, and I believe this is the stock-in-trade of all of them.

"A new bus may be ideal for long routes, but what if he doesn't agree so? What if he agrees but was not allocated the route

103

by his colleagues? We should not forget the quarrels that route allocation causes among them from time to time."

"Unless he doesn't like it," Ineso begged to disagree, "if he likes a route, he knows how to get it."

"And those – their disputes over routes – are what I don't quite understand," said Emmanuel. "If we drivers don't have them, why should they? Whether the routes are long or short, there are just many of them to share among only nine of them."

"I too have always wondered why," agreed Lela, "until I witnessed their last fight, which resulted in the latest arrangements. Now, I know it's because of what the routes mean to them. Not only that, different times on the same route, on the same day, mean different things altogether to each of them."

"Lucky you," said Ineso. "And they allowed you to witness a free show? Don't tell us you refereed the fight."

"No, I spied from a safe distance, using my two ears."

"Tell us what you heard from the meeting then," urged Ineso.

"I heard my boss asking to be withdrawn from our route through Hycie to Regin City, and have it substituted with another to the same Regin City, but through Fali Point and Gemmo being plied by most of them. He was told to wait one month but he refused, saying the bad road on his current route would have finished his bus in another month. In the end, Ike Elfans invited my boss to join him on his current Togana route, which was shorter, had a well rehabilitated road, and was always full of passengers."

"Oh what a thing I would have loved not to miss," said Ineso.

"But who would drive your new bus?" Lela asked yet another question.

This question Emmanuel understood very well, but chose not to fall for the inquisitiveness of his colleague. So did Ineso understand Lela's question, but equally chose to be silent in order not to be seen as being all-knowingly forward.

In split seconds that ran into whole units, the inquisitor now surveyed the two faces. He saw only two sealed pair of lips on two brightly radiating faces. "Emman, who is its driver?"

"You are right. Who," replied Emmanuel teasingly, but without Lela suspecting anything yet.

"Who?"

"Yes, that same person you just mentioned, I said. It is Who – Mr Who – that is the driver," Emmanuel confirmed un-seriously.

Ineso could not hold himself any longer. He turned his face to a side and burst into laughter, which immediately betrayed the joke. Next to join in the laughter was the leg-puller himself. The last, though unsmilingly and without a choice at that moment, was the quizzer. Emmanuel had successfully dodged the question.

Ineso took the next moment to direct the heat at Lela. "But, rumour has it that Chief Tolp too had just taken delivery of, e-e-m two buses, and that they are also blue like ours. Is this true?"

"Ineso," Emmanuel called in astonishment before Lela would confirm or deny the allegation. "Where and how did you come across that?"

"Yes, it is true," he quickly replied, "– two new buses to beat ours. One of my passengers saw them. I mean, saw the two. The passenger claimed to be a good friend of Chief Reduaram's family."

"Ah, Ineso!" interrupted Lela. "You know what? One of these days, you are going to cause trouble with these rumours you love to gather onto your dinner plates. Which two buses? Which blue buses? I heard of only one, and I have not set my eyes on it, talk less of knowing its colour. Did the same passenger also remember to tell you how much was paid for them, which routes they would be made to ply, and who the drivers would be?" he mocked.

"But without me answering those questions, you have now confirmed I have my point," said a happy Ineso. "Besides, when the finger has done its best by pointing to the direction, it leaves the sighting to the eyes, and the approach to the legs."

"And you didn't even tell us that before you turned on poor Ineso," remarked Emmanuel to Lela. "So, you have got two new buses!"

"There was no time yet to call everybody. Your boss knew almost three weeks ago."

It was true – that Carlos Retfil knew what Isa Reduaram planned to do, and did three weeks ago. He knew *a courtesia* of Ineso and of what Ineso knew how to do best – sniffing and shopping for truths, half-truths and sometimes, for outright falsehood which he would panel-beat to his own advantage.

Whenever in the garage, Ineso would move from point to point, gathering news and information. At the steering, as he glued his eyes to the roads, so he set his ears ready for what could be whistling in the gushing winds and what his passengers were discussing. Whenever there were topics of discussion he could not get a fair gist of, he would ask his conductor for possible re-caps. And whenever off duty, he would claim he forgot something in the garages and use it as an excuse to come in and nose about. Late in the evening was his favourite time to sneak into Carlos' house and report what he felt pleased to report. For this, his colleagues nick-named him 'the post-man'.

However, smart as Ineso claimed to be, the regular breakdowns, together with unnecessary scratches and dents that usually occurred on any bus he drove made both his colleagues and his boss' wife doubt his professional competence. Since joining Carlos' employment, his driver's licence had gradually journeyed from being clean to being dotted with offence points.

Whatever Ineso handled – be it passengers, freight or news – as long as the best in financial dividend kept coming to Carlos, Carlos cared less for what anybody called his informer-driver. Quite undeservedly, Ineso was promoted next to Emmanuel within a very short time, over and above two other better drivers.

So, as far as Isa Reduaram's plan on the acquisition of a new bus was concerned, it was already leaked to Carlos who then mandated Ineso to keep a continuous tab on the news and let him have further developments as they occurred. It was in an attempt to extract more facts from Lela that Ineso fooled Lela into a confessional defensive, by asking him openly about certain two buses instead of just the one he, Lela, already confirmed.

"Who are the assigned drivers then?" Emmanuel asked, this time, taking sides with his junior – against poor Lela.

"I told you, we're expecting just one," said Lela defensively, facing both men with a shrunk face that suggested his disappointments with the men. "And Ineso here now, was the first to tell me what the colour is. How then can I answer your questions?"

As the men traded and countered questions that early hour of the morning, Isa Reduaram's car appeared at the gate. It was Ineso who saw it before it could draw level enough for Kresta Ali to see from inside the gatehouse.

"Look. Over there," Ineso whispered strongly. "Your boss, Chief Reduaram, is here – at the gate."

"Where?" Lela swiftly responded as he took a simultaneous dash away from the men. He realised he must have been talking for over an hour; and that the time then must have been about seven, the usual time Reduaram used to get to the office, and one which he expected his staff to have gone far in ticketing-in the passengers for the first outward journey of the day. Despite Lela's evasive actions, Isa still caught a glimpse of him in flight, but believed it would, by that hour of the day, be an additional waste of business time to call and chide him.

* * *

Within the next two hours, full life had descended on the station; it was as if every station user agreed on a lower limit of time to commence the activities of the day. While some buses were still loading, a few had loaded and were already *en route* their

107

destinations. Others from outside NA had arrived and were off-loading their passengers and picking up additional ones to replace those disembarking.

From one particular area within was coming a sweet aroma of delicacies that were already in place as breakfasts. It was the area with the restaurants like the *Original TeeCoff*, *Hungrieman* and the medium-sized *Angel Restaurant*.

Mrs. Popeye, travelling that day, walked hurriedly past the gate and the restaurants, and reached the *left-luggage*. She opened the small wallet in her left hand and took out a small ticket, which she handed over to the attendant at the counter.

"Yees, yees. Row two. Bocs two," the attendant spoke directly to the ticket, raising it to the level of his upper eyelashes. "Just a moment, madam," he added as he walked to the extreme left corner and brought down a small suitcase already strapped to a trolley. He scribbled something on the ticket, made a turn, and handed both ticket and suitcase to Mrs. Popeye.

The speed with which Mrs. Popeye walked across with her luggage to where Lela Adamu and his conductor were checking in the passengers was one clearly out of character. It was the type for someone chasing something, or being chased by something. Because she observed that the queue at the entrance of the bus was short, and was intimidated by the red flashing and revolving lights on the bus, she believed the bus was about full and ready to depart. She therefore abandoned the feeling of the emptiness of her stomach and the dryness of her throat, and of the strongly inviting aroma coming from the restaurants, to get herself fast enough for her check-in.

Mrs. Popeye was in her late sixties, but her small size made her look a full decade younger. For this journey, she had worked to avoid the unpleasantness the rigours of preparations could cause someone within her age bracket. The day previous, she came to the station with her luggage, obtained her ticket, and deposited it at *left-luggage*. She was going to Gemmo.

"Regin through Gemmo?" she gasped as she asked the conductor who still had six more passengers to check in.

"No, madam," replied the man at the door." That one had just left. This is to Gemmo only, just provided to take the passengers who couldn't go on that."

"Bless you," said Mrs. Popeye to the conductor. "Aren't I lucky after all?" she added with a sigh of relief.

"Yes, indeed ma'am. Your ticket please?"

Mrs. Popeye handed over the ticket, and then, the luggage still strapped to the trolley. And, as if doing a necessary favour to a passenger too big for the doorway, the conductor moved to a side to allow the lady to climb in. Once inside, she slowly made an n-turn of her head, starting from her immediate left, to look for a seat she would take. She could see, to her displeasure, that the bus being almost full, had got all the window seats occupied. She reversed the look and was almost at the point she departed from when, on the second row from the front door, she noticed that a lady by the window had an empty seat beside her. Her mind immediately told her the lady would be her row-mate.

"Good morning," Mrs. Popeye greeted the younger lady. "Is this seat free?" she asked pointing to the lady's left.

"Yes, ma'am, I think so."

She slowly crabbed nearer through the space created between the row she was to sit and the back of the one she was to face. At the seat, she palm-felt the softness of its velveteen-upholstery seat, brought out a lightweight handkerchief from her handbag and engaged it, quite oddly, in gentle seat tapping. Fully satisfied of its dustlessness, she took it.

In her more than six decades of existence, Mrs. Popeye had been fortunate enough to see the good, and unfortunate enough to see the ugly phases of transport business in NA.

From babyhood, she grew into the era where mules, donkeys and horses were used in transporting men and goods. She knew how, as children, they loved to feed these strong and gentle animals with bean chaffs and hay. She knew the pleasures and displeasures of trekking to the farms, villages and towns. She knew the excitement brought about by the arrival of bicycles, and how she was the first among the citizens of both sexes to know how to pedal. The day she deflated an arrogant male, a schoolmate, by alluring and carrying him on the frame of her bicycle before their school friends and mates, remained especially indelible. To her, even though this period might not quite pass as excellent, but definitely, it was good enough.

She knew the time Chief Daniel Daniels resigned as a civil servant in NA and began the first transport business with a lorry. Its body was wood-built, and the engine had to be manually stirred like an on-the-fire pot of porridge, using a long and specially angled metal rod, before the engine would start with a big, smoky roar. She knew how the citizens, conscious of their safety, were at first sceptical of going in Chief Daniels' lorry, and how Chief Daniels encouraged them on. She knew how the encouragement, together with the good fortune of Chief Daniels, progressed to the chief's introduction of long buses, which were driven by former office boys, Ral Ralgrub and Carlos Retfil. She also knew the day a prayer of dedication was done in NA for a bus Chief Daniels sold at a giveaway price to his good servant, Ral Ralgrub. She knew how, soon after that, Chief Daniels treated Carlos Retfil the same way. To her, that was the height of the good era.

She knew how, with the sole assistance of Chief Daniels, other local people got into the business, and how these people started to get swollen headed to the point of offering rough rides to the passengers. It was definitely an era she hated to remember.

She knew how Chief Daniels, as the sponsor of the local transporters, ferociously fought them to curb their growing excesses to their fellow citizens and passengers. She knew it was the curb that led to the provision of neater buses, the building of the new bus station, and to the current civilised operation of the system. And, though now she felt great, she could not be sure if it was really happening and how long it would last.

Thus, as she was about to take her seat, a part of her knew the seat was likely to be clean; but then, her stronger subconscious brought out the handkerchief, stuck it into her fingers grip, and commanded the hand for the cleaning. The hand was just obeying when she realised she was in the new transport age, stopped, and sat.

"Did you also miss the bus, dear?" Mrs. Popeye asked her row-mate.

"Yes, madam, but I was told, by about three minutes."

"Oh, poor you, dear. Just by about three minutes? We are definitely in a new era, a good one that's impossible to think of some years ago. Now, they have the timetables and operate them strictly. You miss a bus, and another is swiftly provided to facilitate your journey. Ah! Dear, can you imagine this magic?" She paused impatiently as if expecting an affirmative answer to the question. "And sorry, dear, I am Mrs. N. Popeye. N is for Nancy."

"Mrs. Popeye? That name sounds familiar."

"Really?"

"Yes, ma'am, it does. I am Tina Macaulay – Mrs."

"Tina, dear, it is nice meeting you."

"Thank you ma'am."

Mrs. Popeye used the next minutes again to gaze round the number of passengers inside the bus, and ended it with one to her wristwatch.

"What is the departure time, Tina, dear?" she asked.

"Might be as soon as the bus is full. The conductor would be in a better position to know."

"Conductor, please," Mrs. Popeye called on the man at the door.

The conductor reduced the distance between where he was and Mrs. Popeye on her seat, without actually getting to her. "Can I help you, madam?" he asked her.

"Yes please. When do we depart?"

"Soonest, ma'am. Give us another three quarters of an hour, and we should be full and gone."

It was not that Nancy was so much in a hurry to depart NA now that she had secured a seat, but was interested in arriving at where she could solve her burning internal problem – that of hunger and thirst.

"Can I rush a cup of tea at the café?" she asked the conductor.

"Certainly, ma'am. Take your time; but listen in case there is an announcement."

"Oh bless you, dear," she said with another relief.

"Which journey is ever enjoyed with an empty stomach?" Nancy used to ask herself before embarking on any journey. "If there is going to be one – circumstantially forced for that matter – it had better be on a smooth road, one smoother than any of those in Gemmo and NA," she would conclude. So, she never travelled or advised anyone to do so without first filling up his stomach. She believed strongly that for every journey that was being made with whatever medium, two journeys were in fact taking place. One was by the medium, the main carrier; and the other, by the traveller himself. Both needed a timely oiling, greasing and a thorough servicing in order to counter the effects of potholes, bends, hills, valleys, winds, temperatures and so on along the way as they both went along. Thank heavens now, that unlike in the immediate past, there was no need for any traveller to embark with hunger. One who could not eat at home could balance up the equation at the new bus station with its good restaurant services. Any traveller, she further believed, who could not do either of these, had nothing and nobody to blame other than his own negligence. These were her strong beliefs for which she regularly prayed would never suffer a reversal.

Quite a number of other passengers who directly or indirectly heard the discussion between Nancy and the conductor decided to partake in the opportunity initiated by the old lady. Among the number was Tina Macaulay herself. She accompanied her to *Original TeeCoff* while the others fanned out to *Hungrieman* and *Angel Restaurant.*

"Usually," Nancy started to tell Tina as both ladies settled by their tea and doughnuts, "I feel incomplete embarking on a journey from here without first tasting its tea or coffee. Do you also always feel the same?"

"Sometimes, yes; but my favourite here is the mini-market. I love to stop there and select some sweets for my daughter and her friends. The assortment is always cheap and fresh."

"Have you tried their *Angel Restaurant*?"

"No ma'am."

"Oh dear, you need to taste their rice and spaghetti. They even taste better than what you get in Shanghai or in Pisa – they are just perfect. Thrice we did it – my husband and I – and he labelled the restaurant 'a mini-home away from home', and the station itself, the ISP, meaning 'ideal starting point'.

"I shall try it next time I am here. It must have been very good," Tina agreed wholeheartedly.

By this time, some of the passengers who followed them out were seen returning. The two ladies, having finished without a rush, joined them into the bus.

* * *

Lela Adamu returned to the bus from his boss looking sulky and melancholic. He called on the conductor to ask for the current state of the loading.

"Are we ready, and is your bus full?" Lela asked the conductor.

"Not quite ready. It is not quite full."

"How many seats remain?"

The conductor checked the number of the tickets still not torn from the booklet.

"Four. Four tickets still remain."

"How many of those sold are full tickets?"

"All, except two – taken by two small girls."

"How about the luggage – all in place?"

"Yes, they are."

"Other routine checks all done?"

"Yes, we are fine. Carried out already."

"Then, that's fine enough. What's the time?"

"Just past nine. Nine fifteen. I already told them we might be here for another half hour, and they don't mind."

"You know, we don't have to wait that long. Nowadays, the passengers look for excuses to complain about anything – even about favours done them. I have heard enough of the chief today. He saw me with Emmanuel early this morning while we were talking. I didn't even know he did. He just finished telling me off about it. Just shut your doors and we go. There would be more than four passengers at the bus-stops."

From the garage to *Metro*, the second bus stop, usually took about five minutes. During this time, the conductor did not bother to sit down because of the duties he had to perform.

First, at the gate, he came down the bus and completed certain formalities for his boss, Lela; then, Kresta Ali's men allowed their bus out. As soon as the bus was out on the road, he moved up and down the aisle, fixing the luggage he felt was not safely rested on the top racks. He was about getting to the end of all these when the bus approached *Metro*; and so, he suspended this temporarily. Lela slowed down the bus while the conductor moved to the rear door, ready to open it; this, he promptly did when the bus completely halted at the bus stop. Correct to Lela's prediction, four passengers – two men and two women – rose from the sofa they were sitting on and joined other passengers in the Gemmo bound bus.

An hour had gone since passing *Metro*, and the bus was now about sixty kilometres out of NA. With the legal speed adhered to by Lela, the journey became even more enjoyable. From the visibly gentle movement of the living green leaves on the branches to the quiet settlement of the dead brown ones on the ground, it was easy to confirm that the wind was gentle enough. And it would have remained so but for the continuous disturbance it experienced coming from the bus being powered along by Lela. The disturbance created a continuous whirlwind, a part of which forced itself into the bus through the side windows; and which in turn, forced Tina and other passengers with window seats to adjust by fully or partially shutting the windows. Before long, some of them either dozed or slept off.

Tina's was a doze. She opened her eyes at *Seven Palms*.

"So, ma'am," said Tina to Mrs. Popeye on ascertaining their present location, "we are already at *Seven Palms*. This is wonderful."

Seven Palms was seventy miles from NA. It derived its popularity from two things. The first was from its sharp left-to-right bend that was so sharp that it nearly created an island, and the second, and quite conspicuous, was a group of seven tall palm trees that the bend almost totally encircled. The trees were planted on the bend long ago by raw oil- and kernel- eating animals. Their number started with more than seven, but only that it was seven that survived the last six decades when the route became popular with the natives who then be-fittingly named the spot *Seven Palms Corner*, conveniently shortened to *Seven Palms*. In the past, the bend used to serve as a resting point for travellers on foot, donkeys and on horses. Now, hardly did passengers pass the spot without asking questions and telling stories that were related to the landmark.

"Yes, Tina," replied the old lady. "We are almost gone past it too. The driver is doing well. He is good."

"Indeed he is. I was already in another world before we were out of NA. Not even the *Long Bridge* jolt was able to bring me back. Within such a short time, I wouldn't have thought we've reached *Seven Palms*."

"Yes, we have long passed the bridge. We even stopped there temporarily to allow some stallions and a bus to pass before we climbed on it. The conductor said the bus was one of Mathew Rebbor's returning from Regin City via Togana. It was quite an interesting moment – one when animals confidently led a bus full of humans to cross a known danger. Those of us awake were amused."

"Oh poor me, I missed it. But madam, don't they say that horses are very intelligent because they carry large skulls?"

"Hm-n, no. I, for one, would not believe that. Rather, I believe intelligence is never proportional to the size of the skull or to the largeness of the frame. The other bus created the chance for the horses to lead by giving enough space for them to move; ours reinforced the overall safe passage by being patient on our side of the bridge. You see, it's possible to bring men out of animals."

"Oh thank you ma'am. Now, I see and totally agree with your thoughts. And further, talking about the same bridge…"

"Which? The *Long Bridge*?"

"Yes, ma'am. Both ends of it had been bad for as long as I could remember. I wonder if it was because the driver was good as you earlier said, or that the repairs had been carried out on it that I didn't wake when we were there. It has always been in a bad shape since I knew it."

"Yes, you were asleep when we got there; but then, I, who was wide awake, felt no jolt either. Actually, almost all the bridges in NA are just as caved in. The important thing is to recognise a bad road where there is one. The user who recognises one and plies it with care saves self from the torments of journey-aches. There is no road that is all smooth. Even, on this one we are on now, we already passed scores of caved in spots besides that at the bridge, and yet, neither of us is complaining of the journey itself. Or are you complaining, dear?"

"Oh, certainly not. If anything, it is that I am impressed by the good speed of improvements to the journeys."

"So, dear we must pray that the improvements continue. Once, there was no bus; now there are many. Next, it was the selfish owners; now they are straight. Then, it got to the bad garage; now it is homely. And now, you are talking about the *Long Bridge* and scores of other bad spots; hopefully the repairs will come soon. At present, there are more reasons to be optimistic than to despair. As the Chinese would say, 'the longest journey starts with the first steps'. So far, it appears the firsts of the first steps are firm."

* * *

Just the peaceful way the discussion between the two ladies was going, so were other talks among the passengers; and so was the journey proper progressing. The chitchats were sometimes serious, sometimes jovial, but all the time, very lively. It was all a balanced mixture of generics and specifics of proven and assumed facts, all energetically delivered, on sub-topics that ranged from the transport operators to their staff, from the relevance of the local history of transport to that of its local geography, from the state of the roads to that of the quality of efforts being put in place for their improvement, from what they saw as the pitiable limitation of the owners to that of how the non-owners could commensally complement their efforts, and the like. They were at the periphery of Fali when one of the two girls interrupted the peace of the ride. "Mummy is sick! Please help her!" she screamed, banging as hard as she could on the headrest of the man-passenger directly sitting in front of her mother.

From the front came the man whose headrest was being banged. Both the conductor and the security assistant coming from the aisle joined him. Another lady, a nurse, also came from the back and promptly seized the care captainship. Then she retired the two bus staff so that the job wouldn't be overstaffed.

"You will be alright," the nurse assured the sick lady without asking her any question. "Don't worry. Everything will be all right."

With the assistance of the man, the nurse adjusted her properly on her seat. Her feet were carefully parted about a foot and half, and her upper half gently tilted forward to the point where she could look perpendicularly down between the knees. Correctly, the nurse anticipated more vomiting. She was right – when she did, it all went onto the floor without getting her clothes further soiled. Next, the nurse sped back to her seat and dragged out her bag. She removed a flask of hot water and a face flannel she wet up and shook out to lower its temperature. She then applied the terry to wipe the expelled ingestion off the sick lady.

"Jago, do I stop?" Lela asked his conductor. "Please check with the ladies."

"The lady in charge is a nurse." Jago replied. "She said they are okay, that you should go on."

"Won't they require something from the box?" He was referring to the first aid box.

"It doesn't appear so."

"That's fine then," said Lela. "Anyway, we shall soon reach a lay-by."

Five minutes after being told to continue, they were at the lay-by. Lela saw no sense in going any further until he had self-ascertained the lady's condition. He gently veered the bus into the designated space and stopped.

"Now, let's see the lady, and see if she would need something from the kit," Lela still insisted to Jago. He jumped out and walked round and up to the two ladies. "Sorry, ladies, how can we help?" he asked them.

"She was throwing up," replied the nurse.

"Eaten or drank anything unusual in the last twenty-four hours?" he asked the lady again.

"No. I haven't. Just the usual tea and some biscuits before we left NA."

"Bus-sickness prone?"

"No. Never."

"Would you like to take some mixed kaolin or pectin?"

"No, thank you. Thank you all. I think I am getting better. I am just recovering from a minor operation. I left the hospital yesterday."

"In that case, you should not have undertaken so soon, a journey like this," said the nurse.

"That is true. I was to remain in NA but something happened, and I have to return to Gemmo after just a night of the operation. Just one night, if it could worth being called a night, because it was almost a sleepless one."

"You need to come out for a bit of fresh air," Lela further told her. "It will also be easier to wipe your clothes cleaner, together with your seat and he floor. And, if you don't mind, you can have a hot drink of tea, chocolate or orange. We have them all here."

"That is very kind of you," she said as the two ladies led her out.

It was as if the stoppage was meant more for the other passengers than for the sick lady. No sooner had Lela stopped than they all trooped out either to ease up at the loo erected at the lay-by or just to have their bodies stretched and exercised. It was also the space and peace Jago used to pack the vomit and clean both floor and seat with water and disinfectant.

"But driver," the nurse called Lela before the driver would climb back into the bus, "you are certainly prepared for this type of incident, aren't you?"

"Yes, we are. I used to be an ambulance driver. And since being here, I have undergone first-aid refresher courses."

It was past midday when Lela reached the fuel filling station before their intended destination. Slowly, he pulled in, in a version that seemed to say: 'Well, I have made it'. As the near-zero speed started to wake the sleeping and alert the woken passengers, Jago made the all-important announcement: "Ladies and gentlemen, we are at Gemmo. Please, be up to hear when your bus stop is called and to identify your luggage. Thank you all."

The first to disembark at Gemmo did so at the first stop after the fuel station. She was the sick lady together with her little girl. She looked much brighter as she stood up to get down. Jago noticed her and walked to her.

"Thank you, sir; and how much do I pay for the care?" she asked, handing over the blanket the driver earlier ordered out of the first aid kit for her to cover up with.

"It costs you nothing. We take care of that. Just take good care of yourself." He collected the blanket, and with the assistance of the nurse, folded it.

At the stop, Jago carried down the little girl, and had her mother's luggage passed to him by the nurse. As a show of gratitude on her way out, the lady tearfully hugged the nurse; and did the same to the conductor when she got out to collect her luggage. After there, the next stop was the final one – inside Gemmo garage.

The garage itself was not in any way as big or as modern as NA's, but it was senior to NA's in the attainment of modernism and adoption of some norms. While NA was just getting used to how a good system should be operated, Gemmo, being long in the zone of Daniel Daniels had adopted and adapted to the system more than half a decade ago.

Another bus was shutting its doors and about to depart Gemmo garage when Lela's arrived. It was Lela who first noticed it when completing his arrival formalities at the gate. He signalled Jago to get down and run to its driver to deliver a message that was mutually beneficial to all parties – that he had with him a few passengers going to Regin City.

As the passengers picked up their luggage and disembarked, both the driver and his staff were pleased to see a true sign of satisfaction on their faces.

Len Epoh's was particularly radiating. He was a twenty-six year old passenger whose mother had come to fetch home from the garage. When asked by her how the journey was, his response was how he personally saw it: "Mum, it is a nice welfare package."

Period Three

CHAPTER 5

The Greed

If there was anything Joseph Tolp gained and appreciated from Chief Daniel Daniels, it was the chief's method of accounting – that of fine identification and classification of what he received and spent. At first, Joseph regarded the chief's method as a waste of time; but the lessons and the bullying that Daniel gave him when he was heavily in debt soon changed such perception.

First, it was the chief's method that showed him how he, in those early days of business, continued to incur a loss over the unserious and epileptic running of his buses. Secondly, he was able to see the high cost of embarking on an interruptive project like the house he was secretly building while at the same time staying in arrears in the repayment of the loan he took on his buses.

Thirdly, through Daniel's tutorage, he got down to knowing the value of labour and wages, and got convinced that by continuously showing off his wealth through reckless spending, he was foolishly paying some smart people for services they had not rendered to him.

Immediately after the encounter with Chief Daniels, he provided himself with two notebooks. One was for recording all the daily revenues from each of the buses, and the other, for all the daily expenses. When the new house was completed and rented out, he provided himself with yet another set of two notebooks to take care of the rents being collected and the expenses on its maintenance. And still, when he had more money and added a third line of business, that of running two taxis, he wasted no time in adding one more set of financial report notebooks.

Of recent however, Joseph Tolp was getting increasingly stressed out in meeting his financial obligations. "Business is going on fine, but where is the money?" he would ask himself.

One day, having asked himself the same question in the office without being able to find an answer, he carried the question home to his wife, Mariom. She showed no interest.

"I am talking about something very important," he said, "and you keep ignoring me. Why is that Mariom?"

"But Jossy, what do you want me to say to this talk of yours that is very important? Did you not warn and forbid me from interfering in this business you called your own exclusive? And that I could only complain if I was not getting whatever I asked for?"

"No, I didn't."

"Yes, you did – and added that unless I was invited."

"But now, you are."

"No, Jossy, I refuse to be. You cannot invite when you wish and expel when you wish. Remember that the invited or the expelled is also a human being, and at that, the unfortunate one who bears the heavier part of the burden of disruption."

"Well, Mariom, I agree you are right, and I am sorry. But against another time, you should know that words and deeds are ever basically relevant to the immediate situations and…"

"What immediate situations?"

"I mean the immediate situations and circumstances surrounding one's saying them or doing them. They never last, and where they do, it is never forever. The time you are referring to is past; this is a new one, Mariom."

"A new one, that allows the participation of your wife?"

"Sure, Mariom. Feel free – as my darling wife."

"Okay now, tell me what you see and why you think there's no money in spite of the business going on well."

"I felt it," he said, and admitting, "– that it is not coming in as it should. It is now having a bad impact."

"And if I may ask, have you checked your records well? All of them? I believe you should start from there. The records are bound to point to something, somewhere."

Joseph was grateful as he went to bed thinking about it. In fairness to him, he, before his wife gave the advice, considered giving the books a thorough check and analysis, but somehow thought it should be deferred by two months to coincide with the time he fixed as the end of his own financial year. Now, with Marion's advice, he decided to discard the idea of waiting. Here could be some loose stitches, he thought as he lay on the bed gazing at the ceiling. If there were, he was sure they were likely to be few – one, two or three, at the most. But would it be right to postpone the spotting and mending by another two months? The broken stitches might have turned into tears open enough to make him, the likely wearer, look insane before other eyes that would see them on him. Two essential jobs – sending the vehicles on their daily routes and checking the books – were therefore programmed for the following day, with that of checking the books given a priority.

As early as eight in the morning, all the books Joseph wanted to check were already on his table, arranged according to their ages or the length of time they were opened for the particular businesses.

The two books for the buses were the oldest, and were on top. Hand-written on one of them was BUSES-IN, and on the other, BUSES-OUT, denoting income and expenses respectively on the buses. The two for the house followed in the middle, while those for his newest additions, the taxis, were placed under them. As soon as the last of his buses departed for the day's destination, he returned to his table.

Had anyone at one time done any of the entries for Joseph, he would have had causes to suspect a mischief. Without any dispute, he saw that every entry was made in his own handwriting: day of the week, day of the month, month of the year, and of course, year of entry. In fact, on occasions in 'buses-in', he indicated the exact hours his chief driver came to deliver the takings. He took a fresh sheet of paper, a ruled foolscap, to summarise the findings from his scrutiny.

The first set of books started with a low income that steadily worsened against a moderate 'expenses'. Then, income started to rise, and expenses decreasing. The overall performance for the buses sector was a small profit.

At the start of the second set of books, the revenue was very high as a result of two years advance rent he collected from each tenant. It was thus followed by a period of nil revenue. The overall result: gain the day the tenants paid, but loss when the cost and the maintenance of the building, together with long period of nil rent collection, were considered.

For the third set, a fair income and very high expenses were recorded, ending in a comparatively huge loss.

At first, Joseph Tolp refused to admit discovering the reasons for the financial problem he was gradually sinking into. But then, here they were, before him on his desk, and staring him in the face. "With two new taxis, why can't I and my family enjoy a few goodies?" he asked, forgetting how he acquired them.

Originally, he was going to purchase just one for cash, and as a trial. He however thought the prices were good, and so took a second on expensive terms to be liquidated in only twelve monthly instalments. Inevitably, he was robbing the buses to pay for the taxis.

Joseph then pounced on the easy scapegoat he already identified. The current fare discounting!

In the last twelve months, three other men, Luz Inina, Ecaf Lawrence and Lela Adamu, joined the ranks of the members of the bus owners association, with one bus each. They were younger and talented; and with their membership came a definite and irreversible impact on a system being monopolised by just a few. No sooner that they came than they introduced 'discounts' on established fares. It was a product the old transporters believed would prevent the successful take-off of the three men. When instead, it actually boosted the take-off, the old transporters reluctantly joined in.

Five o'clock that evening, and Joseph Tolp was still in the office. By then, he had seen the problem in his own way and resolved not to blink at it. He was in business both for profit and good life, and would allow no one to take these from him. If anyone should stand in his way, he would face the interrupter man to man; if it were a group, he would muster a bigger and more formidable one against it. He paced up and down his small office, and walked out to the larger office of Carlos Retfil nearby.

"Is Chief around?" Tolp asked the over-forty years old man to who life still wickedly bestowed the title of 'office boy'.

"He is not around sir," he answered.

Joseph returned to his office, feeling some sort of anger, which he himself could not decipher at whom it should be directed – himself, the office boy, Carlos he couldn't meet, or the three new discounters. In another half an hour he was back at Carlos' office again.

"Where is Chief? He is still not on seat?"

"The Chief, sir?" asked the office boy.

"Yes, Chief. You heard me right. Or, how many Chief Retfils do you have here?" Tolp's dough of anger started to rise.

"I am sorry sir, he is not yet around."

"Oh gracious, 'not yet around, not yet around,'" Tolp went into a long, angry wink that totally closed his right eye and almost the left, and causing confusion as to whether his face was naturally ugly or unfortunately deformed. "I can see that, can't I? That is why I am asking you where he is!"

The 'boy' waited a little before uttering the next words. In that little time, he looked at Mr Tolp and could not see why Tolp should display such a fit over the current issue. He wondered who was more foolish – himself who said his boss was out, or, the idiot of a rich man who, despite neither meeting nor seeing a whole human being in a room, still asked if the man was not on seat. Had it not been for the sharp difference in their status, he meant to give Carlos loud and clear, the answer he deserved.

"Well?" said the office boy. He believed Tolp had been answered to the best of his ability.

"Where did he say he would be going; did he tell you?"

"No. He didn't tell me where."

"Was there any mention of when, if he would be coming back to the office today?"

"Yes sir. He said I must remain here till he would come back, that he would definitely be back before seven."

"Could you then please let me know when he returns, since you are going to be here?"

"Yes, that's no problem. I will." As he answered Mr Tolp, he wondered if Mr Tolp lost his right senses at the start of his inquiries and had just found them towards its end. "If his wealth made him loose them, I am happy my indifference has made him to search for them and find them," he said to himself.

It was six-thirty when Carlos Retfil returned to the office; and the first message he received was that of the repeated caller, Joseph Tolp. He therefore sent the office boy to call him.

"Yes, Mr Tolp," Carlos said, showing his guest the chair facing him at the other side of his table. "I got the message that you were here many times. I hope there is no problem."

"Thank you Chief; really, there is none. But I need to talk to you, to seek for your usual fatherly advice on a number of things that are mostly personal, but which I don't understand. Like our Lord said: seek, and yee shall find."

"My dear Tolp, you are going round and round again. What is it exactly that you would like to know from me? Urgent? Or you could leave it till tomorrow when there would be more time?"

"That is okay with me, if you say so. But what time tomorrow?"

"We better make it earlier than today's. Four o'clock?"

"Well, Chief, but can you accommodate around seven?"

"Seven?" Retfil tried to consider that time, and immediately followed it with shaking off its possibility with his head. "Tomorrow I don't intend to remain here this late. By seven, I hope to be already in my house."

"Then, if you wouldn't mind, I could come down to you at home by seven. The atmosphere will just be fine for the discussion by that time. Can I come by seven?"

Carlos paused and pondered a little to enable him make up his mind on whether to allow Joseph's suggestion. He eventually did – Joseph should see him at home the following evening, by seven.

* * *

As scheduled, Joseph Tolp's car pulled up at Carlos Retfil's gate by seven in the evening. Zaki let its august occupier into the yard after taking permission from Mrs. Retfil. She already knew Joseph would be visiting her husband that evening. She then took over from Zaki and led Joseph into the parlour where her husband met the two of them. Next, she went for a bottle of whisky, lime, and glasses, placed them before the two men, and intentionally left them on their own.

"Now, Mr Tolp, what is that you want to talk about?" Carlos asked his business colleague.

"Chief, I would like to start with the personal – that of my own business."

"Oh, I see," responded Carlos. "Which of them because we are now talking of three businesses you currently direct?"

"Well then, all of them – as one – if I may say so. I suspect there is a problem."

"How?"

"Money doesn't seem to be coming in as much as before, and yet, it's going out faster than before. I don't know what I am doing wrong."

"Have you ever tried to know?"

"I made serious attempts, but could not go very far."

"Where, did you reach?"

"I got as far as the books – checking the accounts."

"And what did the books tell you?"

"It was all confusing. In one, money was coming in – and going out. In another, more was going out than coming in. And yet, in another, nothing was coming in at all. Upon all, the fares are lower. I don't know. It's all confusing."

"How, Mr Tolp? You have to explain more."

Joseph Tolp gave as good as he could, what he thought was a fuller explanation, repeating the same things over and over again.

By the time Joseph finished with the last round of explanation, Carlos had already, very much inwardly, started to congratulate himself for his own calculated patience and endurance. He too had long felt the arrival of the three new transporters into the 'club' had initiated a not-so-rosy period for the business. His own daily takings from both the medium and long distance routes were also being adversely affected. He was not pleased they came in to swell up the number, and hated them for introducing the discounts on the fares. He had wished his colleagues felt the same. But then, he admitted that three reasons wouldn't make it dignifying for him to say or do anything on the issue. He possessed by far, more buses than any other member; and if these other members did not complain, he too should not be seen to be grumbling. The total number of buses – only three – controlled by the new comers was small, and the public would view any protest by him or his colleagues for that matter, as groundless. Lastly, the new entrants were younger age-wise, and any confrontation with them could be viewed as both jealousy and an act of wickedness planned to hinder their growth. Now that someone had come into the open to complain, he could typically exploit it and build on it, using tactful and pretentious neutrality. Definitely, he was not going to miss the chance.

"Oh, Mr Tolp," he called out light-heartedly, "I was expecting something very serious, something more serious."

"But Chief, how much serious do you want it to be? The whole thing has started to worry and absorb me. It, already, is very serious, Chief."

Carlos knew it was serious with his colleague, but was only pretending not to know. He knew Joseph must have reached a certain limit of performance elasticity before he could come out openly with what was supposed to be private to him. Carlos burst into a calculated laughter, which though loud, was not enough to disallow him watch Joseph's face. He sipped from his glass of whisky, and was ready to probe further.

"You see, Mr Tolp, business is full of its ups and downs; and whichever comes and whenever it does, we must try to tackle it. If we don't succeed in doing so the first time, then, we must try, try and try again."

"But for how long does one continue to try?"

"For as long, and for as many times as it takes. Look at the new transporters you were referring to. You know as well as I do, that they met with many problems, and put up with many trials before they finally overcame."

"I wish they didn't overcome," snapped an angry Joseph. "Their discount, or whatever they name it, is the source of these problems."

"If I were you, I would sound it out to others. They may not have a similar opinion on this discount thing. You just find out.

Besides, Lela was your man; he underwent a period of apprenticeship under you before you released him to Isa Reduaram where he finally met with the luck that turned him into one of us. I expected he discussed it with you, and that you advised him accordingly before the group introduced it. Or, didn't he?"

"Chief, he didn't with me or with Isa. If he had told me, I know the answer I would have given him. Probably, he too knew it; and that could be why he didn't.

"Since the time Lela was on his own," he continued, "he has not tabled anything, not even one as small as a joke, before me. Nothing, regarding this business of ours. He preferred doing things with his new friends. Isa complained he is being treated the same way.

"Of course, I don't blame him, because he is a boss just as I am a boss. And how many bosses do trust each other? We could be far from the shores of Sicily, but we all honestly know the facts."

"But that would be a distrust coming too soon and going too far. You really did very well for him."

The meeting lasted for about an hour and half, and both men were happy it happened. Joseph was satisfied to know that he spotted first before others – however correct or less correct – the negative impact of the new men together with their sales drive on transport business in NA. He was grateful to Carlos Retfil for his advice on in-town taxi shuttle management; even though Carlos gave none on the problem he had with the management of the new house.

Carlos, on the other hand, felt pleased that he partially cut the cord of loyalty between Lela Adamu, now a boss, and Joseph Tolp, his first boss. He successfully pushed Joseph into bearing the torch of hatred and grudge harboured by the old transporters against the three new ones. Above all, he could now transform his personal animosity against the three daring new comers into a war on them, through his colleagues. He could now, without anyone being able to point an accusing or suspecting finger at him!

By 08:30 p.m., Carlos Retfil saw his visitor to his car where he openly wished him a good night while inwardly wishing himself a better one.

* * *

Like on many of the operational days, Ecaf Lawrence was taking his bus by himself on its route this day. By six in the morning, he was already at the park selling the tickets. As usual, he was offering a ten percent discount on the first ten of the tickets to be sold. Five of those tickets had already been purchased from the ticket office the night previous, while three more were, by seven of the morning. He was sure that by seven-thirty, all the bargains he had to give out would have gone; and by eight, he would have been on his way. He was correct – all through.

Among the people who saw Mr Lawrence departing and returning with passengers from and to the garage respectively was Carlos Retfil. The owner-driver was going out of the gate by seven in the morning when Carlos was arriving to resume the day's work. By two-thirty in the afternoon when Lawrence drove in from the return journey, Carlos was along the corridor outside his office; and he saw Lawrence. Carlos monitored the movement of the younger man within the garage like a hungry lion would a gazelle it wanted for food. He watched him as he entered, parked, discharged, shut up and returned into his office. Five minutes later, Carlos executed the foot-sluggering he already fashioned out to take him as far as the office of Mr Lawrence.

"Hello, Mr Lawrence," Carlos loudly greeted through the opened office window, about six feet before the actual office door he was walking towards.

"Hello sir," Mr Lawrence replied enthusiastically, flicking up his head in the direction of the window to catch a glimpse of the man whose voice he was already familiar with. By this time, Carlos was already opening the door to Lawrence's office.

"Good afternoon, Mr Lawrence," he greeted again with his head already popped in through the door he had now opened halfway.

"Good afternoon sir, and thank you," Lawrence answered, rising as a mark of respect to Carlos Retfil.

"Oh that's a' right. Please sit down and carry on with your work. I was just passing by when I noticed that you were already back from the day's trips."

"Thank you very much sir. But why don't you come in and have some soft drinks to mark a rare visit?" The young man was appreciative of Carlos' 'pop-in', just as Carlos was happy that his laid out plans were on course. Carlos finally entered and stopped near the door.

"Well, thank you; but I am sorry, I can't wait," he carefully responded in a manner that would not make the young man feel belittled. "There will be many good times for that. Right now, I have got an appointment outside the garage, and I don't want to miss it or keep the people waiting. But ah, you know what – what are you doing this weekend? I mean tomorrow or on Sunday evening? You can pop in to my house around four, and we can have plenty of time together to relax and gist. How about that?"

To Mr Lawrence, this was a rare honour coming from a man as rich, as powerful, and as respected as Chief Carlos Retfil. For the first time, he would be able to see the inside of Carlos Retfil's home, as well as know the whole household! He readily agreed.

"It is fine by me sir. Tomorrow, I am free from two."

"Oh that's great. Make it three then." Both men shook hands, followed by Carlos modelling a hurried exit.

Had a bit of Satanism permitted him, Carlos Retfil would have been an Auguste Comte of sociology. His perfect understanding of his colleagues and of the citizens of NA clearly elevated him to the position where he was generally being felt without been seen, and thought-of without been missed. As Carlos left Lawrence, he looked eagerly forward to seeing Ecaf Lawrence in his house as agreed – for the chance to whip into line, the recalcitrant trio of Ecaf Lawrence, Lela Adamu and Luz Inina.

Long ago, Carlos Retfil developed himself into hating those, who by his definition, fell within what he termed the 'middle class' – the exact class the three newcomers had constituted themselves into since owning their own buses, and one he was once a clever member himself. He didn't mind his own type of 'elites,' and would not have bothered about the three constituting themselves into the latter group. His experience of 'elites' had shown they were not as harmful, and could not afford to be, because they looked forward to advancing into the class of 'nobility,' and eventually into that of 'aristocracy'. For these reasons, they would not risk a romance with the poor.

But for Carlos Retfil, it was a different case with those belonging to his version of middle-class. He always remembered he was also once a member of this group for being a driver to Chief Daniel Daniels. The membership positioned him uniquely between Chief Daniels in the upper class and the passengers in the lower class. Then, messages and aspirations from the boss to the passengers and vice versa had to pass through no other way and no other person but himself. Many times, he had doctored the messages to suit himself or whichever party he wished to favour. He was thus in all aspects of everybody's existence; and inevitably, both sides courted him for services and support. He regarded it as a most dangerous class where the members could successfully make things hot and cold, make peace and war, aid attack and defence, and influence chaos and orderliness – between the upper class owners and the have-nots, between the buyers and the sellers, and between the would-be-selectors and the candidates. They were therefore a class that must neither be ignored nor allowed much freedom. He believed the continued romance of the three new transporters with unnecessary business ethics meant they were not prepared to grow. Therefore, and bluntly, the three represented a tripod of troublemakers and spoilsports against who he now had the opportunity to manoeuvre up the ladder of elitism for a short-term peace, or seek to destroy for a lasting one.

"So, you are here at last. Did you find here difficult to locate?" Carlos said to Ecaf Lawrence when he finally arrived.

"Oh, no, Chief. Who would find it difficult to find this place? Can any place be more popular? No."

"Good. Now that you are here, what would you like to cool down with: whisky, brandy, gin, wine?"

"I would not mind some gin and tonic, please."

As they sat and drank, they touched on the general aspects of life, especially in NA.

"Yes, I have an idea," cut in Evi, "why don't you take your friend round our humble place?"

"Thank you madam, I would love that."

The excursion, which could neither be attributed to Carlos' willingness nor to his reluctance, took Mr Lawrence to a swimming pool, the small library and their large kitchen, from where they went out to the back garden. From the garden, another door was opened, and they were all in Carlos' large private bus garage. As they walked from one of its corners to the other, Ecaf wondered how one man perceived as being very simple and quiet could gather so much wealth, so quietly. He had no doubt that Mr Retfil was highly conservative, but he immediately discarded the assumption that Mr Retfil was elusive. He had never before had an encounter with Mrs. Retfil, and was most surprised at how she lavishly complemented the warmth of a man regarded as being richly out of touch.

They were back at the back garden when Carlos asked his guest if they could shift there for a good shade and more fresh air.

"Good idea sir," agreed Mr Lawrence.

"Okay," interrupted Evi, "I'll get your things out for you."

"Thank you dear," said Carlos to his wife.

Evi, serving more as a maid than a wife, first went in and brought a small camping table, unfolded it under a mango tree, and went straight back for two if its chairs, which she unfolded for her husband and his guest. Lastly, she fetched them the tray bearing their drinks and glasses.

"Would you like some cakes to go with it?" she asked both men.

"Yes, sure," her husband quickly replied. "That's very kind of you. You trust I never say no to your bakes."

Evi disappeared inside, and reappeared with a whole round cake, about a foot in diameter. She told Mr Lawrence it was a Saffron cake, and that she baked it by herself using a recipe from Togana.

Mr Lawrence marvelled at both the cake and the wisdom of its baker. He remembered how many people knew that Mrs. Retfil was for a long time friendly with the wife of Chief Daniels, her husband's mentor, and that baking must have been one of the things she gained from her.

"Now, how has the business been treating you? How are you coping?" Carlos asked Ecaf Lawrence as soon as Evi left them.

"Well, so far so good, even though it is tougher than expected.

"And how about your friends, because I know you all compare notes regularly?"

"I believe they too are okay. We are trying to survive."

"You call that only trying to survive?" he teased. "No. You have survived – unless you would change the definition of survival. If, within this short period, the three of you could come up with all these bright ideas that are so useful to all of us, and are most beneficial to all the passengers, it means you have survived."

"But chief, I humbly don't think so. A bright idea, at most, could only be a healthy seed in hand. It still needs to be planted, and the seedling successfully nursed to growth and fruition before any chest could be beaten."

"Don't worry yourselves about that. You are all doing marvellous. It's my belief that if you continue to go steady like this, you would, within the next five years, excel than many of us. Within the decade, we expect you to have turned our trade into one of envy in and outside NA."

"We shall try sir – with your fatherly support."

"Mine? My support," he gave a short laughter of assurance, "you got it already – fully, and in any way you still want it. Did you know I was the first to ratify your applications, and so gave the others no room to dissent?"

"Really?"

"Yes, I did it because of the two of you I knew very well – you and Lela Adamu.

"I know Adamu served both Joseph Tolp and Isa Reduaram diligently; and that's why they assisted him to become independent. And you Mr Lawrence, I keep remembering your brilliant performance at the launching when you were the MC. Your arrangement yielded handsomely for us. From that day, I knew you would one day make it big in business; and that if it's one like ours you chose, that I, for one, would assist you. Besides, when you were in civil service, you helped us fight against multiple taxation that was being used to harass us.

"Luz Inina, I didn't know so well; but then, I never heard anyone talking ill of him."

"Oh thank you sir."

There was a short pause.

"That particular idea, the discount, really had an effect – a big one – on the business. Who originated it?"

Ecaf Lawrence suspected neither a trap nor a probe in the question. He could not, because it had been praises galore and all the way from Carlos Retfil. He believed his answer would ensure their continuation.

"Chief, it was a joint effort," he said with modesty. "Could you remember the time of the taxation – when many vehicle owners and businessmen dodged and refused to pay, and those who paid were not prompt? Then, a lot was spent to chase the taxes about, but still, the achievement from the exercise was negligible. But as soon as there were reductions and waivers relative to time, every dodger showed up and paid without being chased. That was my first experience of what the effects of reductions and discounting could be. I never forgot, and I related them to others.

"Luz too had one that was almost similar. There were some selective tax cuts in his area; and according to him, they boosted their revenue beyond belief. This was how it started. We convinced Lela."

"I see. If you had let me know by then, I would have got a thing or two to contribute. For example, I see it as a seasonal thing – one that could be appropriate only at a time like now when the weather keeps the passengers indoors. If it should continue into the peak season, then, we would all end up cutting our own revenue to please our passengers."

"Chief, it may not be necessarily so. In every full year, there are types – different ones – that are bound to suit its different periods."

"But then, I foresee a war effect. We, as transporters would start to undercut and injure ourselves."

"Sir, this too may not be so, because each person would reach a true, personal limit which, even if he wants to, he cannot pass. Business will then settle and be governed by individual efficiencies. That is competition. It will give us an edge, either as individuals, or as a group, over the neighbouring and distant transporters."

Carlos was most astonished at the arguments put up by Ecaf; and he recognised it at once, as a determination of the trio to stir up a system the nine of them had put in place at costs, and one they were handsomely benefiting from without a challenge."

"But Lawrence," Carlos said, laughing with concealed seriousness, "that's destruction, not competition. You would agree that I have seen more days in this business than either you or any of your two friends. So, I will donate to you some of my experiences. I know you would value them because you are intelligent, certainly, the most intelligent among the three of you. That's why I'm happy to have you here this afternoon. If you've been a member of the association for as long as any of us, your intelligence would have catapulted you to a level much higher than where any of us is today.

"Now, I will ask you two questions and would like you to answer them: What's business, and why is it done? Please, give me the answers."

"Well...eem...well..." Ecaf tried to get out answers to the set of impromptu questions. "Eem, in as much as I believe, it is many things to many people; and many people do it for reasons best known to them. But broadly and personally speaking, I would like to define it as what one buys, sells, or produces to maintain one's life. As for the reason: interest, profit?"

"And for what else?"

"Well, profit and interest, especially."

"Good, Mr Lawrence. The answers you gave require no further arguments and no addition. The first denotes that it's what Mr Lawrence does to maintain Mr Lawrence, and certainly not what Mr Lawrence does to maintain Mr Retfil. Why should it not have been what Mr Lawrence does to maintain Mr Retfil or Mr Adamu or the passengers inside Mr Lawrence's bus? So, you see, it could never have been the other way round. Even the dog that attacks an intruder does so in order to maintain its own life first, albeit through protecting its master's.

"Then, to the second part, you said interest and profit, in that order. Sometime ago when I met you, you were going fishing, meaning you were interested in fishing. Maybe you were interested in other things too, correct?"

"Yes, correct, but not so seriously – just to relax whenever I have the time after the garage, or after my routes."

"That's perfectly correct, Mr Lawrence. The question now is why, over your other interests, you should devote more time to the garage and to your routes."

"Simple that is, for me to answer: it is because it pays me more to devote it. I have to survive, I want to expand, and I need to make enough money to enable me do both."

"And don't you know that this money you need to make is called mister profit?"

"Yes, it is profit. Can't be the capital or the assets I struggled to assemble!"

"Thank you, Mr Lawrence," said Carlos triumphantly, raising his two hands as high up as was conveniently possible, and then, dropping both on the table before following it up with a sweet smile and an audible whisper of triumph: "Now, I rest my case."

Ecaf Lawrence sighed heavily and took a deep breath, and then a look full of amazement at Carlos Retfil. He was just starting to see the best of the chief's wisdom, which to him, was more of his cunning. But then, the chief was yet to finish with him.

"So, you see, that thing, profit, if you earn it, you will only survive; if you make it, you will live; and if you live, you will expand. In any business, that same profit is what people struggle to make. And it's never too much. Never."

"Oh Chief," said Ecaf, now nodding his head in complete agreement, "were you once a teacher?"

"Teacher? Why not ask if I was once a barrister?"

"Because a teacher is more likely to direct his pupils rightly just the way a barrister is likely to misdirect the jury."

"You are clever. I have never been a teacher *per se*, but have always been, and will ever be a student. I only voiced out some of what I learnt. Mr Lawrence, I like you and want you to adopt the same stance. Profit guarantees your interests; but factual and funny enough, discount is anti-profit. That was why your discount was an idea tinted with a bit of inexperience – not very bright, really. But now that we are already in it, there is nothing drastic we can do about it other than to let it gradually guide our future actions. Therefore, next time you are planning to introduce something for all of us, I will appreciate it if you would confidentially and personally let me know of it before you let the whole group know.

"And who knows if you people are thinking of another new idea this very moment."

For the second time within a very short time, Ecaf Lawrence looked at Carlos Retfil with incredulity. He wondered with admiration at the extraordinary gift of intellectualism that kept enabling Mr Retfil to explore, and to correctly zero in, on both exhibited and hidden intentions. True enough, there was in the trio, another hidden product; and Ecaf was not sure whether he should open or close his mouth about it. But probably because of his admiration for his host, or because of an apparent beginning of inter-trust, or because he was getting a bit overtaken by the gin and tonic, he decided to admit its existence.

"Yes, Chief, in all honesty, we have another we are already thinking of."

"Can you brief me about it – in confidence?"

"Yes, it is called *excursion.*

"How does it work?"

"It involves organizing mostly short, but sometimes long, group travels to various destinations for the sake of pleasure and discoveries."

"Which means it would be dearer because special organization is involved?"

"No, Chief, the opposite is the case. It will be cheaper because many people and more trips are anticipated."

"And where are these certain destinations you have in mind?"

"They are not clearly mapped out yet. They could be parks, mountains, games, beaches, and so on. The plan is not yet fully finalised; but we have a clear idea of what it would look like, and of how it would work. We know the people will love it."

As usual, Carlos Retfil showed the initial goodwill by instantly praising it. The praise was followed by a systematic hole punching targeted at luring away Mr Lawrence, and possibly his group, from the smart idea. The climax of the discussion came when Mr Lawrence confirmed to Retfil that, like the reigning idea, this product was an idea first raised by him.

"With rare ideas like these, you stand to profit more by operating on your own than by sharing and commune-sharing them with your two friends."

"Yes, sir, to some extent I agree; but there is no way I could operate by myself at this stage. I am far from that position. Presently, I am not in a position to run as many normal routes; so, how could I add special and pleasure ones? It is not only more buses, but also more money that need to be committed in order to identify and develop these spots to the satisfaction of leisure seekers. That's why we join hands."

"Like I said, my love for you can always make me give you any support you may need. Seeing you as a young and promising businessman, I can arrange two more buses for you and guarantee the loan. The only snag is that with three buses in your hand, like you and your friends currently combined, you may find it difficult saturating them with work unless you operate them independently of your friends. For you to grow right in business, this communism of an idea and style has to stop. If after that, you still think you cannot cover all your routes, or that you need my temporary coverage of certain routes, I will be ready to assist. But it's important you operate independently. What do you say to that?"

For the third successive time, Mr Lawrence was stupefied and lost. Here, he remembered himself as a former civil servant, albeit in the taxation department, who had risen from the position of a collector to that of its image-maker, a very senior position that afforded him some good tutorials in the art of diplomacy. It was the diplomatic aspect that taught him never to say a clear yes or a definite no to an approval or disapproval. He had been born, grown and lived in a place known more for its hardships than its comforts, and where hardships had made the citizens, or at least, those that mattered, to shun fairness for unfairness, and equity for naked greed. He quickly decided what to do – and what to say:

"Chief, sir, I cannot believe your kindness and generosity. What else can I say other than that I am extremely lucky to be here today? The terms are simple and self protecting enough; and I take them all."

* * *

Isa Reduaram was the first of the co-transporters that Joseph Tolp spoke to after his visit to Carlos Retfil. It happened two months after the visit when, one day, about 04:00 p.m. Joseph, on his way out of the garage, noticed a queue of passengers at the booking office. There Isa was, together with his conductor and his chief driver, issuing the tickets and loading up the bus. Perhaps, he thought to himself, the opportunity for discussing the current goings-on about discounting and its apostles with Isa was suddenly presenting itself. He had been looking for it for the past month! He reversed his car and drove to the spot. "Hey, chief," Joseph called out, "is it now this bad?" It was the last words of the question that entered Isa's ears.

"Hello Chief Tolp, what did you just say?"

"I asked if the business is so bad that you have to load this late, and could not leave the loading to your paid staff."

"No, it does not exactly go that way. You see, it is a case of the dancer starting to dance as soon as he meets the drummer. If the passengers are there, and they are paying their money, and the bus is available in good condition, what reason do I have not to load and put it on the road for them? This should not be new to any of us anymore.

"As to why I didn't leave it to them, we can call it a case of all hands being on the deck. Besides, DIY is becoming the fashion!"

"You see, this is what everybody is talking about," Joseph said, constituting himself, Carlos Retfil and probably Carlos' wife into 'everybody'. "That the passengers are paying their money is arguable. We don't believe they are paying. If they are, their payment does not buy the tiniest drop of our sweat. The so-called discount has eroded everything – every profit. Apart from this, have you considered the actual cost of you being here, straining the executive physique in the name of discounts? I hope you too haven't started exchanging the ignition keys with your drivers. This is what everybody is saying."

"What is it that everybody is saying? You keep repeating it, but I still don't understand you."

"That the introduction of discounts is taking a high toll on our business – it is making us overwork, it's wiping out our profits, and that very soon we could be in a position where we would be unable to maintain the vehicles. And God forbid it that such situation does not arise, because if it does, our passengers would be the first to switch to using the buses belonging to other zones."

"But every zone is doing it. It could eventually work well with ours too."

"But then, the eyes that would see one through the old age don't start to ooze spores from the owner's infancy. Consider our inputs now, and you would discover that the passengers are getting the better of them. That's its current and future as it stands now. Our colleagues in the other zones must have been doing theirs with different methods. We have all along been using our experiences to grow; why now should we use their inexperience to wither? Must we allow our business operations to be hijacked by three raw idiots?"

Between the two men, the conversation went beyond the normal time of departure for Isa Reduaram's bus. Isa argued that if the transporters of Togana and Regin City could successfully do discounting with their passengers, they in NA also should be able to do it. He noted that more people in NA now made use of the buses as their means of transport, and that the local buses formed their first choice – which was good and reassuring enough for earnings and future re-investments. However, true as these beliefs were, they were, like the hollow of the bamboo, solidly nodded at short distances by Joseph Tolp who had prepared himself very well on how to block the views of his fellow transporters, himself Isa, including.

In the end, both men agreed to share the job of seeing other colleagues to win them over at all cost. Without knowing that Carlos Retfil had already convinced Ecaf Lawrence, the two men singled out Ecaf, Luz Inina and Lela Adamu as the three to be kept in the dark.

Within a period of one month, Joseph Tolp had spoken to Mathew Rebbor, Ike Elfans, Papah Feiht and Ral Ralgrub. The only man Isa spoke with was Olu Duarf. But Olu had his strong doubts, and so, headed the same evening for Carlos Retfil's home for Carlos' guidance.

* * *

From the moment Olu Duarf was allowed into Carlos Retfil's yard by Zaki, Olu suspected that there was a problem in the house.

First, he could hear some verbal exchanges where the voices involved clearly included those of Carlos and his wife, Evi. He concluded that it must have been because of the exchanges, that quite unlike Evi to her visitors, she did not come out in person to meet him at the door with her pleasant greetings. It was his evidence number two.

The third evidence he saw was in the face of the gatekeeper. Despite the man's self imposed exhibition of superficial smile, the face remained basically in sad wrinkles that were so apparent. Olu had to gather the courage to ask Zaki mildly, if something was going on wrongly there; and if Zaki shouldn't have allowed in any visitor that time.

"O-o oh no, sir," Zaki went into an unusual stuttering. "Nothing; I don't think there is anything serious," he went on, re-establishing that falsehood of a grin – with more energy. "They told me a while ago that I should expect you; and this has just started. I hope your arrival at this point in time, if anything, would be beneficial."

Zaki led his boss' guest into the lobby and asked him to take a seat while he went to inform him of the arrival. He, Zaki, was of the opinion that the current situation made the extra action necessary.

In the ten minutes or so that Olu sat down alone and Zaki went to seek a final clearance, Olu saw the fourth and the final confirmation of what he sensed was badly going on in the house. As there was now a reduction in the distance and the number of wall barriers between the lobby where he was and the main parlour that was the spot of the commotion, he could distinctly hear the arguments and identify the voices.

"You are now satisfied, aren't you?" he heard Evi asked. "Congratulations to you now that you have achieved your diabolical objective."

"Calm down, Evi," Carlos' voice followed. "Please, stop blaming him."

Olu was now sure it was not his friend but a third person who was being accused of a diabolical act by Mrs. Retfil. He was also sure that his friend was acting as the defender of the accused.

"Who then should I blame? Tell me if not him!"

"Please calm down I say. Don't blame him."

"I will blame him. I am blaming him now. If you don't see why as you should, I should; and I do. Who was it that was bringing false stories? He was. Who was it that was telling lies against Titoloujou? He was, this man here. But who will carry the ugly consequences? It is you, my poor self, and our entire household. Even, a blind bat in the broad daylight can see that!"

Olu Duarf listened with worrying attention, wondering who the third person was. Could it be one of the many drivers or other staff of Retfil? What false stories were being brought? Could it have been an attempted or effected fraud by someone with a link to Emmanuel?

"Please Evi, I say you should calm down; we will sort it out. It is not as bad as you are making it out to be."

"Sort it out indeed! Like you've done so far – without considering the 'how' and 'when'? Like you believed the lies of a new man? Did I not warn you that this would be the result? See who is right, and see who has fooled who. This man, Ineso, had successfully fooled you!"

The name, Ineso, caught the attentive ears of Olu Duarf on his seat. He now knew that the other person with Carlos and Evi was Adnata Ineso, the next man to Emmanuel among Carlos' drivers. What the serious fooling was all about, he still didn't know.

"Look, this is not a case of fooling; it's purely that of disloyalty and lack of dedication. And this was what Emmanuel was guilty of."

"Carlos, you are just fooling yourself more, and I hope you can mend it before it is too late. You have chosen to forget that Emmanuel has been with us from the time when there was nobody. Day and night, sun or rain, Monday to Sunday, in your presence and in your absence, he willingly devoted his time to us. What then is your definition of dedication and loyalty? You were the judge, and Ineso, the jury, albeit, biased ones. Oh Carlos, you are making me angry, and I don't want to see this man here now! He should just get lost – and out – NOW!"

As the unwanted Ineso dashed out of the house through the lobby, Olu sensed the time was right to return from the lobby where he had remained unnoticed to intervene; and he quickly did that. As he went in, both he and Ineso passed each other without exchanging a single greeting.

"I am sorry," Olu told the couple as he met them. He took a look at each of the warring faces, and immediately warned himself against repeating the look, especially at Evi. If her eyeballs were not literally hanging out due to anger, at least, the redness made them look so. The visible, glazed shine on each sclera also indicated her tear glands were rendered active – she must have been crying. "I hope I am not intruding and that there is not much problem."

For the next few seconds, the couple, still on their feet and breathing abnormally on the fast, remained silent in speech and motion; and it was in its continuity that Carlos Retfil signalled Olu Duarf to the chair.

"Thank you," responded Olu, "but the two of you need yours first. Why don't we all sit down?"

Carlos Retfil was the first to take his seat, followed by his wife. But before she would, she went to a shelf, lifted a white envelope, took out the folded paper inside it, and handed it to Olu Duarf. "Here sir, please read. This just came from Titoloujou, his chief driver. Ineso, the trouble, brought it."

Olu Duarf could not imagine what to expect. He adjusted himself on the chair, and anxiously went through the paper:

Dear Sir,

I want to inform you that as from today, I resign my appointment and withdraw my services from your company.

This was because recent happenings, the climax of which happened this morning, confirmed that falsehood is powerful, and at times, so powerful that it could easily overpower the truth and ride the truth for as long as it will take mother luck to arrive and set the truth free, if at all it ever would. Fortunately, people say it would eventually set it free; but unfortunately, no one was able to predict the amount of damage that falsehood would have inflicted before the time for such an eventual arrival and freedom would come.

I feel sad leaving, but brilliantly happy that I, to the end, valued and practised the game of honour and morals; and anywhere I find myself, the sort of Inesos or not, the sort of his backers or not, I will continue to be myself.

I thank you, and thank madam especially. She was always kind and helpful. I hated to disappoint her or disappoint anybody for that matter, but I don't want to wait to be torn apart. The very moment the dog that wags its tail to welcome you starts to bark at you is the right time to withdraw and retrace your steps.

Again, thank you sir.
EMMANUEL TITOLOUJOU.

CHAPTER 6

The Warning

The spread of the news of Emmanuel Titoloujou's resignation took the dimension of a harmattan fire. Tee-Jay, Olu Duarf's head driver learnt of it as early as six o'clock the following morning when Tee-Jay came to take his master's bus to the garage. It was Olu who asked Tee-Jay if he knew his colleague, Emmanuel, had left the services of the Retfils. The negative was the answer because Tee-Jay could swear anytime and anywhere that the colleague loved both his boss and job so much that one would easily doubt the possibility of what he had just been told. In fact, as far as Tee-Jay knew of Emmanuel, he was a man all fellow drivers constantly derided to die one day as a chief driver, or, as any other thing, as long as such other thing was in the service of the Retfils. Since to see was to believe, Olu maintained the story to his head driver. He told Tee-Jay that not only did he directly overhear it, he saw and read Emmanuel's letter of resignation that to him, carried a mark of irrevocability. Olu also added that although he was unsure of the extent of Ineso's involvement, he was a witness to the blame being put on Ineso by an angry Mrs. Retfil. Tee-Jay had no choice other than to believe his boss as he took his own bus and drove to the garage.

"Is it true?" Tee-Jay asked Ineso impatiently for the full story of the resignation on getting to the garage.

Ineso understood the question very well, but typical of his trickery, he did not show he understood who or what Tee-Jay was talking about. "Is what true?" Ineso asked back.

"That Emmanuel has resigned?"

"Oh, if it is that, then, it is true. He has not only resigned, he has gone." He was radiant.

"But, why?"

"I wouldn't know exactly. It must have been for something between him and our boss."

"Were you not there when it happened?"

"Yes, I was – at the one that happened yesterday. But it was nothing unusual. I saw the chief got angry with him for giving unauthorised discounts. It wasn't the first time in the recent that they would argue over such; so, it was not strange. I saw Emmanuel also walked away in annoyance. But then, they must have reached a compromise because Emmanuel came back and gave us the normal day's directives, and thereafter took his bus on its normal day's route.

"We both returned about the same time. At the close of the day, he gave me the day's takings together with the letter to give to our boss. I least expected it was a letter of resignation."

"So, it's purely over discounts?"

"I believe so. You see, I have no doubt that in this our type of job, it would be wrong to call a child by any name other than the one the parents gave it. It amounts to sheer arrogance to give out what you neither possess nor was given. I also believe that when you are before your boss with a wobbling case, you pray and plead, and not justify and claim equality with him. Anyone can imagine a situation when you have two captains on a liner…"

TJ – and Bose – listened very patiently, spurring Ineso to rap on one-sidedly on what he saw as the areas – almost all of them – where Emmanuel went beyond his boundaries; how their common boss had been patient and lenient; how there ought to be firm limits to patience and lenience; and how Emmanuel's waywardness had clearly pushed their boss beyond humanly acceptable limits.

"But I also heard that you were somewhat connected – that you did a lot of fuelling up before Chief Retfil, and behind Emmanuel."

"No, that was not true. How could I? How would I? If anything, it was Emmanuel who kept inciting the passengers against our boss. I did not need to add to it; otherwise there would have been an explosion of the most destructive kind. The business is not mine, so I didn't have to give any instruction to anyone to carry out."

"Okay, Ineso, but will his sudden departure not adversely affect your operational arrangements?"

"No. That, I know, will not happen. Nobody is indispensable. Jobbers will always come and go; it is the jobs that will always remain."

What Brenda-O Teews saw of the incident was different. Brenda-O was the manageress of *Original TeeCoff*, the midi restaurant where Emmanuel loved to have a cup of tea in the garage whenever time permitted him to. It was to her restaurant that Emmanuel came to cool off immediately after he had the arguments with Carlos Retfil. For the first time then, she saw Emmanuel's face not wearing its usual smile. He was red-eyed and visibly angry. Hesitatingly, she asked him what the problem was. After his answer, she sat him down and offered him free, a cup of tea to cool him down with. After the tea, he went back to the bus, completed the loading, and went on the day's trip. So, about two hours later, when Bose from *Hungrieman* rushed into Brenda-O's to inform her of the resignation – of course, according to Ineso's version – she, Brenda-O, was able to dispute it authoritatively. "You got it all wrong," she told Bose. "Though I did not know it would end up this way, but I wasn't surprised it did. I was right here, in this place, when Mr Titoloujou stormed in immediately after the arguments. He told us the whole story; and I was the one who calmed him down enough to return to his job. The story was not how Ineso or whoever told you, said it was."

"What happened then if it was not like what Tee-Jay told me?"

"What Mr Titoloujou told me, to the hearing of others here with me that yesterday morning, was that the time he was busy with the booking, two passengers, a middle aged man and the minor accompanying him, asked for assistance so that they could come on his bus. The man, a regular commuter with him, pleaded that certain problems prevented him from having enough money on him for the two's return journey, and sought the permission to pay at the destination. Because he was a regular, Emmanuel agreed to the 'p.a.d.' and made out two tickets. He however kept the two tickets until the man would make the full payment at the other end. Shortly after, Ineso disappeared from the line, to be strangely replaced by Carlos Retfil. Carlos climbed the door, announced who he was, and demanded to see the passengers' tickets one by one. The inspection stopped at the intended target – at the commuter who was to pay for two at the destination. Without listening to any explanation, Carlos rudely ordered him out together with the minor. As he did so, he shouted at them his version of how not to undertake a journey without having an exact fare ready, and that the circumstances that made one not to have that exact fare should also have made one not to venture out for that journey.

"Next, he turned to Emmanuel and gave him a dressing-down, the sort that befitted a top rogue. He reminded Emmanuel that the bus was his and not Emmanuel's, and would not have been there for Emmanuel to support his life with if he, Carlos, had been packing passengers in it *per gratis*. He told Emmanuel, as if Emmanuel did not know, that there was a distinction between business and charity, and that he, Carlos, was in for business and not for charity. Emmanuel could set up his own, opt for a full-time and round the clock charity if that would fill his table.

"Digressively too, he told Emmanuel that despite the lingering problems of discounting, that Emmanuel continued to offer it and pay for passengers to show he was a generous driver. If Emmanuel would pay for all the day's passengers, that was his bloody business, but it must be done without blackmailing him, Retfil, or his business.

"Emmanuel attempted to explain, but he was not given a chance because Carlos had already planned how far he wanted to go with him. Emmanuel tried to show his boss the unreleased tickets he already made out, but Carlos told him he was not interested – that Emmanuel could have the tickets and let him, Carlos, have the money.

"At that point, Emmanuel furiously drew out his purse, removed some money, and counted out what was the total on the two tickets. He then threw both the money and the booklet of the ticket stubs down in anger, and walked out on him, to this place."

"So, that was how it happened?" marvelled Bose at Brenda-O's story.

"Yes, and there was every reason to believe it."

"It means Ineso planned it all!"

"Yes, every right thinking person would think so. The witch screams this day, and the baby dies the next, who wouldn't suspect that it was the witch's scream that killed the baby?

"In addition, according to Emmanuel, Ineso even lied that it was four passengers that were allowed in for a free ride. Emmanuel alleged that these days, Ineso was particularly fond of telling lies on him, that he regularly gave unauthorised discounts; and yet, there was never a time his daily return differed from the total of tickets sold."

"Pity, what a pity," said Bose, "that a man like Emmanuel had to be the first causality of their price war. Had he been a bus owner like the rest of them, it would have been more understandable."

"Pity indeed," Brenda-O agreed. "It is a warning."

"Warning?"

"Yes – for everybody. The death that takes an old man is warning others in his age group of its imminence. And to Ineso especially, if only he could understand that the same whip used on the horse would still be in the keep for use on the mare. I just pray that they limit their nonsense to themselves and don't extend it to us."

* * *

Moments after the departure of Olu Duarf and Adnata Ineso from his house, Carlos Retfil began to realise the impact which Emmanuel Titoloujou's resignation would have on his personal self, on his household, and on his business. In particular, his being totally isolated by his wife hit him hard; but he had in his wisdom, neither contested nor appealed against it. He couldn't as at then, even if he wanted to. Rather, he took it bravely, thinking of how he could get out of it all.

Bedtime came, and he walked into the joint bedroom as its only occupant for the night. He changed into his pyjamas and returned to sit on the left out corner of the bed. Then, he shifted to its right. From there, he paced haphazardly to each of the four corners of the room and each accessible side of the bed, twisting his mouth left and right at irregular intervals. He arrived back at his bed, but this time, on his back, looking through the nothingness of the clear air to the cream painted ceiling which he, in reality, did not see because his mind could not coordinate his sight. For the whole night, his brains remained too unsettled, and his eyes too clear for a sleep. Soon, his lips began to flipper up and down alternately like a tilapia's out of water – he was murmuring unknowingly, seriously thinking whether the action against Emmanuel was morally wrong or business-wisely inevitable. He later agreed he should not have treated Emmanuel the way he did. But then, it was already done; and the only thing left for him to do was either to bring Emmanuel back, or, to leave it at that.

He considered recalling Emmanuel; but that would require somebody to work on Emmanuel first, he thought. He wondered who should be more suitable: himself, Carlos, or his wife, Evi. He was sure his wife had a better chance of success; but then, Emmanuel might become more loyal to her and the home than to him and the business. Besides, Ineso, now badly exposed, might face retaliatory torments from both Evi and Emmanuel – and so, might be squeezed out of service in the long run.

On the other hand, if he, Carlos, was to work on Emmanuel, it would mean he had swallowed his pride and self-respect, especially after the open disgrace reciprocally melted on him by Emmanuel's open walkout at the station. Emmanuel might become swollen headed and embark on doing more things without prior clearance and authority.

The other alternative, of letting Emmanuel go, was full of even more entanglements. To start with, some of his methods and secrets of operation would be exposed by Emmanuel to other bus owners. Two, even if only at the initial stage, the job itself was bound to suffer without a diligent presence of the like of Emmanuel – he, Carlos, knew Emmanuel was head-above-shoulder higher in intelligence and dedication than any driver or head driver in NA. Three, others in the association could see him as an ingrate, and as one who was easily corrupted by backbiting. Four, Lela Adamu and Luz Inina would see him as someone with cold enmity to them and their ideas. Five, he would remain at odds with his wife for a long time; and however successful the face-mending he would do with her was, echoes of Emmanuel's forced departure would always re-appear, particularly at every mistake of Ineso's. Six, should Emmanuel be allowed to go, other drivers could assume there was no amount of diligence and loyalty to their bosses that would save them in times of trouble; and so, they could start plotting their own departure before any pressure to do so would be exerted on them from within.

As to his first fear, he would rather wait and watch Emmanuel very closely. He was happy that Emmanuel, unlike Lela Adamu, had not got a bus of his own – he owned only a taxi. Not having a bus to drive anymore would mean that all Emmanuel learnt from his organisation would sooner die with him since he, Carlos, would ensure no other bus owner engaged his services.

To overcome his second fear, he, Carlos would spend more time at work in the new station as well as in the garage inside his backyard, without getting physically involved in actual driving. He hoped Ineso would learn fast and fill the vacuum quickly.

For his fear number three, he would personally take up a PR job before the rest of his colleagues and staff.

For his fourth fear, he would not be bothered about the feelings of Lela Adamu and Luz Inina because both men were after all, a major cause of this problem. In fact, he would not forgive them, and would wait for a good time to avenge both the discounts and Emmanuel's departure, on the group.

Overcoming fear number five he knew could be difficult, because more of the efforts would rest with Ineso himself. Ineso needed to, and must change from being a talkaholic to being a workaholic, and from being cunning to being a really clever man. In this way, he, Carlos, would not have to regret Emmanuel's departure for too long, while Evi would sooner be inclined to be softer on Ineso.

For his sixth fear, he was sure of using it to draw a solid support from his colleagues against the new trio. He would raise a false alarm among his fellow owners, alleging that Emmanuel wanted to corrupt their staff through Luz Inina and Lela Adamu. With this, he would be able to carry the fight to the doorsteps of the two new transporters on behalf of the old ones. In his opinion, the new were like young fighters who, relying on their endowment with physical power, arrogantly challenged the old ones to a duel, forgetting that the old ones too have their own endowment – in their wealth of experience!

157

It was therefore not surprising that within two weeks, Carlos perfected his package of fight and blackmail; and using one of the new owners, placed it right on the door steps of the three new transporters.

* * *

The bright morning made this Saturday look like being destined to be pleasurable to the passengers, the transport staff, and the garage staff of NA, as well as for all the journeys planned for that day. The station was active and full of people moving in various directions and speeds that ranged from slow to fast, but definitely with vigour, having just started using some of the energy gained and stored from the immediate past night's sleep. A few buses from outside NA were either exchanging or discharging their passengers, while most of the local ones were loading up. Among those loading up was one of Luz Inina's two.

From a fair distance within the yard, one's attention was easily drawn to it through the deep sonority of a hand bell being jingled in-between an intermittent loudspeaker announcement: "*Weekend Rider* – Togana and Regin City; *Weekend Rider* – Togana and Regin City!"

The Weekend Rider was a type of discount package introduced by the new, but now reluctantly embraced by the old bus owners, for weekend bus travels only. It was available on Fridays, Saturdays and Sundays in two versions. In the first, one could purchase a cheap day return ticket to any city on a Saturday or Sunday. In the second, the traveller could obtain a much cheaper return ticket to Togana and Regina City any time on a Friday and return the following Saturday to Monday.

All the same, both the advertising bell and the noise instantly turned Luz Inina's loading stand into a centre of attraction. To those with journeys in their hands, the combination prompted them to make Inina's bus-stand their first place of call. There, some of them found the innovation quite impressive, and others, disappointing, depending on whether they were for Togana, Regin City, or for any other places not listed for cheap fares that morning.

Kong, Tapeta, Akiya and Urison, were among the first to be in the queue for the *Weekend Rider*. The design among the four men was that Akiya and Urison would buy day return tickets to Regin City, while Kong and Tapeta would buy following day return tickets to the same city. While Kong and Tapeta obtained their tickets and boarded, Akiya and Urison abandoned the queue shortly before it was their turn to obtain the tickets, got out of the garage and went towards Satellite Street. They returned shortly to the same queue and spaced themselves out in it, with Akiya to the front and Urison to the back.

Within minutes, it was the turn of Akiya to purchase a ticket. When eventually he collected it, he directed a serious look at it and fired some questions at the seller. "But mister conductor," he embarked on an accusation, "why should my ticket cost more than the one obtained by the last man you served? Or was it with counterfeit money I made the payment?"

Apart from the multiplicity of silly questions, two other things prevented the conductor from ignoring Akiya. First, Akiya had blocked him away from the next man in the line for ticket. Secondly, the answers to the questions were not farfetched.

"Yes, you are both going to Regin City, but he is returning tomorrow, while you, today."

For any lost mind genuinely seeking a way out, the conductor's answer would have been satisfactory enough. But for one like Akiya's, bent on making mischief, the answer could only serve to harden it into attempting a double effort nullification of the conductor's explanation.

"But," Akiya took off again, "why should that have anything at all to do with it? We are both booking into the same bus, at the same time, the same day, and to the same destination. My friend, there should not be excuses, but uniformity and fairness."

Assisted by his own intelligence and job training, the conductor could see in Akiya's eyeballs something well beyond an honest ignorance – a trouble in the making. He was however confident he had enough guts to handle it.

"What I just gave you was the correct explanation, not excuses," said the conductor. "With the same destination and return day, the fare is the same; but it is not, when the return day is different. We also value the good worth of you, our customers, and we try to be fair at all times as many people would testify."

"No, not at all, mister conductor, you are both confusing and confused – like one who doesn't know what he was doing and what is to be done. Since nobody is on his knees begging for a discount, why don't you scrap it if you can't do it properly? When there was none, people travelled with peace of mind and without these types of confusion."

"Okay sir, it appears I am not yet clear enough. Please hold on to your ticket, and I will come back to you. Let me first book in the last two to fill the bus, and I will be with you. Your seat is reserved."

The queue was now becoming distorted as a result of its occupiers wanting to know the cause of the noise that was growing louder. The attention of those already on the bus was also getting drawn to the outside scene.

"Look, mister conductor, you have a problem you haven't solved, and you want to attend to the next two people, and so end up with two more problems, to make three in your hands. Will that not mean more confusion? I am in the front of the queue and you must attend to me first." It was an order.

"He said you should give him a chance," interrupted Johnson, the next man to Akiya, "that he would come back to you. Let him attend to the others first. There are three more seats, and that number already included yours. He would have as much time as you wish for you."

"If I may ask, sir," Akiya snapped back at his perceived intruder, "what has this got to do with you. You look neither like the conductor, the driver, nor a booking officer? The discussion is strictly between me and him."

"But we all have places to go – and you are delaying us unnecessarily. That is what and why it has got to do with me and with everybody here." Johnson had a bagful of goat meat he was going to deliver to his customers in Regin City.

At this point, more of the sitting and queuing passengers decided to see what the problem was; they moved closer. Among those who came down was Kong, leaving Tapeta inside with others; and among those who came from the queue was its very last man, Urison.

"You have places to go? Akiya shouted. "I suppose it is not hell! And if it is, that is your own cup of tea. I am protesting against being cheated, which is more important than your so-called delay. What delay? Is anybody forcing you to make the journey? If you have nothing useful to contribute, just shut up."

"You don't have to be so rude," interrupted a young man, one of those who came down from the bus. "There is nothing wrong in what the conductor and the last man said. If you feel cheated, or you are too much in a haste to listen, you could take a refund and give peace a chance. You have to see reason."

"I saw it already. It is some of you that are too thick to see it – because you are blinded by the urge to get everything free of charge. And if you don't believe I already saw it, or, that it is you that is unreasonable, repeat that again, and I will make the layer of soil higher than you."

As the commotion got more uncontrollable, three groups of people appeared to have emerged. There was the noisiest made up of Kong, Akiya and Urison. The actions of its members were inter-complementary enough to show a single purpose – that of delaying or preventing the day's trip by Inina's bus.

Tapeta was in the second silent group. He sat in the second bus, quietly ahead of his programmed hour of strike. Others in the group remained on the line, hardly moving except when trying to avoid, or react to, a push. The members' silence however rendered their numerical superiority ineffective.

The third group was made up of about six other passengers, which included Johnson and two women, and was more for persuading the group of Kong, Akiya and Urison to see reason. The more the members tried, the stronger became the conspiratorial determination of the first group to install chaos.

At a point, Urison, then already self-propelled to the centre of the argument, asked the conductor if he, Urison, had not just heard him saying that the bus had only three more seats to be filled. When this was affirmed, he insisted that he must be one of the three because he was on the queue earlier before an emergency compelled him to abandon it for some time. "Who among us here is master over the unseen and the emergencies?" he asked the conductor, and without waiting for an answer went on, "and if there is none, then, everybody must be sympathetic to it; and you, the conductor must restore my earlier position."

"You should have obtained your ticket and reserved a seat before you went away," remarked a lady passenger from the top of her voice in order to make it triumphantly audible over all the noises.

"Yes, she is right," shouted the young man who advised Akiya Lewis to give peace a chance. He was Johnson again.

"Who said she was right?" bellied out Akiya. "Where is that person?"

"I, – I said it," shouted back Johnson. It was the last clear sentence to come from the second, or, for that matter, from any group, as a rain of slaps from Kong and Akiya drenched Johnson's I-will-be-brave face.

The free-for-all fight that started was a most violent one; with the instant use on the passengers, of daggers by Kong and Urison, a hammer by Tapeta and of a handgun by Akiya.

A garage employee ran to Luz Inina in his office to alert him. Both the call and his arrival served no useful purpose to the chaos. Sighting him presented the four thugs the rare opportunity of hitting direct at their intended target.

By the time it was over, two of the passengers had been inflicted with gunshot wounds, while three others, one of them the lady who earlier on challenged Akiya, were left with stab wounds. Even though a gunshot missed Luz by the whiskers, he had two stab wounds in addition to receiving a beating so thorough and merciless enough, and they all rendered him unconscious. He was in that state when Akiya pulled him up and dragged him to a front bus tyre that was already ripped apart by a member of the gang. Akiya sat him up with his back rested against the tyre before finally chalking MR DISCOUNT across his forehead.

While all this was going on, Tapeta, the man sitting quietly in the bus, had the opportunity to show what he was there to do. Drawing out a small hammer from his trouser pocket, he embarked on smashing the glass windows of the bus he was sitting in. After smashing all of them, he moved on to Luz's second that was parked next to the one he was in and smashed them all too.

Then, the four of them fled.

Curiously, the policemen arrived late. In a habit that was fast giving them more notoriety than respect, they forced long identification and exoneration processes on both Inina and the remaining passengers before they would allow the wounded to be taken to the hospital.

Of the four members of the gang, only one, Urison, sustained a visible injury. The hill on the cheek-bone below his right eye was shaved clean of its salty flesh by Johnson, using his lateral and central incisors as he, Johnson, rolled with Urison to prevent Urison from repossessing the handgun he just knocked off Urison's hand. Miraculously, the chunk Johnson bit off managed to exclude the eyeball, the supporting lower eyelid and tarsal gland.

Johnson was one of the passengers Inina had never met before, but who still visited Inina at his hospital bed. He introduced himself to Luz as one of the passengers who the trouble prevented from travelling that day, and offered his sympathies for being so cruelly treated as a person and in business. He was sorry he did not realise early enough that the four men were purposely there to make trouble; otherwise, he would have talked more of the passengers who remained passive in the name of avoiding trouble, into standing up against the four vagabonds. He would have convinced the passengers that a trouble that one doesn't stand up against would continue to chase one about and put one on the defensive for as long as it takes one to call its bluff. He urged Luz not to be dejected or be disappointed, and hoped that next time, the people, with whatever means they had at their disposal, would rise and defend themselves against anything, person or group attempting to wreck their opportunities. Johnson showed Luz his joy at being able to knock the gun off Urison's hand and thus denying Urison a further chance of shooting. He was equally pleased to let Inina know that he left a serious wound that would leave an everlasting scar on the face of that same thug.

Carlos Retfil also made regular visits to Luz Inina at the hospital. During his first visit, he was surprised many people felt concerned for Luz, and were waiting their turns to be allowed in to his bedside. The people included garage staff, drivers and colleagues he worked with before he became a transporter. Carlos found it impossible to ignore the intensity of the hostile glare they all directed at him.

"This was definitely the handiwork of people alien to NA," he tried to convince Inina. "This was why none of the passengers could give the police a perfect description of their faces beyond saying they were masked." He told Luz he had already arranged to pay from his own pocket the full cost of the treatment of all victims, Inina principally including.

Deep down, Carlos Retfil was satisfied that going by the seriousness of the incident, fear and division had been successfully created not only in Luz, Lela and Ecaf, but also in the other transporters – except of course, Joseph Tolp with whom he co-planned the attack on Luz. The softening up now successfully accomplished, Carlos made the next move towards delivering the first killer-blow to the discounts. He pushed his colleagues to accept an immediate suspension of discounts until a suitable guarantee could be found for the safety of the transporters. Next, a meeting where the issue would be discussed must be held.

Exactly a week after Luz Inina was discharged from the hospital, the transporters sat for the meeting.

* * *

Initially, Luz Inina was not going to attend the meeting. Lela, however, offered to take him, having convinced him he had to come in order to see what the old transporters were up to. Besides, Lela told Luz, their joint presence would deter the transporters from planning more evil. He saw it equally significant that Luz should not be the absent victim or complainer to whom it was always easier to apportion the blame.

From the car to the meeting room, Luz coped with the pains as he minded every step he made with the support of his friend. As Lela assisted Luz to cope, Luz felt glad he temporarily brushed aside the terrible state of his face and body that were untidily busted like rotten tomato by the assault, and were now patchfully responding to the doctor's medical mummifications.

As usual, the chair arrangement was u-shaped, but with the closed side nearer to the entrance door. This side had the chair for the day's chairman. On entry, both men took the first seats they came across, apart from the chairman's, and awaited the arrival of the others.

165

Much sooner, the other transporters were all in their seats, their arrival being as punctual as that of one compelled by a law court summoner.

Conscious of the unstoppable flight of time, Papah Feiht was ready to move the gathering forward. "Gentlemen, shall we now start what we are here to do?" he threw at them the question. There was a unanimous 'yes' extended by an addition of 'we can' by some, and still yet, by a further 'what else are we still waiting for?' from a corroborating lone voice. It was all the consent Papah needed. He rose from the chair he was on among them, and moved on to occupy the one at the closed end of the arrangement.

"Good morning," greeted Papah Feiht, "and thank you gentlemen for attending this meeting. Please, let us put God first by calling on Chief Ike Elfans to lead us with a short prayer."

They all rose and the prayer was over in about half a minute.

"Again, gentlemen, I thank you very much for coming at this very short notice. And on behalf of every member of this association, I particularly welcome our brother and friend, Luz Inina, and sincerely wish him a full and speedy recovery.

"It is gratifying to God that he is with us in this meeting, and that the wicked death that attempted to take his heart two weeks ago only succeeded in taking his hat. May the good God continue to be our shield against those wicked souls that are ever stalking us.

"No doubt, you all know of the ugly incident. It was the type we have never experienced before, and one that we pray never to experience again. It is for this that this meeting has been called, that we can discuss its probable cause and the way it was handled. We shall then arrive at how we can avoid such a horrible situation in future.

"Secondly, our brother, Inina, has suffered a lot. We shall consider with him, how best we can assist him. After all, everyone of us here should be able to boast of, and count on this association in times like this. Therefore, I now call on Luz Inina to give us his own side of the story as much as his health would permit him. After him, we can contribute.

"And lastly, for any address he may wish to give, may I please remind Mr Inina to remain seated throughout."

The theme of Inina's response was on thanking his colleagues for the support and sympathy shown him. Also as far as he was concerned, what was most important was for him to fully regain his health. The confinement to the hospital had not permitted him to assess the extent of the damage to the buses; so, he would not say anything about them. He would evaluate the damages when he recovered well enough, and from there decide whether to stay in the business or quit it altogether. He re-emphasized how happy he was to be alive and recovering.

At the end of Luz Inina's response, Papah Feiht, the meeting's director called for contributions from the members present.

Linus Isho was the first to rise. He wanted certain clarifications from the victim.

"Did you ever," he started, facing Luz, "I mean, ever suspect any reason or person for the attack? And were you able to identify anyone? Also, was there any warning – direct or indirect?"

"No," replied Luz. "No, is my reply to all the questions you asked me. I knew neither what the motive was nor why they came when they did. And those who did it? Only God knows them; then wasn't a time to seek identification."

As Luz Inina extended the negative to all of Linus' questions, Linus scornfully gathered his nose in readiness for more. However, at the very end of Inina's answer, Joseph Tolp was able to beat Linus in the race to make the next comments.

"That doesn't sound good, or should we say, good enough," said Joseph. "For something as serious as that to happen without a warning and without a pointer is quite funny. It should always be our duty to take care. The crab, which Mother Nature provides with a pair of compound eyes mounted high on the stalks, should have nobody but itself to blame for not watching over her flat body. Individually, we should apportion certain responsibilities to carry out ourselves. Where we don't, or we don't take it seriously, we only have ourselves to blame."

The meaning of Joseph Tolp's contribution was clear to everybody at the meeting, and there was hardly anyone of them who did not turn his body either in agreement, disagreement, or surprise. Mathew Rebbor, using a combination of his hands and looks gazed for the reaction of Ral Ralgrub sitting beside him. He got one – that of 'deserved, serve him right' – coming more as a reciprocated genuflection than a murmur.

Ike Elfans was surprised at Joseph Tolp's unkind remarks, but happy that they did not come out of his mouth.

It suited Carlos fine, though he would have preferred a milder tone of questioning and fault finding at that particular time. Carlos gazed at both Joseph Tolp and Luz Inina and returned his eyes to his desk without saying anything. His silence was understandable.

Lela Adamu, on the other hand, could not believe his ears. Lela believed the actions and utterances of Joseph Tolp, and apparently supported by some other members of the association, were nothing but a direct inhumanity to a fellow human. He knew some of his colleagues were wicked but did not know they could be so openly blunt, apolitical and satanic. He successfully sought permission to speak; and with a carefully concealed anger, he rose to attack Joseph and Linus.

"Mr Tolp and Mr Isho," Lela called out after a brief preamble, and without any regard to the men's seniority to him in the transport business, "why are you so insensitive and wicked on a matter like this...to your very own colleague? How can you make this period one to query instead of one to sooth and love? You both sounded disappointed that Luz escaped being murdered. Is this a plot? Were you and Isho involved? To me, sirs, you are both a big disgrace and disappointment."

And so, the meeting developed into a theatre for personal attacks.

Papah Feiht wasted no further time in calling both Joseph and Lela to order, using the method he and his colleagues inherited from Chief Daniel Daniels – that of banging the table severally while ordering them to stop arguing.

When the situation came under control, the chairman corrected Joseph that he had no right to talk to Luz the way he did. If anything, Joseph owed it a duty to sympathise with Luz; and that if Joseph saw anything funny, a poor victim like Luz should be the least to be suspected. "Why would Luz want to destroy his business, or commit suicide? Impossible," he asked and answered by himself. He then passed the baton of speaking to Carlos Retfil, who he said should afterwards pass it on to two other people who might want to contribute before they would round up that subject and go on to the next topic they had to discuss.

By the time Carlos was called to speak, he had speculated on what could have made Lela Adamu mention the word 'plot' in his response to Joseph Tolp's. He hoped it was just a non-investigated opinion of Lela's – and that nothing had leaked out, and no one had been suspected, really. If there had been a suspicion, then, he thought, was a good time to erase it. He had to steal the show from the day's chairman.

He started by thanking Papah Feiht for using his wisdom to restore peace. Next, he appealed to Lela and Joseph to harbour no bias or doubt in their minds against any association member. Lela, he emphasized was and should be in a better position to encourage Inina. Lastly, to confirm their joint solidarity with Inina, he said each transporter had willingly agreed that something be done to assist Inina to return to business soonest.

For that particular moment, Carlos recognised himself as an ordinary participant just like any of them, and therefore considered it as being out of place to announce the cushioning package agreed on for Inina, when the day's able and honourable chairman had not specifically, constitutionally or dictatorially empowered him to make the announcement.

Because Carlos' expression was deliberately and carefully laced with more of satire and sarcasm than frankness and compliment, it drew both the laughter of the members and the attention of the chairman. It's just what Carlos wanted.

"Come on, Chief Carlos," the chairman interrupted Carlos, forcing Carlos to stop briefly. "What other empowerment do you need when the chairman had already permitted you to talk? No other one. Go on and let Inina know what we have for him. If you miss out anything, we shall remind you."

Carlos cleared his throat and went on. "First, the association will repair free of charge, your two damaged buses. *Capital Garage* has been contacted for the repairs. It promised to complete repairs on the first bus within two weeks, release it for operations, and then take in the second for another two weeks."

Papah Feiht ordered a round of applause.

"Second, the association will make available to you, an interest-free loan of up to five thousand to run the business. It will be made available as soon as the first bus is ready for the roads."

There was another round of applause, this time, without it being ordered.

"Third, the association waives your garage dues for the next twelve months."

And off went yet another round of applause.

"What we can call the fourth is that if there is any other thing you may require to aid your business or physical recovery, feel free to ask now. If you cannot think of it now, ask whenever you can – through the chairman or my humble self.

"These are just the few we can do. We wish you good luck and a quick recovery."

Papah Feiht ordered a special round of applause again.

As one announcement of an offer followed another together with the stage-managed escort of applauses, Luz Inina and Lela Adamu started to smell a rat.

"No, I can't believe it," Lela loudly whispered to his friend as clapping followed the offer of free repairs.

"Strange. Can't believe it either," marvelled Luz who, at the announcement of the second offer, was quick to ask Lela the next question: "What really is going on?" As an answer, Lela could only tell his friend that they both had to wait and see.

"But for how long shall we wait?" Luz asked as the dues waiver was announced.

I wish I know and can tell you," Lela replied, summarily concluding as dubious, the chests and brains of his fellow bus owners, starting from those of his two former bosses to that of the intractable Carlos Retfil.

"But pray I am wrong," added Lela, "all this can't be for nothing," he confidently predicted.

He was right; it was not.

Papah Feiht wasted no time in going to the next topic for discussion. He called it 'how to avoid a similar occurrence in the future'. But Mathew Rebbor quickly reminded him of how inappropriate it would be to treat that topic without knowing first, the causes of the last incident. Papah Feiht, in the end, ruled the next topic would be a joint one: 'causes and remedies for attacks'.

Ike Elfans, the first to attempt solving the problem, saw no need to waste efforts on discovering both the causes and the remedies – they were all simple enough to see. The causes were the effects of modernization on the environment and the ingratitude of the citizens of NA.

Elfans accused the citizens of not making the correct use of the opportunities the introduction of a modern transport system presented to them. He reminded the old and lectured the young transporters of how everything was peaceful in the days when there were no buses. That time, he told them, the God-given *footwagen*, asses, horses and later, bicycles were the only competing kings of the roads. Then, it was rare and almost impossible to see any of these objects being misused or maltreated. So was it unthinkable then to ask for a discount from their owners. "But now," he started the rebuke, "because there are big buses and easier means of movement we kindly provide, the excitement has erased NA's sense of history to the point of demanding for discounts, and assaulting our members for not giving them in time."

Evans concluded that he was sure that very soon, there would be more of such assaults, and the only remedy that could halt them was to stop giving discounts altogether – and immediately.

Ecaf Lawrence saw to the reason of ingratitude as presented by Ike Elfans. As a former tax collector, he wondered if the passengers would ever make such troubles should they know how high and many, the taxes paid by each transporter were. Probably if they knew, they would be humble at asking, and reluctant at attacking. "It is only fair that 'please' begets 'thank you'" he said, "and he who is incapable of expressing thanks does not deserve to be pleased." Doing further the biddings of his new benefactors, he supported the immediate cancellation of discounts.

Carlos Retfil was the last to speak. He wanted Papah Feiht to have a final say on what they should all do, but after his own modest contribution. He saw real senses in what all his colleagues had said, and would not disagree with any of them as such. However, to him, pointing accusing fingers at the citizens, technology, ignorance, or even, weather for that matter showed only one thing – a tactical shying away from a self-indictment. Neither the citizens nor the technology sought any discount before every route was flooded with discounts. Because the citizens did not seek them before they were given, the citizens did not and would never know their true value, and hence the extent of the misuse. Carlos then went angry. "How would they know the true value?" he asked again. "Deprivation gives value for wants, just as hunger for food and thirst for drink; it's never the other way round.

"Before the advent," he roared on, "everything was so peaceful. But then, we discounted ourselves away together with that peace. Therefore, to have that peace back, we must wake up and do away with the root cause.

"As I have said, it's the chairman who should give an opinion. For me, I will fully support anyway he sees it," he concluded.

The chairman's verdict, which followed, was nothing but an extended summary of the wants of the old transporters. He told them their case was like that of Shakespeare's Emperor Caesar – that the fault was not in the stars of the passengers, but in the transporters themselves.

He proudly went further to narrate the story of Uban, a small community where some local philanthropists pulled together and supplemented the source of the drinking water, a small well, with a mini reservoir. Soon the people to whom this reservoir was donated started to misuse it. This resulted in continuous, high cost of maintenance by the donors who, at first, did not want it abandoned for the fear of being given a bad name. In the end, the donors were forced to find a final solution. He asked if any of his transport colleagues knew what that solution was. Because none of them appeared to know, he asked what solution they would proffer should they find themselves in the same situation.

Without hesitation, the first answer came from Joseph Tolp. "Earth-fill the damn thing!"

Tolp's style of the abruptness drew the others' laughter.

"And what will they drink?" asked Ike Elfans.

"What they were drinking before," answered Joseph, "and from where they were getting it."

"You don't mean the inadequate water from the old, small well?" asked Linus Isho.

"But what else would Tolp mean?" jumped in Carlos. "That's all they had before – all that they needed, and all that they deserved."

Papah Feiht was impressed. "Mr Tolp," he called, "it was the correct answer you gave. That was exactly what the donors at Uban did. They filled it, and so, blocked the loophole once and for all. Ideally, a big donation is always more useful when both the donor and the recipient are more prepared for it.

"With us," he went on, "we continued foolishly to create loopholes and make things difficult for ourselves. With this meeting, we are blocking them once and for all."

He then rolled out the resolutions:

One: The destiny of the citizens of NA will continue to be improved by us.

Two: All discounts are cancelled.

Three: Further discounting is banned.

Four: For auditing, all used ticket booklets must have the stubs returned to the Central Ticket Office.

Five: Individual or group transport policy must not be practised unless approved by the association.

Six: Anything doubtful to any transporter must be referred to the association for clarification.

Seven: This is a joint decision that could only be reviewed at a joint meeting of the association.

* * *

At the end of the meeting, Lela took Luz in his car to drop him at home. They progressed silently amidst near-miss accidents, each man full of internal self-curses. They thought it was bad they had directly been privileged to feel real poverty and wealth, that they would have been comparatively happier knowing one in its entirety without the other. There were curses too for being in the same trade with the lot. Lastly, there were, for attending the meeting. They were in this state of mind when Luz Inina's shaking voice interrupted the in-car silence.

"I am captured," he cried. "Really captured."

Lela heard him, but somehow, could not pull himself together enough for a response. He just drove on absent-mindedly.

"Lela, I am captured, and in their chains!" Luz screamed out, this time, his red eyes starting to rain tears.

"Luz, you are not," Lela responded soberly. "You must have none of such wishes for yourself." He too was wilfully holding down tears with the stronger urge to drive on.

"I am. I am. I know I am. Look, my business is ruined. I was physically smashed. And now, I am being gagged and made to lose my morals. Oh my God!" He was now sobbing profusely in hysteria.

"Calm down. Neither of us was captured. Let whatever they did affect your body and never your soul. There was nothing we could have done in their midst more than what we did."

"I should have refused the offers," said Luz without realising the transporters had pre-planned the meeting to end that way. "It was prostitution on my part. I must go back to return the offers and accept what happened to me as a judgement of nature and of my own luck. I just have to. It is not too late."

Again, Lela was speechless. His immediate response was a sorry headshake before he finally found what to say.

"Luz, I am your friend, and will never be a pimp for any price. Never. This must not make us loose our senses. Your rejection of the offers from the association will not only make you a captured person, but certainly, a killed one. Then, it will push a lonely me next to be killed or be forced to join them."

Lela, now overwhelmed by the seriousness of the discussion, automatically allowed it to take over his performance on the steering. He stopped at the lay-by he created using a quarter on the road and three quarters of the pavement. "Tell me Luz, how and when would you survive if you should reject these offers now? Have we considered these?" he asked. He switched off the engine.

"You have to take the offer," Lela continued, "and so must it remain. I am with you, I swear; and I am sure you will make the best

175

use of it. Can't you see this is a common show of the power of the rich and greedy over that of the fair and skilled? Didn't Papah Feiht's story of the well tell you something? In my opinion, we have to stoop and plan along. Didn't you see how twisted they were in their suggestion for the reason for the attack?"

"Yes, it was shameful," said Luz. "Only the wicked could do a thing like that, and the luckiest could get away with it. It's even more shameless of them to have reasoned that way."

"To them it is not. Stopping the discount is exactly the same as filling up the well; and I fear they would do something serious to anyone who attempts to oppose them. This is why, for now, we have to tread carefully. Quietly and with no shame whatsoever, take any offer, whatever the source. With focus, the end will justify the acceptance."

CHAPTER 7

The Bonds

Two friends, Len Epoh and Alan Yop, were about thirty steps to the main gate of the bus station when they noticed a man on a ladder leaning against the wall fencing.

Two things made his presence conspicuous, even, from a distance. With him and the ladder jointly forming a spot of double external aberrations on a neat wall, the resultant ugliness was quite easy to see. Secondly, the position of the man and the ladder was at where one colour ran into another in a manner too offensive for any pair of sharp eyes to ignore. The man himself was a painter, actively engaged in his trade, covering up the original cream with reddish brown.

The feeling of actual arrival at the gate inspired the two young men to stop for a deserved short rest. They shrugged their shoulders and eased off the rucksacks mounted on their backs. Almost simultaneously, they both exercised a long body stretch to relax and release into position their already load-distorted muscles.

"At last we are here," said Len to his friend.

"Yes, we are," responded Alan, "and in good time too – if the departure time will be half nine as you said."

177

"Why not? It will be," assured Len. "Remember, you are talking to a regular of this garage, and of this route," he boasted.

"Okay boss," Alan belched, sighing and stretching again before turning to the direction of the man on the ladder. "Look, Len, what the hell is this man supposed to be doing? Look at him."

"Eh man," snapped Len, "one thing at a time. You want me to look at him, or to tell you what he is doing? That man you are asking about happens to be painting the wall – with a pain-int brush. Understood paaal? Anything stran-nge?"

"But you can see, can't you, that what he is painting on is new and brighter. Or is it supposed to be an undercoat?"

"Maybe and maybe not. Nowadays, they tend to change the colours regularly on both the outside walls and the buildings inside. It keeps the place glittering, which is nice, and the painters busy."

"And probably, busy making their money too."

"Not necessarily. The general belief – and a proven one at that – is that you can't make money from the transporters of NA. Instead, they will take it off you, however clever you think you are."

They lifted their sacks after a laugh, mounted them on to their previous positions, and walked inside, to the area allocated for passengers for Regin City. There, they took two empty seats under the shed, and beside another passenger. They awaited their bus.

"Please sir, when do we have the next bus to Regin City?" Len asked the man they sat beside. He wanted to reassure himself.

"E-e-m," began the respondent as he drew back the left cuff of his shirt and turned round the loose chain strap round his wrist to display the round face of a heavy stainless steel watch with the hands showing a perpendicular to the left. "Exactly in half an hour's time. It's nine now, and it should be near – hopefully."

"Thank you sir," said Len.

It would be about twenty-five minutes before the bus would arrive, and both men decided to use this time to look at the pasted timetable.

"Which one did he say we are taking?" Alan asked Len.

"This," he answered, pointing to the line that started with 09.30 p.m.

"And which one did we miss?"

"This one," pointing to a more upper line that started with 07.30.

"But it was a big miss – never a near one like you said at home. There was no way we could have caught it."

"How could we have, Alan – with your centipede-like speed of preparation this morning?"

"See who is accusing who. Anyway, don't you worry, I'll wait till next week when again, neither I nor the alarm clock would wake you up."

"Eh, look," shouted Len. He turned abruptly and started to pace towards their point of departure. "That is the bus. Joseph Tolp's. Wait till next year if you like. Len is go-o-o-ne!"

They both moved fast enough to secure places to the front of the queue the intending passengers formed outside the bus.

"Fares please," called out the man wearing the brown tie. Brown was the colour allotted to Joseph Tolp; normal ties were for the conductors and bow ties for the drivers.

Incidentally, the middle-aged man at the front of the queue was surer of what were supposed to be his fare and his destination than he was of both the ticket and the change he received from the conductor. He looked at both on his palm and slowly raised his head up to the issuer – he was about to say something.

"That is the normal fare sir; no discount today," the conductor quickly did a pre-emption of what he was sure the passenger wanted to say. "So, there is no change to return to you sir."

The explanation at first shocked the passenger; but almost immediately, he became indifferent. Without uttering a word, he entered the bus and took a seat.

The next 'next' call saw Alan Yob tendered two notes and some loose coins to the conductor for both himself and his friend.

"Ten more, please. What you gave me was two-ninety. It is three hundred for the two of you."

"But it is supposed to be a hundred and forty-five each," cut in Len who was a regular taker of that route. The same day of the previous week, he was on the same route. "Since when has it changed?"

"Since ever," replied the conductor, "the fare has never changed, only there is no discount anymore."

"But that is how much we have with us now," said Len. "It is your normal fare for this day of the week."

"It is not, my friend. You probably misunderstood it."

The queue was now changing into a crowd.

"There would have been nothing to misunderstood if you have notified us, and in good time."

"Look, gentlemen, it is not all that need to be known that need to be announced – better certain things are discovered. Besides, by the main gate, you find the announcement already placed. Please, pay, or you let the next man."

"Why can't you just pay him," added a new voice. "The queue will never wind up, and the bus will never depart," it added.

"How much have they got, and how much more do they say they need?" asked yet another new voice. Now it was that of the elderly man next to Len on the queue.

"They are to pay a total of three hundred," replied the conductor, "but they said they have only two-ninety, making them ten short.

"Okay," the elderly man said, "take the two hundred and ninety, and here is ten."

The joint 'thank you sir' of Len, and the 'God bless you sir' of Alan was closely followed by the conductor's own 'thank you'.

By ten-forty, the bus was ready to depart, having been fully loaded. As a last routine, the conductor set out to inspect the tyres and the outside body. He was on the other side of the bus, well away from a convenient view of other passengers still in the queue, when two men came to him.

"Please conductor, we need your help," one of them commenced pleading. "I am Puma and my friend is Mando. By now, we are supposed to be in Lal Town for a most urgent case, a serious one. We don't know, and cannot be sure of when comes the next bus. Kindly allow us to come in this."

"But it is already full, as you can see," he pointed at the bus.

'Please' of one begged after that of the other.

"All seats are occupied. There is nothing I can do. I wish there is."

"Please, if you want to, there is," said the first.

"I can't put you on my lap; the world has not come to that. I can't put you on the driver's seat because he has got his own job to do. So, you see. Nothing."

"We won't mind to stand, okay?"

"But stand where, and for how long, on a long journey like this one?"

"We can stand by the door for the entire journey, and we shall still pay you in full," the first man said again.

The conductor initiated a deep inhale of oxygen and exhaled a corresponding quantity of carbon dioxide. He wondered what type of problem could be so serious as to compel them pay full fares and still choose to remain standing for the length of the journey. As standing on such a journey was against the rules, he quickly wondered how his boss would take it should the news get to him. Before they would take off, the driver might even refuse the final permission anyway. The conductor therefore sought further within himself, a way of refusing the men's requests.

"Incidentally, that zone, the aisle, has been allocated to an essential staff we must neither move nor replace," he told them.

"Good then," said the same first. That makes three of us, a good company. We shall pay you in full."

The conductor saw no other way of escaping the two men. He concluded that if the two were foolish or generous enough to pay full fares only to stand all the way, the boss should be happy with him and the driver for making the extra money for the business. He therefore took the case to the driver and successfully convinced him to agree.

Within thirty minutes of its departure, Joseph Tolp's bus was completely out of NA, cruising freely along the countryside towards its destination. It was this relative tranquillity of the countryside that caused a good attention to be directed at those standing along the aisle of the bus.

They were three. One, the security assistant, was in a uniform completed with ranking; he was the one who entered the bus last and then shut the door after himself. Despite the availability of a small, newly attached seat near the front door, he remained standing by the seat, now folded up, as if intentionally displaying his presence to the passengers.

The other two were the seat-less latecomers who earlier begged their way in. Sometimes, the two drifted in the same direction, sometimes in different ones. At the end of such movements, like two weighty objects attached to each of the two ends of a thread of rubber, they recovered again at a point. At first, they were to the front, near the doorway where the uniformed man stood. From there, they drifted to the middle, holding on to the overhead roof bar and leaning for support on the seats' outer edges. In the end, the drift became so much unbearable that the passengers had to stare, gesticulate and finally voice out protests, which sent both men to the rear doorsteps which they stubbornly stayed on because they could go no further.

"Excuse me," protested the female gender of the couple whose turn it was to have her view partially, blocked, "why don't you take your seats?"

"We are sorry," responded one of them, apparently on behalf of the two.

But the response did not go beyond those words; the duo neither moved on nor got seated. They seemed satisfactorily reserved to their position with indifference, which was infuriating to the lady and her husband. The lady however managed to endure it for the next five minutes or thereabout.

"Look, gentlemen," the lady started to protest again, "get yourselves seated. We need breathing space. Your being sorry does not provide it."

"Sorry, we apologise," the first man appealed again.

"But that is not it! An apology doesn't solve it. I need breathing space!" Her voice was now raised to the clearer hearing of the nearer sitters-by.

"Breathing space?" asked the second man, as if unsure of either what he heard or of its meaning.

"Yes, you heard me! Breathing space – of fresh air – round me here!" she affirmed to the unsure inquirer at her full volume, and with whirlwind fury.

"I cannot just understand," came back the second man, now in a more determined mood. "We are standing, you are sitting comfortably; and yet, you are protesting that we don't give you breathing space. What else do you want from us? What are all these that surround you?" he asked, smarting an arm swerve gesticulation through the vacuum between the rooftop, through the aisle, and to the exit door next to them.

"Who exactly are you," angrily intervened the lady's husband. "Are you a rude person, or just an ordinary passenger who could not afford a bus fare? What do you find so offensive in being told to take your seats? Instead, you keep moving from door to door like the oscillating pendulum of a grandpa clock, disturbing the peace of the passengers!"

At this point both the conductor and the security assistant abandoned their positions at the front and paced to the rear to intervene. "Conductor, can't they afford to pay for their seats?" continued the lady's husband. "Can't they, conductor?"

"You better go back," retorted back one of the duo, "– to whatever or whoever deceived you into believing that we cannot afford the fare! And from there, have your information corrected!"

"Please, gentlemen," appealed the uniformed man from the rear. "Please cool it."

"Please bear with us," the conductor pleaded to the couple particularly. "It was because they were in a certain hurry that we allowed them to come with us. It was just to help them – by being our brother's keepers. Please, they will soon get off."

"In that case," replied the lady, "since they knew they were in such a hurry, they should have either be in the garage early enough to take an earlier bus, or be early enough to secure a place on the front of the queue. Or better still if you want to help them, you have your own seat; you should allow them to take it, probably with your driver's.

"We have paid in full, and without any discount you know; and yet, you are overcrowding us all up with unreasonable excuses. I am sure your management must not know of this nonsense."

Eventually, the efforts of the two arbitrators paid off as the commotion gradually died down to give way to mixed reflections among the parties directly concerned, as well as among some of the passengers.

Now the conductor was self convinced he erred by allowing the two men on board. He saw the error further magnified by the resulting loud quarrel, and wished Joseph Tolp did not find out about it.

For the two standing passengers, they knew they were just trying on a reservation experiment, and that they were not actually in a hurry, otherwise, like the lady said, they would have arrived earlier at the station. They were quite satisfied with themselves that they successfully twisted their way in, but wondered at the type of help and brother-keeping the conductor claimed to have rendered. They giggled at each other, mocking the self-acclaimed brother-keeper who, without considering any aspect of brotherhood, had already taken his full payment in cash and kind.

However, the driver, Gebu, felt no doom or threat to his job on account of the standing passengers his conductor allowed on the bus. The very moment his conductor was reaching an agreement with him, he thought of a good-enough defence he would put up in case of any eventuality; it would be his ace of an answer should the boss hear something and complain about it. Gebu wasn't going to disclose it to his conductor.

* * *

Heron, Lee and Olga were two other men and a lady respectively united by the same trip. Heron and Lee were about thirty while Olga was in her fifties. By accident of choice, they occupied the three seats forming a right hand side row, exactly two from the last row. Quite a large part of the recent drama had taken place near them. Now, they were enjoying a relative cease-fire, which, like other passengers, they hoped would become a permanent peace.

"Ah," puffed Heron to no one in particular as he shook his head, "can't just understand...how some people behave... A journey...what is in it? One from where eventually and inevitably, everyone of us will part to head for his or her own home?" He was muttering, getting louder, grousing.

"How do you mean?" asked Lee who felt the style and tone of Heron would not mind an intervention from someone like himself sitting nearest to him. He was to Heron's left, sitting by the aisle.

"I mean all that noise and how badly the couple handled it. What is so much in a journey that if the wife wouldn't behave properly, that the husband couldn't correct her?"

"Certainly it is more than that," replied Lee. "A journey is much more than getting on at a point and getting off at another. It is a total of all these and more."

"But still," Heron was adamant, "everyone of us will sooner or later leave this bus. So, there is no reason why a passenger should not tolerate a co-passenger. Is it not a matter of accommodation – temporary accommodation? Where is the reason for a fight?"

"Sorry to interrupt," cut in a reluctant but interested lady, Olga, to Heron. "It is also more than tolerance and accommodation. Where do you place your preparation, your route, the vehicle, the distance, the time taken, post-arrival time…the driver and much more? Where do you place all those?"

"What about your safety" complemented Lee, "and your comfort?"

"All of which may compel you to compare and contrast before making a decision. And pray you have the chance to decide and select, so that you are not made to pay for what is imposed on you, like this sort of rubbish," completed Olga.

"Come on, you two, and be practical. But one can't expect to have the best of all you have listed." Heron was still not convinced.

"But then," Lee said, "can, and should we expect some?"

"Yes," answered Heron, "nothing is wrong with that. Yes. Some."

"You want to mention – which ones in particular?" Lee asked again.

"I don't know. I can't say. But do we have to fight ourselves over it? Where is our sense of accommodation and friendliness – as human beings?"

"What we have in our hands now," Olga came again, starting to analyse, "is a case of a seller deliberatively offering the buyer a poor product after taking a full payment, calculating to get away with it because the buyer would raise no questions for the fear of being labelled unfriendly. In clear terms, the seller had taken the buyer for a fool. In reality, both man and wife were fighting for their rights which they had paid for. Remember, others along the aisle did not allow the two to swallow them up. Only a fool would have allowed it."

"In that case, they should have started with the conductor who booked them in," judged Heron.

"Doesn't matter," said Lee, "and you are correct that both the conductor and the two men deserved being caged inside the same guilt bracket. Yes, it won't be out of place that in trying to shake the leaves, to start by the very branch."

Heron went no further in the argument with Lee and Olga. Instead, he gradually went down the slope of silence, enabling the two co-passengers to make a satisfying ascent of further teaching him more of what he was yet to know as regards transporting and the transporters. As he assimilated the verbal lessons from the two, his original brave face gradually got invested with remorse maggots despatched by his own brains. Bravely and silently, he consoled himself with the fact that his guilt had got nothing to do with any intention or collaboration; and that he argued in good faith.

Heron could now see how devilishly and selfishly human minds could push human actions; and how arrogantly confident the cheat could be at times, by basically believing that the cheated was incapable of suspecting, detecting and confirming simple trickeries.

He could see how less effort it could take the cheat to exploit others' gullibility and carry others along with him in the short, which could extend into a fairly long run. His own initial sympathy for the seat-less two – and for the conductor – was an innocent example.

He could see how good communication could aid the right education and transform a pre-held belief, and how a good communicator was always the effective guide and teacher. Within himself, he felt happy he met the likes of Olga and Lee.

He could see how education could liberate both body and mind from the sharp clutches of unjust impositions; and could now find the appropriate definition for an imposition – as an application of the un-notified, un-discussed, un-agreed, burdensome, and normally unacceptable. Allowing one of these, he now believed, would lead to a floodgate of others, which might eventually require more noise than was already witnessed inside the bus, for a true restoration to normalcy to be achieved.

Next, Heron went on to review his former understanding of tolerance and accommodation. Firmly yes, that they meant putting up with certain situations and adjusting to a downward difference respectively. But definitely no, that both should only flow from the less to the highly privileged. And, definitely no, that the privileged should so cleverly design these to cause confusion and hatred among the unsuspecting less privileged.

Finally, before Heron slept off in his seat, he formed his own distinction between compromise and friendliness. He knew each of them bore a chord of attachment to peace; but one, compromise, from the point of weakness, and the other, friendliness, from the point of humanity. Ironically, unfairly and tragically enough, it was only the poor passengers that were made to exhibit the two properties. Excepting the driver, his conductor, and the security assistant, Heron saw all others, himself including, as belonging to this class of poor, silly, compromising, but friendly passengers.

* * *

It was now four hours since departing from NA, and they were at Lal Town, the last major town in the zone controlled by the association of the NA transporters.

Comparing either the outlook or the functional aspect of the garage of Lal Town to that of NA was at most, an exercise in finding something only to keep the senses busy. Good basis were not just there; its wall was white, low and capped with wire mesh, the size was merely a third of NA's, offices and shops were by far numerically inferior, and the services available were very much curtailed. Probably because more taxis and motorbikes than buses patronized it, the floor space allocation was not definitive; and there was hardly any memorable shine on its gate. However, its inside housed a fuel pump, a car-bus wash zone and two pit ramps – one for the buses, and the other for taxis needing underneath attention. It was straight to one of the bus ramps that Gebu took his bus.

"Thank you ladies and gentlemen," the conductor's voice of Micho greeted as soon as the bus was brought to a final halt. "This is Lal Town. We are stopping briefly for some passengers to disembark. We shall also top up our fuel and check the tyre that has been giving some warning signs. Anyone wishing to stretch and relax can do so. But please, don't go far because the stop is going to be a brief one."

He then turned and leaned towards the driver, and both men exchanged words with their eyes. Somehow, the exchange took a similar form with an earlier one they made when the bus crossed the gate into the garage – very sinister one. Both men alighted and headed for the garage office, leaving the door opened for the passengers to disembark, under the hidden surveillance of Akiya, the security assistant.

"How was the road," Jojo asked the driver. Jojo was the station officer.

"Fine, really fine. Where are they; aren't they here?"

"No, Gebu," replied Jojo, "I am afraid they are not. Only heaven knows what is happening. But they must be near."

"Near? They are supposed to be here already! And the boss ordered that I must not leave them behind."

"He told me the same too – that I must remind you to take them with you by all means. But he assured me the three would be here in good time."

The three passengers being awaited were Joseph Tolp's cousins going to Regin City. Joseph had already given them free tickets that reserved their seats from Lal Town.

"Now they are not; what do we do?"

"What can we do?"

"Nothing, but wait," interrupted Akiya.

"But a longer delay would make the passengers go funny," said the driver.

"Okay," said Micho, "let me get Prampa, and together with Akiya we can set out on the tyre check, and possibly make changes. It won't be so bad once they could see us doing something about the checks we told them we are stopping for." Prampa was the garage's junior mechanic.

"Yea, brilliant of you, Micho," commended Jojo, "while on that, I'll take someone along and go and look for them."

The seriousness with which Prampa and Akiya set to work pretentiously on the twinned right hand rear tyres was one that could not be faulted nor suspected. Within minutes, both of them were in their trousers and vests, having removed the shirts. Within minutes too, the make-believe touched on their sweat glands which in turn, visibly let loose its salty fluids all over their bodies. So, liars too do sweat!

For a little over an hour that both the mechanic and the conductor tactfully played about with the tyres, there was neither a sight of Jojo nor of Tolp's cousins he set out to look for. Gebu locked up the office and set out for both fuel and water top-ups, none of which was actually required. The stroll saw him into the den of the angry passengers.

"Thank heavens, he's here at last," remarked a male passenger amid the tumult that was already brewing. "So, you remember us at last!" he shouted at the driver.

"My apologies please, ladies and gentlemen. It is not our fault," Gebu was explaining. "First, we encountered a problem with the tyres; and then, we are almost out of fuel."

"Y–e-e-e-s," interrupted another passenger, "yes, and so what? Which of the problems have you solved so far? None! You felt unconcerned and walked away – only to come back now and give excuses!"

"But we are trying our best," the driver sought to resume his explanation. "Already we have…"

"Yes, you indeed have started the journey late," the last driver cut the driver short, "have inconvenienced the passengers, have got us stranded here, have left the tyres unchecked, have not done the so-called topping up. You have failed to, to, to…"

"And you all wait," interrupted Len Ipoh, taking over from his angry co-passenger. "I tell you the only thing he has not failed to do: he has not failed to remove our discount and charge us exorbitant fares!"

"Yea, yea!" echoed others led by Alan Yob. Their anger was clearly aroused, and Akiya knew that something must be done about it very fast.

"Look, gentlemen!" the security assistant shouted with a firm voice that concealed his own fears, "the driver has explained and appealed. Why can't you show some courtesy?"

"Cour-t-e-sy?" responded Alan Yob again with a weird mocking laughter. "Look, our dear security man, you need to go on beyond that word 'courtesy' till you reach up to 'jury-sie', lawyer-sie' and finally end up at 'prison-sie which you should belong!"

"Yea e e!!" There was another round of cheers, but this time, higher and heartier than any of the previous.

The arguments carried away the passengers and staff so much that they were shocked into a hurried scatter when a blue car with four occupants, two of each gender, screeched to a stop at their feet. The man at its steering wheel, another of Tolp's drivers, swung open the door and ejected himself. He had spotted Gebu from a distance; and so, as soon as his feet touched the ground, it was to Gebu he turned. "Sorry to have kept you and your passengers waiting, Gebu," he said breathlessly like someone who has just completed a short distance race.

Gebu quickly signalled the apologiser to say no further before the passengers would notice what was happening. The passengers had been deliberately kept in the dark over why they were made to wait; in fact, they had been deceived. An apology over the true reason, if noticed by the passengers, could only fuel their protests!

It was however too late for the apologiser to understand, and he went on: "We did not mean to bring them late."

"So, it was for these people you have held us all down and all day here," Len said in annoyance. "Incredible. All of us, and a whole journey, for just three people?"

The next few moments were those of near chaos, where to a greater extent, arguments succeeded in invoking furrows of ugliness on the faces of the participants. Orders were yelled against orders with none being obeyed, and pleadings poured over pleadings with all meeting a maddening deafness. Even, Akiya, the chief peace overseer, was at first totally immersed and lost. Later, he managed to get himself back enough to resume his primary duty. "Well, that is it! The journey is cancelled – stopped here!" he shouted the order.

"No way," rejected another disgusted passenger. "You can't do that; you horrible people!" The speaker was moving a pointed finger towards the eyes of Akiya.

"I have done it. And it is done. It is my duty to. I am stopping here. And the journey stops with me. Right here! It stops further problems!"

"Go ahead then," challenged another voice that had been silent since the start of the protests. "Stop it; but remember to first refund the fares you collected."

"Not only that," added Lee, "since you won't take us to our destination, then return us to our point of departure where you collected the fares; and there, return our money. A nasty surprise awaits you if you don't. Remember, you are only three among us," he threatened.

Surprisingly, all angry or frightened faces fell into a silence, which another voice, Olga's, came forward to exploit.

Sharply and briefly, she called the bluff of the security assistant. Next, she turned to fellow passengers with an appeal for calm, urging that Akiya's arrogance and empty threat should be ignored. She explained that the suffering they were already made to undergo had by-passed in value, any refund the officer could ever make. Unless the journey, already delayed, was allowed to continue, they, the passengers, would be at a total loss. For the three privileged passengers, she pleaded they were allowed on board as a last of such privileged cheating; a repeat of such brazen high-handedness anywhere along the remainder of the journey would be resisted. In all, it was an intervention that was most acceptable to both the crew and the passengers.

"That was brilliant, Olga," Heron leaned across to address the lady pacifier as soon as the journey resumed. "Had it not been for you, probably we would have still been there, or the journey could have terminated altogether inside that garage."

"Yes," agreed Lee. "We would even have been lucky to have it stopped at that. We might have gone beyond that to rioting. We were almost there – just a few steps away."

"That," responded Olga to the compliments, "is the least one could do to be ahead of them. They are nothing but night soil-men who have no respect for your clean clothes. You have to balance a safe distance from them. You just have to do it." She paused and continued. "Fortunately, we succeeded – at least, this time."

"You mean it could have gone the other way?" Heron asked.

"Certainly. It could have. The interests were contradictory enough. We wanted service that we paid for; they wanted the undeserved privilege that someone gave to them. These are two different things for which you cannot blame any of the conflicting groups for defending."

"But we were defending the right, and they, the wrong," Heron noted. It was a statement Olga was pleased to hear.

"Who told you they believed you were right, or that they were wrong? They didn't. And as far as the transporters are concerned, they are the only ones who are always right – they, and their staff. Full-stop."

"Which means they won't accept any responsibility for this system turning gradually chaotic? Is that what you mean – what it means?" Heron curiously asked. He wondered what had started going through Olga, an intelligent counsellor to them all since the commencement of the journey. Did she consider the actions of the staff correct and blameless? Heron did not realise that Olga was only carrying them further towards another base of re-awakening.

"Yes, my dear Heron, that is what it means. It could mean worse; and it is hopeless."

"Then, we would be fools not to face them with our fists should they ignore whatever we tell them from now," snapped Heron.

"Fools? But are you not?" She managed a derisive smile and clapped five times. "Are we not?"

For the second time on the journey, the weight of Olga's utterances rendered Heron speechless. He struggled to pull himself together for an answer but couldn't do it. Next, he made a swift turn to Lee as if to find that answer from him. When such wasn't coming either, he looked at Olga with a hazy smile and a pair of moving lips that were unable to utter a single word. Finally, he resigned himself to another period of silence and reflection on this matter of the moment. Fools, he thought they, the passengers, were; but wasn't quite sure. Then, he thought they were not, but that it was pure circumstances that made them look like some. He wondered if such circumstances could ever be changed, and believed they could be, and should be. Without such a change he believed, their redemption would not only be far away, it might never come. The meditation zeroed him back on education – its inevitable role before the passengers would be successfully redeemed from the claws of the transporters.

* * *

In the latest round of discussions going on among the trio of Olga, Heron and Lee, the conductor, Micho, considered a few things he was able to pick up and became convinced that the three men were unfriendly. Slowly from his seat, armed with a probing look, he turned round to scan the faces of the three passengers he strongly suspected but could not discover a thing on them. He was extending the probe to other faces when his eyes met those of Puma and Mando. The two men, having taken two of the seats vacated in Lal Town by some disembarking passengers, were sitting comfortably beside the elderly couple they earlier obstructed. Micho's brains made a swift calculation of the product of the men's sitting, standing and disembarking. Multiple deceits came up as the answer; he walked up to them.

"But what are you two still doing here?" he asked. "You were supposed to have disembarked at Lal Town. And here you are, now occupying the seats you did not pay for. May I please know why?"

"We did not realise it when we reached and passed Lal Town," said Puma. "We overslept and couldn't help it. Sorry about it," he ended apologetically.

"Overslept? The two of you overslept? How could you have?" The conductor was thoroughly baffled. "I don't believe you."

He was right not to believe them. He remembered the stop in Lal Town was not only long but was also rowdy – so much that both attributes attracted the hostile participation of nearly all the passengers. Incredible enough that a man uncomfortably standing on his feet all the way to his destination was at the same time fast asleep at the very point of disembarkation, no amount of magic would have made the same things to happen at the same time to two people in the same circumstances. Micho therefore believed the two were just playing cheeky and smart.

"Sorry, gentlemen, nobody will believe that crap," he said.

"But it is the truth," added Mando, "and you have to believe it."

"I will; but that is after you have paid the excess."

Micho moved closer to them in an anticipation of exchanging his tickets with their money. It was a vain move, one that yielded neither the payment nor a hope of doing so by the duo.

To some of the passengers including the elderly couple, it appeared another round of trouble was about to start. Repeatedly, the couple exchanged looks, the satisfying type that clearly rejoiced that the same evil, which once bonded the duo to the conductor, was now giving them a breakup.

"Please, you have twenty-five each, fifty altogether, to pay," came again Micho, but this time, with a firmer voice.

"After all that we have paid – without a seat?" inquired Puma.

"You chose it. It was a kindness I risked doing for you."

"Okay, we appreciate it," said Mando, "and we thank you. And now, please complete the kindness."

"What exactly are you saying?"

"We have explained how and why we passed Lal Town," replied Puma, "and you are still insisting we pay. You shouldn't. That's what we are saying."

"If we should give you the money with us now," said Mando, "how do we return? With what money?"

"You did not sleep. Passing Lal Town was intentional. Please, you have to pay. Others paid without excuses."

"No, they did not," said Mando boldly, "not those three who held us up for hours. It was there for all to see," argued on Mando.

"Oh, and how did you yourself know that? From your sleep? Anyway, that should not be any of your business."

"Why not?"

"Simple. Because other passengers did not make yours theirs when you were boarding."

"Aha, simpler then. In the same way, this, our payment thing, shouldn't be your business either," said Puma.

196

"But it is mine, and you will soon find out. The bus will be ordered to stop anywhere, anytime now, for you two to get out and find your own way."

"That is braggadocio," said Mando. "You can't, and won't be allowed to do it."

"What will stop me?"

"What will, certainly will," Mando replied. "And if nothing does, I will."

Mando's statement sent Micho's brains into a state of madness. He would take none of the defiance and threat from the two. Not when they still owed him!

"You, really?" the conductor angrily asked. "But before then, we shall see." He bellowed a call and beckoned for support to the security assistant who was already on his way to them anyway. A few steps before Akiya would arrive at the spot, Micho reached out to Mando, the last speaker of the duo, and pulled him off his seat. It was swiftly followed by an attempted rescue cum support by Puma before Akiya could reach Micho for the needed reinforcement. While the two staff were bent on either collecting the fares or getting the duo ejected, none of the duo would tolerate being roughened up, talk less of being dragged down by the bus staff. The particular situation that the couple dreaded had now been re-started. It forced the driver to make an abrupt stop.

Had the stop been made at a point properly allocated for that purpose, perhaps it would not have caught the sight and attention of Chief Carlos Retfil who was driving his car in the direction of where the bus was coming from. He made a u-turn and went to it. Parking beside it, he ran to its rear door.

"Stop it," Carlos shouted upon discovering that turning the handle would not open its door. "Bham! Bham! Bham!" he banged repeatedly on the body of the bus with his fist. The commotion didn't allow anyone to respond from within. The erratic and violent brawl in the bus he could see, and the noise there-from he could hear, but his anxieties to impose peace on them, they could not see.

"Wham! Wham! Wham!" he slapped the body of the bus. "Open the door. I say open the door!"

Attention now started to emerge from inside the bus. Micho who was nearer to the door looked out, and on seeing the chief, started the disengagement at once. He let his hands off the collar of the man held sandwiched between himself and the security assistant, and descended to open for Carlos Retfil. It was an advantage promptly taken by the duo of Puma and Mando to land many blows on Akiya now sandwiched in turn between them. Gebu's leap off the driver's seat was equally useless, as the angry passengers promptly blocked him from reaching Akiya.

"Stop it. Everybody, let go!" commanded Carlos. He rushed up to separate the fighters. The order was slowly obeyed and a complete disengagement finally achieved.

"It is these two," shouted the security assistant. He was vigorously moving forth and back, the pointed right hand index finger pivoted all the way from the elbow, like an enraged cobra attempting to succeed at a difficult strike. "They started the trouble. They won't pay up, and won't get off."

"Liar. That's not true," said the innermost of the two passengers. "How many times must you make us pay?" he questioned angrily. "How many times? For every bus stop of the journey?"

"Who wants your money for every bus stop? Nobody," the conductor asked and answered himself. "But if you offer to pay for every half-stop, why not, I will take it. Yes, I will – happily."

"Yes – you heard him sir?" interrupted one man, a passenger, addressing Carlos. "That was the root cause of the trouble on this nightmare of a journey. The bus staffs are very greedy. They certainly made a pact – an unholy one – with these two, at the expense of all of us here. Now it has boomeranged and they are trying to outdo each other. That is how fast evil can catch up with its doer!"

"Now, you driver," said the chief, "I am disappointed. What have you got to say to all this, and what kind of report do you want to carry to Chief Tolp?"

"There is no time to table any case now," said another male passenger. "So much of our precious time has been wasted on this journey – just the same way we wish the gods to waste these so-called staff's too," he cursed. "The favour you can do us is to tell them to start immediately and let us go. It's already late."

"It is true," said the man who earlier paid for Len Epoh and Alan Yob in NA, "that due to some of the behaviours of the bus staff today, we have spent more time than normal. To save time, please ask the conductor how much exactly he wants again from these gentlemen."

"I think you heard him, Micho," said the chief. "How much do they owe you?"

"Twenty-five each. Fifty in total."

"Okay, come here and take, and let us move from here," the man said, as he reached for his wallet. "You can tell the driver," he addressed Micho, "to start while you write out your tickets as we go along."

"Thank you sir," said the chief to the man as Micho proceeded to take the note for the requested amount. "And let me have a quick word with the three of you over this bad behaviour of yours," he commanded the staff, "so that you don't cause this type of problem again."

He summoned Gebu, Akiya and Micho down the bus fairly angrily – at least, apparently to the passengers. In the short time he talked with them, not only was Carlos Retfil able to ascertain all that had happened, he was also able to give his own candid opinion on the matter.

The two members of the bus crew were surprised he did not apportion them any blame. Instead, he praised what to him, was their smart and business-like guts that enabled them to carry extra passengers, keep them standing on an inter-zonal route, and yet, collect full fares from them. He however warned them against further carrying extras and keeping passengers standing inside Daniel Daniels' Zone 2 they would soon enter, because the penalties there attached to both illegalities were very stiff. His last act was re-entering into the bus to thank the passengers and seek their cooperation for the remaining part of the journey. He was making the final exit when he spotted the man who paid to settle the quarrels, and he concluded that he deserved another offer of thanks.

"Oh thank you again, sir," he went and told him. "You are so kind. By the way, I am Chief Retfil, and every staff on board is known to me."

"You are welcome, chief," responded the 'kind' man. "I am George Ubuloino. I know how it feels because my son is also a bus driver. I myself hope to go into transport business very soon."

It was just about two minutes after the journey was resumed, and most of the passengers were busy discussing the last incident. "Another one for you, gentlemen," Olga turned to Heron and Lee, "what is your opinion of this last one?" she asked them.

"You mean this last palaver?" asked Lee.

"Yes, the last drama."

"Well, it is just another of our lucky escapes," he answered.

"Yes, it was," agreed Heron, "courtesy of the same man. He was definitely Godsent – an angel."

"Which same man?" Heron asked.

"The one who paid for the cheats."

"What made him an angel?" Olga asked, keeping her own different opinion to herself. "Do you call this a holy mission then?"

"Not one as such," replied Heron, "but, twice, and for two sets of defaulters, he had paid," Heron justified the generous qualification he just awarded the man.

"That didn't make him an angel," countered Olga. "No, it didn't."

"I too agree," said Lee, "it didn't. Why should it? Another kind passenger would have paid if he didn't. Generosity does not necessarily start and end with a single person or a single source, does it?"

"I don't mean it that way," said Olga. "There was no generosity there. He must have belonged to the group of those with more money than sense. It was therefore relieving that no one else was foolish enough to make the payments. Had he laboured to obtain the money, he wouldn't have embarked non-stop on senseless charities. We could do without such people."

"I don't quite understand you," said Lee. "Do you mean it was senseless of him to have donated the payments?"

"Of course, it was – unless there was a motive," Olga answered. "And it shouldn't be a surprise if there is one.

"On both occasions,' she continued, "what the old man did amounted to giving more sympathy and understanding to the transporters and their agents. For reasons best known to him, he believed the transporters were entitled to whatever fares they charged, and that the only duty the passengers owed the transporters was to always pay them up in full, or otherwise keep off the buses. The first lads tried to resist the cheating, but his payment killed the resistance."

"But the second case was different, wasn't it?" Lee asked without any real disagreement with what Olga just said.

"With that, it was almost the same thing," Olga continued. "The same man supported the immorality of both the terrible duo and the bus staff. The support assisted the bus staff and the duo to get away with the cheating. More ignorantly than deliberately, the man was unable to figure this out."

"But all said and done," Heron still believed, "we could still have been unable to leave that spot, talk less of reaching our destinations."

"But then, up to now, which of the two have you accomplished? None. The take-off was bad, and the part of the journey undertaken so far was worse. For the arrival at the destination you mentioned, look at what the time is already. I can predict it will definitely be worst.

"Gentlemen, there is an important fact you ought to know about these transporters. More than how they want your money is how they want more of it; therefore, they hate any delay. But they know that the depth of the passengers' reasoning won't reach the level of discovering this fact. In any standoff or argument, they hold on as long as possible, expecting the passengers to blink first. They know the higher the number of eyes, the more achievable this could happen in their favour."

"In which case, a lesser number of eyes is more reliable?" asked Heron again.

"No, but comparatively, it has a lesser number of blinks. But, had the higher number realised the enormity of light it could generate at a time, and generate same purposely, it would have totally subdued that lesser number with the intensity."

"Now, I see," said Heron, "and understand why instead of praising him, you judged him guilty."

"Actually," said Lee, "it wasn't the man alone who was guilty. He led and we followed. We should all share in the guilt – all of us in the bus."

"Yes, that is correct," accepted Olga "– for being passive. A more intelligent person among us, if there was one, could have told him to use his surplus money, if actually he has got some, to start a better bus service for the teeming passengers."

"But that is not too late to do," assured Heron who had now learnt another lesson and acquired more sense. "Leave that to me."

* * *

It was almost another hour and it was getting darker. *Mazinda*, the last major village in the zone, was passed with five passengers getting off the bus at the mini-stop along its main road. All of a sudden, a completely unlit car hurled itself on to the front of Gebu's bus, narrowly missing being hit by the bus. The resultant jolt pushed Gebu to switch on his lights – brake, front and rear's – to enable him view and note the detail of the car, and intimidate its driver reciprocally. "Idiot!" he swore, turning to the direction of his conductor. "Micho, did you see that?"

"Yes, I did; but not until after it was about finishing the overtaking."

"Lucky bastard, wasn't he?"

"I suppose we were all lucky," Micho replied. "He would have delayed us."

"Hmn-n, I suppose you are right," conceded Gebu, "as if we haven't had enough already. And by the way, is anybody doing the internal checks yet?"

"Not yet," answered Micho, I will start after the bend."

"You might just as well start it now – you and Akiya. We shall soon reach *Deeceepee* and there could be plenty to put in place after all the problems we encountered. We must avoid further delays."

Micho agreed, called on Akiya, and they both set to work.

A necessitated brainchild of the authorities of Zone 2, *Deeceepee* – actually coined from DCP – was the specially demarcated point of crossing into Zone 2 by all buses coming from Zone 1 on New Angel – Regin City route. When it was discovered that most serious road accidents were being caused by the drivers of Zone 1 with terrible spillover effects on the people of Zone 2, the latter's authorities banned all buses from Zone 1 from entering their region. On the subsequent pledge of safer driving by Zone 1, the ban was lifted on the condition that each time, each of these buses was subjected to certain safety checks of Zone 2 at the point of entry. Four huge speed breakers were thus erected across the first fifty yards of road inside Zone 2, in order to slow the buses down sufficiently for these checks.

Later, for more effectiveness and in order to ease the burden of the checks in Zone 2, the transporters of NA were compelled to arrange and carry out similar checks on their own drivers and buses inside their own zone before they would cross into Zone 2. This was how an extension, complete with its own speed breakers, was erected on Zone 1 side, and the entire area got to be called *DCP*, for 'double check point'

"How was the journey?" one NA traffic policeman commandingly asked Micho who had already alighted from the bus as was the custom. "Everything in compliance?"

"Fine sir," replied Micho, like an errand boy feeding back a boss with an answer. "In very full compliance sir," whatever that meant between them.

"All spares and documents in order?" the officer asked again.

"Yes sir."

As if the officer still had his doubts, he climbed into the bus, added the rays from his torch to an already lit inside, and glanced over the overhead luggage racks before coming down through his same point of entry. He went on to shine the same on the body and the underneath of the bus until he reached the driver. "How was the journey...?" he started all over again like a pupil poet rehearsing a memory verse for perfection.

Surprisingly for Gebu and his team, Ral Ralgrub's bus also arrived at the checkpoint and stopped behind theirs. It left NA before theirs and was supposed to have reached its destination and embarked on its return journey. Micho walked back to its conductor who was already equally out on the ground.

"Where have you been, and what are you still doing here?" Micho asked him. "We long expected to meet you returning. Any serious incident?"

"We have been on the road," Ral's conductor yelled with happiness, "or where else could we have been? Incident...incidents? Yes, good ones. We had a diversion."

"How?"

"I mean we had to create one. At *Tadpole* stop, we met a load of passengers going to Ojja; so, we faked a reason for diversion and picked them up."

"And the passengers you were coming with allowed you to go off course?"

"Yes, that was because of how cleverly we presented it to them. Those of them who were too much in a hurry opted to get off and continue in taxis at their own expense. Anyway, we are back on course now." There was some laughter of triumph, which was interrupted by another traffic officer, a more senior one, of NA. He walked to Micho and his colleague from Ralgrub's bus.

"Isn't this Chief Ralgrub's bus?" asked the officer.

"Yes sir," replied its conductor.

"He just passed by us a little while ago; do you know that?"

"No sir."

"Okay," he started to zero in on his intention of coming over to them, "just tell your driver to move back a little and pass by the side of this and move on. We are confident your bus is okay, always okay – just like your boss. Alright?"

The two conductors fully understood what the officer was talking about. Ralgrub's conductor quickly dropped the conversation with Micho and marched to his driver to deliver the instruction before the corrupt boss of the road would change his mind. The driver moved the bus backward, outward, backward and finally, outward again, and with all the lights, including the revolving orange one on the roof fully on, he drove forward into the Zone 2 sector of the *DCP*.

The next checking, that is, at the Zone 2 sector of the point, took around the same length of time as the first, but the items checked and the methodology of the check were different.

Quite politely, the checker went to Gebu, and collected the documents he required from him for an on-the-spot, physical inspection. Where there were his pictures affixed, he merged such with the owner's physical resemblance.

205

At the same time, another colleague of the checker went to examine the fire extinguisher on the bus, knocking on it a few times to enable its sonority to tell him if it had suffered any leakage. Then, he inspected the spare tyres, calling the conductor's attention to what he perceived as low threading, and advising him to effect a replacement soonest. As his colleague was finishing up with the driver, the inspector climbed into the bus to welcome the passengers to Zone 2. He asked if they had a nice journey, and finally wished them a pleasant stay in both Regin City and in the entire region. His was a pleasantry which, at that late and horrible hour, successfully concealed from the faces of the passengers, what they would have naturally displayed – resignation, frustration, tiredness, hunger and regrets.

"If only they could do the same at NA, at the start and end of every journey," the elderly lady of the couple turned to tell her husband as the inspector went out of the bus, "it would have kept the passengers in high spirits."

"Unfortunately dear, they wouldn't."

"But it didn't use to be as bad," she lamented.

"Yes, it didn't. But that is NA for us now. The good days have gone into history, fairness gone into the past. We can only hope they come back before they go too far for a retrieve."

"Hope?" asked the lady. "Anyway, that word makes me look forward to tomorrow. Besides that, it has no other significance," she concluded with pessimism as the bus finally left the last inspection point and crossed into the last zone of the journey.

* * *

"Did you notice that bus?" Alan Yob asked Len Ipoh.

"Which one?"

"The one that met and left us at the first checkpoint."

"Not particularly."

"That, flashing the rooftop lights?"

"O yes, o yes – the one moving back and forth with the huge flasher?"

"Yes, that one."

"What about it?"

"It was the bus we could not catch, that I said left in time – two and a half hours before we got to the station, and three before we actually departed."

"Wwhaat?" exclaimed Alan in disbelief, his voice sending the waves into the hearing of many passengers who now responded by turning to the discussants. "You don't mean it. And we still finished Zone 1 before it?"

"Yes," said Len Ipoh, "that is how they move nowadays. They disrespect the time-table, the route, the fares, the passengers – all."

"Anyway, it has overtaken us now and gone."

"But don't trust how far it would go," warned Len. "We left later but arrived earlier; it left earlier but arrived later. Then, we arrived earlier, we left later; and it arrived later but left earlier. Confusion galore. Needs clearing!"

"Hopeless situation. And who does the clearing?" asked Alan.

"You ask me?" asked Len.

"Yes, lads, I know," interrupted Heron from the other side separated by the aisle. He started to boil with anger. "If the passengers won't, then nobody ever would, because this lot won't – not when you have some making reasonable protests, and others, countering them with unreasonable payments to appease the bus robbers – like we have all witnessed twice on this journey.

"An – an," he stammered with anger, "and you see some selfish cheats and shameless opportunists stealing advantages and so on. It is we innocent passengers who must clear the confusion, and if possible, clear these heaps of rubbish with them."

There was a moment of complete silence. Slowly and simultaneously, all the faces currently on Heron found somewhere else to turn to – the positions of the old man, of the troublesome duo, and of the three cousins of Tolp who joined the bus at Lal Town.

* * *

The first sign of arrival at Regin City came a few minutes before midnight, in the form of an announcement from the conductor.

"Please, is there anybody for *Burial*?"

Burial, actually, was a bus-stop that passengers usually felt quite reluctant to answer to – because of what the vocabulary denoted. Usually, they felt embarrassed that it meant they were going to be buried!

The conductor exercised a thirty seconds pause to allow for responses. There was none.

"Anything or anybody for *Burial*?"

Still, there was no word heard as a response. Almost everybody looked at the announcer, some with hate capped with hisses of assorted drags.

"*Burial*, anything or anyone for *Burial*?"

Another period of silence was just going past four seconds when a barely audible voice punctuated it.

"Here."

Almost all those who were earlier on startled at the conductor's calls were now even more startled, and they turned round to see where the response came from. The same man, George Ubuloino, who paid for four of the passengers, was seen supporting his own feeble answer with a passively raised left hand. With relief, and derision, many passengers burst into uncontrollable laughter, that old George had now acquired the identity of a corpse ready or made ready for the burial pit!

"Any stuff coming down with you sir?" asked the conductor again, but this time with the question directly put to the old man.

"Please, two small suitcases – up here – are to come down." He pointed to their position above him on the overhead luggage rack.

"No problem sir. Please wait till the bus stops there."

Two minutes later, and at a point approximately three miles from the centre of Regin City, Gebu slowed down the bus and stopped at a lay-by separated from a massive clearing. The clearing had a shed with a bold inscription 'CEMETERY BUS-STOP' written below a small 'Regin City Authority' centrally sign-written on the running board. The clearing was the city's horticulturally beautified cemetery.

Out of generosity and for easy accessibility, the authority in Zone 2 once allowed the cemetery to serve other communities outside the zone. However, no sooner it was established that drivers of other zones caused most of the road deaths occurring inside Zone 2 than all other zones were banned from its use. Then, as a forced alternative, Zone 1 had its own ten miles before *DCP*. It had neither a shelter nor a bus stop, and its exact size could not be clearly known from the road because both boundaries and area were overgrown with weeds. Nonetheless professional and private undertakers always besieged it.

Because there was a road junction – more significant for being the first on arriving at Regin City than for forming a tee directly opposite the cemetery – the authority of Regin City decided to have its first bus stop there. Initially, it was named *Junction* before it was changed to *Eternity* and then, to *Burial Ground* that the transporters loved to call out with mischief as *Burial*. Even though it was further changed to *Cemetery Bus-stop* to beat the rudeness, the transporters still stuck to *Burial* at the expense of the passengers who usually felt shy to answer to it because its meaning implied either they or theirs were dead and ready to be buried.

"Just these two, sir?" Micho asked George, getting down the suitcases for the elderly passenger.

"Yes, those two; thank you. Can I go down and you pass them to me?"

"Certainly sir," Micho replied.

At *Burial*, Akiya opened the front door of the bus and George went out. Akiya then gently passed the first suitcase to him, while Micho returned for the second. The security assistant was lowering the last suitcase down the bus steps to George when George changed his mind on his final bus stop. Now, he wanted to stop at the city garage instead of the *Burial*.

"Look, Security," he said to Akiya, "please, it is too late and too dark here. I am following you to the city bus garage." He lifted the first case to hand back to Akiya at a time the second being passed out by Akiya was almost on the ground. Using the loud idling noise of the bus as a source of pressure on himself, Akiya threw down the old man's second suitcase and shut the door, while the bus dangerously took off, leaving the man with his useless shout of 'wait, wait' before the tombstones.

Olga, Heron and Lee were among the passengers who saw what happened. Heron and Lee believed he deserved it. Heron in particular was highly elated that the man would have the horrible experience of being alive and yet made to stop among the dead – which was just one of the ordeals the transporters of NA were making the passengers to suffer. He wished the ghosts in the dark cemetery actually pulled George to their domain for a taste of hell.

Olga, on the other hand told Heron and Lee to have nothing but pity for George because the last incident had confirmed and punished him enough as a genuine fool after all.

At 12.30 in the night, the bus stopped at the final destination inside the garage at Regin City. As soon as the bus staff threw open the doors, most passengers realised they had been forced to face another ordeal – how to finally make it to their homes and intended destinations at that hour of the night.

Some of them believed they had paid for, and undertaken a journey of no good dividend. Others thought that instead of a journey of discovery and fulfilment promised them, they were dumped among the dead, and made to get lost in the dark forever or till another daybreak, which they might or might never see. Yet, to others, having anything to do with any route or destination in Zone 1 was one of the biggest misfortunes that could ever befall a living soul. Whichever way, the feeling was a bad one.

One very good thing though – as seen by Olga: bitter experience had started to bind the victims together!

Period Four

CHAPTER 8

The Grab

That Joseph Tolp saw Gebu, his head driver, that day in the mid-week – first, in the morning before Gebu set out on the day's trips, and then later in the evening when he returned with the bus to base – was not unusual. What was strange was the type of question Joseph posed to Gebu in the morning before Gebu set out for his first trip.

"You frequent the canteens, don't you?" he asked the head driver who had come to him to signal his readiness to depart for Regin City.

"Yes, sir, I do," replied Gebu, "especially in the evenings."

"Good. Then, which of them is better, or, is the best?"

"Ah, for someone like me with a deep pocket, *Hungrieman* is the best. Besides, it opens till late every day of the week."

"Look, I am not talking of any deep or shallow pocket. For you, Gebu, to require a very good meal for yourself in this bus station, or for you to arrange one for me, which of them would you go to? That is what I want to know."

"In that case sir, my choice will be the *Original TeeCoff*. Brenda is expensive, but the nerves, mouth and stomach pay good respects to whatever comes out of her pots. She has no rival."

213

"Are you sure about that?"

"Yes sir, very sure."

"Okay, on your way now, can you tell her to please see me?"

"When?"

"Now, if she is already there. Or, as soon as she is in, if she is yet to arrive."

"Yes, I will deliver the message straightaway."

Gebu just reached the door on his way out when his boss called him back. He wanted Gebu to arrange it that all his buses returned to NA as early as possible the same day of the following week so he could hold a short meeting with all the staff.

At the *Original TeeCoff*, Brenda-O Teews was yet to arrive, and this left Gebu no option than to leave the message with Alice, her assistant, to pass on. Gebu hardly finished giving Alice the message when Alice showed a greater interest. "Is there any problem?" she asked.

"No. I don't think so."

"Come on, man, but why would he send you at this particular hour, and when the office boy is still on his payroll?"

"Well, I think either he himself, or the office boy will be in a better position to answer that.

"Then, you asked if there was a problem. Supposing there is, what can you in particular do about it?" he asked, treating himself to mocking laughter. "If you can do nothing to save these poor live fish," he said, pointing to a large aluminium bowl filled with water and holding about two-dozen large catfish, "from ending on your customers' dinning plates, how could you save your boss in case she had a problem with Chief Tolp?"

"You wait there and be surprised. Do you know how well I, Alice, know your boss?"

"You little braggart," continued Gebu with the jokes, "when will you stop bluffing? How well could you have known him? I can

214

see you clearly; and it doesn't show on you – not in the least. A dream of yours maybe!"

"Clear out, you cheeky something. Your bus and passengers are waiting for you!"

Joseph Tolp was exceptionally happy to see Mrs. Teews. He showed her to a chair, the central one of the three facing him on the other side of his desk. He then grabbed a piece of scripted-on paper he reserved on the desk, and went straight to the point.

"I have a job to give out," he declared, "and you have been recommended as the most suitable for it."

"Oh thank you Chief; what is this job?"

"To prepare a good dinner for my staff. Twenty of them."

"Against when?"

"This day next week. 5 p.m. okay?"

"What would you like for them? This would determine if that day and time would be okay."

"The best on your list would be fine by me. I am not particular as long as it is the best."

"They are all bests. Chief, just say what you want."

"In that case, I leave it for you and my head driver to sort out. Then, you give me the bills."

"That is no problem sir. Is there any other thing?"

"Only that everything will take place in your canteen. I want the tables specially zoned out and well decorated for the occasion.

"And then, you add another plate – for me."

Brenda-O was surprised at the request of Joseph Tolp, but she put up a successful effort to hide this away in her response to him. She could not understand what qualified her for the job and honour of preparing dinner not only for his staff, but for him as well.

"That will not be a problem, Chief. I will arrange with Gebu, and if need be, come back to you."

Another person Joseph Tolp was particularly happy to see that day was Akiya, his former security assistant, and now the substantive Head of Security, HOS. It was late in the evening after the day's job was over. In order to make the encounter direct and private, Joseph intentionally set aside his position as the boss and hid in a sort of ambush for Akiya outside his own office.

"Good evening sir," greeted Akiya when he was finally before his boss.

"Oh thank you," in a lowered voice accompanied with an extra wide grin that sent both corners of his mouth to within a short distance of his earlobes. "Did you have a nice day?"

"Yes, thank you."

"I haven't seen you for almost a week to ask how you are coping with security affairs. Anybody or anything creating problems?"

"Everything is fine sir, as far as the department is concerned. There is no problem whatsoever."

"Anyway, I have always trusted you will manage well. You are not only smart in uniform, but also smart all round. And if you can keep it up, as far as your progress is concerned, the sky is the limit."

"Thank you sir. I will try my best."

"And by the way, did Gebu tell any of you anything special today?"

"What about, sir – like a new operations directive?"

"No. About me looking for the lady at the canteen or something of that sort."

"Yes, in the morning. He used the excuse of being sent by you to call Mrs Teews as being responsible for his late return to the bus for our departure."

"Is that all – anything else?"

"E-e-e-m," he started to shake his head very slowly, making surer of the answer with each side turn. "No. Nothing else sir."

"And how about this evening – did he say anything?"

"Nothing before we parted."

"Not to worry. He will soon inform all of you." He made a fast but careful look round where they both stood. "But for now, you move closer and listen."

Akiya complied – as reasonably as courtesy would allow him.

"You have always been loyal and hardworking. And like you earlier heard from me, very soon you will have a reward far greater than you enjoy now – one that you would least expect.

"One day next week, there is something you will do for me. And keep it to yourself. Understand?"

"That is alright sir. Which day will that be?"

Joseph Tolp decided to appear uncertain of the day. It would be too risky and early to leak out any part of the detail of the job he had in mind.

"Right now, I am not very sure which day it's going to be," he lied. "But what is sure is that you are the one I trust to do it, be it next week, or the week after the next."

"And what is the job, sir, so that I can get myself prepared?"

"For now, don't worry about that also. I will tell you next week, or, as soon as it is time to do it. No preparations as such will be required. It's easy – won't require chalk, blackboard or classroom!"

Monday before the day of the dinner, Brenda-O reminded every member of staff to keep her poplin tabard uniform clean and on for the special evening reserved for Joseph Tolp and staff. She gave the supervision of the cooking and table setting to Alice, leaving the overall supervision to herself. When the Wednesday finally came, it was obvious that Brenda-O and her staff were fully prepared, as all the arrangements seemed to work perfectly.

The table layout started with a head-to-head placement of four white-linen-covered rectangular tables of the same dimensions to form a row. A second similar row was spaced out parallel to the first. Two single tables of similar dimensions placed across to join the two ends of the two rows completed the rectangular setting. And for the first time in a while, Brenda-O personally complimented the snow-white linen-covered tables with flowers of yellowish cream petals and white sepals, as recommended by Alice, to blend with the linen.

Gebu was determined to get to the canteen earlier than any of the staff so that he could, among other things, direct each person to the seat earmarked for him. The arrival however proved not early enough, as Raful, another conductor of Joseph's, was already at the restaurant watching all the goings-on when Gebu arrived.

"Hello, Raf," Gebu warmed up to the early bird, "you are very early. How long have you been here?"

"About ten minutes."

"So, you really meant to beat all of us to it – to the arrival here," he started to joke.

"Well, since all of you decided to keep to the local, instead of to the standard time."

"But Raf, when was the last time you actually kept to this standard time you are now boasting of? You never did, except on an occasion like this one."

"How do you prove that?" Raful responded with laughter. "That I never did. Or, that I did only on occasions like this? It means I always do!"

"I mean only on special occasions."

"It means I know occasions – know when they are special, and treat them as such."

"Hm-n, you never miss it, not anything that is free."

"Correct, Gebu. But who would prefer either what is good but costs or what is bad but free to what is good but free? No sane person would! I wouldn't, certainly not. Would you?"

They both went into prolonged laughter as more of their fellow guests started to arrive.

At the end of the cooking, Alice wanted to make the service even more efficient. She decorated a large table at the corner of the hall, and temporarily set on it the glasses, cups, plates and all that would be reservedly needed to go onto the main table.

As soon as a guest took the seat to which he was directed, Alice would move to him at once to hand over a copy of the menu, and asked him to make his choice ready for when she would come back for his order.

Joseph Tolp had instructed that he be served last by the virtue of being the host. As he was being served, Akiya watched both Alice and his boss probingly, and concluded that the past boast of Alice, claiming a sort of familiarity with his boss, was an empty one. He was convinced that his boss paid special attention neither to her nor to what she served him. By 07:00 p.m., Alice had successfully served every plate and the guests were ready to dine.

Joseph Tolp believed the best time to address his staff was before they got on with the dinner. He would not risk having their attention shared with what he had used his money to provide for them. As soon as the last plate, his, was placed on the table, he cleared his throat, rose, and called for their attention.

He acknowledged their attendance and punctuality, especially after the day's hectic job. The dinner, he said, was arranged as a token of his appreciation of their loyalty and dedication. They should continue in the same way, and he too would always find means of compensating them. It was important they stayed ahead of other transporters; and so, whatever business method his organization should adopt through them, his dear staff, they must never pass it to anyone outside the organization. But should any of them, through friends, be familiar with any good method being used by other organizations, he should not hesitate to come and share it with him directly. Thanking them again, he concluded by inviting any of them with something to say to stand up and say it. Each comment however, should be as brief as possible so that their primary time to enjoy the delicious food and drinks would not appear stolen.

Only Gebu responded to the boss' address. On behalf of his colleagues he was grateful for the timely dinner. He sought the full cooperation of his colleagues to serve the boss better. Their boss, he said, usually rubbed their backs, and they too must jointly continue to rub his. This was why, unlike other bosses, Chief Joseph Tolp deliberately closed his eyes while they made extra financial gains on the sides, on his buses. A man with a heart big enough to do this for them deserved being given his full daily returns, he concluded.

From a hidden distance, Brenda-O watched the men as they dealt with their dinner and she felt contented with herself. She noticed on Raful, a soft, but radiating smile which she could not determine whether it was there to welcome the mountain of food in the plate before him, or as a result of certain jokes being shared with those sitting nearer to him.

Gebu sat with his back partially turned towards her direction. Though both the distance and the solid wooden back of the chair he sat on prevented her from seeing the whole movement of his back between the back-neck and the buttock, but from the sides, she could see the successive projections of his elbows as they showed and disappeared alternately in front of the head that bowed and recovered. She was particularly delighted that with every bow, Gebu's mouth was sentencing into disappearance, a piece of meal that had come from her kitchen.

As for Joseph Tolp at the other end and facing her direction, she was surprised to see him very relaxed among his employees. As he ate, he humbly cracked jokes to which everybody made a response, even when such a response only stopped at the lower limit of passiveness that would make a boss feel happy.

She nodded in joyous acceptance of how happy everyone dining at her tables was. The sum total of it all, she told herself, was that she herself was more than basically good for her profession. Her mind went to the story often told her by her father – that of the redheaded he-lizard. He emerged from a wall crack and saw an insect high up a tree. He ran up the tree, caught the insect, and devoured it outright. Instantly after, he jumped down from the height, landing on his belly without the slightest feel of indigestion. He looked round to see if, from anywhere, some applause would come for him. In the absence of none, he nodded his head repeatedly in self-acknowledgement of the rare feat he had performed.

At this time too, Alice, in the course of performing her special assignment passed by Brenda-O, still in her hiding place. "Where are you going – is there any complaint?" she asked Alice, pulling her gently.

"Thank God, there is none," replied Alice as she quickly recovered from the mild shock from Brenda-O's sudden touch. "I am going for more drinking water; what is left there will soon finish."

"Good girl. Well done, and run along," Brenda-O complimented her and moved away from the hiding place.

But the happy and peaceful table Alice left was not what she met on her return with the jug of water. By then, every guest had abandoned what was left of his dinner and was instead, attentive to Akiya who was covering his mouth with both hands. Dramatically, others, led by Joseph Tolp, were assisting him.

Alice dropped the jug and ran to Akiya to see what was wrong with him.

"Stones!" Joseph Tolp shouted to Alice. "There are stones in the meal. He cracked one…this." He pointed to a crystal of almost the same size and colouration as that of the brown boiled rice on the plates before them.

"Oh my God," she said with fright. "But how can?"

"Please somebody, just call me Mrs. Teews," ordered Joseph. "She must come at once."

Brenda-O's response was fast. Looking ahead from about twenty steps from where her attention was required, what she saw sent her into a state of fright and confusion. She saw Akiya made a throw-up that fountained up before splashing down over three other plates of food. And so abruptly, the dinner stopped, leaving Brenda-

O and Alice thoroughly bewildered. They were lost as to why their efforts that deserved to be a credit had to terminate in a confounding disgrace.

* * *

Within two days, the incident at Brenda-O's canteen was the talk on every lip inside NA bus station. Joseph Tolp was particularly pleased; and he spared no effort in spreading it as fast, and as far, as possible. When on the third day of the incident Carlos Retfil called him to ask for the confirmation of the story, he quickly convinced Carlos that it was a serious matter that was better related face-to-face with him; he would be coming straightaway to him in his office.

"So, Chief Tolp, what is this story, that has been making the rounds?" Carlos asked as soon as Joseph's head was inside the door to his office.

"Chief, that is how I saw it – how it happened – unfortunately," Joseph answered.

"How did you see it; and how did it happen? Please sit down and tell me."

Joseph, looking angry and deeply upset, took the chair shown him by his host.

"Right before me," he went on, "I saw my guests eating stones and pebbles instead of the dinner I ordered and paid for. I have never seen anything so humiliating and embarrassing. Not in my entire life."

"Really?"

Joseph seized the golden moment. With deliberate seriousness, exaggeration and falsehood, he blew up to Carlos, the story of the incident he, Joseph, designed in the first place.

Joseph started with how his heartfelt desire to give his staff a treat for their dedication to work had driven him to the idea of giving them a good dinner. Mrs. Teews was recommended as being the best in catering services in the garage. Even though he had on occasions heard some negative reports about her canteen, he never expected the extent of the decay to have gone beyond rearing the maggots. It was with reluctance he agreed to the recommendation to use hers. And if Mrs Teews were the best, he wondered how horrible the general situation must have been with *Hungrieman* and all other canteens inside the station. He prayed that not even his worst enemy would ever encounter the type of loss and embarrassment he was made to suffer in his quest to show kindness.

"And such worst enemy doesn't include me I suppose," Carlos said jokingly, trying to calm him down.

"You?" Tolp asked, now smiling and shaking his head. "God forbid, no. You are a good leader, father figure, friend, confidant...you name it. You can never be in the category of an enemy to anybody in this world," he concluded with ovation and laughter.

"Are you sure about that or you are just pulling my leg?" asked Carlos, with more laughter.

"Serious and honest about it; you have always been all that to all the transporters in this city and beyond. That is why I also felt that this incident at *TeeCoff* would affect you personally when in fairness, it shouldn't have."

"How?"

"Of course, through the reputation of the garage that is being soiled. You are the number one in the garage – in the system. Everyone knows that."

"Don't tell me that."

"Yes, you are. Neither you principally nor any of us could dissociate himself from the garage or its activities."

"Yes; but we could, from the canteens. For example, no one would ever mistake me for Mrs. Teews, her *TeeCoff*, or for any of the other canteens for that matter."

"That is correct sir," Joseph agreed, "but only to some extent. The same people would remember we own the whole structure and allow them to run the canteens. Nobody talks only about the bad river without remembering its source. The people who are worse affected are either our staff or our passengers, and they need our protection."

"But how?"

"These people in the canteens were given several chances to improve but they clearly misused all, as evident now. I suggest we have to stop relying on them, take our destiny into our own hands, and run the canteens by ourselves."

"But who would have the time for all that?"

"We never can say, Chief. I, for one, can make out time for it. And I believe many others among us can, too. The worst of us is bound to be better than the best of them."

"That is easier said, Joseph. It has never been tried or confirmed."

"For now sir, all that might not be necessary; I mean, with the kind of urgency required to solve what is before us. These people put in very little to make fortunes; yet, they couldn't bother to give the basic services."

"You see, Joseph, this, we are discussing now, is a serious matter – so serious that a careful handling is necessary. Certainly, you have your reasons. But the consideration shouldn't just be between you and me. Again, do discuss it with others and hear what they think about it. Or, you can bring it up during our next meeting."

* * *

The next meeting came six months later. Its call was disguised as one for the consideration of the Mathew Rebbor Committee report on the growing complaints from the passengers after the discounts were cancelled. Before the meeting, Joseph Tolp had sought the views of his colleagues, and made them see everything his own way, such that they preferred that they ran by themselves, the canteens and other business outfits within the station. Pressure was also exerted on the passengers, such that discounts were forgotten, overcrowding in the buses was accepted, and irrational diversions were unchallenged by them. The transporters were pleased to see their own fortunes increased at the expense of the passengers they ruthlessly subdued through harassment on the buses and in the garages.

The meeting, at the usual Majesty Hotel, had a full attendance. Carlos Retfil, this time the first to arrive at the venue, swiftly purchased the first respect for himself by pre-paying for all meals and drinks that would be required by the participants that evening. By turn, he was the meeting's chairman.

The last to arrive was Luz Inina. His was not a serious lateness; he missed only the usual opening prayer.

Carlos, as chairman, had the only copy of what was to be deliberated upon. He told them that the meeting, being an impromptu one, allowed him no time to make copies of its programme.

He had no doubt that they all knew what the meeting was all about – that three weeks ago, the Mathew Rebbor Committee that was raised to study the passengers' complaints submitted its final report to him. He had used the first week to study it page by page before calling the meeting for that day. He found it a thoroughly researched document, and was sure it achieved its goals. Because it was a more-confidential-than-before document, he warned them not to divulge anything about it, or about the meeting to a third party. It was the least favour they could do for themselves, he said, and asked if he could count on their support for his request for the secrecy. Their answer came as a mixture of yeses and nods of assorted rapidity.

"Okay then," Carlos said, "since the tongue is more suitable than the cheek to lead the talk, I now call on the committee chairman, Chief Rebbor to formally present the report to this meeting.

"It is important we follow him as he reads it topic-by-topic and subheading-by-subheading, so that we can arrive at taking correct actions. I am however sure that hardly are we going to get any part of it rejected."

Mathew Rebbor rose to the call and was greeted with applause.

He was grateful to Carlos Retfil for the encomia showered on him and his committee, and to the transporters for the faith they had in his ability before entrusting him with the big responsibility. He was of the opinion that the passengers wouldn't have initiated any trouble in the first place if they had taken time to find out and know that they, the transporters, were businessmen operating the system legally and humanely. He thanked the other three members of his committee for their active contributions, without which it would have been impossible to produce the report. He hoped that at the end of his presentation, the committee would not be a disappointment.

Mathew Rebbor commenced the reading of the full text of the committee's findings:

"One. Delays: Observation showed we could not be held responsible for delays. The passengers hardly arrived in time for the check-in. They ignored the fact that the timetable existed, among other things, to eradicate delays. They failed to realise that once one starts late, one is almost certain to finish late, unless something pays for the lateness during the course of the journey.

"We received three complaints on delays caused by rains and floods. This was when the sky and the roads were covered with water so much that driving could not be risked. Therefore, we could not be liable for a clear act of God. We actually asked one of the protesters why he could not brave the rains and venture out of the bus while the downpour lasted. Expectedly, he went dumb.

"Fifty delays were caused through the passengers having unnecessary arguments with our staff. Of this number, our staff could be blamed for only two.

"There were ten complaints on the delays at the checkpoint. Who were we to order the inspectors not to carry out their legitimate duties? However, we recommend that we take this up with the respective chief inspectors. We also recommend that in order to speed up our take-offs, as well as to give prompter assistance to passengers, the number of conductors on every bus should be increased from one to two.

"Two. Diversion: It was difficult to know what they meant between diversion and delay. We guessed they meant that buses at times, before arriving at final destinations, passed through places not originally specified from NA. Some even complained that sometimes, the original carriers stopped halfway through the journeys, while some alleged they ended at different destinations altogether. But we are fully satisfied that no passenger ever complained of not being put on alternative carrier that would get him to his intended destination. Neither did we see a single record showing any passenger who was surcharged for a diverted journey. But we hereby confirm that we are within our legal rights to choose routes and destinations for the passengers and their goods.

"For our protection, we suggest that we specify only the points of departure and the final destinations on the time-tables, continue to arrange for alternative carriers when necessary and without demanding payments for transfer services, and three, cut the number of diversions on a single journey to not more than two.

"Three. Fares: In all the five zones, we confirm our fares to be the lowest. Zones 3 and 4 charge whatever they want per mile and per kilometre, while Zone 2 employs a method too difficult to verify. We, on the other hand, charge according to the smoothness of the road and the number of the bus stops we cover. What could be fairer?

"Even though our roads are smoother now, the passengers forgot it was mostly our money that was used to repair them.

"In reality, we suspect that the complaint about fares was being mixed up with the cancellation of discounts. Fortunately the grumble is dying out.

"Currently we are twice cheaper than Zone 2, and about thrice than each of 3, and 4. In fact, we suggest we make an upward adjustment as soon as possible, especially on the NA - Regin City route. Or better still, we could raise all, and when there are murmurs, lower them a bit, so it would look as if we are doing them a special favour.

"Four. Discounts: We confirm that by introducing the discounts when they were neither required nor requested, and later cancelling them, we unnecessarily imposed the problem of passenger complaints on ourselves. It was like we introduced free honey into the mouth of the lazy, and the sweetness encouraged him to gather enough strength to attempt wrestling its pot off us. Our investigation confirmed that since the attack on the buses of Mr Luz Inina, two other incidents of violence had been recorded. Fortunately, the damages inflicted on these two buses, though bad, were not as serious; and more significantly, none of our staff was injured. Also, within the same period, eight more passenger protests took place but the bus crews successfully handled all of them.

"We therefore recommend that all buses starting from Zone 1 – whether owned in the zone or not – should not be permitted to issue discounted fares. After a period of six months from now, discounting could be considered for pre-booked, family travels only.

"Five. Conclusion: We recommend a total overhaul of our logistics in order to cope with current and future demands on our invaluable services. Unless we do this, the passengers will start new rounds of problems, and see to it that we do not enjoy the fruits of our labour and investments. Now, they believe we are making too much profit, but they are not interested in knowing how much we spend on maintenance, staff, inspectors and even, burials. It is we, who know. It must be we, who are to keep things balanced at all times.

"Thank you all."

Carlos Retfil called for another round of applause for Mathew Rebbor and his team. He then invited comments from other participants.

Isa Reduaram said he was not surprised that the findings vindicated them. Right from the moment the committee was inaugurated, he knew it would, because the complaints of both the passengers and the citizens were silly in the first place. He did not agree that they, the transporters, were making money, but that they were only trying to survive the harsh times. "Who doesn't deserve profit and happiness from the only profession he knows?" he asked. He wanted the plan to raise the fares to be set in motion at once – that a committee should look into it and make a recommendation that would be implemented, all within one month hence.

Luz Inina did not however see any sense in increasing the fares. He believed it would be too soon after the discounts were removed. He also saw no good purpose served in comparing their fares with those of other zones.

"But how can we be sure other zones haven't compared their fares with ours?" responded Carlos to Inina. "You all should remember that they even compared their cemetery with ours. We are bound to learn from making comparison." He then overruled Inina and upheld Reduaram's suggestions, adding that the terms of reference of the fares committee should include the possibility of creating additional bus stops within Zone 1 only.

Ecaf Lawrence wanted them to take very seriously, the protests of the passengers. Protesters must be identified and their names sent to all garages for all drivers, conductors and security assistants to note. The ringleaders should then be banned from travelling on any of their buses for as long as the transporters wished.

Linus Isho saw the complaint on delays as some unreasonableness coming from idle mouths and minds. He lampooned the passengers as the ne'er-do-wells, and asked to know what they would have done if the transporters have not rescued them

229

from their old gigs and energy-sagging tandems. The statement drew prolonged laughter and applause.

Having heaped enough insults on the citizenry using the committee report and individual comments, they adjourned for a short tea break.

* * *

The second and final part of the meeting was reserved for topics other than the report of the Mathew Rebbor Committee. Joseph Tolp was the first to rise for an address to his colleagues.

"I have a very serious observation and some complaints to make," he started. "It is about the quality of the services being rendered in the garages in the name of the association. I take NA as an example, and our canteens as specific.

"I am sorry to reveal that all of us here are already sentenced to death by slow poisoning, by no other persons than the canteen managers and supervisors. In fact, we are all already serving the sentences." Then, to sway his colleagues, he joined up the complaint he fabricated with the incident he plotted to happen at the *Original TeeCoff*.

"Therefore, the whole house, I respectfully put it to you: What do we do before the undertakers start to import our coffins?" he concluded with the strongest of emotions.

A complete silence engulfed the room.

"Set up a committee and let us have a report," Isa Reduaram suggested.

"And what if the committee members don't live to write one; or we, the transporters don't live to get one?" Joseph Tolp asked as a reply.

"God forbid, though you could be right," said Isa Reduaram. "But what else can we do?"

"I think there is a way out, the best for keeping ourselves and our reputation intact. It should not have been allowed to get this bad. I suggest that all the canteen operators are suspended immediately, together with whatever staff they may have. Then, the committee can work unhindered."

"But then," asked Lela Adamu, "how do we get food for our passengers, our staffs and ourselves?" He could not understand how one of them could make such a suggestion.

"What happens if we don't have a single canteen?" Joseph answered Lela with another question. "In fact, since that day of my bad experience in their hands, I have made up my mind on a suggestion. It is that since these people don't care, and are more interested in selling us mouthfuls of stones instead of, of food we pay them for, why must we allow them to continue? We might just as well run the canteens ourselves."

"That will never work," Ike Elfans swore. He was the only friend Joseph Tolp could not see to convince before the meeting. "First, how do we pick one of us to become a canteen runner?" he asked Joseph scornfully.

"Secondly," Ike continued, "our number far supersedes that of the canteens available. A balanced distribution among us will therefore be impossible to carry out."

Joseph Tolp at once saw the technical correctness of Ike's input, and of the mistake of his, not to have seen him before the meeting. But he had no time at all to sulk, or to blame himself.

"Chief Elfan's observation is absolutely correct, gentlemen," Joseph quickly came in. "But to be honest," he continued, "from what I hear every day, it is not only the canteens that have problems. Almost all the retail outlets also have their own; and very soon, they will ripen to bursting stages as the canteens have just done."

"We will not damage our reputation by waiting till that time comes before we act," shouted Isa Reduaram. "I suggest we take over all the shops and retail outlets now. It's then no one would blame us."

"I support it," said Joseph very readily. "It means everyone of us will be guaranteed an additional outlet to run."

"But before you support it," Luz Inina cut in, "have you thought of what would happen to the lives of all those currently working in the outlets – how they would survive, how they would manage?"

"How have they been managing and surviving?" sharply asked Joseph in his usual manner. "None of them was born with the garage, and the garage was not established because of any of them. I, or any person here today, would be too prying and inquisitive to try knowing how they manage. It is – and should be – their own private affair."

"Please, gentlemen," the chairman interrupted, "let us go back and consider what Luz Inina reminded us of. I think it reasonable that we think of their security. Is that what you have in mind, Luz?"

"Yes, mister chairman, sir, – the security of those to be laid off – income-wise."

"That is fine," said Isa Reduaram, "I would rather prefer the meeting starts with considering the security of the members. We must learn to protect our own eyes first to enable us see others' that would need our protection."

"But chief," Luz said to Isa, "what other security do you still need in addition to what you have now? None. Unlike those poor ones, you need none whatsoever. Everything is good and intact for you, and you still want to acquire more of what you can definitely do without. Crazy, isn't it?"

At this point of higher emotions, the chairman, Carlos Retfil, made an observation. "Gentlemen, do not let our meeting of today or of any other day for that matter, degenerate into personal attacks and accusations. There ought to be tolerance and understanding. This is how we can achieve something." Then, he called Joseph Tolp who was signifying to talk.

"Mr Chairman and colleagues," Joseph started, "still, on the same issue of security – call it of job, of Mrs. Teews, of whatever, or, of whoever. I believe I have an idea that has something for everybody, should all those we are talking about be sent off our outlets. It is radical, but definitely not crazy. It is that if any of them is still interested in selling, we should permit him to bring his wares into the buses and sell along to the passengers – completely rent-free."

"Oh my God!" mildly screamed Lela Adamu. "How more crazy could an arrangement ever be? What will the inside of the buses look like – shopping malls?" He rose at once to oppose the suggestion.

"No, none would look like a shopping mall," expatiated Joseph. "If we could agree to this, it would be controlled in terms of items and style. More jobs are what we want, and more jobs are what it is going to provide."

"O yes," said Olu Duarf, "I buy the idea too. It should keep their big mouths shut."

A long debate took place before a 'yes' vote for a total take-over of all outlets in Zone 1 garages by the transporters won the day.

In the end, the chairman, Carlos Retfil, happily read out the resolutions and agreements as a reminder to his colleagues:

"One: All recommendations made by the Mathew Rebbor Committee Report are adopted.

"Two: Due to the irresponsibility of the former operators, the Association takes over the direct management and supervision of all leased retail outlets, including the canteens, with effect from two weeks from this day.

"Three: Two newly inaugurated committees – Outlets Re-distribution Committee headed by Chief Joseph Tolp, and, the Fares and Routes Update Committee headed by Ecaf Lawrence are to submit their reports within a fortnight.

"Four: In order to give better services to passengers, two security assistants are to work on every bus, together with a conductor and a driver.

"Five: Any operator who so wishes may permit in-bus sales and commerce during its journey in Zone 1 only. Such activities are not permitted beyond Zone 1."

Once more, he reminded them of how critical the day's meeting was to the winning of the war with the passengers; and so, how important it was that the contents of their adoption were kept within the members only.

Lastly, he thanked them for their contributions and urged them to stay on for the free dinner he had ordered for them. Together with Papah Feiht, he walked to the hotel canteen to let the chef know they were ready for the dinner.

* * *

Carlos and Papah were walking back from the kitchen when they bumped into someone Carlos least expected, coming in the opposite direction. He was Emmanuel Titoloujou; and Carlos was particularly shocked.

"Hello, Mr Titoloujou," Carlos greeted, pulling his eyebrows. "What are you doing here?" he asked suspiciously as if Emmanuel was in a no-go area.

"I came for Inina."

"That's good," said Papah Feiht, "do you know he is in a meeting?"

"Oh yes. I brought him in the first place."

Carlos Retfil looked into Papah Feiht's face.

"And have you remained here since then?" asked Carlos again.

"Oh no," answered Emmanuel, "I went away and just returned here about half an hour ago."

"He would not be ready for another hour or so; will you call back for him then?" asked the former boss.

"I can't. I will wait."

Carlos looked at Papah Feiht's face again

"And how is the business going – passengers behaving?" Carlos asked his former chief driver another question.

"Business, on our own taxi scale, is fair enough. I can't complain."

As both men continued back to their colleagues, and Emmanuel to the bar to wait for Inina, Carlos' countenance suddenly changed – worries and anger manifested on his face through his eyeballs. Why, he debated with himself, should Emmanuel be there on this day of the meeting: to eavesdrop? Why did Inina not bring his own car: to justify Emmanuel's coming? Why had Emmanuel been there since the past half hour: to monitor their movements? Why did Emmanuel have to come for Inina when Lela, another friend was there with his car: to enable a meeting of the three where they would plot over some bottles of beer? Why wouldn't Emmanuel maintain a complete break from the transporters after his protest resignation: to effect revenge? Yes, he was self-convinced there's a sinister motive behind Emmanuel's presence.

"Did you believe he actually went away and just came back?" Carlos asked Papah Feiht.

"Yes, most likely he did. He wouldn't park a taxi for a whole day for a friend's meeting? No, I don't think he would."

"Let's hope so," said Carlos unconvincingly, as both men entered the hall to join others for the dinner.

By Carlos Retfil's design at the end of the meeting and dinner, he and Joseph were the last of the transporters to leave Majesty Hotel. Carlos had called aside Joseph Tolp and quietly notified him of the presence of an uninvited guest. "Did you know Titoloujou is at present here with us?" he asked Joseph.

"Really? Where, and since when?" Tolp asked back with acted concern. The depth of the hatred Carlos had for Titoloujou's earthly existence equalled exactly the depth of fear Joseph had for the same man's name.

"He has probably been here since the beginning of the meeting."

"Doing what?"

"Doing what God knows – gathering information on our strategies I suppose."

"But this man Titoloujou, why won't he leave us alone?" asked Joseph.

"That is exactly the first question I asked myself too. And I couldn't find a single, justifiable reason. I wish I knew why.

"When I saw him outside the bar, he said he brought Inina down, went away, and later came back for him. But honestly, I neither believed nor trusted him. Why did he have to undergo all the trouble when Lela was with us and could take Inina? I don't believe him."

"I don't either. No part of his body should be believed. Yes, Inina wouldn't need him to come. It's fishy."

"That is what I thought," agreed Carlos. He paused for about five seconds. "But he resigned by himself; why won't he leave me alone?" he asked, fighting unsuccessfully to suppress his anger. "Why?"

"The reasons I can now think of are legions sir," Joseph answered with clear eagerness to enumerate them. "One, he has his friends as sources of inspiration to make trouble. Two, he still loves publicity at its cheapest – to continue painting us black while appearing nice to his past and present passengers. Finally, through his friends, he finds it easy to collect information and disperse it against us. These are the reasons why he and his friends will not leave us alone."

"You probably get it right, Mr Tolp. It means today's meeting is already in the network, isn't it?"

"I am afraid, sir, probably so. They are all very fast actors – dangerous ones."

"But for how long shall it continue?"

"E-e-em, for as long as e-e-em..." Tolp was lost for the conspiratorial words he would have preferred. "Yes, for as long as they continue to infiltrate."

"But it must stop. Stopping it should be our joint responsibility." Carlos made an unusually long pause, thoroughly dejected and angry.

"Chief Tolp, you know me – that I give you my regards every day, and that it is only you I trust in the Association. This must stop. I mean all the three of them. Two have excuses to be at this venue now; one has none. And the one with none has to be stopped first, and then, the tripod would start to collapse for good. Then, we can see it from there, and thereon know what to do."

"You mean Emmanuel sir?"

"Yes. Yes, Emmanuel Titoloujou."

"How then do we stop him first? Will stopping him stop the other two together with their sympathisers?"

Carlos Retfil paused and then started to produce in parts, the difficult answer he had concealed within himself for a long time. He could not hide it anymore as it had now come head-on to the unfortunate – to the criminally inevitable.

"He has to be the first," said Carlos, "because his job and obsession gave him more time among the locals – before he would sway them. It is usually more difficult to conquer in a war that starts from the locals than one from the outer. Emmanuel must be prevented from getting more locals on the side of the three of them.

"It will stop the other two, together with any number of sympathisers they might have. Did it not work during the era of their discount nonsense? It did then; so it will now.

"Tomorrow night, see me at home. But before you come, get it all sorted out with Akiya. He has to be involved. I don't want to get direct with him because you understand him better.

"But assure him: as soon as he successfully completes the task to be given him, he becomes a driver, even if that means with me. And three months later, he owns a brand new bus to himself –

absolutely free. It is a promise, and it holds if the whole project is delivered within a fortnight from this day."

CHAPTER 9

The Total Control

Lais Dorman's farm sat within the semi-tropical vegetation, mostly made up of Legon Forest, which surrounded the town of Little Angel. Her husband, Fadey, started the farm long before he was ordained. The farm, by the time he died, and with the active support of Lais, had grown to become a major source of goat breeding and meat supply. The Majesty Hotel and many members of Dorman's congregation were among the farm's best customers.

Lais, having finished her packing at the farm cottage, was anxious to leave for home – together with Johnson as soon as he returned from the animal shed. To kill the time before he would return, she carried the rocking chair out under the shady cashew tree outside the cottage, and was reading the Bible. Habitually, it was the only book she enjoyed reading.

Five minutes into her reading, she paused and looked up at the sky. There was the low, shining but weak sun, a confirmation that for that day, they had already rendered the job that was for the farm to the farm, and should get home early enough to render to the home, that which was for the home. It was almost an hour she remembered, since Johnson had left for the goats shed, and she became worried over what must have kept him from returning within the initial ten minutes he had promised to return. She lifted herself off the chair, dropped the Bible on the chair, and headed for the shed.

"Johnson!" she called out immediately after she walked past the two hundred metres or so of cleared farmland that separated the cottage from the shed. She heard no response.

"Johnson!" she repeated as she moved towards its door, "where are you?"

"Yes mum, I am here!" replied Johnson.

"Where? I can't see you."

"Here. I know you can't see me; I am on my way back!"

The sixty feet square goats' shed was lower walled; from outside, one could almost see its occupants. For safety, it had the space between the top of the wall and the roof barb-wired. Externally, a ridge of tobacco plants of special scents the Dormans believed would keep the snakes away was made round the shed. A small rectangular area off its interior right corner was further walled off with a door opening to the larger area. Johnson closed this door, hooking-on an open padlock. He then walked to and out of the shed's main entrance to his mum.

"Is this your ten minutes? So, what's holding you?" asked Lais.

"Sorry mum, a goat got injured by another. I had to clean up the bleeding eye and had her separated to the small room."

"Yes, you will always find something to do, and many reasons to do it," she said, laughing. "Are you ready now?"

"Yes mum – ready for NA!" Jovially he held his mum by the left arm and slowly turned her to the direction of the cottage in a playful attempt to drag her along. As Lais, now laughing, shook her arm off him, he knew he had successfully removed her anxieties.

"Just let go my arm, boy," she commanded with a voice devoid of anger. "Supposing I have not come to call you?"

"Then, probably, you would have ended up listening to a bad story, of a blinded he-goat or of a dead she-goat."

They both laughed.

At the cottage, Johnson hurried in and out, carrying inside first, his mum's rocking chair and book. He pushed his Suzuki 100 forward off its stand and started the engine. "Come on mum, let's go," he called.

Lais stared at the motorcycle as she listened with hate and reservation to the sound of its running engine. The louder Johnson fired the engine, the clearer she remembered that scores of citizens were already killed or injured on motor-cycles in NA; and the more she blamed herself for keeping this particular one in the first place, after the death of its original owner, Fadey Dorman, her husband.

Originally it was offered to her husband free by the church, as a further encouragement for his pastoral excellence. He just had it for a year when Ral Ralgrub, driving Chief Daniel's bus, fatally knocked him off it as he rode with Tonga, his younger son he carried behind him. Tonga survived, but had a broken right leg. Family and friends strongly believed it was an act of wilful murder because it happened two days after Fadey, for the first time in the church, publicly called the attention of Chief Daniels to the careless behaviour of his drivers. When, because of his past selfless services, the church left the motorcycle to his household, Lais refused to sell it off. Instead, she covered it up for the future use of Johnson and Tonga who were then sixteen and fourteen years old respectively. Such preservation and eventual passing over she thought, would keep alive the memory of a good father and a loving husband. On occasions when she expressed some motherly fears, Johnson would convince her of its harmlessness, liking it to a gentle horse which would only floor without respect, one who rode it without respect. He would assure her that the only dangerous 'something' on the roads were the bus drivers.

241

"Anyway, take it easy, and no speeding," she reminded Johnson, as she was about to climb up behind him.

"Of course, I won't speed, mum. There is no need for it; we have plenty of time."

"No, we don't," Lais replied. "We ought to have gone, and perhaps reached home. I have preparations to make at home for tomorrow, Sunday. So, where is the time?"

True, the significance of a Sunday to Lais Dorman reached the point of sacredness. According to the doctrine of Holy Repentance Church where her late husband was a respectable pastor, Sunday, and not Saturday, was the day regarded as the holy Sabbath; which, for its members, started from the sunset of the previous Saturday! The members believed it was the day God took a rest after creating the entire universe, and therefore, one when no one must work but assemble in the churches and offer their prayers. This was why she loved to be at home early every Saturday – so that before sunset, she would have cooked what the whole household would eat on Sunday, got ready the clothes she would wear to the church, and had time to study the Bible verses she would discuss with other women in her group, at the church assembly. This, to her, was how best to maintain the trust and respect the church had for her as a worthy flag bearer of both the church and of her late husband.

"Oh mum, what do you mean – that we should speed and hurry to get home?"

"No, Johnson. I am only talking of the time – that we don't have much of it. You are the one talking of speed."

"But both time and speed go together; neither is best expressed without the other."

"Well Johnson, do any analysis you want, but get mummy home safely now. Clear enough?" she issued a joking order.

Lais climbed up and made an almost unending self-adjustment on the seat. They both headed northwards home, to NA.

* * *

Three intruders – one natural and two artificial – were prominent in the surroundings of NA. The natural one was River Ada which formed a moat round three quarters of NA; while the two artificial ones were two roads, one going north and the other going south from NA.

These days, big business-wise, the road to the south on which they were returning became busier because it led to other towns and places every citizen desired to go for one reason or the other. Prominent among these were Regin City, the most commercial and the most organised city of Zone 2, and Togana, a most peaceful city in Zone 3, and one that was popular for its business and educated citizenry.

As an important gateway, the southern road was recently widened at some points and rehabilitated at some others, so as to improve the flow of transport that had grown from mainly the use of horses, bicycles, motorcycles, and cars to that of long passenger buses. Unfortunately, the bridge on River Ada was largely omitted in the scheme of such repairs.

Constructed many years ago through the solo efforts of the people of Zone 2 in other to boost both commerce and communication with NA, the bridge now appeared like a thin, bony neck between a fat chest and a fat jaw in its narrowness with the two widened ends of the road it linked up.

Apart from this, its two ends constantly developed distinctive cracks at the points where the soil met the iron fabrication. Although the cracks were filled up with soil at the repairs, continual ascents and descents of traffic soon had the soil eroded, leaving the grounds on both sides lower than the bridge level. Usually, therefore, two rude jolts informed the user that the bridge was being reached and passed.

Five years ago, when the late Pastor Dorman first received the motorcycle from the church, the road was a quiet one. Now, with the increase in the volume of traffic – of that of the buses especially – its passage had become very risky to the same old groups of users.

The dreaded narrow bridge, being on the immediate bend before NA, also did not help matters. Thus, as soon as mother and son rode past the narrow bridge and negotiated the bend to view from a distance, the signboard announcing the welcome to NA, Lais heaved a sigh of relief with her usual "thank God" expression.

"Oh mum, how many times do you have to thank God on this spot?" asked Johnson, bored of his mum's regular practice.

"For as many times as we are able to pass it safely," she answered. "Look at what the signboard says – welcome to New Angel. It means it's not all who passed it going out today that were privileged by God to be alive and well enough to pass it returning. You and I are lucky exceptions who God welcomes back to NA."

"Anyway mum, better to leave you and this signboard," surrendered Johnson as he took a glance at the conspicuous roadside object that, even though he knew to be extremely beautiful, he loathed for being equally unnecessary.

When the signboard was first erected, both Johnson and Tonga loved it. Its newness, colossal size and colour actually attracted them. And like many other youngsters, they once walked down to it, stopped at it, and admired every detail of it.

The board stood seven feet high and eight feet wide, on the right hand side of the road.

Because of the big and reflective lettering used, the red lettered NEW ANGEL could be seen twenty yards away, gleaning in the centre of the board. A nearer approach of about ten yards revealed a careful combination of pure arts, pictograms and alphabets. The oval, top central bit carried 'welcome to' in bright green. A round, one and a half feet diameter design encompassing a cow and a wheat plant, followed the big name of the town. Below this was the last line, another phrase, 'the land of plenty' in the same green.

At the reach proper, a concrete slab about three and a half feet high, and two inches thick was revealed. It was beautifully slotted into the goblet shaped top of another slab four feet high from the ground. All the wordings and pictures were cast and raised before being painted in the respective colours. After the painting, they were traced with tubes of neon lights. With a flat background of neutral light grey, all pictures and words could be easily seen in both day and night.

With every passing day, the two brothers saw the mini-structure more as a grand deception planned by the transporters ahead of a deception, to boost their egos and win the trust of the citizens of NA. They believed there were more important things they could have used the money to provide within the township. So, they grew to hate it.

"The land of plenty?" the brothers would ponder and laugh over that line whenever they passed by or thought about it.

"Yes," said Johnson one day to Tonga, "these people are masters of ambiguous jargons."

"You mean of deceptive nonsense, brother."

"It's amazing how the citizens could claim to understand it and embrace it."

It was the same negative opinion of it Johnson had that moment he was carrying his mother past it. Land of plenty? But, plenty of what? To who? For who? It must mean plenty of goodies to the transporters who erected it, and plenty of misery to the passengers who passed by it. The goodies must have been supplied by the passengers, and the misery by the transporters. Johnson felt unmoved by Lais' exaltation and sigh; instead, he chose to tease her.

"But mum," Johnson called after passing the board and about reaching the point where the long, posted road changed to the next.

"O yees?"

"Won't you also thank God we are passing the valley?"

"Which valley?"

"This one we are in – and about to pass."

"You mean this hill?"

"But it is no more a hill, mum; it is a deep valley."

Lais, turning sideways, looked at the two engineered walls on both sides of the road, and at the artificial floor surface they were passing on, and laughed amusingly behind her son. At the same time, Johnson smiled into the opposing brushing air and awaited the comments that would come from his mum. Lais, knowing that Johnson was right, quickly reminded herself of the pointlessness in using maternal authority and wishes instead of good reasoning and understanding, to deal with his lads, now young men. She knew where Johnson was going and she kept mum.

In all fairness, both mother and son had their points. The long stretch of road was once hilly, terminating at a peak about four poles after the point where the signboard was erected. That was before the idea of modernization came into the heads of the authorities, spurred by the transporters. Then, that area of NA called Eddea Hill was very much virgin, and a few citizens who regarded themselves as being more far sighted were the first to move in there. They anticipated enjoying a good area, a good view, out-of-town peace, and easy access to a destined-to-be-important road. Fadey and Lais could be said to belong to that group. But because they were not quite strong members, they were cheated – fortunately too – out of the first plot of land they jointly acquired there, by a wealthier neighbour called Gibs Asida. Fadey and Lais had to move away to their present site, far inside on the right, just after the peak. It was shortly after the move that the authorities in NA came up with the idea of taming the hill, or bringing it down to its knees, for easier ascent. Caterpillars and earthmovers of various sizes were brought in and used to cut through it in a manner that, to the likes of Mr Asida, caused the pest to laugh and the farmer to weep. Asida's house that was normally accessible from the hilly road before the 'taming' now became inaccessible after the same road was sharply cut about twelve feet down.

Therefore, to Lais, her son's challenge called for neither a further argument nor a debate. Rather, it called for another sigh and 'thank God'; and this she humbly did again. Finally, they turned right towards Fruits Street of Eddea Hill where their own house securely stood.

* * *

At weekends, Tonga was never far from home. This was more so since he had his accident and took up the crutch. The farthest he would go was their church, two streets away; and that was on Sundays, and when he was in the mood. He preferred to pass the time with Yemie, daughter of Emmanuel and Minat Titoloujou, who was of his age group. Both families moved to Eddea Hill about the same time. It was on the advice of the Dormans the Titoloujous quietly took their present plot instead of wasting time and resources fighting the grabber, Gibs Asida.

The different professions of the husbands – Dorman in the church and pastoral, Fadey in driving and transporting – inevitably kept them apart more than they would have loved to be. But the case was different with the wives, Lais and Minat, who cultivated within them, an exchange of good neighbourliness, friendship and regular visits from years ago when both of them were the only landladies on that street. Their children – Johnson, Tonga, and Yemie – grew to meet the friendship, and so grew to become friends among themselves too. It was therefore no coincidence that Tonga found going to Yemie's very convenient now that he could not move round as much as he used to.

Sometimes, Tonga would go to Yemie on his two crutches, sometimes, only on one; and on few occasions, he would hop the short distance. This day, he went with one, and was not long returned when his mother and brother came back from the farm.

From the kitchen where he was doing the washing-up, he recognised the distinct sound of the family motorbike and knew his mum and brother were back. He went to the main door to let her in while his brother took the bike round to the back of the house.

"Hello, mum," greeted Tonga as he pulled the door handle. "I was just wondering if you decided to remain on the farm till tomorrow morning for the Sunday church service," he joked.

"Remain where? I wish that was possible. We have to wait for you to establish a branch of the church over there first. Amen. But for now, tell your brother to be mindful of the time. He kept us this late."

"Don't worry about that, mum. Let him park the bike and come in first, and I will deliver your message. I hope he too would not have his own complaints."

"Complaints? Never. What would he have to complaint about?"

"I hope he would not attribute the lateness to you stopping at the signboard to pray!"

"Oh my God," she said, laughing as she passed him and went into the kitchen. "Your two minds work the same! Just imagine that. Your brother never gave me peace between that signboard and this door."

Tonga followed her in.

"Anyway," she continued, "you ask him and he's already got his answers ready for you – the story of his goat, its eyes, its nose, its mouth, and so on."

"Oh mummy. His goat? Its eyes? Its nose? Its mouth? I don't understand."

They both laughed more.

"Anyway, thank you," she said, "I could see your efforts in the kitchen." She was referring to the washing-up he did. She knew how very untidy she left the kitchen when she and Johnson were going to the farm.

As soon as Johnson entered, the executions of what Tonga was to clarify with Johnson was carried out with jokes between mother and sons. Soon, food was ready, and the table set.

"Come on, lads, I am waiting. Come over to the dining!" Lais called on her sons.

Both Lais and her husband used to refer to the dining table as just the 'dining'; it was the lads who called it 'the table'. In the lads' much younger days, they used to giggle at their parents for the reference they believed was funny, but silent enough to ensure the parents neither saw, heard nor suspected the giggles.

The Dormans' house was a modest, three-bedroom bungalow. On entering it through the main door, the large, moderately furnished space to the left was the parlour. On the first right was the first of the bedrooms, Johnson's. Going anti-clockwise, and next to it was the kitchen, followed by the second of the bedrooms, Tonga's, at the end of that side of the house. The third room, Lais', had its door directly opposite Tonga's but separated from it by the continuation of the passage that started from the main entrance. Next was the spacious parlour. Its immediate space next to the sidewall of Lais' room had a large, well-polished rectangular wooden table surrounded by six wooden chairs, to make the 'dinning'. Two chairs facing the table along the longer and outer side backed the passage and faced two similar chairs at the table's opposite side. Its other two sides had one chair each, one backing the direction of the entrance door, and the other, the left hand sidewall of Lais' bedroom.

Above the chair nearest to the sidewall hung a half-yard square, framed picture of a pair of clasped and supplicating hands, with the inscription 'give us this day our daily bread' printed below the pair. Lais, already on this chair, was about to call her sons when Johnson came out of his room with a tray of empty cups and saucers for the kitchen. "Johnson, get your brother here, or we are all going to end up with cold food!" she promptly told him, interrupting his passage.

"Mum, I heard you," Tonga voiced from his room. "I am ready too!"

Johnson dropped the tray and joined his mum on the table. Within seconds, Tonga joined them.

"We should not waste more time," said Lais, "so, let us pray."

They all dropped their heads and closed their eyes.

"We thank You God for Your mercies in providing this food," she started. "As it goes in through our mouths and throats, may it not come out through our noses and oesophagi. Let it be useful to our bodies. And in the end, may we have the honour to dine with You in Your everlasting kingdom. Amen."

"Amen."

"Amen."

Fadey Dorman believed in the 44, and he encouraged every member of his family, starting from Lais, do the same. He believed the more the number of voices joined in saying a prayer, the earlier the prayer would be answered by God; hence, his constant advocacy and practice of group prayers both in the church, among friends, and in the family.

As a young Christian of twenty-five, his special talent in praying got him noticed in the church, and consequently led to his being ordained early, five years later.

On becoming a pastor, he blended his talent of prayers with that of sermons so perfectly that his moments in the pulpit were never dull. At the end of every sermon, and whenever he observed some fatigue on the faces of his congregation, he would enliven their spirits by asking them a series of the definitions of God he had previously taught them. "Can anybody remind me of the true meaning of G.I.G.?" he would ask.

"God is good," the crowd would answer.

"G.I.G.?" he would ask again as if he didn't hear them.

"God is great!" they would shout.

"G.I.G.?"

"God is gorgeous!" they would roar.

"G.I.G.!!?"

"God is good!" they would scream.

"Gee Aai Gee!!!?" he would finally ask, with both hands widely opened and highly raised to signal his call for a final answer. Among fellow churchgoers, Fadey thus became Pastor GIG, and his wife, Mrs GIG.

That the three of them were able to have the prayers and dinner together that evening made it very unnecessary for Lais to remind her sons of that aspect of prayer their father cherished and expected of them.

"Johnson," Lais called out as they were all about to finish having the dinner, "can you please get me to the church a bit earlier tomorrow morning?"

"I am sorry mum," Johnson replied, "but I don't intend to get anywhere near the church tomorrow."

"Tomorrow is Sunday; do you forget? What prevents you from coming tomorrow then?"

"We have decided to be at the farm."

"Who is 'we'? To be at the farm for what? We were there all week and all day, up to just a few hours ago, weren't we?"

"We are going to examine all the other goats, to see if any other was injured. The one injured must have fought with another; and I did not have time to look for it before we left. Besides, we have to look at the state of the wound, and supply the feeds."

"But that shouldn't require the two of you to be there."

"Mum, I am going with him," said Tonga. "He will need the usual assistance of his brother."

"Look boys, you are getting drifty nowadays. Remember your dad? He wouldn't have liked it."

"On the contrary, mum," said Tonga, "that wouldn't have worried your husband a bit."

"You mean he would have gone to the church and made excuses for not taking along his sons?"

"No mum," said Johnson, "our dad would have carefully packaged tomorrow's sermons around Luke 14:5, Mathew 18:12, and the ants."

"Which are what?" she asked Johnson.

"In Luke, Christ warned that no ox that fell into a well should be left un-rescued under the guise of a Sabbath day. In Mathew, He warned that you must not leave one sheep uncared for simply because you had ninety-nine others. And lastly, dad would have likened us to the wise and industrious ants whose mode of living was worth emulating. In other words mum, Christ and Pastor Dorman who are our Fathers in heaven now would not have minded our absence from the church tomorrow morning.

"Tomorrow mum, you too could make this your theme when you talk to your group at the Sunday school."

A thoroughly amused Lais could not readily find any objection to what her sons had just sermoned. For the second time that day, she was beaten in the mother-son argument. For about six seconds, she fixed her eyes on Johnson, then shifted them to Tonga, and finally, to one of the two pictures of her husband hung on the wall, before she could find what to say.

"You see, boys, that is what I mean. You could make better pastors than your dad. That's why the church needs you every Sabbath. Could you therefore try and make it to the evening service?"

"Oh yes," Tonga swiftly replied, "That is a possibility."

"Good night then, boys."

"Good night, mum."

"Good night, mum."

Both lads disappeared into their rooms, leaving their mother behind to complete her preparations for the following morning. The preparations consisted of ironing, selecting the topic of discussion for the Sunday school and tucking the tithe inside the special envelope. It was midnight before she switched off the lights and retired into her bedroom.

* * *

At first, it sounded to Lais like some drops of water intermittently falling on a dry leaf. She fought to sleep with it. Then, the sound grew heavier and louder to the point of actually keeping her awake. She switched on the light in her room to see what time it was; it was two in the morning. For the next five minutes, the sound stopped. She switched off and laid back on her bed, hoping that nothing again disturbed the few hours she had left before she would get up for the church.

"Tap, tap, tap. Tap, tap, tap, tap." It now sounded like knocks.

Because she was already fully awake, and it was in the deep of the night, the knocks echoed clearer. She was able to determine which house door was being knocked, and that it was that of the Titoloujous.

"Open the door. We are policemen," she heard followed the knocks.

"Funny," Lais thought to herself. "What would the police be looking for in Titoloujous' household this hour of the night that they could not wait till the daybreak?" Though Lais knew Emmanuel Titoloujou suffered some harassment in the period that immediately followed his resignation from Carlos Retfil's services without being able to pin down anybody to it, but the Titoloujous as well as she herself believed that time was past now.

"Police, from where?" she heard Emmanuel questioned.

"From NA. Would you open the door please?"

"Who do you want?"

"A young lady by the name Yemie Titoloujou. We have the warrant."

"Warrant for whom?" Emmanuel was heard asking again after about four seconds.

"For Yemie Titoloujou – here, at number seven, Fruits Street."

There was another interval of five seconds.

"For Yemie?"

253

"Yes. Yemie Titoloujou."

Another five seconds of quietness followed.

"Okay, just give me a couple of minutes."

From her position of alertness where she heard the conversation, Lais could not remain lying down any longer. She got up and tiptoed to the kitchen. Quietly, and without turning on the light, she opened the window that faced the empty plot separating her house from the Titoloujous' low-fenced compound. She looked out but saw only the darkness. It was one of those many nights of the week when the streetlights packed up due to the problem of energy generation and distribution, or to an outright switch-off by the operators in other to save costs their own silly way. She was sure more of the commands and knocks would follow because she heard Emmanuel urging his unwanted guests to wait. She opted to wake up her two young men, starting with Johnson whose room was nearest to the street, and whom she believed must have been listening to the goings-on.

"Tap, tap, tap," she gave Johnson's room door a half-closed knuckle. Due to the effect of Johnson's previous hard day at the farm, Johnson, deeper into sleep, heard no knock, and his mum no answer.

"Tap, tap, tap," her knuckle went against his door again, this time harder, with each tapping accompanied with a call of his name. Still, no answer came. She worriedly twisted the door handle, entered his room and went straight to his bed, meeting him fast asleep.

"Wake up Johnson," she patted fast and firm. "There is a problem," she patted again. "Aren't you listening?"

"Oh mum, what's the matter?"

"There is a problem. The police have come to arrest Yemie."

Johnson's eyes cleared to the point of being reasonably able to understand his mum. "Did you say the police arrested Yemie? When?"

"They are over there now. They have been banging the door to get her. Get up and listen while I light up the lantern."

Johnson, duly obeying his mum, got up and off the bed. Lais was hardly gone out of the room when Johnson heard the knocks resumed, with a voice firmly threatening to break down the door if it was not opened. The voice warned they had already had enough of the waiting.

"I heard them, mum," Johnson said as he rushed out of his room and met her. "They are ready to break down the door. Can I go down there?"

"No, wait a minute," she ordered. I have looked out through the window and it was very dark."

Just then followed Emmanuel's voice, loud enough for them to hear. "Did you say you are from NA station?"

"Yes; from NA Central."

"Is Inspector Elo Neason with you?"

"That is not for us to answer, sir. Elo Neason doesn't have to accompany every officer for every arrest, or to every investigation."

"Okay, just a minute."

"But your minutes are already running into hours. You either open now, or we force your door."

There followed another moment of silence, one of fear and helpless anxiety for Lais and Johnson.

"Mum," called Johnson with a firm whisper, "They want to force the door. Did you hear it?"

"No," replied Lais. "Are you sure? Get your brother up first – and quick."

Johnson went for Tonga while Lais went to peep again through the kitchen window. She was most frightened now that she saw or heard nobody outside intervening. She ran back to the parlour to meet Johnson and Tonga.

"Tonga," she said breathlessly, "did you hear what's happening? Yemie is being arrested."

"Mum," said Johnson, "it must have been more to it than that. This time of night, a normal arrest wouldn't attract all these harsh words and threats. Something is happening, and somebody has to go in there to see."

"I will go," said Tonga.

"No, you won't," Lais ordered. "I looked out and could not see a sign of any of the neighbours."

"But how would you," Tonga asked, "if all neighbours are acting like us? Besides, mum, you know what type their nearest neighbours are. They wouldn't raise a finger to assist them if they could get away with it. We all in this house know that."

Yes, Lais knew that – and that her son was right – that Mr and Mrs. Dalaf would be the last persons to come out to the aid of the Titoloujous, if they could safely escape it, even though their houses were next to one another's.

Mr Dalaf was a driver and a colleague of Emmanuel Titoloujou, but serving Linus Isho when Mr Titoloujou was serving Carlos Retfil. Mr Dalaf loathed Mr Titoloujou purely out of envy because of the latter's good relationship, and thus, highly privileged position with the most successful and the most fearfully respected transport magnate in NA.

Secondly, Mr Dalaf, like most of the other drivers, believed that Emmanuel's acknowledged trust and popularity among the passengers and citizens of NA was attained through carrying modesty to the point of eroding the self-esteem and high class of the drivers. Dalaf therefore equalled him to an immaculately white egret that chose to bathe in brown sand and mud, and should therefore be isolated by other white egrets to prevent their feathers from being stained by those of the self-disrespecting egret's.

Thirdly, as soon as Emmanuel resigned from the services of Carlos Retfil, other transporters, having been twisted by Carlos, privately but sternly, warned their employees who would like to keep their jobs, to stay away from Emmanuel. It was an ultimatum taken seriously by both the givers and the takers. Thus, even though some of them lived around the Titoloujous, they publicly refused to go beyond exchanging short and hasty pleasantries with Emmanuel.

"Okay boys, come, let us pray first," Lais directed.

"Mum," said Johnson, "let's go there first. There is no time."

"There is no time for prayers?" a stunned Lais asked. "Never is there any time more appropriate. Never is there a mountain prayers cannot flatten!"

Verbally, she dragged them to the sidewall where the picture of her late husband was hanging. It was a large one where he was in full pastoral regalia, and holding a copy of the bible. It was the spot she used to go to, or make her sons come with her to, whenever she wanted to make special prayers. She believed it was the right place to stay in other to have family prayers complete with her late husband's spirit. They knelt down, joined hands, closed their eyes and Lais went on:

> *Our dear God,*
> *God of Isaac, God of Jacob,*
> *God of the Titoloujous, God of the Dormans,*
> *Omni-present, Omni-merciful,*
> *Omni-protective, Omni-conqueror,*
> *We, Your children, Your very own,*
> *We kneel before You this hour of the day –*
> *Oh sorry, this crucial hour of the night,*
> *To seek refuge, first for the Titoloujou family…*

She humbly called on God to put the Titoloujous under His protection. She prayed Him to deliver them from the evil that had traced them to their home – in the same way the biblical Daniel was delivered from the lion's den, and Jonah from the shark's belly. Where the attackers, now with the Titoloujous had turned into lions, she asked God to sheathe silly their claws and lock firmly their jaws. Where they turned into serpents, He should break their fangs and dry their poison.

She quickly remembered her own household, and prayed God not show to these attackers its direction, talk less of the house itself.

Then, she ordered a joint recitation of Psalm 23, followed by the *nostrum padre*. She ended it with a strong grace:

> *May the grace of Christ the Lord,*
> *The sweetest fellowship of our Saviour,*
> *And the mercies of the Holy Spirit,*
> *Be with us now,*
> *Be with Emmanuel now,*
> *Be with Minat now,*
> *Be with Yemie now,*
> *Be with this household now,*
> *From this very crucial hour,*
> *From this very minute,*
> *This very second,*
> *Now, and forevermore.*
> *Amen.*

"Amen."

Johnson and Tonga had scarcely finished saying amen when the three of them heard a louder voice of Emmanuel Titoloujou challenging the person he must have opened his door to. "Why are your faces covered? Where is your warrant? You are not policemen!"

"Shut up!" they heard one of the intruders yell.

"Now, finish him!" they heard another order.

There was a burst of gunfire lasting for about three seconds. Immediately following it was the shrieking voice of Minat. "Help! Everybody, help! They have murdered my husband!" it went on.

Johnson, defying his frightened mother, disappeared into the outside darkness through the back door – to Eddea Hill police sub-station about half a mile, but three streets away. He made special efforts to dodge the gunman pacing and watching between

Emmanuel's gate and the actual front door. He just went past the house when he heard another burst of gunfire. The burst propelled him to run faster, and to wish he had more than two legs to put into use.

Lais and Tonga were the first to be at the Titoloujous. Lais who was ahead of Tonga managed to catch a glimpse of the gunman outside as he disappeared into Mr Titoloujou's house. 'Let them kill us all if they could,' Lais said to herself as she raced in through the door, hoping to meet with the gunman inside before more damage would be done. Tonga hopped closely behind.

"Minat, where are you? Can you hear me?" Lais called out loudly. There was no answer. She ran down the passage and peeped into the kitchen. "Minat, Yemie, Emmanuel, where are you?" she screamed. Still, there was no response.

As she then ran towards the back of the house, she saw the last of the gunman scaled the back wall. "Minat, they are gone! They jumped over the wall!"

"Yemie," Tonga called out, "it is us. They are gone!"

A distraught Yemie furiously ran out of her room past Lais and Tonga into the parlour. As she burst in, the first thing she saw was her father's body lying face down, and bleeding from visible holes the gunshots drilled out of his back. She looked at the body, turned to look at Tonga, and passed out.

While a bewildered Tonga was holding on to Yemie, an equally bewildered Lais ran out to the front of the house to call on the neighbours to come out and help, that Emmanuel had been murdered, and that the murderers had scaled the wall and escaped.

Between the Dormans and the first set of neighbours to answer her call for help, frantic efforts were made to revive Yemie back to life. As soon as she was semi-conscious, she was carried to her room to stop her from seeing again, the sight that caused her to faint, while Lais arranged a cover over the body.

Between Lais and the neighbours too, Minat's body was found inside her own bedroom. She had been shot in the mouth severally when she went hysterical on hearing the shots fired at her husband. Lais and her son however won the support of the neighbours to keep the news away from Yemie whose condition, they were convinced, could irreparably worsen should she be told of her mum's murder at that particular time.

* * *

At the police sub-station – or station, as it was preferably called by its occupants – Johnson received a treatment that at first appeared too efficient to be true. It was as if the officers were expecting the like of him and his problem that very hour.

"Calm down, young man," Inspector Evans reassuringly patted a distressed and sweating Johnson's arm. Evans was the newly appointed chief posted to the station from NA Central. A known protégé of Inspector Elo Neason before Elo was prematurely retired from service, his actual last substantiated rank was that of a sub-inspector; but the rank and file found it nicer and easier to pre-fix 'inspector' to his name.

"But time sir. It is the time," said a trembling Johnson.

"Yes, time, young man – that's what we don't have enough of now to waste," the sub-inspector said more firmly. "You must calm down and explain what happened so that we can get out at once.

"Paula," he called a female officer at the counter, "please get the young man a glass of water."

Paula did not only comply, she made Johnson take some sips.

"Dido," the sub-inspector called again, "get the patrol jeep ready at once, together with two armed officers."

"Yes sir," replied Dido, a reckless police driver, "we are ready, and the jeep is ready."

"And Caspian," the man called again, "take one motorbike and leave one for me. I am coming with you myself."

As his orders were being complied with, he switched his attention to Johnson again. "Now, and as quick and as accurate as you can, I want you to tell me how many the attackers were. Did you see them? Did anyone assist the man who was shot? Was there any other thing you know that might assist us? Calm down and tell me."

As calm as he could, Johnson commenced supplying answers to the inspector's questions: Because it was dark, and because he didn't go into Mr Titoloujou's house, he could not see all the attackers, and could not ascertain how many they were. He saw just one of them keeping watch outside Mr Titoloujou's front door. He heard shots fired on two occasions, but did not know exactly who was shot; so, the situation of him assisting whoever was shot did not arise.

"Any other thing?" the inspector reminded Johnson at the end of the account.

"The man outside the door wore a mask, and was dressed in a full police officer's uniform," Johnson added.

All of a sudden, Inspector Evans' coolness warmed up. "Masked?" he asked. "In police uniform? Isn't that incredible, young man? But you said it was dark; how did you see the police and the uniform? No police officer would be out there doing that sort of thing."

"There was a reflection of light coming from the inside through the opened door he stood by," Johnson affirmed. "I actually dodged him to cross to this side of the road."

Inspector Evans, suspecting Johnson had seen too much immediately terminated the inquiries at this point. "Now, to Mr Titoloujou's quarters; everybody, dispatch," his final order went.

"Caspian, you lead. And all of you must approach from the back road. That's likely where they would take."

"Inspector, sir, can my bike take the front route?" asked Caspian.

"All to take the back route!" yelled the inspector. "I am coming through the front. But use the siren. It would melt them down before you pick them up.

"Paula," the inspector again turned to the female officer, "take care of the station and of the young man; and put his mind at rest. He will be safer staying here until we return.

"And don't contact the Central Station yet. We shall do that if, on getting there, we would require some assistance."

And so, in a mood that to Johnson appeared enthusiastic and determined of Evans and his team – using two motorcycles and a jeep – the policemen roared out of the station in a bi-directional approach to Mr Titoloujou's house.

They were just gone when Johnson approached Paula and sought permission to leave, since he was not under any sort of arrest. Paula unconditionally granted the request, contrary though, to Inspector Evan's instruction.

Half way between the station and Fruits Street, on the same front route taken by Inspector Evans, Johnson saw three men approaching from the opposite direction. As they got closer, it became apparent that they were in police uniform. They were not really chatting; and because they wore no masks, he could see on them what appeared to him as happy, satisfying faces. He believed they were some of the men of the sub-station, and decided to seek a further help from them. He crossed over to their side of the road.

"Good morning, officers," he bravely greeted them. "Please, which way are you going?"

"Of course to the station," replied one of them.

"There has been a murder or a robbery or both at Mr Titoloujou's quarters; did you notice anything on your way?"

"No," replied the same man. "We have just finished the patrol duty, and are returning to the station."

"Can you please come with me to the scene?"

"Sorry, we can't," answered the same man who had taken on the job of the three's spokesman. "We got some assignments just given to us by our inspector. By the way, he is already on his way to Mr Titoloujou's quarters. He will sort it out the proper way." With that, the men walked towards the station, while Johnson continued to the Titoloujous.

Caspian and his colleagues arrived at Titoloujou's before the inspector. Along their route, they came across no one, and saw nothing suspicious. Perhaps, this was due to the sirens they were ordered to use – the same way it could keep an obstructer off their route, so too would it hide off it, any smart criminal.

The situation they met in the house was rowdy. The neighbours, including those who acted ignorant when the attack was going on, were already there. They were, partly due to Lais' call for help, or to a belated morality imposed on them by their environmental proximity to the Titoloujous.

First, Caspian led the men to the parlour where Mr Titoloujou's body was covered-up. The unhelpful neighbours, as well as the genuinely traumatised ones surrounded it, unable to answer questions. From there, Lais took them to Minat's room where yet another body, that of its owner, was covered up. There, despite the deep distress Lais was going through, she remembered to warn the policemen that Yemie was still dazed since seeing her dad's body and so, she must not be told of her mum's murder yet. It would have to be so until she recovered enough to bear both losses.

Next, they met Yemie in her room. With her were three neighbours, one of who was Tonga, holding her up on a settee. She wasn't crying, and she wasn't frowning. She was hardly blinking, and obviously looking at neither a person nor an object in particular. She was alive, but not living.

Inspector Evans was not quite ten minutes in Mr Titoloujou's house when Johnson arrived. Johnson met him asking the junior officers the same questions he threw at him at the station, and which the junior officers had asked those they met at the scene without obtaining satisfactory answers. For the first time, Johnson learnt of the murder of both Emmanuel and Minat Titoloujou.

"But, Inspector," Johnson cut through the session of Evan's questions, "there is no way you would obtain the right answers to your questions now – now that the murderers have escaped, and the victims who are not dead are barely alive due to shocks. Can't you see that?"

"That is appreciated, my young man," said the inspector, "but we need to know something first, to be able to start somewhere. We need the cooperation."

"It is not that others don't want to cooperate. You can see for yourself that there's tension everywhere, and grief on all faces. Everybody needs more time. But for now, I can tell you the little I know."

"Yes, that will be fine and be appreciated, my young man."

In the presence of the neighbours, and with more anger and boldness, Johnson again told Inspector Evans the whole story as known to him and his family. The only new addition was how, on his way back from the station, he met three policemen who claimed they were aware of this attack through the inspector himself; and that the inspector had just left the three of them while on his way to this address.

Conclusively, Johnson bared it that in his own opinion, the assassins were either policemen, or people with very strong connections with the police. Honestly, he would not be surprised if these three policemen he met were directly a party to the double murder.

From the reaction of Inspector Evans at the end of Johnson's story, it was clear he was rattled. He needed to put up a defence for himself, his station and the force.

"Look, young man," Evans cautioned, "we as members of police feel sad for these catastrophes. Get that clear. But that doesn't mean you shouldn't guard and guide your tongue." He was angry at Johnson's highly implicative inferences. "That some people claimed they were aware of the crime through me?" he foamed on.

"Impossible! What do you think the police force is all about?" He was furious.

Neither the inspector's countenance nor his fury frightened Johnson a bit. Johnson knew he was saying what he truly saw and heard. If anything, that the inspector continued to disbelieve and misunderstand him annoyed him so much that he became angrier with the dreaded representative of the law.

"Inspector, it is not only me," Johnson blasted, with anger. "From the general experience now, if you should ask each person here the same question – what he thinks the police force is for – the answer you would get would be the same: that it is for force and force only. Ideally, it should include being for honest and neutral interferences. I have risked a lot to tell you what I saw and heard, and yet, you refuse to believe or investigate. What type of cooperation are you then talking about?"

The blunt truth Johnson packed into his outbursts filled the hearts of its neighbour-hearers with contentment. Shamefully, it put Inspector Evans and his men on the defensive.

"Okay, young man," said the inspector, "we shall now go and look for these your three policemen. I hope you still remember where you met them."

"Yes, I do – where I met them, and where they said they were going to."

"Okay then, we all go now," said the inspector.

"But Inspector, sir," Johnson started to ask another question, "how about the three people lying down dead or down alive; are they going to be left there like this?"

"Don't worry, we are taking care of that," answered Inspector Evans. "My men are seeing to that."

"They should have long seen to it first."

Inspector Evans seated Johnson on his motorcycle, and instructed Caspian to take one of the neighbours coming with them on his. Together, the four of them headed to where Johnson would direct them.

A few yards to the point Johnson had in mind, he noticed some smokes rising slowly into the sky from the spot he was taking them to. The four of them eventually got there and stopped. They discovered that what was burning was an unknown number of police uniforms. There was also an identification card that was melting and glowing, and Johnson quickly used a long stick to isolate it. Already, its carrier's name and passport photograph were burnt, but its police logo was still clear enough. He bent down and picked it up. As he turned and inspected its two sides, he was sure he needed no professional to confirm to him that something was wrong. He handed it over to the inspector and curiously awaited his reaction. In the end, it was still Johnson's that came first.

"Do you now believe in the need for a neutral investigation?" Johnson asked the inspector.

Inspector Evans turned his face into a half-smile, the type that is more of self-derision of an exposed conman than that of the satisfaction of a bright cop who had just made a breakthrough. "Yes, I do," he crumbled.

CHAPTER 10

The Dead-end

From when Ral Ralgrub's bus knocked out life out of his father, and one leg out of his brother, Johnson had maintained, almost on a daily basis, the knowledge of current news on bus garages and bus owners around NA. He would ask any known garage user what life was like in the garage on the day of his use, and ask any known traveller what the condition of the road was at the time of the journey. That, in his own way, was how to insure himself and the rest of his family against further tragedies on occasions any of them would need to travel by bus.

This day, four weeks after Emmanuel Titoloujou's murder, and six after the last transporters' meeting, was one of those inevitable occasions. Tonga had to go for his quarterly therapy in Regin City; and as usual, Johnson was to accompany him.

NA garage wore the new thuggish look that was gradually becoming familiar to both the road and garage users. By eight in the morning when Johnson and Tonga entered the garage, they met it full of people, mostly disillusioned passengers, standing around in groups that varied from few singles to small clusters. He knew the period of orderliness was gone, and was not so surprised at the situation they met the garage.

One could not help spotting one particular group that qualified for a medium size crowd. In its centre were three buses, of blue, green and yellow colours, respectively denoting Mathew Rebbor's, Ike Elfan's and Linus Isho's.

"Oh Johnson, is that it then?" Tonga asked as he suddenly stopped on his crutches, necessitating his brother to also stop.

"Is that what?" Johnson sought to know.

"The new crowd peculiarity they said has taken over the garage."

"Yes. It was said to be worse for most of yesterday when there were fewer buses running. At least we can see three now."

"But that doesn't confirm they are running, does it?"

"Okay, you can go and sit down there," he pointed to a half occupied sofa, "while I go and see what the situation is."

Tonga moved to the nearest fence wall instead, while his brother headed for the crowd. He rested his back against the wall and hung his impaired leg on the crutch. From that position, he watched his brother as he disappeared into the crowd.

About fifteen minutes after Johnson had gone, Tonga began to become more worried than tired, wondering why his brother was still over there. Perhaps, he thought, he was having problems securing two seats. He dreaded the only two options before him should there be no bus available. The first was that he would have to miss the long awaited doctor's appointment with no hope of when he would secure another. The second was that he could allow Johnson to take him on the family motor bicycle he dreaded so much. He drifted further in thought and arrived at a graphic replay of how he lost his father and the use of his own leg: leaving the church on the bike on a bright evening after the choir practice, talking of early morning visit to the farm and a late evening return to the choir practice the following day, the sudden roar of the bus behind them, his father's slowing down to enable the bus pass them, the bang from behind, the blank. The strange hospital bed environment in NA, the pains from the silencer burns, the partial mobility of his left leg! Then, the presence of his mother and brother – with the puzzling absence of his father! The tears!

"Tonga, you're sleeping," Johnson's voice suddenly came. "I'm back. Why didn't you take the seat? Are you alright?"

"Yes, I am okay." He recovered from the initial shock of Johnson's voice as well as from the sight of a third and strange man in their midst. "Was there any trouble down there – why you didn't return in time?"

"One can say that nothing unusual is happening. Anyway, meet Ebino. He and his friend, Heron, down by the buses are also going to Regin City. I just met them. They are nice fellows. They told me all that was going on; and I told them already about us."

"Within that short period?"

"A ha, haven't you just said I've gone for a long time?"

"Oh Johnson, I don't know what else to say."

They all laughed.

"Anyway, I am Tonga, his brother," he repeated his name. There followed a short exchange of greetings.

"Johnson," he resumed again, "but you still haven't told me what is going on! What is it?"

"Brother, simple. What we predicted and what we suspected – that's what's going on."

"Lack of buses or increase in fares?"

"Both. Not enough buses; and fares are gone up on every journey that starts from NA."

"But the increases should have made more buses, and thus, more seats available," argued Tonga.

"Normally, yes," replied Ebino. "But normality has disappeared from this garage for over a month now. Many passengers don't seem to care about the fare increase, since they

269

have no power of their own to choose. Anyway, there are more, even though few, buses today.

"Sad, isn't it?" asked Tonga. "How many of the buses do you say are available now?"

"Only two," replied Johnson.

"But how about those few others that are scattered about?" Tonga inquired again.

"They are all dead," replied Ebino, "and awaiting mechanical repairs and revival. Pity isn't it – that it is come to this?"

"Indeed, it is more than pity," said Tonga, "it is frightening. Does that mean we might not be able to go?" Tonga asked, visibly worried.

"We are going. We cannot afford to miss your appointment. Not when it is this long we have been waiting for it. Calm down, there is still time."

"Don't worry, Tonga," assured Ebino. "It could be difficult for you to get into any of those two; that's why we stopped trying. We understand another two – one of Retfil's and the other, of Tolp's – will soon arrive and load. We left Heron there to obtain tickets and secure all the four seats we would need. Your brother can be here with you while I do the shuttling between you two and Heron."

Fortunately for the worried young travellers, the shuttling did not go on beyond half hour when the two loaded buses took off, and the two being expected to arrive and load up arrived.

First to arrive and for loading was Joseph Tolp's, driven by Gebu.

Ebino and Heron were the first to beat the rush. As soon as they obtained four tickets, Ebino came for Johnson and Tonga. Heron took four of the six seats of the first two rows, physically sitting on one, and using two caps and one handkerchief as symbolic objects of occupation on the other three. Upon the brothers' return, and because of Tonga's condition, he and his brother were given the first two of the three first row seats behind the driver's; the third by

270

the aisle was left empty. Ebino and Heron sat on the second row, directly behind Johnson and Tonga respectively.

"Thank you very much e em...?" Tonga wanted to know the name.

"Heron," Ebino volunteered the help, touching Heron who was sitting by his left.

"Thank to you both, Heron and Ebino. I am Tonga."

"Yes, we all know you are Tonga," said Heron, "Your brother has told us. He is very friendly."

"Yes, thank you. That is why he is with me – the type of person I need most on a day and journey like this."

"Oh sorry, he said you are going for therapy," added Heron.

"Yes, at RC, to go and have my limb re-checked, hopefully for a better fixing."

"That is good. We pray everything works out well for you."

"Thank you."

The last passenger to board was one huge man likely to be in his late thirties. He took the only remaining empty seat, the one by Johnson on the first row. As he took the seat, he raised the bag and rested it on his lap with an adjustment that prevented it from touching Johnson's lap. Apparently, the bag was old, as confirmed by the countless number of peels, bruises and squeeze lines that reduced parts of its area from its original colour of dark brown to tan, fawn or cream. Its age? Probably, half his.

Almost immediately after that, the driver was heard directing the conductor to get others inside and ready for departure. Tonga and Johnson were among the first to be relieved by the driver's directive. It was ten in the morning, and within minutes, the two brothers were having the first direct experience of the horrible transport system that had taken over in NA.

* * *

The bus was hardly out of the garage when Heron drew the attention of the friends to the presence of the security assistant and the two conductors. Unlike him, they were not alarmed because they already knew that every bus now carried up to two of each. However, a certain high-pitched call-out by the conductor standing to the rear door was unexpected.

"Ladies and gentlemen," the voice called, "*Emmanuel*. Have I got any *Emmanuel* here?"

Many, including the brothers, turned round to see who that *Emmanuel* was while some did not bother to turn because they were already aware of the conductors' adopted method of announcing the bus-stops.

"Please, Kamar," shouted the same conductor to his colleague standing near the front door, "call out *Emmanuel*."

"Who the hell is this *Emmanuel,* that they won't let us have some rest because of him?" Heron asked Johnson. "Do they think he is deaf and dumb? Probably, they left him behind in the garage."

"Don't mind them" replied Johnson, "it is the first bus-stop."

"But common sense and common economics," said Tonga to both Johnson and Heron, "should have told them no person who just paid for and started on a long journey like this would have disembarked at its first local bus-stop. A waste of money, wouldn't that has been?"

"Anyway," said Johnson, "they don't care if you waste more than your money, as long as what is out of your pocket goes into theirs. The same bus-stop was a pick-up point for taxis until two weeks ago when it was turned into a bus-stop."

"Please, excuse me, young men," interrupted the lady sitting and listening silently by Ebino's right, "now that they want to start with these unnecessary stops at every bus-stop, when are we going to reach RC?"

"They won't stop at all the bus stops, but they will stop at a number more than before," Ebino replied her.

"Besides," he continued, "they now charge according to the number of stops they pass – which is why they've created many new ones."

"But then, more stops will mean longer delays," the lady reasoned. "Does that mean the longer the delay the higher the fares they charge us?"

"In effect, yes."

"May God deliver us."

"Only if we could try delivering ourselves first. We should remember we are not the only creations of God, and must not monopolise Him.

"Anyway, they will still make up time for the stopping. Trust them for that, ma'am. They love their money and will never sacrifice any of their rounds for it."

No passenger got off at *Emmanuel*, but six got on, and remained standing along the aisle together with the conductors and the security assistant. They were in the same standing position when they reached *Eastout*, the next in-town bus stop, half a mile from *Emmanuel*. The driver stopped in front of its group of waiting passengers.

There were seven of them, and were all allowed in. Five first climbed in by the rear door, among persistent appeals from the conductor to those already standing from *Emmanuel* to move forward and create space for their fellow co-passengers. The other two had to make use of the front door, after pleas from Kamar and the man sitting next to Johnson.

Carlos Retfil's bus, driven by newly elevated Akiya, which they had left behind at NA, caught up with them. Drawing parallel with Gebu's, it went into a crawling speed as if its driver had some action to watch in Gebu's bus. "Hi boss," Akiya shouted jokingly, but as loud as he could, "you keep taking our passengers! You won't take the next!" He sped off without clearly hearing Gebu's own shout-back of "get lost and face your way!"

Tonga watched the drama and was going to say something when Heron's voice beat him to it. "I didn't know it's this bad," he said, principally directing the observation to Johnson and Tonga sitting in his front.

"It's grown worse in the past two weeks and at this rate, I can see it definitely getting worst," Ebino supplied the pessimistic prediction.

"But this is appalling enough," said Johnson. "I least expected this scale of decay, and wondered how the passengers can take it."

"You are one of them – one of the passengers now," said Heron. "Just as I am, and just like all those blind bats who entered, knowing it's already packed full. Now, you have seen it. You will see more; there is no doubt about it."

"I am seeing enough now," said Johnson again. "Yes, Heron, I have seen so much of these men and their business. I have seen my father murdered, and my brother injured in a so-called accident. I have seen passengers stabbed, shot and left to die. I have seen buses destroyed. I have even seen children being gagged and cheated. What else haven't I seen? I have seen so much that I wouldn't like to see more, because the next possible thing to see would be blindness itself. They are getting too crazy, Heron."

"I suppose you are right, Johnson. But with these people, nothing could be ruled out completely. Of course, many of us knew about some of your encounters even if we didn't know you in person. The accident was discussed in all churches, including mine. Then, our church leaders convinced us it was due to a genuine fault of the driver, a local brother who should be forgiven."

"No, no, Heron," Johnson disagreed. "It's never a normal accident, just as what we have seen so far on this journey makes it not a normal journey. And what type of local brother would that be, the Cain on Abel type?"

"And we are not normal passengers either," snapped Tonga as he remembered he had a question for the man sitting by his brother's right. "Excuse me," he said, leaning across to the huge man, "are you a conductor or a builder?"

"Conductor or builder?" the man responded in astonishment. He could see neither a reasonable correlation between the two professions nor any reason why they had to be related to him by Tonga. Whatever he currently was in addition to being a co-passenger, he would soon tell them. That he was formerly a garage shop assistant, but now favoured to sell in the buses for collaborating with the transporters, he wouldn't.

"Oh no, I am neither of the two. But why?"

"Seeing the way you co-directed the boarding of the two passengers that were just picked up, one would believe you were a senior bus conductor – that you merely kept your uniform at home.

"Are you a builder of some sort then?"

The huge man now became baffled.

"But why asking all these questions? I don't understand."

The conversation was now drawing the attention of those in their immediate area. Some of them could remember that the man was on the side of the bus staff, especially at *Eastout*.

Tonga took a quick look at the dense pack of living bodies that stood in the aisle. It reminded him of a wall partitioning that just stopped short of the ceiling. He wanted to assure himself before throwing his analogical sarcasm.

"Take a look at the aisle, he told the huge man. The huge man obeyed. "This human wall of partitioning which you helped the conductor to erect and reinforce could never have been done better by a non-mason."

The comment drew a burst of laughter from the passengers and better-left-undisplayed anger from the huge man.

"If you must know," he started to brave it up with a fabricated smile, "I am only a small sales manager of a consultancy firm."

"A small what?" asked one lady among those standing near him. "Oh my God. You must be – and you really are – a typical Sales Manager. You are big; and your mouth is honey-coated."

There was another round of laughter.

"Yes, ma'am. And that is why here today, I am going to be highly selective of who I allow to kiss my mouth and taste the honey!"

And yet, another round of laughter.

The huge man was satisfied that his wits had got him out of potential trouble that would have rendered him unwelcome among the passengers he targeted to sell to, the contents of his old bag.

The next bus stop was called *Bridge*.

"Ladies and gentlemen, *Bridge* bus-stop!" shouted Kamar.

"*Brie-ie-dge, Bridge* bus-stop," the back conductor relayed the call. "You are now at Brie-ie-dge bus-stop!"

"But for goodness sake," shouted one man from the other side of aisle, "why can't you please reduce this noise? If there is anyone for the bus-stop, he would have answered you."

"Please, don't blame me," replied Kamar. "When we don't call, it is you the passengers that get us reported. You report us for everything."

"No one tells you not to call," said the lady who challenged the so-called sales manager, "but if that is your passion, please be moderate at it. That's all."

"Thank you ma'am," replied the conductor.

The driver still slowed down anyway, and was about to stop at *Bridge* when the huge man spoke, this time without supporting the bus staff. "There is no passenger for *Bridge*," he shouted to the driver.

Gebu drove on – until he was at the start of the long road that had another bus stop at its end. He saw Carlos Retfil's bus that overtook him at *Emmanuel* parked at this stop. A line of passengers was filing into it. Before Kamar could confirm that no passenger wanted to disembark there, Gebu slowed down and stopped in front of the parked Retfil's.

"Kamar, see if they are dropping some for us, or taking all," he instructed.

Kamar opened the front door and dashed out to the conductor of the other bus before the protests of his own passengers could become audible enough.

"We can take them all. Who waved you to stop?" mocked Retfil's conductor.

"Aha," said Kamar, "that was why you sped past us – to be here first to pack them all!"

"So, you beat us to it," shouted Gebu before his conductor could finish, leaning his head out of his window.

"You are greedy sir," Akiya jokingly rebuked his former boss. "Where else do you even want to put them: on the roof?"

"You wait till the next bus-stop to find out!" Gebu drove off.

"That is if we are not there before you!"

It was doubtful if the wind and the noise allowed Gebu to hear his former boy's shout distinctly. But what wasn't was the passengers' growing awareness of the drivers' crazy objectives. They could see that the drivers were bent on dangerous overloading that ignored the comfort of the passengers. They could also see they were all in the race not to arrive on time at their destinations, but to out-drive each other to populated bus-stops where passenger were likely to board.

"Mister driver," shouted a passenger sitting two rows behind Johnson's, "why did you stop at that bus-stop? Where, on a bus this packed full, do you expect more passengers to stand? Or, can't you see it yourself?"

"Sorry, I can't see it; my eyes are on the road."

"And you also couldn't hear it – that nobody answered to come off – despite your conductors' big noises?"

"That was why I stopped – because I couldn't hear anything," he lied. "Anyway, I am sorry!"

"Yes, I think you really should be," said another.

Gebu saw no reason to give a further response. He drove on.

* * *

The huge man, noticing the frayed nerves had calmed down a bit, took it as an opportunity to do what brought him into the bus in the first place. He lifted his huge frame, turned to the passengers, put his bag on his seat, and loudly cleared his throat. "Good morning, ladies and gentlemen," he greeted, clasping his hands.

Even though he paused, he was not really looking for any verbal response, and the suddenness of his greeting guaranteed he got none – at least, not at first.

"Good morning I say to you all again," he raised his voice higher.

"Good morning," responded two or three voices as if they were doing it on behalf of the other passengers. Many, however, turned to his direction to see who was delivering the greetings.

"Thank you. Thank you very much to those who responded to my greetings – and to those who didn't. Above all, the greatest thanks to God who has preserved my and your lives to this moment of our meeting inside this bus of our kind transport chief, under the kind control of our able driver and his team.

"I am Krespie, the particular one many of you have either met or heard of, and whose services many of you have been fortunate enough to enjoy one time or the other. For those of you meeting me for the first time however, I have good reasons to congratulate you, because surely, today is your lucky day. Okay?

"Therefore, you are to please listen attentively, and ensure none of the passengers sitting, standing, leaning or bending besides you sleeps, dozes, sneezes or murmurs. Okay? Where he does any of these, don't slap him. Instead, just shake him back to life and to alertness in my very name," he added jokingly the tall order. "Okay?"

There was a general chuckling response by the passengers who were beginning to see more of Krespie as a jester than a salesman. Amidst the chuckles came a lone, serious voice.

"You are not Krespie, the singer, are you? If you are, why aren't you singing anymore?"

"Oh no", he replied. "That is another Krespie. You see, it means there's usually something great with everyone of us Krespie," he started to boast. "But we both have one thing in common – we make you people happy. Okay?

"The love I have for you all brings me here," he went on, quickly abandoning the escapist comparison so as to get back to his job.

"Not at all," replied yet another lady among those standing. "You mean the love you have for money and for yourself." It drew more laughter.

"Okay. Whatever you say. You are the boss. Okay?"

"Yes, you should have known that," agreed another passenger.

"Okay, in order not to start killing a wobbling snake with a wobbling stick, let me go straight to the two products I have for sale to you today. They are both special health products, which before now, were only available from very few stores inside NA garage.

"In fact, the people who were buying them kept the knowledge of their existence to themselves in order to monopolize their consumption. This wasn't fair, and hence, my determination to spread the good news around. Okay?

"The first of the products is called *choco-menthol*. Okay?"

Krespie paused and brought out a small nylon-covered packet from inside his bag. He, like a performing magician, raised it up with his left hand and then urged the passengers to take a good look at it. Next, he tore it open and poured unto his right palm, some of the fifty or so wraps of lemon colour sweets it contained.

"This is *choco-menthol*. Can you see it – from here, from there, from the sides, from all round? Okay?"

Some passengers managed to look at what he had in his hands; others did not bother. Among those who looked were most of those he faced on the same side of the bus; among those who didn't, the bulk of those partitioned off to the other side of the bus by the thick wall of standing passengers.

To most of those who heard him, they knew he must have been joking somehow – that it was impossible for everybody he had called upon to see him or the sweets he had in his palms.

"It was made to serve three categories of people," he resumed. "Do you know the three?"

There was a mixture of noses, 'we don't' and 'I don't'.

"Do you want to know?"

There were clearly more 'no' than 'yes', and neither with 'thank you' or 'please'.

"Never mind," he quickly proceeded, "but I still have to explain the three categories to you, so that you can know if you are qualified to start taking the advantages. Okay?"

Surprisingly, none of the passengers with 'no' countered him any further. He continued.

"The first group it is made for is that of workers and walkers, or simply, the *2Ws*. Okay?

"Yes. Yes for that group, because everyone in it has one special thing in common. Okay?"

He went on to say, how what they had in common was 'energy' which had to be spent irrespective of whether one was working or walking. He was very much unconcerned about how his listeners would rate his logic or reasoning, if at all they were capable of doing so.

"Consumption and burning of energy," he said, "meant taking in and expelling the air at a rate corresponding to the speed of working, walking, or even running.

"Having a drop of *choco-menthol* kept in your mouth is the easiest way of taking in the air because it ensures the air rushes in not only through the mouth, but also through the nose, ears and anus. The overall result is that the lung is never starved and the licker can live longer and healthier.

"The second category *choco-menthol* is made for is that of Returnees and Visitors, the *R and V*, Okay? For example when you leave your children at home and go after a business or pleasure, and later return home to them after the mission is accomplished, usually, the first question the children would ask you as soon as you walk in through the door is 'Mummy – or daddy, or sister, or auntie – what have you brought back for us?' Certainly what they are indirectly asking for – and deserve – is a bag of *choco-menthol*. Okay?"

There was laughter.

"Or, you now decide to visit a friend. When you meet such a friend, hugging is not enough. What is more loving is to first unwrap and drop a *choco-menthol* in his or her mouth to do the kissing. It would be loved so much that your friend would refuse to let you go off him or her from the hug."

There was more laughter and broad smiles.

"The last category of people that *choco-menthol* is good for is that of smokers. Have you ever heard of nicotine?" he asked the people he had now captured to his attentive audience.

"No," a few of them jointly replied.

"*Tobacotine*?"

"No!"

"*Cafetine*?"

"No!"

"That's strange indeed. And *Teafetine*?"

"No!"

More of them were now more ignorantly than honestly showing interest in sharing the marketing nonsense with Krespie.

"Okay? These are poisons that settle on your teeth, in your blood and on your chest when you smoke. They start you up with cough and end you up thin and weak. The cough is always non-stop – day and night – that if you turn right, you cough; if you turn left, you cough; if you look up, you cough; and if you look down, what do you do…?

"You cough!" they answered complementarily.

"If you are in the park?"

"You cough!"

"If you are in the market?"

"You cough!"

"If you are with your friend?"

"You cough!"

"And even if you are in the bus?"

"You cough!!"

"Thank you all. You cough, cough, cough, and co-u-gh… that nobody wants to be near you. You and your cough become isolated – like a leper in the market place.

"Does it then worth it? No. That is why you need *choco-menthol* when you smoke.

"Smoke whatever you will, but lick as many *choco-menthols* as possible. Then, your blood, teeth, lung and throat will all be as clear as rainwater.

"And one last thing: I have come across some smokers who claimed that they smoke special cigars and filtered cigarettes that are poison-free; and that as such, they would not need *choco-menthol*. Ladies and gentlemen, I really feel sorry for these people. Unless they take our product, even if they have their houses build near Jean Nicot's, they will not only end up coughing out mucus and blood, but will also thin out like a praying-mantis – with shapeless abdomen, thin legs, thin neck, but all head and eyes."

More laughter.

Those who could see Krespie were now enjoying his talk. It was just what he wanted them to do, to enable him bring more overstatements and irrelevancies that he needed to clinch his sales.

"So," he went on, "if you are a smoker, lick my *choco-menthol* regularly to save and prolong your life. It is particularly recommended to you if you smoke any of these brands: Rothmans, Camel, Three Rings, Sweet Menthol, John Players, Gold Leaf, Peter Stuyvesant, Lucky Strike, Marlboro, Sovereign, Silkcut." He paused to regain his breath.

"Go on. Is that all?" asked an amused passenger – one of many – who wanted him to go on singing the names of cigarettes.

"Dunhill," Krespie resumed where he left off, "Panama, Hamlet, Benson and Hedges, Gold, Kent, Richmond, Chrystal, Mayfair, Solo, Maddison, Royals, Regal, Embassy, More, Lambert, Butler, Bexley, Maxim, Craven, Raffles, Lincoln, Classic, Taaba …"

As the roll got longer, the passengers who marvelled at his knowledge of the brand names clapped widely.

"Thank you. And how much is this good product after all? Fifty, just fifty per bag! No more. Okay?"

"And yet another thing: when you buy more than one bag, pay me just forty-five per bag. Therefore, I advise you buy more than one because you pay less; and besides, you might not find me when next you want me. Okay?

"Only twenty bags reached here with me today. I am sending nineteen out to you and keeping one to myself. A doctor is neither good nor wise when he gives out the entire good drug to his patients, without reserving a part of it for himself.

"As soon as your own bag reaches you, just send me the fifty; it is as simple as that. Okay?"

With the assistance of some of the passengers, the nineteen started to find different parts of the bus.

"Please, listen to another piece of good news," continued Krespie. "For every bag you buy, I am giving you two loose wraps entirely free – so that you can reach your destinations with the bags you bought still intact. Okay? But as I give it free to you, you will have to do one thing for me please: you will please remember not to swallow the wrappers with them! That, I strongly disallow!"

The general reaction that followed Krespie's advertisement was of the hilarious type. Not a single one of the nineteen bags was returned unpaid for. He would have easily sold the twentieth if in fact it existed.

As he took the money a buyer passed to him, he sent in return to the buyer, two wraps of *choco-menthol* together with thanks and prayers. Well satisfied with himself, he went to the next product he called *multivitaron*.

"My next product is one that is fast gaining popularity among men and women, young and old. Its packaging is smart, its potency is high, and its price is rock bottom. It is called *multivitaron*, and I will show it to you all now. Okay?"

Krespie dipped his right hand inside his bag and brought out two flat packets that he now fanned out in his raised hands.

"This is *M-V-R* multivitamin manufactured in England in March of 1980, to retain its potency for a whole half century... or, let me see..." he pretended to be reading off the packet in his right hand, "oh sorry, 2030; it expires in February, 2030, a whole fifty years! Okay?

"What does it do for you? It is a blood tonic, the best on the market today, and one that highlights quality and not quantity, potency and not idiocy, strength and not size. It purifies your blood and guarantees its level is correct in your system.

"Women especially need it after child birth, after menstruation, and after the day's hard work.

"For men, physical jobs ranging from how to make the ends meet in the family, to how to satisfy the wives' main wish behind locked bedroom doors make *MVR* indispensable. Okay?"

"Oh my God, save us from these salesmen," came a loud-laughing female voice from among the listeners who were now thoroughly amused.

"Why is this product so potent? It is because of the strong ingredients it's made of: twenty-five of them, that *MVR* offers to you in one.

"These ingredients include Vitamin A, Vitamin B, Vitamin C, Vitamin D, Vitamin E, Vitamin F, Vitamin G, Vitamin H, and Vitamin I, meaning iron – not the type used to make the garden implements or the type used to build the bridges across the rivers though. It also contains milk richer than the cow's, and eggs ten times better than those of the ostrich. Okay?

"This is why for the carpenter, it is ideal; for the policeman, it is ideal; for the road sweeper, it is ideal; for the farmer, it is ideal; for the boxer, it is ideal; for the clergyman, it is ideal; for him, it is ideal; for her, it is ideal; for them, it is ideal; for you, it is ideal; for me, it is ideal. It is ideal all round for the living!

"As for the price, don't be frightened. One packet of thirty capsules to last a whole month at one a day, costs you only two hundred and fifty. Okay?

"I also consider those of you meeting me here now without a fore-plan for it, and those not carrying enough cash on them. For them, I will sell half a packet for one hundred and twenty-five, and a strip of five capsules for fifty. Okay?

"Ladies and gentlemen, I have just ten packets left. Okay? If you want to be among the lucky ones to get them, please let me see your hands up so that I can dispatch one to you in the comfort of your seat or the comfort of your feet. Okay?"

There were no takers.

"Where are you, ladies and gentlemen? Let me see your hands up. You don't have to feel shy, or wait until you see someone's hand up first. What we are talking about is good health you know – which is more important than riches. Okay?"

Slowly, two hands were raised.

"Thank you. Those are the wise people – people who know how to reserve water against the time of thirst, those who know the value of being in good health."

285

He released the two packets to two passengers near him. "Please pass these on to the lady and that man for me.

"Anyone else?"

There was another hand, the third, raised. It instigated another, then another, and another. In all, there were about twenty.

"Just wait," said Krespie, smiling, "I will get to everyone of you."

"But didn't you just say you have only ten left?" asked Heron.

"You see, this is where I am a different man. I always have something in reserve for everyone, be he the vocal or the quiet, the forthcoming or the shy. In my type of business, you come across different kind of people. Okay?"

Krespie sent his hands into the bag again, and got out more packets of his capsules to the passengers who wanted them. He was busy exchanging his products for their money.

One packet of Krespie's product had a temporary stop before a man who read for himself, the list of its ingredients as printed on the wrapper. "Excuse me please," he sought the attention of the salesman, "there is nothing like Vitamins F, G, H and I, and they are equally not written on any of these packets."

"They are all there. Sometimes they are written out in different forms."

"They are not and never written in any form other than the standard."

Krespie took a hard look at the man he feared could easily spoil his show. "If I may ask, sir, are you a doctor or a nurse?" he smarted a question.

"Yes, I could be. But who needs to be any of those to read what is written on the packet? Are you also a doctor, or a nurse?"

"Well my friend, I don't have to answer that question. But if you want to know who I am, just turn to all the numerous people who have gladly purchased my products. They are in a better position to tell you. Okay? They are my answer."

Apart from Krespie, there was another salesman in the bus. He called himself Doctor Toronto. He was among those standing. Hung firmly on his left shoulder was what served as his office, another wretched looking brown leather bag. After a familiar style of self-introduction, he announced his own product, *'Dental-go'* powder.

He let it be known to the passengers that it had taken many years of expensive research to produce the powder. Its researchers he said, started with the study of the properties and constituents of both the dog's and the shark's teeth. These teeth were chosen not only because they were very white, but also because they were always sharp and strong – enough to crush any bone or tear any flesh. Besides, they were never seen by man to rot. He assured them that all the elements – much more than calcium – that were present in the beasts' teeth were extracted, and later combined with some other elements, to produce the powder. Therefore, the combination guaranteed its user a white, sharp and strong set of teeth till his dying day! *Dental-go* powder would also prevent mouth odour, tooth odour, toothache, tongue-ache, throat-ache and holes. Any hole in the tooth, however big, would stop aching forever, once it was filled with a paste of the powder, and left for thirty minutes before being rinsed out with warm water or any type of wine."

At this point, one man thought he had heard enough.

"Look here my friend," he called on the salesman from where he was sitting on the right hand side of the bus, his voice showing the clarity and sternness of somebody provoked into a near-brawl. "What you have been saying all along is not true. It is all rubbish – all rubbish and arrant nonsense."

"It is true," countered the self-laureate Doctor Toronto, "a truth that could be sworn to. Nothing but the truth."

"No it isn't."

"What isn't out of it – the length of the research or the important animals that were used for it?"

287

"Neither. For your information I am a fully qualified dentist. I spent seven years in the special institution and have practiced for another seven since graduating.

"There was nothing like that research, and there is no approved product in the name of *Dental-go* powder. You people had better go and look for something better to do before you kill every innocent person."

Doctor Toronto was shocked and ashamed but would not show it. He knew that any apparent show of these would not only evict him at the next bus stop, but could put paid to his source of daily bread. The dentist, he knew was right; but still, he must be countered. He paused a little and came up with a question.

"With due respect to you, the dentist, sir, could you be kind enough to tell me how much on the average you do charge your patients. Would you say about fifty, sixty, or even seventy, going to a hundred?"

"It will depend on the treatment required and given. Consultancy could be free, actual treatment could be as low as forty."

"That is it – what I expect to hear from you, sir. You see, my product, the *Dental-go* powder, costs only twenty per bottle – content, packing and delivery – and it can last you a whole six months.

"You dentists don't like people like us, who are capable of competing with you, because you know you will always loose out."

"Compete if you will, but don't lie to kill. Can you tell us specifically when and how you got your sharks and dogs for experiments, and who actually led your research team? One of you was just caught grinding up broken china and peppermint to produce a type of toothpaste! Both you and those who allowed you in here are fraudulent cheats! And make no mistake; people are becoming more aware now. You are nothing but another fake! Get out of this bus!"

In the end, both the sales attempt and the ensuring debate saw Doctor Toronto a looser. At the next bus stop he left the bus, prematurely.

Up till now, the in-bus hawking system had produced two net gainers. The first was the group of the transporters using it to cover up the greed manifested in the take-over of the retail outlets, through acting as the providers of livelihood for those they displaced. The group also used the act to divert the minds of the passengers away from realizing the new extent of exploitation and humiliation the transporters made them suffer on every journey. The second group was that of the bus staff. On a regular basis, they received free product samples, cash and support from the hawkers.

Of course, the hawkers made some monetary gains, but this was offset by the uncertainty in the continuity of the hawking itself. Besides, only a handful of the displaced and cheated ex-shop owners were allowed to benefit from the in-bus selling. On the whole, they were losers.

In the greatest looser group however, were the passengers. It had moments of easy shopping; but more often, every item paid for was over-priced, of poor quality or poisonous. It was also difficult for its members to see the overall danger and discomfort in the journey because of the hawkers' constant use of wisecracks, exaggeration and outright lies. For example, it was as a result of the last effect on the passengers that it was only Johnson's group that noticed an incident at *Lona* bus stop, twenty miles before Lal Town.

There at *Lona*, Gebu had stopped the bus despite the fact that no passenger had signalled to disembark. Then, the passengers were still laughing hysterically at Krespie. Johnson, the first to observe the stopping, made a head swerve at the laughing *house* and then, at Heron sitting behind him. "Why has he stopped?" he asked.

"Who knows?" answered Heron. "We better ask him."

"Why are you stopping, driver?" shouted Johnson, leaning forward to the point where the back of the driver's neck could almost feel the carbon dioxide coming from his mouth.

"Sorry, we won't take five minutes please," was Gebu's evasive answer as he quickly jumped down to talk to two ladies standing by their luggage. He made a very brief negotiation with one of them and hurried back to take some papers from his driving seat.

"You are not carrying these people, are you?" Johnson asked him.

"No, no, no; just one of them. The other is waiting for Akiya's bus close behind." He hurried back again, joined by both conductors and the security assistant.

Within the next few seconds, the four men were busy loading the luggage of one of the ladies unto the rooftop of the bus.

"Why do these people behave like this?" Ebino asked his friends. "Is this bus not full enough?"

"They do it because it means extra money for the driver and his staff," replied Johnson. "The more overload they carry, the more underhand money there is in it for them to share outside their normal wages, and off record!"

"Yes," said Tonga, "and at our expenses and peril. What a shame?"

It took less than ten minutes to load up ten bags of rice and one basket containing ten live chickens. Throughout the period the loading was going on, hawking went on freely, with the passengers being conned into parting with their money while they laughed their heads off. At the end of the loading, the new lady passenger followed Gebu to the steps leading to the driver's cubicle. There, Gebu assisted her to climb up into the cubicle proper.

"Is she taking over the driving now?" Ebino asked.

"Oh no," replied Johnson, shaking his head, "doesn't look the type."

"Can anybody really put anything past these people?" asked Tonga.

"Really, no. No one can," replied Heron. "Let's see what they are up to."

They watched as Gebu dragged out a makeshift stool by his seat and guided the lady to sit on it. They could now see that it was reserved for that purpose – such a purpose!

"Driver," called out a bewildered Tonga, "you can't be serious. Having somebody sitting down there while you drive? Do you want to cause an accident?"

"I am sorry, gentlemen," Gebu quickly went apologetic as usual, to enable him achieve his goal. "She is not going beyond Lal Town. Just a few miles, and off she disembarks. I have put her with me so that nobody out there is disturbed. And until somebody disembarks, no passenger will be taken. In addition, I am assuring you of your safety."

Like the rest of his group who heard the driver, Tonga wished the driver could keep to his promises. "We hope that would be possible," he said.

"It would," cut in Heron, "only if and when your speed is reduced and overtaking is cautious."

"Don't worry about those, I say," he re-assured.

But unlike his co-travelling hawkers and buyers, Heron's group was actually getting more worried. The reasons for being so were real, and apparent.

About ten miles to Lal Town, an event put the assuror cum re-assuror together with his promises to the test. It started when Gebu took the usual momentary look at his side overtaking mirror and saw Akiya closing in fast behind him, the roof top of his bus, like his own, equally loaded with luggage he was sure belonged to the other lady he could not carry.

The thought of him having to drop some of his passengers and goods at Lal Town came to his mind. Ideally, such goods and passengers needed to be simultaneously replaced, preferably at Lal Town. If Akiya should get to Lal Town before him, getting these replacements from there would be difficult or impossible. This time therefore, he was not going to allow Akiya to overtake him. He looked at the mirror again and depressed the accelerator pedal as far down as it would go. The passengers who were already on alert found the sudden change in speed easy enough to notice.

"Why has he just taken off?" asked Ebino. "Tonga, you are nearer to him, please tell him he is going too fast."

Tonga relayed and repeated the warning to Gebu. He was repeating it the third time when Akiya levelled up and started to drive past him. Even though the ensuing noise of the two engines prevented Tonga and Ebino from knowing for sure if there was a verbal response from Gebu, it was clear that there was no reduction in the high speed being complained about.

The closeness and near parallel level of Akiya's bus with theirs prompted reactions that ranged between fright and excitement among the passengers and crews. Hawkers in both buses were so excited that they exchanged hearty greetings and waves as the two buses drew level.

Members of Johnson-Heron group were among the frightened. Joined in the verbal protests by a few other passengers, they succeeded in pressurizing Gebu into letting Akiya drive past. They also stopped Gebu from a later attempt, as they were about entering Lal Town, to re-capture the front position he had lost to Akiya. In that particular attempt, the chicken basket on the bus-top opened and some birds escaped to their everlasting freedom.

To Akiya, beating his old boss to Lal Town garage was a source of joy. It guaranteed him a complete sale of all seats and spaces vacated by the disembarking passengers.

In grudging but silent anger, Gebu later arrived inside the garage and parked near Akiya. He walked to the garage office, leaving his three assistants to see to the offloading. He was eager to know if there was any remnant of passengers or goods he could take from Akiya's leftover. He knew Akiya won the round but was determined to exact revenge as soon as another chance arose between Lal Town and Regin City.

Heron and Johnson joined some of their co-passengers to alight and stretch their legs. First attracted by the colour of Olga's dress as soon as both men commenced strolling, Heron took a keener look and knew it was Olga even though it was a long time since he last saw her during their journey to RC. Both men walked towards Olga and a young lady who accompanied her, and stopped as a surprise before them. "Hello, Olga", Heron beamed the greeting.

"Heron?" she asked him, wanting to know if her sight and memory were right.

"Yes, Heron."

"Oh, nice to see you again," she hugged him, "and what are you doing in Lal Town?"

I am on my way to RC – from NA."

"Is that? From NA? It's surprising we didn't see you at NA. We would have come in the same bus. I am coming from NA too; and by the way, with my daughter, here, Laura. We are returning to RC."

"Hello, Laura."

Laura acknowledged Heron's greetings.

"It must have been because of the rowdiness in the garage that we didn't see each other," Heron guessed.

"Probably so," she agreed. "Your friend?" she further asked, pointing to Johnson.

"Yes, sorry. Johnson, Johnson Dorman. I got carried away and forgot to introduce him. We met in the bus."

"Hello Johnson," she shook his hand. Any relationship with Pastor Dorman, the GIG?"

"Yes, my late father," replied Johnson.

"Oh, I am sorry. God bless a brave and holy soul who had to end like that."

"Thank you. Well, there was nothing we could do. Mum always reminds us to put it behind us – without realising her constant reminders always put it before my brother and me; and probably, before the church too."

They all laughed.

"Are you also going to RC?" she further asked.

"Yes", replied Heron on Johnson's behalf, "together with some other friends who are too tired to come down."

"Who wouldn't be tired," agreed Olga, "going with these people? You see, look…" she dipped her hand inside her handbag and brought out an aluminium sachet of tablets, "this is Panadol. It is the first thing I take before and after going with them. I find it relieving."

"That's clever. You always are! Last time, you correctly predicted this situation – that it will get as bad as this and even worse, unless people have the courage to stand up and stop it. Today, the congestion is excessive, the fares taxing, the speed reckless, the overtaking senseless and the whole thing hazardous.

"That's right Heron, and can you see their present speed competition?"

"Yes, I can. It has been going on without a challenge."

"Of course, it was met with fierce challenges – in our own bus. Otherwise these crazy men would have done something worse."

"I guess the same thing was true of our bus too," said Heron, "only that most of the challenges were directed at the hawkers. Did you have them, the hawkers, too?"

"Who would they ever allow to escape having them?" said Olga. "They stole everybody's peace, but they were challenged anyway. A lady taking her sick husband to RC actually pulled down one of them, a lady hawker, who claimed to be the chairman of so-called mobile doctors; her noise was making her husband restless. Surprisingly, most people backed the lady with the husband. The backing gave me hope.

"And Heron, can you guess what – guess who was in the same bus with us?"

"Have no idea. Who?"

"A brother of Lee Waters who was with us last time; his name is Sien Waters. By chance, he sat next to Laura."

"Interesting. Did he say anything about Lee?"

"Yes, a lot of things. He was said to have led a successful boycott of one chief Mathew Rebbor's buses."

"Oh, but how?" Heron asked with eagerness.

"Toot! Toot! Toot!"

All the four turned to the direction of the blaring. It was Akiya's bus, inelegantly top-loaded like an ass at *Al-Azbakiyah* on a market day. It was ready to go.

"That's your bus calling," said Heron to Olga, "I think it is ready to go."

"Okay, thank you, gentlemen. We'd better run down. That's what the blaring is all about. We will probably meet at RC. Nice meeting you both."

"O yes," remembered Heron, "I still have your address, and will get in touch whatever."

"Good. And safe journey. Get in touch and there'll be time for the full story." She and her daughter paced down and into the bus, which readily took off.

Twenty minutes after Akiya, beaming with satisfaction, had driven out of Lal Town garage, Gebu also left, full of anger and grudges. Gebu's fears were already confirmed by the lack of enough passengers and goods to fill up the empty seats and spaces he was leaving Lal Town with. With every yard he went, the anger pushed his recklessness to higher limits.

"Take it easy," shouted Johnson. "This driving is bad."

Gebu raised his head stubbornly and sped on, his ears totally blocked.

"*Coconut*!" shouted Micho. The bus was approaching the first out-of-town bus stop after leaving Lal Town.

Gebu did not have to stop because none of his passengers wanted *Coconut*, and there was not a single passenger waiting to board.

"*Austin*! Anybody for *Austin*?"

Another bus stop, the next after *Coconut*.

Also, luckily for Gebu, there was no passenger for *Austin* and so, Gebu took the opportunity to overtake Akiya there as Akiya was discharging some goods and passengers. As Gebu raced past, he almost brushed Akiya's bus with the side of his own.

"Are you deaf or just pretending to be deaf?" Johnson shouted at Gebu. "The more we complain the more you ignore us. Did you know you narrowly missed brushing one side of the other bus?"

"No," said Kamar, "it was the other bus that nearly brushed ours. Instead of parking it well off the road, its driver just stopped there as if the road was meant for him alone."

No, Gebu was not deaf, and he heard them; but then, their complaints were, as far as he was concerned, insignificant. They or their complaints would never fill up the empty seats in his bus.

"*Moonlight!*" suddenly called out Gebu himself. He was alive after all. "Micho, all of you, get ready, we are stopping at *Moonlight!*" Gebu had already looked ahead and seen a good number of people standing. He prayed they were passengers. They were; and he stopped.

"Now, driver, shouted a man from other side, "I hope you drive carefully now that you have got more than you can carry." More passengers filed in, squeezing themselves up along the aisle as Akiya regained the front position.

"And don't bother to overtake that bus again," added Tonga with a sternness fit for an able-bodied man, "because both of you drivers have been going crazy today."

"Mind your tongue, my friend over there", warned Micho. "You don't have to be rude."

"There is no rudeness in that. It is the plain truth – and a favour," replied Tonga.

"Who is asking for your truth or your favour? It is pure disturbance, which is never a favour to the mind of anyone driving."

"Please gentlemen, that man was correct," one lady added, siding with Micho, the last speaker. "We should do nothing to divert the driver's attention so that he can concentrate."

"But madam," snapped another man sitting beside her, "warning is not a diversion, and recklessness is not concentration. I am sure that if it were your lad driving or being driven like this, you would say something. This is crazy."

While the verbal exchanges went on among the passengers and between Johnson's group and Gebu's staff, Gebu took the chance and went reckless – until he caught up again with Akiya. This time, Akiya had stopped in the middle of his lane and was talking with Pepperoni, Isa Reduaram's driver, who was returning to NA from RC. Because vehicles were held up and unable to drive pass due to the way the two buses stopped, vehicle queues quickly formed in both directions of the road.

"This is what we have been saying madam," Heron angrily turned on the woman who believed Gebu was being disturbed. "Do you call this concentration? Who and what could be more crazy?"

"I think we all here are the more crazy ones," promptly replied Johnson, "for allowing some thuggish Shylocks and their spokeswoman to drive our lives this way and this far."

The lady looked away in shame, unable to say something.

"I am glad no one can accuse us this time. It is those two," shouted Micho at the passengers.

Gebu as well as other drivers held up continued to blow their horns with rage. Eventually, Akiya moved on – only for his lawless position to be taken by Gebu.

"Now, conductor, you see your boss?" Heron asked angrily, facing Micho. "Just now you were accusing the other driver in front of you. You people have to be careful today. You cannot expect us to keep putting up with you while you endanger our lives and journey. We are not as crazy. If you people don't move now, we will move you."

All the same, Gebu managed to rush through all the inconsequentials with Pepperoni while the queues got longer, and the horns louder. Pepperoni, on the other hand, remembered to tell Gebu that the day's business was bound to be juicy because many passengers and goods were waiting to be lifted from RC to NA. "Can't you see the inside from there?" pointed the informer-driver to his bus for Gebu, to show how it was full beyond having the doors closed.

Then, Gebu remembered that a passenger among those sitting immediately behind him just threatened and was still threatening him. He turned round to see who it was. In Heron, he was self-convinced that he saw nothing but a mere loud mouth of neither power nor authority, and of neither means nor a back up. Somehow, he felt sorry for Heron and drove on, his mind immediately returning to both RC and the return journey to NA. Then, his timepiece read three o'clock. In another one and a half to two hours, it meant he would have already been on his way back to NA, fully loaded. Easy as it first appeared, he realised he had some hurdles to cross before the full return load would be realised. The first was that Akiya was still ahead of him, and that this time around, he must overtake him and arrive first at RC.

The second was that Gebu believed Pepperoni had given Akiya the same passenger situation report as he had; and so, Akiya too would try as much as possible to maintain the lead to RC. He, Gebu, must give it all it would take to enable him beat Akiya to RC.

Thirdly, he remembered that two buses left for RC before his and Akiya's. With a total of four aspiring buses, would there still be enough passengers for him to bring back at that time of the day? Yes, there would be, he believed, as long as he could reach RC before Akiya.

Therefore, he and his staff had a lot – a tough! – to cover, otherwise the goodies in the daily deliveries to their boss and to themselves would not be fat enough. The anxieties from these facts completely erased from Gebu's brains, any remaining feelings of care he had for his overpacked passengers. He must seize the single key to all his aspirations – arriving in RC ahead of Akiya.

* * *

After a short while, another hawker started a fresh disturbance. Initially, some passengers who were fed up with the bothers hauled some hostilities at him, and wouldn't let him talk. He sought a way out by emphasising that he was a man of God who only wanted to pray for a safe journey and deliver the gospel for free.

"We have heard and seen many of you," said one voice. "Christ warned us about you."

"Yes," said another, "the fakes that would take over towards the end of the world."

"But maybe we need prayers," still, another said, ahead of a final heart softening plea from yet another, a woman. "Why can't we listen to him? If he should defile God, then, that will be between him and God Himself," the woman said.

When in the end he sneaked his way into their hearts, he called himself Pastor Silvanus Antonio of Holy Repentance Church, and ordered everyone in the bus, "except the driver", to close his eyes for a special prayer. The prayer turned out to border more on asking for wealth than for asking for a safe arrival at RC. He led a chorus that many sang with him before he finally landed on his actual objective.

Johnson grew sceptical of this in-bus pastor he had never met before even though the church he claimed was the same as the one he and his family attended, and one that was served by his late father. He however let off the pastor when the pastor claimed to come from Chief Daniels' Togana, and that he knew the popular *GIG*.

Silvanus Antonio announced he had with him a few tracts of some selected self-help words of God. They were meant for sale but he wasn't going to sell them. Rather, he would give them out free, for token donations from those who managed to get copies.

The distribution was progressing prayerfully when there was a serious jolt caused by a dangerous manoeuvring of the bus by Gebu. At a daredevil speed, Gebu had overtaken two cars at a time and had almost collided with two other buses coming from the opposite direction. Gebu had to duck the two buses while forcing the two cars to a stop. The incident extended, without room for objection, the so-called prayers of the up-standing man of God. At the end, the donations he collected on his tracts were fatter than token ones, especially because many passengers believed that it was his timely prayers that had just saved their bus from having a serious accident.

Gebu did not stop at *Flower Peak* bus stop, at least, not until he was forced to, and that was after he had sped past it. About five hundred yards before the stop, Micho and Kamar made one call each for passengers who would like to disembark. Two women responded, but then, Gebu in his type of concentration, claimed ignorance of their responses. For him, what mattered more than anything else was to arrive at RC ahead of Akiya.

"Conductor, here!" one of the ladies shouted. "We want to get down!"

The driver responded with increased speed.

"Stop please!" screamed the other lady. "You are carrying us past where we are going!"

"Gebu, please give them a second to get down," intervened Micho who was to the front of the bus.

"But where have they been all these years?" Gebu asked at the top of his voice, still driving on. "Were they sleeping? Or did someone padlock their mouths?"

The rude questions infuriated Ebino. Instantly, he felt it was wrong of the transporters and their staff to so treat the passengers. He was angry the passengers were never allowed to find the fares in peace, to pay in peace, to board in peace, to travel in peace and to disembark in peace! Why should they be made to suffer insults upon injuries all the time? Squeezing past Heron and Ebino, and turning past Tonga's left, he landed himself by the driver's seat.

"Stop!" he commanded. "You son of a bitch. Stop I say, and let them come down. Before I open my eyes…one…two…"

Micho saw the danger and quickly struggled to walk pass Krespie so as to get to his boss. Unlike Micho, the security assistant hanging by the door had no chance of passing through the fully packed aisle to get to Gebu who was being threatened.

"Stop there. You can't pass," Johnson told Micho and pushed him back with all his strength, balancing him on Krespie. "Tell your boss to stop and let the ladies get down or else, today…"

Gebu saw the great danger he had put himself in – one that could upset his other plans too – as Johnson stretched out to grasp the steering wheel.

With his ego badly bruised Gebu stopped. He looked back at the face of his boss of the moment and took the wise decision of saying nothing. He was most astonished to see that almost all the passengers were against him, and in defence of those he saw as mere women. This to him was a new phenomenon, quite new.

The irony of this particular passenger arrest was that only a double bend separated it from a near similar arrest being imposed on Akiya by his Olga-led passengers. It came about when, despite many protests from the passengers about his excessive speed, Akiya had entered the first length of the double-bend so roughly that some heads were knocked against each other, and some, against the body of the bus. They were not fully recovered from the pains when he went into its second length in a similar manner. This time, the repeated recklessness of Akiya's driving sent many of those standing in the aisle crashing to the floor. Olga was the first to walk to Akiya and grip him by the backneck of his shirt before rousing others to stand up and save their own souls.

Apart from her physically forcing Akiya to stop, her call on fellow passengers also resulted in them dragging down Akiya's unruly security assistant for a thorough beating that first seemed to him a dream than the reality it was. It was while the security assistant was being dealt with that Gebu caught up with Akiya. Gebu was ordered by his new commanding passengers not to stop for an intervention.

So, Gebu drove on, angry with the passengers, as well as with himself. He was angry with the passengers for what he perceived as their growing disobedience and violence towards the bus staff. Why on earth should they hold him hostage, rough-handle his staff and then go further and beat up another security assistant? Why should they interfere to force a journey to stop or continue? Why should they influence the time and speed of a journey? He saw no justification whatsoever. He was burning inside with rage.

Very soon, he feared, both the transporters and their staff would lose their authority to the insubordination of the passengers. Sooner after still, usurpation would finally legalise itself!

The small relief for him was that it did not happen to him alone. What he saw happening to Akiya's team in Carlos Retfil's bus was clearly worse than what he suffered – and that was despite the fact that Akiya's was a team well known for no nonsense. But whatever was the case, he would not take such from anybody again. Never, never – never again!

He was just five minutes away from his zone's cemetery. He felt like stopping and throwing out on to the road, and into the bush, all he regarded as troublemakers inside his bus. He wished he'd found a way of making them pay on the spot for their rebellion. Anyway, he quietly resolved, he would go on and wait till any other time they would come again with such bravado. Then, he would not lose the opportunity to take the score from the current $0 - 2$ to $1 - 2$; then, level up at $2 - 2$, and eventually go ahead and win the fight.

Finally, he wished Akiya too didn't get depressed, and that he was able to overcome the situation as he, Gebu, had just done. But as it turned out, Akiya certainly resolved the situation much earlier, as confirmed by his sudden appearance on Gebu's overtaking mirror. He had caught up with his old boss and was seriously looking for a space to nose-in enough and overtake him. His arrival suddenly sent Gebu back to his old self – the experienced, reckless and rude of the road.

* * *

And so, Gebu went on, this time maintaining the mad lead towards DCP, which he hoped to reach and cross in the next fifteen minutes. Thereafter, he would have only *Burial* to pass, and would finally arrive at RC within another half hour.

Soon, he was only five minutes away from the crossing, cruising as fast as he could on the plains that were before two hills separated by a deep valley. So too was Akiya – closely following behind and making frantic efforts to overtake him.

Ascending the first of these two last hills, Gebu put a strong firing to his bus in the middle of the lanes and blocked Akiya.

"You have been warned," shouted Tonga, "and you people are starting again."

"Are you going beyond RC?" shouted another lady passenger to the driver. "You can stop and let me get out if you mean to continue like this."

But 'stop' was what Gebu neither liked to hear nor do. To stop at DCP compulsorily, yes; but at other places before RC garage, no. He must beat Akiya to RC, to pick up enough passengers to take back to NA.

Akiya flashed his lights and blew his horns to tell Gebu to stop blocking him. Gebu acknowledged him by doing the same thing on his own bus but without allowing Akiya to pass, in what became a perilous mixture of fun and seriousness between the two drivers. Next, Akiya stretched out his right arm and waved happily to Gebu; Gebu, seeing him in his mirror did the same thing back to Akiya, still, without giving up his lead.

"Drive well and stop racing with our lives," warned Heron. "You can't go on like this. You won't be allowed to," he threatened.

Other members of Gebu's staff heard what was being said and so, repositioned themselves at the points it would be easier this time to assist their boss in case trouble returned.

As Gebu's bus started to make a rapid descent of the first slope, Akiya moved closer behind him yelling with laughter. Then, Akiya tactically slowed down to create a longer gap between his bus and that of his former boss. It was just like a fighting ram that moved back after a horn batter – to gain more strength and go again.

Gebu merely crossed the valley when the superior roll-on speed of Akiya put Akiya's bus almost parallel with his. Another couple of seconds, and Akiya was clearly overtaking in a move that Gebu resisted with everything he could think of. Nevertheless, a quarter of Akiya's bus surged ahead towards the very summit of the second hill as both men were negotiating the final left before the summit.

Heron got up instantly to repeat the kind of confrontation he earlier had with Gebu. Micho moved fast pass Johnson, throwing Johnson down before moving on to clear out Heron, now in the driver's cubicle. Gebu stubbornly squared up to the intrusion, as well as to Akiya in the other bus.

At first, the superior fighting capability of Gebu and his staff thwarted the efforts of the resisting passengers led by Heron, Johnson and Ebino. But a few other passengers joining on the side of Heron started to change the struggle in favour of the passengers.

Johnson used the chance and space to invade the driver's box again in order to force Gebu to a second stop. He met a well-prepared Gebu who gave him a terrible elbow to the groin. With a sharp and painful groan, Johnson collapsed into what could not be immediately adjudged an outright death or just a momentary unconsciousness. Tonga, still to the front would not have it. He raised one of his crutches high above his own head, and with all his strength of desperation, crashed it on Gebu's skull, instantly knocking out Gebu inside a vehicle that technology was yet to endow with an automatic co-pilot. Akiya was then half-a-bus length ahead at the very peak, going on to complete the bend ahead of Gebu.

From the right hand side of the road, Gebu's bus, now unmanned, rammed Akiya's right in the middle, sending Akiya's rolling down on its sides – severally down the steep slope, on the left side of the road. It was completely out of sight where it stopped some two fifty meters away. There, it exploded and went into flames.

Gebu's, on the other hand, first landed on its right side, and finally on its back, with three very loud bangs – if that of the ramming it initiated was included. There was a severe earth disturbance that in turn, sent huge balls of dust into the immediate atmosphere. Through the dust could be seen about half a dozen tyres rolling very fast on their axis, like the blades of a wind vane caught up in a monsoon.

CHAPTER 11

The Victims

It was one of those days Luz Inina took his bus by himself for the trip to RC. Up to the cemetery at Zone 1, everything was fine; and he looked forward to crossing the *DCP* in the next ten minutes. He was about completing the ascension of the last hill before *DCP* when suddenly, he saw ahead of him, four cars parked dangerously by the roadside.

As he drove closer, he wondered if the owners were some kind of ignorant-of-the-code picnickers. Coming just a bit further, he saw four men, obviously from the cars, standing and using their hands, presumably in addition to their mouths, to talk to each other. He knew they must be the owners of the parked cars.

Two of the men flagged him down to a stop. As they walked towards his window, he noticed they wore extremely worried looks.

"Is there any problem gentlemen?" Luz was the first to ask.

"Yes sir, there has been an accident," said the first man.

"It involved two passenger buses," added the second.

"Oh God of Mercy. Where?"

"Here. Just now. That's one of the buses," replied the first man again. "Over there," he added, pointing to Gebu's bus resting on its back about twenty metres off the right hand side of the road.

Luz anxiously followed the direction of the man's fingers with his eyes, and ended up on the sprawling object. At once he knew whose it was, but was not sure who the crewmembers were. After Luz had exhibited a comportment of immediate shock, the same man directed him to where he could park so that his staff and some of his passengers could come out and join them for the rescue operation.

A motorcycle was also heard roaring up the hill from the direction of *DCP*. Luz parked, and was with the four men when the bike reached them and stopped.

The rider, Police Inspector Nicolo Jonas, had with him one of his officers, Sergeant Fred Sati. As soon as the accident had occurred, one of the car drivers closely following the two buses had gone straight to *DCP* to alert the policemen on both sides of the checkpoint about it. Consequently, Nicolo dispatched an officer in the patrol car to *Motherwell*, the hospital at Regin City, to alert it and ask for ambulance services. The same officer was also mandated to alert the main police station headed by Chief Inspector Tserra. Next, Nicolo arranged two other officers to look after his side of DCP and took Fred with him on the motorcycle to the spot of the accident.

Both officers were sweating as they walked up to the three men. "Where are the vehicles involved?" Nicolo asked.

"Here, and down there, burning," replied one of the men, first pointing to the bus on its back and then, to the direction of the smoke and fire.

Nicolo yelled to those wishing to join them from Luz's bus to hurry up. He put two of the men to man the two directions of traffic flow, stopped more vehicles and asked their passengers to alight and help.

The helpers swooped on Gebu's bus, trying to upturn it amidst the banging, screaming and crying of some of its trapped passengers. The helpers first attempted to turn the bus right over onto its side but were not strong enough. So, in order to reach the trapped, they resorted to a careful, one by one breaking up of the windows nearer to the ground.

Nicolo left that group of rescuers as soon as the operation commenced. With another handful of them that included Luz, he rushed towards the Akiya-driven burning bus, following the path of destruction it created as it rolled over severally downhill.

The site was spectacularly gory; and the smell, thickly acrid. The fuel was burning, the luggage was burning, the air was burning, the leaves were burning, the soil was burning; and they all combined to give little or no chance at all to piles of human and animal flesh – they too, like chunks of fresh but fatty meat in a barbecue, were burning fiercely.

The fire virtually blanketed any call by the victims for help from being heard. So did it at first blanket the colour and thus, the ownership of the bus from Luz, until he took a harder look and established its orange hue. He was able to ascertain the bus was Carlos Retfil's, and that among those burning must be Akiya and his staff. The outlook was certainly grim and hopeless.

By now, more vehicles had stopped. Among them were Chief Olu Duarf's returning from, and, Linus Isho's going to RC.

Nicolo and Luz raced up and down the road summoning for more volunteers to join the team further down the slope. Painfully, the team found it could do only very little to save what had already happened. Most of the victims were either dead or unconscious by the time the bus stopped rolling and bouncing to its stop position, and so, were unable to cry or crawl out. Just eight other passengers were found far down the slope. Four of these did not need a doctor to be certified dead, two were seriously injured, and two looked well enough.

Of the sixty-eight people made up of four crewmembers, forty-nine seated passengers and fifteen standing ones in Carlos' bus driven by Akiya, six were unhurt, six were rescued injured, forty-six bodies were recovered, while ten passengers completely burnt to ashes. Akiya himself, a conductor, Laura, the police's son, the lady hawker, and a sister of Chief Carlos Retfil were among the fifty-six passengers who perished on the spot. The police officer, Elo Neason, was among the injured, and Olga among the physically uninjured.

Inside Joseph Tolp's bus driven by Gebu, and carrying four crewmembers and fifty-eight passengers, huge framed and fatally squeezed Krespie, the dentist and the preacher were brought out dead. Forty-five, among who were Gebu, Tonga and two standing salesmen were seriously injured. The remaining fourteen, which included Heron, were unscathed.

Very impatiently, the rescuers awaited the ambulances. Ironically, they were being expected from RC as organized by Nicolo, even though he knew the buses involved were Zone 1's, and that the accident had occurred inside Zone 1, just outside his own Zone 2. He was aware of the fact that the transporters of the zone believed more in bus acquisitions and money making than in providing good backup of security and ambulance services. He was also aware that in their thinking, provision of services like these would parasitically eat into the wealth they already created. Had this not been their general belief and stand all along, nothing like this mismanagement of the passengers would have occurred, and accidents like this would have been avoided. Where it happened, assistance would have arrived faster, and internally, from Zone 1 officials. But, as the situation was, and under normal circumstances, a decent person like himself and a decent society like his Zone 2 should and would allow humanity to prevail.

Tonga and Johnson were among the first to be rescued from Gebu's bus. They looked particularly bad. Johnson was rescued first and stretched out in the open; he was alive but unconscious. When

Tonga was brought out, he too was stretched out about six feet away from his brother. He looked at Johnson in desperation and wanted to reach him; but realised that his other leg, the right, and his spine were broken and impossible to move. He attempted to roll over but it was useless. He stretched out his hand as far as it would go but the distance could not be covered. In despair, and believing Johnson was dead, he passed out – just moments before fresh air breathed life back into Johnson.

When Johnson came round, he attempted to join Heron and the rescue crew but was disallowed. He was however useful in resuscitating his brother, who he assisted to join the first batch of the wounded taken to *Motherwell*.

Olga, wailing among those lucky enough to escape any injury, could be heard expressing ingratitude to her luck for sparing her life while taking away Laura's. Johnson, later self-discharged from amongst the rescued, joined other rescuers to console her. She broke from them and ran to where her daughters' body was laid, flung herself onto the charred body and sobbed hysterically. She wished the question of death and survival had been in favour of her daughter and given her a chance of knowing how and what a good journey of life should really be. Though as its strong campaigner, she knew good time would soon come because passengers were already taking the issue seriously; but she felt bad that her daughter who would have partaken in it was instead, violently sacrificed for it. Her sobs, as well as the horror of what was spread about on the ground triggered some of the passengers and rescuers to sob with her.

When, during the course of the rescue operation, both Johnson and Inina met, it was apparently difficult to know who of the two was the happier. Deep down though, Luz thanked God for sparing the life and physical health of Johnson, who he could never forget as a rare, good person.

"But excuse me sir, how did this happen?" one of the rescuers from Luz's bus now had time to ask Nicolo.

"No idea. But it is the worst I've seen," Nicolo answered, following the assertion with a big breath, "the worst ever for them too." He was referring to any singular loss or fatality among the notorious drivers of NA.

"Someone attributed it to overspeeding. Could that be so?" the man asked Nicolo again.

"Look sir, this is a time of emotions, and it doesn't allow for either a reasonable thinking or a just action. For now, let's all concentrate on evacuation and treatment. The time to look for causes, reasons and probably, remedies will come – hopefully."

In all, six ambulances – all from RC – arrived one after the other at the scene; and the unofficial paramedics who included Nicolo, Luz and now, Johnson, instantly teamed up with the actual paramedics to load up the ambulances with the dead and injured from where they were assembled on the scene.

The fourth ambulance was being loaded up when Johnson noticed the face of the injured man he and another rescuer were carrying inside it. There was a nasty scar under his right eye. He looked, and looked again – to his own eyes and brain contents – at this man who was too weak to open his eyes to see who was staring wildly at him. Johnson noticed he had a chain round his neck, and that the badge attached to the chain was half-hiding somewhere under the blood-soaked uniform he had on. Curiosity and anxiety took over Johnson. He wanted to know who exactly the bus staff was.

After the man was rested on the gurney of the ambulance, Johnson tactically stopped behind for the other carrier to leave. Then, he pulled out the chain to see what was at its end. It showed that the injured man was a security assistant. Pretending to be adjusting his neck, Johnson removed and pocketed the badge.

Next, Johnson approached Luz and asked if he could, in addition to the five uninjured passengers already allowed on his bus, be allowed to come with him to RC.

"Of course you can, Johnson. But you ought to have gone with the ambulance to the hospital. You know you are overdoing things now – after such a lucky escape."

"Thanks Luz. But irrespective of what condition my health is, now, my spirit feels well, very well; and this is what counts. Besides, I have got something serious to discuss with you."

"Since when?"

"Since now. That's the reason why I stayed behind to come with you."

Luz was anxious now. He wanted to know what was so important to the point of preventing an accident victim from going straightaway to the hospital for a check-up and treatment. The anxiety wouldn't let him wait.

"Since now?" he asked again. "Can't we discuss it now then?"

"No we'd better not now, because we won't have enough time. But for now, I show you something."

Johnson brought out the badge he removed earlier, and handed it over. "Here, keep it very safe. We discuss it when we get to RC."

Before sunset, the site was already cleared. Luz, with his passengers was among the very last to leave.

* * *

The rest of the journey was more sober and quiet, except for the initial outbursts of some passengers at its commencement. First, and at Luz's humble request, one passenger sitting immediately behind the driver's seat agreed to vacate his seat for Johnson. Luz wanted him to be near so he and his staff could keep an eye on him. This last part of the journey also saw Luz's passengers displaying various levels of shock as well as of the analysis of the accident. Some remained rigidly seated and lost in thought, while others kept their minds cast on the ugly scene itself.

One man continuously sang praises to his God. He was one of those uninjured inside Gebu's bus. Another man, his co-lucky traveller, was cursing the two drivers as loudly as possible for being the cause of their problems. "They were warned," said he angrily, "but just won't listen. Everybody was like a dog to them. May this sort of sorrow they put on us befall them too – befall them together with their families. Amen."

"It is alright," said another passenger, a lady sitting by the hysterical man. "Just take it easy and thank your God. Do you know one of the drivers is even dead? He was fatally burnt."

"Dead? Lord's justice. Which of them? Wouldn't even matter. He deserved it – with the other one. May he die many times over. And if he had a soul, may it roast on in the heavenly hell fire."

"That's alright," the passenger pleaded again. "I can understand your feelings. Please take it easy."

"Yes, I will, only if there is anything left to take easy. But there's none. Had it not been for that young man – the brave one sitting over there," she pointed at Johnson, "and some of his friends, it would have happened earlier, and probably would have been more fatal.

"Many of us said the same thing to the young man's group – to take it easy and leave the driver alone. Pity they took it easy for too long. Pity we didn't see it early enough the way they saw it. Now, this is the result. Why should any passenger still and ever be in that kind of silly take-it-easy-group?"

"Sorry, I didn't mean it that way," she pleaded.

"Well, that is not the way it sounded to me."

"That's okay," another lucky man started to appeal to the last speaker. "You see, because they were not there then, they found it difficult to understand and to appreciate what we went through."

That's quite true," said the man who regretted taking it easy. "At the current level," the man retorted further, "anybody who doesn't understand is only pretending out of fear or something else. We need to join up and face the reality now. From what I saw today,

I am fully convinced it is silly running away, and expecting the pursuer to know when and how to stop. Every transport staff in that man Carlos Retfil's zone is as decent as the owner he serves; and every owner as the Lucifer."

"Johnson," called out Luz, gently tapping the seat Johnson was resting the back of his head on, "we are at RC."

Johnson opened his eyes and sat up.

"How are you feeling, alright?"

"Yes, Luz, thank you. I think I am okay."

"The way it is now, it is too late to load and return to NA. So, I am staying the night here. "Have you got enough strength to discuss it now before I take you to the hospital?"

"Oh yes, I have. You see, that badge; bring it out."

Luz complied.

"Can you make a wild guess about it?"

"Well, the guess is that it is an orange badge signifying it belongs to Carlos Retfil's organization – to his security assistant who was either dead or injured on that journey."

"Good trial Luz. Anything else you want to add?"

"Yes the man feared he was dying and wanted you to pass it fast to his boss to enable 'Mr All-important' know his plight and arrange a better treatment that would free him from the sharp clutches of death."

"Again, Luz, good attempt. But the real story is that I have found a fugitive."

"You have found a fugitive? I don't understand."

"Then listen again. Untruth might have been racing along for twenty years, but it will take the truth only a day's stride to overtake and outrun it. Or, Luz, put it this way: however old the evil is, it will always be outlived by the good."

"Come on, Johnson, with all you said so far, I still don't understand."

Johnson then reminded Luz of the day he, Luz, was beaten up to unconsciousness and his buses vandalised over the problem of discounts, and how he told Luz one of the attackers was deeply marked under the right eye, and that he was very sure the injured security assistant he helped carried into the ambulance was the attacker.

It was all too sudden for Luz. He could not be sure. "But how can you be sure it was him?" he asked Johnson.

"I am – because I saw him, I faced him, and I did it to him. I told you I did it to him, didn't I?"

"But somebody like that wouldn't work for any of us. He wouldn't be employed so near. He would keep very far away."

"That wouldn't matter. Remember you were the only transporter there with us that day. How you were mishandled made it impossible for you, or any other transporter for that matter, to know the perpetrators, even if they work under your nose."

"I just don't know."

"I know you don't. You couldn't have."

Then, something cropped up in Luz's mind. He raised the badge up to a better view and took a closer look at the attached passport photograph of its owner.

"But Johnson, there's no mark or scar under any of the eyes. Didn't you say one was deeply marked?"

Johnson followed Luz to look, and came up with another explanation. "I was right then," he declared. "It means he wasn't born with it, otherwise he would have grown with it. He used an old photograph, or took the photograph before you were attacked. Today I saw his ugly face and my mark it carries. Now I can swear it's him. It is Urison."

"It is him then; it is him!"

In the end, they both believed it was the thug. They also agreed that seeing him did not mean apprehending him or getting a confession from him. Any of these would ever be difficult with a man serving a man as powerful as Carlos Retfil. But the two men were prepared to give it a try. They were going to start from the point where Johnson would, that evening, get admitted to

Motherwell. From his bed, Johnson would monitor Urison, and use the opportunity to look after Tonga. Luz on the other hand, as a transporter of NA, would show his kind financial presence at the hospital, pending the arrival of Joseph and Carlos who, by the law of Zone 2 hospitals, would be held responsible for the total cost of treatment.

Luz accompanied Johnson to *Motherwell* Hospital that night and left him there after he had made an initial but handsome cash deposit for the victims' treatments.

* * *

The following morning before leaving NA for RC, Joseph Tolp called at Carlos Retfil's house about the accident that involved their two buses. He did not meet Carlos who had already gone to RC to find out more about the accident. Three places – the scene of the accident, the police station of Inspector Jonas, and the hospital – Joseph had to visit that day, to know what he had to know and what he had to do next.

Accompanied by two aides, his first stop was a brief one at the scene of the accident. He met Joseph Tolp's bus lying on its side not far from the road, with almost all its windows broken.

"This won't be a total loss for him," he grumbled on concluding a brief inspection. "If recovered in time, Tolp will only need to spend on the body, perhaps replace the whole of it."

Carlos then moved across to the other side of the road to look for his own. He saw a large path, the size of one attributable to a herd of fighting elephants. He guessed it was the one made by his bus, and the one he had to follow. Had he not been previously given the exact place of the accident and the exact landing position of his bus, he would not have been able to know that the burnt pile at the end of the path he followed down was once his bus.

In economic sense, there was nothing about it left for him to recover. Some items of clothing were met scattered about, with those they belonged to either already in ashes, or on admission dead or alive inside *Motherwell*. He wished the wreckage he saw first was his.

At *DCP*, Carlos Retfil's next port of call, he did not meet Inspector Jonas who was then on an assignment to the RC office. But there was Sergeant Sati who, after sympathising with him over the unfortunate incident, expressed the anger and shock of both the police and the hospital at the appalling level of mismanagement that must have created Zone 1's worst road accident on record. Sati warned Carlos that the full investigation into the cause was well underway, and it was likely that both transporters faced heavy evacuation and medical costs. He referred him to the main police station in RC. However, Carlos, with his aides, opted for the hospital first.

The first thing Carlos Retfil did at the hospital was to confirm the death of the sister he allowed to travel free on that day. To him, it was the second most painful aspect of the accident, the first being the destruction of his bus. When led into the mortuary where the bodies were stacked, he had no time to see the body of Akiya or of anybody else.

On his way back to the wards, Carlos met Joseph who apparently was just entering the hospital premises. Like Carlos, Joseph had stopped at both the scene and at the *DCP* where he saw and heard the same things as Carlos did.

"Sorry Chief," Joseph sympathized, "I was at your house this morning but you had left."

"Oh thank you," replied Carlos with more hatred than appreciation. "Do you seriously expect to find me in NA with all that has happened?"

"Chief, it is sad indeed."

"Sadder for some still."

"How do you mean, Chief?"

"Have you spoken to Gebu?"

"No, Chief, I haven't. I'm just coming in. But why?"

"He caused the whole problem, didn't he?"

Joseph Tolp was astonished to hear that coming from Carlos Retfil. It was not only an indictment, but also a judgement coming before either a formal investigation or trial. He was not going to agree with it. He himself had been fed with a version that was totally different from Carlos Retfil's, one exonerating Gebu. He wouldn't have any of it.

"No, Chief, far from it. Eyewitnesses said Akiya caused it."

"Who can be better witnesses than the victims?" Carlos asked Joseph in a bid to rubbish Joseph's point of disagreement. "I have been to the wards, and that is what they said. They did not whisper it."

Joseph was adamant in his disagreement with Carlos. He was in fact getting angry. "But which of the victims have witnessed your claim – from your bus or from mine?" he queried.

"What difference would it make anyway?"

"Lots, Chief. They would certainly see it from different sides. You must never apportion blame before any reasonable investigation; it is wrong, very wrong, and disappointing."

At that moment of enraged argument, the first ever between the two men, Luz Inina walked to them, totally unnoticed until he was actually beside them. He was visiting the hospital to see how Johnson and Urison, as well as the other victims admitted were getting on, as he had promised Johnson and the hospital staff he would do.

Luz could see both men were totally immersed in a hot argument, and he moved to break it.

"Hello Chiefs," he addressed both men.

While both men were slightly shocked, Joseph Tolp was glaringly relieved.

"It is only God that brought you at this right time," said Joseph Tolp, now facing Luz. "Thanks for your effort yesterday, which everybody commended.

"Please, since you were there, we would like to know which of the drivers really caused the accident.

"The Chief said it was Gebu. Was that true?"

Luz was surprised to know what the two men were arguing about, and still more astonished that they could engage in that, at that wrong place and time.

"Look Chiefs, what is this argument all about? It is pointless. You could engage in this worthless argument because none of you was there yesterday to witness the seriousness of what befell the poor passengers and crews. Now, it is more important to think of how to salvage the situation, starting with the cases of the dead victims. That is why I am here now, and going into the wards. Better you join me."

"Oh thank you Luz," said Carlos. "You are right, quite right."

* * *

The entourage of the three men, joined with Carlos Retfil's aides, headed towards the wards, stopping first at the Senior Doctor's to thank him directly, and thank his staff through him.

The doctor told them that with the exception of one, all the patients were responding well. The one, a young man, not responding actually did not respond at all and unfortunately, he died a couple of hours ago. His father, a police officer also admitted, was yet to be told. He remembered to thank Luz for the all-evening and late night physical and financial support he rendered.

As the transporters walked among the injured, it dawned on them, or so it seemed, the serious pains their own selfishness had caused. They took their time to see all on admission, and spoke to those of them who were well enough to hear them or talk with them.

They saw Gebu who, according to the accompanying nurse, was just having his first real sleep and therefore must not be disturbed. They also saw Urison who was just well enough to talk, albeit feebly and without clarity. With great pains, Urison managed to relate how the patient next to him gave to him the fruits by his bedside. This inferred a visit and thanks from the trio to the kind patient who happened to be Johnson. Luz was careful not to show any special interest towards Johnson when they stopped to thank him.

The climax of the joint visit came when the entourage was at the mortuary used for the dead passengers. There, the accompanying nurse, as if doing the visitors a favour, instructed one of the mortuary assistants to open the first row for the group to see. When carried out, they saw a row of tagged and paired soles facing them, with the toes up. In cleanliness, each pair varied from *a-one* to almost carbon black; and in placement, from a letter V to a badly written roman figure eleven. They looked at the row from the top to the bottom before it was closed, and another opened.

"Thank you," said Carlos to the assistant, "I think we have seen enough. Just close it. I wouldn't like to see my sister again for now. Oh God." He started to cry.

"Your sister?" Luz asked. "Did I hear you say your sister?"

"Yes, my sister, the second junior. She was well and alive in my bus. Now, she lies in that row," he pointed, "dead and cold." He was sobbing. "I just identified her before you came."

"Oh sorry, about that," said the freezer opener in a crisp and emotionless tone that confirmed he was very much used to that phrase. After all, it was a trade language he had to use many times daily, to many callers to his section of the hospital. All the same, it made Carlos Retfil sob, even more heavily.

Luz watched Carlos crying and could not believe it was happening. "So, the wicked also cries," he confirmed the wonder to himself. Then, he wondered further: How many families have been or would be crying the same way as a result of the present crier's initiated greed and wickedness?

"Sorry Chief. That's alright now," said the nurse. She took the handkerchief from his chest pocket and wiped his face with it. She was doing this when another lady came in, excused the nurse, whispered something into her ears, and then went straight back.

"Gentlemen," the nurse called the attention of the men with her, "Dr Efink just sent the lady to say he knows you transporters are here and he would like to see you now. He wants me to lead you to the conference room."

"Dr Efink?" Joseph tried unsuccessfully to place him, "who is Dr Efink?"

"Oh, I remember him," said Luz, "the medical officer, isn't it?"

"Yes, he is the one," confirmed the nurse.

"Does he want me too?" Luz asked again.

"I presume so, because the lady talked of three transporters."

"It is too late to differentiate now Luz," said Carlos. "You have even done better than the two of us who own the buses. So, we go together please."

In the conference room, Dr Efink was brief and to the point. For record purposes, he introduced the man sitting with him as Isa Aril, the hospital secretary, and demanded that Carlos Retfil, who he knew very well, should introduce his two colleagues.

Next, to create a little bit of life, Dr Efink, in welcoming the three men said he had met with Carlos Retfil before, but never with Joseph Tolp. He also met Luz for the first time only the previous night when Luz was assisting the hospital staff; and that after Luz had departed, the doctors on duty told him of the hefty deposit he left towards the victims' care. He said it was an act that was truly commendable. Next, he asked if the information supplied the hospital on the ownership of the two buses was correct – that they belonged to Carlos Retfil and Joseph Tolp.

"Yes that is correct," answered Joseph Tolp.

"In that case then," the medical officer started, "we shall now tell you what happened to your passengers in our hospital since yesterday, what we have done, what more we have to do, and what you two will have to do."

He narrated how the hospital was put on alert by half past four the previous afternoon, and how the hospital immediately

321

dispatched the ambulances and the paramedics who were able to commence ferrying-in the victims by five. The hospital, he said, received ten dead and fourteen seriously injured, and that unfortunately, one of the injured just died early that morning.

He was pleased that the continuous dedication of his hospital staff was paying off as shown by the patients who were responding to treatment so well that there shouldn't be any more death among them.

Since it was the zone's agreed rule with Zone 1 that the transporters of Zone 1 paid for the initial recovery and treatment of any accident victim of Zone 1 treated in 2, the breakdown and the total cost of the current treatment would now be read and submitted to them by Mr Aril.

Mr Aril went straight to the most important headlines and bold letters of the sheet before him. He said that the document should be immediately scrutinized by the two transporters, and then jointly signed right there by himself, Dr Efink and the two concerned transporters. Highlights:

Cost of evacuation and first aid as 45,000;

Cost of treatment as 80,000;

Cost of pathological tests as 30,000;

Cost of storage and preservation as 45,000;

Total cost as 200,000;

Less Luz Inina's deposit of 20,000 as 180,000;

Balance to pay as 180,000;

Last day for payment: Friday next, to ensure discharges and releases on Saturday.

There was an added footnote:

One: Treatment is costed up to Saturday when all the patients should have been discharged.

Two: Further treatment, if necessary after Saturday, would attract fresh billing.

Three: Pathological tests (post mortem) would be done and completed on the bodies by Friday noon.

Four: Bodies would be released only after all payments were completed.

Five: Conveyance of bodies to Zone 1 cemetery on Saturday if requested would be done free. Bus owners are to supply the coffins, or otherwise, be charged for the supply.

Finally, lines were provided for the dated signatures of C. Efink, the Medical Officer and I. Aril, the Hospital Secretary for the hospital, and C. Retfil and J. Tolp, for the "Owner."

Three copies were pushed across to Carlos for him to read and sign. After the signing, each transporter would receive a copy, while the third would go to the hospital.

Carlos looked through and passed them unsigned to his colleague. Joseph read through and at the end turned to speak to the secretary "Mr Aril, we have seen this, and it involves a lot of money. Can't you please allow a discount before we sign?" Joseph asked.

The two hospital representatives were not surprised at Joseph's request. They were well prepared for it. They would give no concession whatsoever to those they already regarded as the butchers of NA.

"But Mr Tolp," answered the secretary, "you don't negotiate a discount in this type of matter. You preferred and selected a matter of pains. And now that you have it, it is only right that you pay for it. Everybody knows how you transporters of NA don't believe in discounting."

"But still, dear secretary," came in Carlos, "we are talking of a large sum to be paid. Therefore, however small the discount, it is something we shall appreciate."

"Sorry, no," Mr Aril bluntly refused.

"Please, gentlemen, let's move forward," intervened Dr Efink. "Not causing the death and pains would have been the best discount. Can't you think of that now, if you couldn't before?"

Carlos Retfil, with the look of a ridiculed man, saw the determined faces of the last two speakers and felt thoroughly ashamed. He knew he had no alternative but to swallow the educative insult – and, in the presence of Luz Inina! He told Joseph to sign and pass it to him to sign.

As Carlos pushed the papers back to the medical officer, Joseph asked his next question in the form of a humble request. "Now that we agreed to pay the bill, can you give us two weeks to complete the full payment?" he requested.

"Why we can't and will not, gentlemen," responded Dr Efink, "is that unless you pay up in full before or by Friday, our system will be badly disrupted. Remember, if it has been left disrupted in the first place, the benefits would not have been there for your people and ours to enjoy now. Without a full payment by Friday, nothing would be released on Saturday, and you would have to pay more. Good day gentlemen; and see you before Saturday." The two men closed the door of the conference room behind them, leaving the three guests lost and glued to their seats – until Luz broke the trance.

"So what next now?" Luz asked his colleagues.

"Nothing," replied Carlos. "Nothing, other than we pay. An option doesn't exist here."

Luz Inina could not believe hearing and seeing Carlos Retfil running out of ideas – so openly for that matter.

"But there must be something that can be done," Luz told his two beaten colleagues. "Do we call a meeting for tomorrow? We should find something."

"That is thoughtful of you Luz," remarked Carlos. "The problem now is of time. Tomorrow is near, but the deadline of four days from now is even nearer. That is the problem."

"Luz is reasonable, Chief," said Joseph, "We shouldn't miss tomorrow."

"Okay then, Luz, can you please arrange it?"

"Oh certainly. And for what time – ten in the morning?"

"No," said Carlos, "better much later, say about six in the evening. We have an appointment with the police today; and who knows, it may extend to tomorrow. You know the way they do things here. Better we have between now and tomorrow morning for the police and any other matter that might arise from there. Then, there would be enough time to return to NA."

"In that case, while I get on with the arrangement why don't you see the police now?" suggested Luz. "Worry less that it is getting late. It may give you more time for other things."

"Certainly," agreed Carlos. "By luck, the Chief could be there now."

* * *

Chief Inspector S. Tserra was in his office that evening. He had used the whole afternoon to condense the reports he'd gathered from Inspector Nicolo Jonas and his team, and from the field officers who had been dispatched all evening and night to both the scene and the hospital. It put before him, a straightforward case of premeditated mass murder that was borne out of the greed and inhumanity of the bus operators and their agents.

He and his fellow law enforcement agents in the zone knew that such a calamity could befall Zone 1 and spill over to Zone 2 at anytime, the provision of both the *DCP* and a separate cemetery notwithstanding. He and his men were aware of the fact that the drivers of Zone 1 were smartly circumventing the road safety rules. Now, with this unprecedented height of human ruins inflicted onto the two zones, he, S. Tserra, and his team would do more, fairly and ruthlessly, to put the transporters of Zone 1 in check once and for all. It was soon after the CI arrived at this determination that one of his officers entered his office and informed him both Carlos Retfil and Joseph Tolp were at the reception to honour his invitation. He was very eager to see them.

CI Tserra led the two men into his office and showed them their chairs. Then, he called three of his officers to join him. One of the three was Inspector Nicolo Jonas.

"Gentlemen," the CI opened the discussion, "you know why you are here, I believe."

"Everybody in the room except the CI nodded even though the statement was meant for only the two transporters.

"Have you visited the scene of the accident and the hospital?" he directed the question again to the transporters.

"Yes," they responded again.

"Did any of you notice anything?" He looked into the two faces amidst the silence in the room. "Mr Tolp and Mr Retfil, did you notice anything?" he asked again.

"Chief Inspector," answered Carlos, "who wouldn't have noticed something – the serious accident of course."

"Yes, the accident," agreed Joseph, "and the destruction."

There was another moment of deliberate pause from the CI. He used it to scan the faces of his two guests again, but this time, as if searching for where they intentionally hid the appropriate answers. He was disappointed, but not too surprised. Wealth, after all, did not equal sense, he thought; especially where it enjoyed the backing of coercion, cheating and ignorance, as it did with the likes of Carlos Retfil and Joseph Tolp. He found none of their answers involving enough.

"Well, Nicolo, Gasua and Tairu," the CI called his officers, "you were all over the places, did you see the same thing as these gentlemen?"

"Oh no, not the same thing, something most serious," answered the officer sitting next to Nicolo.

"Now you have heard Tairu," the CI told the transporters, and then turned to the officer sitting out next to Tairu, "and Gasua, what do you think?"

"Gentlemen, I still feel sick. Yesterday, I saw the most horrific scenes in the whole of the thirty-six years of my living. I pray I won't see such again, because I know next time I would faint." There was another pause in the room.

"So, my dear businessmen of NA," said the CI, "you have heard the two men. Further asking for the opinion of Inspector Nicolo would definitely amount to asking for a feeling that would damage our appetites, because he was the first to be at the scene, and he saw it all.

"Gentlemen," he continued calmly but firmly, "what we saw yesterday, and which are fully evidenced before me now, were mass murder and attempted mass murder – premeditated, pure and straightforward – including the foolish suicide of a driver and some crew members.

"I have seen and investigated thousands of road accidents," he hammered on boastfully, "but never one so gruesome beyond description like yesterday's.

"So, the question on everybody's lip here, in the hospital and about town, was why and how it was allowed to happen – why and how you carried innocent men from both zones through fire into a collective hell instead of through the smooth journey they paid for. Every lip here asked why you stopped them from reaching the respective destinations they aspired to reach. Gentlemen, it is more than incredible.

"Anyway," he continued, "within the last twenty-four hours, my men went through all the available facts and established the true why and how. Now, listen as I read to you what they discovered:

"One: You co-herded a hundred and thirty passengers into two buses that should carry a maximum of ninety-eight altogether. So, it was easy to have fifty-nine killed on the spot, and one later in the hospital; and to have fifty half killed, living only twenty free of any physical injury.

"Two: As if taking human lives were not bad enough, your vehicles destroyed a number of birds and livestock because you, in the first place, disregarded the law banning them from passenger vehicles.

"Three: The money the drivers and crew made, and would make for themselves and for you the transporters, formed a constant basis for getting them intoxicated. Money drove them to continuously out-race each other to all the bus stops along the routes.

"Four: Up to the point of the accident, your drivers and crews violently disregarded the warnings and interventions of the passengers.

"Five: Up to the immediate point of the accident, which was on a hilltop, there was an unreasonable determination to overtake by the driver called Akiya, and equally an unreasonable determination to disallow it by the driver called Gebu.

"Six: Both buses were neither safe nor roadworthy. Three defective tyres were found on Gebu's, while the inability of the two drivers to stop appropriately on a hill inferred a combination of serious brake and tyre defects on both vehicles.

"Seven: Luggage must have been excessively and poorly packed. In one bus they contributed to the ferociousness of the inferno, and in the other, to the number and seriousness of the injuries sustained.

"Therefore, gentlemen," he continued, "our investigations showed that the *whys* and *hows* were because of complete disregard for simple and reasonable laws governing the transportation system by your staff, and backed up by yourselves – all criminally.

"This being so," he continued, "even though the accident occurred in Zone 1, many citizens from Zone 2 were among those your actions and staffs murdered; and so, the responsibilities became a joint one between the two zones. Without delay, we are sending our recommendations to the authorities in your zone for them to act on accordingly."

He stopped and sought a response if any, from the two transporters. Carlos was the first to give one. "Thank you CI," he started, "and to your entire team, for your efforts during and after this accident. It is all appreciated.

"But all the same, I feel there is need to correct certain impressions you have on how we run the transport system. The fact is that our staff, as well as we, the owners, do care as much as possible for the passengers; and we, the owners try even harder to maintain a good system.

"What happened this time was an accident – something that never has a defined medium, place or time to happen. It will happen through what it will, and when it will, just as unfortunately, it had."

"No" disagreed the CI, "it only will, after due warnings have been given. And in this case, we find evidence they were – adequately. They were ignored."

"Is that your recommendation then?" asked Joseph.

"Yes, it is based on that – very much on that."

"That you still insist on it is a pity," said Carlos "I hope you realise we too suffered serious losses from this accident. Therefore, a further negative recommendation is unnecessary."

"So, what exactly do you expect the authorities in NA to do – to us?" asked Joseph Tolp, now getting angry. "You want them to, or believe they should, hang us?"

"There is no exactness. The recommendations are already compiled and they will be sent," answered the CI.

"And what if they don't see it your way?" asked Carlos.

"They don't have to. But we believe they will do the right thing this time. If they don't, the truth is that you will have all your vehicles removed from Zone 2 – permanently. Not only that, no facilities, except in highly selective cases, will ever be extended to any of you again whenever you run into your usual problems.

"And one last thing," added the CI, "the cost of police operation in this was 20,000. The two of you, as the owners of the buses involved will have to pay it to this office by Friday."

"Twen-tie thousand? By Friday?" Joseph asked, more with rage than with amazement. "On top of the two hundred thousand just charged by Mr Aril? And you want all the two hundred and twenty to be paid by Friday? CI, where do we get that kind of money within that space of time? Or this twenty now is part of the two hundred?"

CI Tserra listened to Joseph in disgust. He wanted to say something – most likely to be rough, rude and explosive. His three police officers expected him to. And so did Carlos, who smartly put in his verbal intervention before Tserra would explode.

"We appreciate your help," Carlos said, "and it has been very kind of you all.

"But it was true, what Mr Tolp said. Today alone, within the last four hours to be precise, we have got a bill of 220,000, all against Friday at the latest. There was a 200,000 from the hospital – without a discount, and without an allowance to spread the payment. Or perhaps, you would be kind enough to do something for us on your own 20,000, to lighten our burdens."

"Which burdens exactly?" Tserra started. "Can you compare them with ours? Are we not the ones now being forced to carry your burdens? So this question of doing something…"

There was an intrusion. Another officer knocked on the open office door and walked straight in. He handed the CI a white envelope. Because of the urgency indicated on its back, Tserra opened it straightaway and read the note it enclosed.

With the suddenness with which he threw down the paper on to the table, anger turned his eyes into red, and he directed the intensity at Joseph and Carlos. "You see. You see, another has just died," he said, shaking his head. "A young man, Tonga Dorman. Do you know him or have an idea of who he was, Mr Retfil?"

"Sorry, no idea of who he was," he lied!

"Anyway, what would that even solve?" Tserra asked. "Poor fellow, he couldn't survive the operation that removed his only leg. You still want something done for you – now that the number you killed has climbed to sixty-one?

"You think you carry many burdens. So, you want discounts or, maybe, outright write-offs. You people are shameless – heartless!" He stormed out of the room, entered his old jeep, and drove off, Nicolas, Tairu and Gasua immediately following him in another. He was on his way to *Motherwell*.

CHAPTER 12

The Awakening

At *Motherwell*, CI Tserra went straight to Isa Aril from who the written message originated. Aril was in the ward, and so Tserra marched in there together with the other three officers who had now caught up with him.

In the ward, some strange voices attracted him to look through into the door-less nurses' room. "Take heart and accept our sympathy," he heard one of the voices there said. It was that of Luz, and Tserra recognised him as soon as he saw him. Luz was consoling a lady blinded by sobbing. Sitting by the lady was a young man being equally consoled by Aril and a nurse. But unlike the sobbing lady, the man wore what looked like a permanent, forced smile.

"You saw our letter?" Aril asked the CI.

"Yes. It came while I was with the murderers – Retfil and Tolp."

"So, they have learnt of the young man's death?"

"I told them, just as they were asking for discounts, extension or what we could further do for them."

"Discounts again? The same thing, they did here. Nasty swines. What discounts? What else do they want us to do – after all the explanations I gave them? Probably, they need to be burnt alive."

"Okay, are they on their way down to this place?"

"I don't know. But perhaps not, because they claimed they could not place who Tonga Dorman was."

"Well, this lady here, Lais, is the mother," Aril said "and the young man, Johnson, is the brother. Johnson himself was one of the victims admitted, but has been extremely useful from the scene of the accident."

"I am sorry," Tserra expressed his grief.

"Lais arrived this afternoon, moments before Tonga's situation ran into complications," Luz told Aril. "It was as if it was all waiting for her to arrive. She and Johnson were at his bedside and everything looked normal. I too was with them. Then, the alarm of his monitor went off."

Luz carried on with the rest of the story: how help speedily came, how the curtain was speedily drawn round Tonga's bed, how he was wheeled back to the theatre, and how in a space of about a quarter of an hour, the doctor came out to tell the mother of the sad news.

Tserra was moved by Luz's story. As Tserra repeated more of his sympathies to mother and son, he noticed that since the time he arrived, Johnson still wore the same fixed smile; and this convinced him that what was on Johnson's face was not a smile after all, but a subconsciously radiated grief imposed on a soul by a sadness too deep-rooted for tears, and too complex to understand.

"They ought to have arrived if they meant to come, shouldn't they?" Luz asked Aril.

"They will not be coming," Nicolo Jonas was becoming surer. "I heard them talking of attending a meeting in NA tonight."

Before Tserra left that night, he got to know more of Johnson and the big tragedy in the Dorman family, now headed by

Lais. With Aril, Tserra arranged comfortable accommodation for Lais and Johnson within the hospital for the night.

After Tserra left, Luz and Johnson were able to consider both the alleged utterances of Carlos Retfil and Joseph Tolp before Tserra, as well as the two's subsequent absence from the hospital that night. They found it extremely wicked of Carlos and Joseph not to have come to the hospital on the excuse that they did not know who Tonga was. Luz and Johnson were angry that the two transporters brushed aside the facts that the Tonga they did not know must have been a jewel to some parents, and must have fully paid not for death or injury, but for a safe journey. Above all, Johnson knew the claim was a lie – the story of Tonga together with his family, the transporters knew so well; the burden of Tonga's primary care, their overall boss still shouldered; and Tonga himself, most transporters still carried as a most difficult passenger. The whole thing hardened more, the hearts of the two men, against the transporters.

CI Tserra thought seriously about the meeting he earlier had with the transporters and became intensively angry with Carlos and Joseph. Particularly, he thought of the two questions the two men bluntly put to him: 'what exactly do you want the authorities to do to us?' and 'and what if they don't see it your way?' He remembered the manipulation and other evils the transporters of NA were capable of, and how they could easily overturn what would have normally been correct judgements. So, this time around, he was determined that the authorities in NA would not be left alone to make their own judgements. He would seek to enforce the rule that since the casualties were from both zones, that single bi-zonal panels be chosen to deal with every aspect of the incident – from police interrogations to the trials – so that neither the suspects nor their backers would take any undue advantage. His zone got him what he wanted, using Zone 2's social, political and economic superiority to arm-twist Zone 1 into obedient compliance.

* * *

As early as six in the morning, Lela, unable to sleep, was already up, thinking about what to do with the news of the accident Luz sent to him the previous night. To him, that the accident claimed innocent lives and injured innocent passengers was sad; that it involved the buses of Carlos Retfil and Joseph Tolp was welcoming; that Carlos and Tolp found themselves on the defensive and at the receiving end in RC, and witnessed by Luz was most interesting; and that Urison's past evil suddenly caught up with him was most exciting. He eagerly awaited the 04:00 p.m. arrival of Luz from Regin City.

When Luz came, he and Lela quickly arrived at a final strategy to be adopted on the issues of Urison and of the transporters' meeting fixed for later in the day. On Urison, both men would first seek the assistance of CI Tserra. Already, the identity badge removed from Urison had established him as a crewmember in one of the buses that killed many citizens of NA and RC. This time, both men hoped the CI and other authorities in RC were going to take the issue more seriously than ever. Additional allegation of a previous attempted murder and a wanton destruction of others' belongings against Urison, witnessed by Johnson, would make it even easier to get Urison nailed, they hoped.

On the proposed meeting of the transporters, Luz would not only go ahead and organize it, himself and Lela this time around, must participate actively in its proceedings. To enable them have their way at the meeting, if necessary, they would stoop either lower than, or to the level of fellow transporters. As long as they were able to achieve their primary aim of exposing the mal-management of the citizenry by their fellow transporters, it would well worth it.

At the meeting itself, the personal resolves pushed Luz to move it that all fines and bills – medical and burial – imposed on the two senior colleagues be paid by the Association at once, meaning the following day, Thursday. The precedence he quoted was the similar bailing out his fellow transporters did for him when his own buses were vandalised.

The meeting recognised the goodwill, rapport and respect accorded Luz on the other side. So, it appointed him to head the RC Welfare Committee, whose job it was to pay the fines on behalf of the two men, liaise with the injured, and see to the peaceful release of the corpses for burial.

There was another *ad hoc* committee, the NA Welfare, inaugurated at the meeting. Its job was to console those who lost friends and relatives in the accident and persuade them to agree to the burial on Saturday since the transporters were prepared to foot the bill. When Lela volunteered to head it, the members were particularly relieved because they knew that over the years, both as a former driver, chief driver, and now as an owner and a close friend of the murdered Mr Titoloujou, Lela had endeared himself into the hearts of most citizens of NA. He was therefore the most qualified to work on them at a difficult time like this.

Early on Thursday, Luz Inina led a three-man team of himself, Linus Isho and Ike Elfans to RC to settle all the payments imposed on Carlos and Joseph. Before noon, it was all done in the manner acceptable enough to the offices of Dr Efink and CI Tserra.

Having successfully carried out the first phase of their assignment, the three men dispersed to re-assemble at the hospital the following morning for the final preparation for Saturday. Later, and unknown to the other two, Luz returned to Johnson at the hospital and had his information on Urison updated. From there, he took the update immediately to CI Tserra.

The CI listened with disbelief to Luz's narration of the story of Urison as it affected Johnson and himself; and of course, he remembered it at once. He remembered vividly how his office was told not to bother itself looking for any marked man from NA because an arrest of such person, if done, was unlikely to lead to his prosecution by the NA's pro-Association policemen. With this additional story, his office would use all fair methods to get the truth

335

out of Urison during an interrogation. He only had to wait for CI Stern, his counterpart from Zone 1, to arrive for the interrogation to take place.

* * *

The first rounds of the interrogation did not take long to conduct on Gebu. Gebu insisted it was Akiya who did all the intimidation as well as the dangerous overtaking; and that despite his late colleague's bad driving, he, Gebu, held on very well until when some of the passengers suddenly attacked him; that was when he veered off the road, out of control.

At that point, CI Tserra asked Gebu if he knew why so many people were killed and injured in the accident. He replied he wasn't sure of the reason. The CI then listed their findings to him: overloading, mixing of human passengers with birds and livestock, speeding, racing, ignoring passenger warnings and defective tyres and brakes. Because some citizens of RC were among those killed, the CI made it clear that Gebu would be tried for both mass murder and attempted murder by a judicial panel jointly drawn up from among the citizens of RC and NA.

The interrogation took the same form with other surviving crewmembers, except Urison. Urison's was the last; and it was an extended one, jointly conducted by Stern and Tserra, and with Johnson and Luz present.

"Now," CI Tserra addressed Urison, "we are going into something a bit different. Do you know who these three gentlemen are?" He pointed to CI Stern, Luz and Johnson.

"I know just two of them."

"Which two?" CI Tserra asked.

"This man," he pointed, "Johnson, my friend and ward mate. And Mr Inina."

"Since when have you known them?" CI Tserra asked again.

"I met Johnson when we were admitted into the same ward. Last month, I met Mr Inina as one of the bosses."

"And this man, the officer, you still don't know?" asked CI Tserra again.

Urison took another look, this time a longer one, at Stern. Stern's face was definitely not among those of a few passengers, bosses or colleagues he could remember.

"No," Urison slowly answered, shaking his head "I don't know him. I am sorry."

"Anyway, CI Stern is the chief of police for the entire Zone 1, which includes NA. He is here because of you."

CI Tserra then put his right hand in his left breast pocket and brought out the bus staff badge. "Can you recognise whose picture is on this badge?"

"Yes. It is mine."

"Are you sure about that?" asked CI Stern, the man Urison didn't know.

"Yes. That is me."

"But where is the big scar under your right eye?" asked CI Tserra, pointing to the position it was supposed to be on the picture. "Okay, wait. Wait a minute." He again sent his right hand into his right side pocket and came back with an enlarged copy of the picture. "This is an enlarged copy of the same picture, and I cannot see that scar on any part of your face. Why is that?"

"It won't be. It is an old picture."

"Was the mark a new one then?" asked Stern.

"Yes, something like that."

"How new? Tserra resumed."

"About a year."

"Can you tell us how it happened?"

"But officer, why asking these questions?"

"Because our duty now demands that we ask them. And it is in your best interest to answer truthfully," Stern carefully explained.

"I really cannot remember exactly. It was a gardening accident."

The answer prompted a scornful smile on CI Tserra's face. "Gardening inside NA garage on...?

Urison was shocked – and speechless.

"I asked you, did you do a bit of gardening inside some buses which you later vandalised, and whose owner and crew you later attacked and shot?"

Urison realised the game was up. He could find no words to say. The CI realised he was within a few steps of Urison's total capture.

"You see Urison," continued CI Tserra, "your friend, Johnson, was the man you had a scuffle with when you sustained the injury; so, he wouldn't make any mistake recognising you. As for Mr Inina, he was the one who personally rescued you from the scene of the accident even when he scarcely knew you. Then, he paid for your treatment. That was the man whose buses you vandalised, the man you shot at and would have killed. Eh? What have you got to say to that?"

"Can I please speak with you in private?" Urison pleaded.

"No, you can't. At least CI Stern will have to be with me. Others can excuse us. Is that alright?"

Urison nodded an acceptance; and CI Tserra directed Johnson and Inina to leave the room.

"They are outside now," said CI Tserra, "Can we hear what you have to say to all these?"

"I did not shoot anyone. I have never fired a gun at anyone. Never."

"That is not what the evidence before us says. Unless you have something else – like who shot Luz Inina and so on – we believe you did the shooting."

"It was Akiya who had the gun, and who shot Mr Inina. Though it's all four of us that were there, but it's only Akiya who carried a gun."

"But Johnson actually wrestled a gun off you," Stern put it to Urison.

"It's Akiya's spare. He gave it to me. I only scared off the passengers with it."

"So you too had a gun," Stern deduced to him.

"Well, something like that; but it was Akiya who did the shootings."

"You said you were four; who were the other two apart from you and Akiya?" asked CI Tserra. "And what did they carry?"

"Kong and Tapeta were the other two. They have long moved out of this area. They carried just knives and their fists."

"How did you get the guns and the knives?" Who gave them to you? And who sent you?"

"Oh my God. I really don't know," he answered soberly.

"Well, Urison," CI Tserra started to infer, "the little you now claim to know – and which we have now known – is quite enough to send you to the gallows. If you admit you know more, and you are able to tell us more – and at no other time but now – that could make the difference between the same gallows and your life. It's entirely up to you."

Urison, wearing a pitiful expression, looked at the face of the last speaker, in a desperate search for the genuineness of the offered conditionality. Then, his gaze shifted to CI Stern's as if to appeal to him to make his colleague uphold the promise should he provide answers to the questions. Finally, his was back at that of the questioner.

"Chief Tolp. He recruited us and gave us the guns."

Both officers looked at each other with shock and in disbelief. They were clearly astounded.

"Chief Tolp?" asked CI Stern. "Do you really know what you are saying?"

"Yes, I do. He gave us enough money for the knives and for our escape too. He said we must not allow any passenger with a cheap ticket to board any of the buses that morning."

"But there, you were wounded this seriously," said CI Tserra, "why could you not be found in any of the hospitals?"

339

"I don't know. Immediately after the problem Inspector Elo Neason picked us up and took me to the police hospital for treatment."

This was another bombshell for the two officers.

"You want to tell me you know Elo Neason?" asked CI Stern.

"Yes, from that day. Even on the day of the accident, he and his son came with us with free tickets authorised by our boss. Might be he is in the hospital right now."

And in the hospital he was – well enough to be discharged in time for his son's burial.

"Okay Urison", said CI Tserra, "we shall let you have some rest now. Later, we shall come back to you.

"But remember, that the level of cooperation we receive from you shall determine the amount of leniency you get from us. And, in your own interest, do not discuss this with anybody, not even with Retfil or Tolp, should you happen to see any of them. From now on, only the two of us here tell you what to do."

Before the two officers came back the following morning, they were able to meet Luz Inina and confirm to him the story he had related.

With Luz, as directed by CI Tserra, the officers arrived at the strategy to be followed in dealing with Joseph Tolp especially. In order that too many things would not be stirred up at a time, Joseph Tolp's arrest would be delayed by a week, till just after the burials were over. It would be for the attack on Luz and the accidents. Carlos', for the accident, would follow later. Principally, Johnson and Urison would be the star prosecution witnesses at their subsequent trials.

* * *

The two heads of committees prepared for the Saturday so well that everything to do with the day's event was ready as early as 06:00 a.m. on the day.

Between his day of appointment and the Friday night, Lela, with Johnson ensured he visited as many bereaved families and friends as possible, and as many times as it required, convincing them to agree to the Saturday burial. This was thanks to Johnson's determination that was strong and cool enough to enable him use his motorcycle. "Since it has happened," Johnson would plead, "let's us all agree to the burials now, so we can have enough time to mourn."

Lela was particularly happy to have Rev. Father Din Peters among those convinced to agree. The Rev. Father was the man of God in charge of Holy Repentance Church, the biggest Christian church in NA. In the accident, he lost an important shepherd from a nearby diocese, Pastor Antonio, who prayed and made collections inside Gebu's bus; as well as Tonga, a devoted son of a late shepherd.

At first, the Reverend Father, a silent critic of the transport system, was angrily indifferent to Lela's requests, and would have nothing to do with any problem caused by the arrogant and callous transporters of NA. He therefore bluntly told Lela: "We warned them before, to stop the hunt. Now that they have killed the game, let them eat it alone. Thereafter, they should be brave enough to come and open their bloody mouths to us to confirm they have enjoyed the cruel pleasure."

However, he changed his mind when Luz and Johnson accompanied Lela to plead with him and release to him, the full list of post-accident events: the determination of CI Tserra and the authorities of RC, the forced cooperation of CI Stern, the findings on the causes of the accident, the discovery of Urison, the confession of Urison, the implication of Tolp and Neason, the loss of Tonga suffered by the family of late Rev. Fadey Dorman, and finally, the joint plan of the three of them with CI Tserra for the cemetery on Saturday. In a rare opportunity like this, the men pleaded with the Reverend Father to go beyond mourning his church members to converting the souls of the devils, and to liberating the uncountable number of those oppressed and caged by the

341

transporters of NA. In the end, he not only agreed to come, he also pledged to mobilise his congregation and other religious groups to turn up. He would officiate at the gravesides' open service!

In the RC sector, Luz with his group equally started the Saturday smoothly. The situation was particularly helped first, by the fact that all the five bodies belonging to RC were released and buried on Friday.

Only those selected by each victim's relatives to collect the bodies were brought to the hospital mortuary by the transporters. They were few, and formed an infinitesimal percentage of those for the cemetery. By midday, they were already there, sad and angrily quiet. By that time too, the thirty bodies to be taken were almost ready; they would be able to depart in another couple of hours in vehicles provided by the transporters and the hospital, under a security escort overseen by Chief Inspectors Stern and Tserra. Every group worked punctually and efficiently.

The superb persuasive abilities of Johnson and the two rebellious transporters ensured that the biggest crowd ever gathered in NA was at the cemetery. It was among Lela's assignments to hold the crowd outside the cemetery until the bodies would arrive. This was to allow the relevant people arranging the flowers, seats and stands at the open service by the graveyard, to do their job.

Starting from cemetery's main entrance, the crowd formed backwards on both sides of the road, and towards the approach the convoy would come from. Every few minutes, Johnson reminded them over the mobile loudspeaker how it was the least respect they could all give. Towards the time of the arrival of the procession, Lela actually went further beyond Johnson's by blaring across, a stronger reminder: "We know, they made them die like chickens; but we must not allow them to be buried like fowls, because they are truly a part of us. We must pay these last respects with everything we have."

It was neither an ideal occasion for a party or for a carnival, but yet, the hymns, drums and trumpets signalled their arrival in clear echoes from a distance of about a quarter of a mile. And because of the clarity and the local popularity of the tune, it was not surprising that the people who lined up from the cemetery gate joined in the singing long before the convoy ever appeared.

At first, it was a lit, escorting motorcycle that was visible from a bend, about five hundred yards away from the cemetery gate. Next appeared the second, on the other side, to complete the leading pair. Then, one, two, three, four big buses, followed. Then, followed ten ambulances of RC, a couple of cars, and lastly, the last two police motorcycles of the procession – all heavily bedecked with flowers.

For many mourners at the gate, the unexpected beauty of the procession was all the remote control they needed to cause their eyes to rain tears. Even, Luz Inina, its master organizer, could not hold back tears from his seat on the leading bus when he saw how very successful the arrangements he masterminded had turned out to be.

There were no tears on Johnson's face. He was too sad and too busy to harbour a molecule of them. At every part of the cemetery, he directed the movement of the people to ensure nothing diverted the programme from the path he, Luz and Lela planned for it.

As soon as the procession passed a point along the line-up, a disintegrating mob would follow it amidst loud trumpeting, drumming and singing. Slowly but majestically, the procession funnelled into the cemetery.

Rev. Father Din Peters and Lela Adamu positioned themselves at the entrance to the venue, a large clearing surrounded by young shady trees. Lela, the head of NA Welfare Committee, was made the official 'Receiver', and Din, the officiating minister, the 'Chief Mourner'. When the bikes-led train reached them, it stopped; and the occupants of the ambulances, cars, and buses, with the exception of the musicians started to disembark. As they did so, four other men, friends of Johnson's, were on hand to direct the

343

close relatives of the dead to the seats at the front rows of the semi-circularly arranged stage. Others who accompanied the procession on foot were directed to the rear seats.

Luz, the last to alight, did so after the bulk of the members of the procession had been seated. He walked straight to both Din and Lela, and gave each of them a slow hug before directing another group of young men to start offloading and arranging the coffins containing the bodies. Johnson's friends were the larger members of this group.

It was a careful procedure lasting about twenty minutes. Coffins numbered one to five were arranged in head-to-toe positions, and central to the first curved row of seats. Another five, numbered six to ten, with number six placed in front of number one, followed them. Next, eleven to fifteen, sixteen to twenty, twenty-one to twenty-five, and finally twenty-six to thirty – all with artistic parallelism from whichever side the thirty coffins were viewed.

About two metres after number twenty-eight stood the wooden, amplified pulpit, for the use of the officiating minister and anyone he might need to call upon to use it. Behind the pulpit, a high chair, also for the use of the man of God, was placed.

Luz next directed the arrangement of flowers round the coffins. Even though the provision and arrangement were specially commissioned, scores of mourners and florists still brought in flowers for free.

The space between the first curved row of seats and the straight line formed by the first five coffins was the first to be bedecked; the shape was that of a disappearing moon.

Next, they filled the space at the far end of the coffins; it was a beautiful triangle.

Next, the area between the front of coffins twenty-six to thirty and the pulpit was done; it was a two feet wide, beautiful block.

Lastly, the near end was arranged. It was a triangle similar to the first, and the arrangement formed a complimentary balance of the entire decoration.

Luz was proud to put the last touch to the decoration. When it was finished, he signalled the music to stop. He paid his last respects to the bodies with a bow and walked smartly to Din and Lela again for a last tearful embrace. He had finally handed over the bodies to the state for both the service and the burial.

Many of those just discharged from the hospital were also present. Although their number was small compared with the sea of heads, the light-coloured plasters and bandages, the slings, and the visibly awkward movements with or without crutches, easily gave them away as those fortunate enough to have escaped being a tragic increase to the thirty bodies arranged on the stage.

* * *

Luz and Lela were particularly happy to discover John Martins among the crowd. He had been mandated by old and feeble Daniel Daniels to come and show the sympathy and respect of Daniel Daniels' organization which was still very much associated with NA. He embraced Luz, Lela and Rev. Peters who were in the front, and quietly whispered a pledge to the families of the dead into the ears of Luz and Peters.

"Please, let everybody rise," Father Peters called out over the microphone, his two arms stretched out and raised to positions just higher than his head and then lowered onto the sheet atop the pulpit. "And let us sing the first of the three hymns on the sheet with you. We are to listen first to the organ for the right tune."

Two mouth-organists from his church took the first two lines of *Amazing Grace*, at the end of which Rev. Peters energetically swung both hands for everybody to sing. The message was received, and with the organists again leading, the crowd started the hymn.

345

At first the tone was dominated by sadness, soberness and to some extent, lack of good knowledge of the song by all. But by the time the last stanza and its chorus were taken, it was obvious that most people had really put their hearts in it.

"Last stanza again please," Father Peters called out, raising his arms before the crowd that was so happy to hold on to the sweet jugular of the hymn.

The stanza having been properly sung, Father Peters said a short prayer, and told everyone to sit down while he sermonized. Now, about two-thirds of the sympathisers had nothing to sit on, the number present having swollen well beyond expectation. Those standing did not mind the position anyway.

"Praise the Lord," Father Peters shouted.

"Hallelujah!" the crowd replied.

"Praise God!" he shouted again.

"Hallelujah!"

"Today is a sad day," he went on, "never mind the music, and never mind the song.

"It is a sad day for all of us here at this hour as we bid our loved ones and relations lying down motionless before us, a farewell."

He went on to admit that it was painful but that two things had soothed the pains. The first was that the prophecy was being fulfilled – that all humans were made of earth, and would return to earth after death. The second was that all the thirty heroes and heroines whose bodies were before them, had departed the wicked world, and were surely already in good heaven where they would sin no more and suffer no more. Death, a compulsory transformation of existence, could happen any day to anyone; and everyone should get ready for that day by being good to neighbours, friends and enemies. He wished the souls of the dead God's acceptance, and prayed that God consoled those they left behind.

He then announced five people would be permitted to eulogize on their dead relations or friends before he would take the service to the next stage.

Chief Carlos Retfil raised his hands. Rev Peters, knowing his involvement in the whole problem that brought them there, called on him to speak.

Carlos told the gathering how important it was for him to be there to share the sadness with the families and friends of the dead. He told them one of the buses involved and destroyed was his; but its loss was not painful to him. Instead, the loss of lives and the injuries sustained by the passengers were the most painful.

He particularly remembered his sister who died in the accident, as a kind and cheerful mother who left a three-year-old girl behind, as one who would do anything to help the needy. He remembered Akiya, his faithful and hardworking driver, who, he would find very hard to replace. If he had known that he was seeing both his sister and Akiya alive for the last time on the fateful Tuesday morning, he would have looked at them very well and said a longer goodbye. He was sorry that death hid all these away from him, he said, as he used his handkerchief to wipe tears from his eyes. At any rate, he would build and donate a big enough hall inside the cemetery as a place of worship, in memory of all those who died in the accident.

Lastly, Carlos said that since the accident had brought enough of its own deaths, injuries and sorrows, he was appealing to the authorities of NA and RC to drop the charges of mass murder, murder and manslaughter being prepared against all the bus staff who survived the accident.

Father Peters beckoned Lais Dorman next.

Lais hoped Tonga could see and hear her wherever he might be. If so, she had a special message for him:

"Darling Tonga. When you survived the first accident – though badly – I, your mother, believed you survived the worst of

347

tragedies in your life. But then, here you are, plucked from life by the second.

"In the first, they claimed the driver was blameless, and his bus perfect." Now, her bravery gave way to her tears. "Might be this time too, the driver, the bus and whoever sent them would be right – because they know you are no more, and the dead are forever defenceless.

"But darling, don't worry, we know you are selfless and caring, and we apportion no blame but praises to you. I take consolation in knowing you will suffer no more; and that together with your dad, you are with our good God, the judge and the saviour. Till we meet again I, your loving mother, and Johnson, your dear brother, will take heart. Rest in peace, darling Tonga."

Johnson and Lela led her off.

Olga was called next. She spoke of Laura's high hopes and hard work, and how the pig-headedness of two drivers had put an abrupt end to Laura's aspirations as well as wasted her own love and expenses on her lovely daughter.

She cursed herself for being born in a zone where people were too stupid to challenge stupidity, and where people foolishly expected intimidating dangers to be tackled only by fate, faith and prayers. She said even though it was her mourning that day, it would certainly be the turn of others unknown among them to mourn and suffer a worse fate very soon, unless everybody was determined to do something about it now. Both the road and the journey could be pleasurable but for the insincerity of certain wicked people, she concluded. Before anybody could suspect her move, she ran to her daughter's coffin, numbered nine, threw herself on top of it and sobbed hysterically. Johnson and Tolp assisted her back to her seat.

The next person Rev. Peters called to speak was Joseph Tolp. He said the loss of precious lives and properties gave him the saddest moments of his life. Joseph claimed to know that all his colleagues felt exactly the same way. He prayed that the souls of the dead rest in peace.

Joseph also expressed a special sympathy for Olga, the lady who spoke last, and for Lais who spoke before her, and prayed that God gave them the strength and courage with which to cope with their sad moments.

He said that the fact that among those being buried was a most dedicated Akiya and Chief Retfil's sister, proved it was an accident that was destined by God to happen. As ordinary mortals, they were in no way wise enough to see or change that destiny. This was why despite the transporters' respect, love and care for both the passengers and the staff, this still happened. He rounded up with another prayer for the repose of the souls of the dead, and stepped off the pulpit while the crowd was responding with amen.

* * *

John Martins was anxious to talk. Twice he had indicated this by raising his hand, but had not been called upon. He was determined to try again after Joseph Tolp even though unknowingly to him, Din Peters wanted him to be the last to be called on to speak. But then, hardly had Joseph stepped off the pulpit when a crutched, heavily head-bandaged man stepped forward from among the gathering and raised his hand. In fact, it was another man standing with him by design who gently shoved him forward. The combined attraction from the bandages and the crutches, together with the timing of his coming out gave the minister no chance of assessing the man's request other than to urge him on, to limp out to the pulpit. He was Urison.

"I am sorry, many people here don't know who I am," he shouted through the microphone. "I am one of those to be tried for the murder of all who died," he continued. "But this should not be so; it is not that I am claiming innocence though. The truth – yes, the truth – is that all what Chief Tolp just told you were a pack of lies.

He didn't take care of anybody – not the passengers, not the staff. Akiya, my friend who died knew what I am talking about.

"Let falsehood be shamed – now! He made us beat them up. I mean the passengers – made us shoot them…to pack them…" He was becoming hysterical.

"Reverend!" shouted Joseph Tolp, already rushing back to where he just left a short while ago, without being called to come forward, "you must stop this man, before he spoils the service. This is not the occas…"

'This is not what?" Urison shouted back at Joseph now at the pulpit, with Din Peters struggling to maintain peace. "I say this is not what – not the time for me to speak? No, I am not waiting until after my execution because by then, it will be too late!

"You instructed us to over-pack the passengers, to beat them up, to shoot them!" He doubled the crutches under the left armpit, and swung the right arm uncontrollably, sweating and shaking.

"Titoloujou! Yes, Titoloujou and his wife! Yes, Luz Inina – he is the only saviour now.

"You too, be brave. Admit it. Joseph Tolp, admit it. You gave us the dirty jobs to do!"

Suddenly, every mind started to shift from the mourning to the highly dramatic actions and utterances of Urison.

Lela and CI Tserra ran out to the pulpit to help save the situation, as well as to prevent Urison from doing more harm to himself.

"Look gentleman," the CI shouted to Urison, "this is a special occasion. If you have something to say, then say it calmly for people to be able to understand, so that this burial is not disorganized."

"Yes, I have; and I will say it!" screamed Urison.

There was a loud murmuring coming from the crowd. It was laced with anger – partly at Urison, and partly at what looked like an attempted gag by Joseph and the CI.

"Reverend, CI," called Lela Adamu again by design, "let him talk. That will cool off the situation."

"No," shouted Joseph. "No, he can't go on with this rubbish!"

"Let him talk!" shouted an angry mourner from the crowd that was now getting impatient. "After all, you have said your own. You can't gag him!"

By now, everybody, with or without a seat was on his feet, eager to see what was going on at the front. The last speaker had caused the people's anger to shift away from Urison; they were beginning to believe Urison needed to be shown some sympathy.

The three gentlemen by the pulpit managed to calm down the two main disputants as well as the crowd. They ordered Joseph to listen and let Urison talk; that Urison should be calm and brief; and that the mourners should put first, their maturity and the main objective of the gathering, which was all about the dead.

For whatever it was – the influence of the piece of land they were on, or the true anxiety to discover the hidden facts, or both – all murmurs and noise were at zero audibility within two minutes. Urison finally had permission to talk.

With as much calmness as possible, Urison related the story of what existed between himself and his friend Akiya on one hand, and Joseph Tolp on the other. His starting point was that it was Akiya who knew Joseph, and how Joseph invited both of them to his house where he armed and paid them to smash up Luz Inina, Lela Adamu and any bus offering cheap weekend fares. He narrated how his gang of four was injured during the attack on Luz Inina, and how Joseph Tolp arranged with ex-Police Inspector Elo Neason to take them to the police hospital for private treatment. It was after that incident, he went on, when Joseph Tolp offered him and his friends full-time security jobs which three of them declined due to the fear of being exposed at NA garage, but which Akiya took. Akiya came to him again and they both met Joseph who wanted them to shoot Emmanuel Titoloujou for being a threat to him and his business.

351

Unfortunately, the job was carried out beyond its design and specification, in that Emmanuel's wife was also shot. After the shooting, Akiya persuaded him to come in as a security officer on a new bus of Chief Retfil where he, Akiya, was being made a driver. The carrot was that they could carry as many passengers as space would allow them, and could keep the fares taken from such excesses. The scramble for the day's private taking from excess passengers they would carry actually caused the speed and pick-up rivalries that ended in the accident.

He also remembered to add that a week before he would start the full-time job, Akiya told him that Joseph Tolp pushed him to sabotage both the cooking and the dinner at the *Original TeeCoff* by secretly putting pebbles in his own plate of food.

Now Akiya is dead, and he too would soon be hanged. Why should only the two of them be the sacrificial lambs in the hands of Joseph Tolp, he wanted to know.

In the five minutes or so that Urison's hot but clear confession lasted, and up to another quarter minute after it was over, both the people, the coffins and in fact every other thing around, except the air, maintained an uncharacteristic silence. And it was Carlos who first broke it, and Joseph who first saw Carlos broke it. Carlos moved to disappear, unthinkably, without his wife!

"Stop him!" yelled Joseph Tolp, his voice almost louder and clearer than the microphone he didn't use. "Carlos Retfil is going! Don't let him! He has answers to Urison's questions. I cannot answer all!"

Carlos paced on, five aides, each of them looking like a well fed bouncer, following him. At the end of the stage, Nicolo stepped out with five of his men, all visibly armed, and blocked Carlos' way. "You can't go," he ordered. "And round up the gang! You are all under arrest," Nicolo roared in a voice that would cause the loudest of slum bullies to tremble. He and his officers aimed the mouth of their pistols to cover any of the gang who would dare foolishly to attempt an escape or resistance.

"But let him pass," counter-ordered one of the aides.

"Quiet you!" Nicolo roared even louder. "I say you are all under arrest!" He ordered the five thugs marched away, and reminded Carlos of his business colleague's invitation to the pulpit.

"But why are you doing all this?" Carlos asked. "Why the arrests? Why can't I pass?"

"You will soon know why, Chief Retfil," answered Nicolo. "But first, just move yourself away from the coffins and the flowers, and take this side to the microphone. After that, you may go."

Before Carlos knew it, his aides were gone and he was already dragged round to the pulpit.

"Now welcome, Chief," Joseph mocked Carlos arrival. "You are in a better position to answer the questions. Killing Titoloujou was your idea, wasn't it?"

"But then, wait; shooting Luz was yours," Carlos countered.

"Wrecking Lela's taxi was yours."

"Wrecking Brenda's *TeeCoff* restaurant was yours."

"Creating more fare stops was yours."

"Not sticking to the routes was yours."

"Promoting Akiya was yours."

"Employing Akiya in the first place was yours…"

"Sh-uut up, you shameless criminals!" shouted Rev. Father Peters, now red-eyed with anger. It was the first time he had ever displayed his anger in the public. He was more than angry, he was mad. "Shut up. We have heard enough!"

"No, you haven't," shouted Joseph. "Not until you have seen this…"

"Whuam. Whuam," and Joseph landed two heavy slaps on Carlos' face. The force sent Carlos crashing down to the ground, taking the pulpit down with him. Joseph then launched himself on top of the floored Carlos.

Instantly, CI Tserra recognized his men needed more assistance to end these men's show of shame. He ran out to the pulpit, followed by Nicolo, Gasua and Tairu, the three officers who, as far as duty goes had no other choice than to try and see if they would reach the pulpit area even before their boss. Stern too promptly joined them.

Between the officers, Joseph was pulled off, and Carlos, up. And to ensure that another free round would not start again, CI Tserra ordered his subordinates to have the two, as well as Urison, handcuffed and taken away.

When the unceremonious exit was in progress, a young lady quickly departed her position near Tonga's coffin and caught up with the march past, one of her shoes she'd removed firmly held in her hand. She was Yemie, the daughter of the murdered Mr and Mrs. Titoloujou. Before anyone could take any notice of her, she seized Carlos Retfil from the back and rapidly landed heel blows on his cheek and face. When Nicolo and his men finally succeeded in disengaging her from him, his face was puffy and bloody. Now, hell had clearly broken itself loose.

John Martins, standing besides Isa and Ecaf remained still and too shell-shocked to believe what was happening before his very eyes. As if to make the situation worse for him, there were a man's shouts of 'yes, they are here!" coming repeatedly directly behind him. They were of Alan Yob; and they almost made him wet his pants.

Martins had scarcely started to turn to the direction of the shouts to his left where Isa and Ecaf stood when he heard slaps being rained on both men as they were being arrested by irate mobs that Johnson was actively directing. Two of Carlos' thugs used the cover of the chaos to seize Martins but Johnson quickly intervened to set him free in a brief and sharp encounter.

In disbelief, and with his arms folded up to his chest, a thoroughly shaken Mr Martins watched the police-led mob drag away two more of the powerful men he knew, together with others he didn't, in the direction the police earlier took Joseph, Carlos and Urison. Even though, unlike his boss, he had certain doubts on the behavioural capabilities of the transporters, but he never knew the level of sadism in them was that high, or that their own acts could catch up with them this quick, and in this way.

He took a look at the spread of coffins and shifted the arm-fold he had to his front, to his back. Many questions about the transporters raced through his mind: With all those efforts of Chief Daniels, why hadn't they realised that passengers were sacred to their business? Even if out of selfishness the transporters had wanted the lucrative business only for themselves and their offsprings, why couldn't they have put in place, a management method that would guarantee the passengers some basic but solid minimum to live on. Why did Chief Daniels waste so much of his time and resources on the lot? Then, he remembered Grandy Ezidie's remarks at the fund raising, that they were not well tutored; but he knew they were – that his boss certainly did his best. He was relieved Chief Daniel was not present to see the huge waste.

* * *

"Everybody, remain in your position and be calm!" blared out Rev. Father Peters over the microphone. With the active assistance of Luz and Lela in the front, and Johnson in the crowd, he commenced to force through, another sermon necessitated by the series of dramatic incidents that had taken place since his first. "Please, be calm!"

At first, it looked as if the events happening at high tempo would not create the atmosphere for anyone to give the Rev. Father's request a consideration. But after about ten minutes, and with the last and several sentences of appeal being repeated over the microphone, the situation was quiet enough for him to proceed:

"It is your loved ones you followed here
And so, you must not follow the criminals out of here.
Because if you follow them out from here,
Neither can the five of us out here do the burial.
Following them would mean doing them in,
And theirs would pollute the holy bodies here.

355

Today is a long day
When we have come a long way.
With you all I sympathise today
The same way I do sympathise with myself.
With you all I rejoice today
The same way I do rejoice with myself.
And if after, I have to sympathise again with you,
It means I have to sympathise again with myself.
But as a man of prayers, you all know,
I pray it will never come to that again.
Amen. Amen?"

"A-y-men."

"Why the first sympathy I have to offer?
It's because of the fools we're made to suffer
Over a long, long time, over and over,
In the hands of those we trusted.
From when they moved to compete with dear Daniel,
We hoped their services would be better,
Or, at least, be of equal goodness.
So, our entire journey we confided
And put into their hands entrusted,
Till they felt we're too good for a comfort,
And brought in loads and goats as our equal.

"Shame, we were cowards for a time so long,
And were ignorant for another so long,
Leaving the solution to the songs.
Pity we did not make earlier protests –
Till we waited to have all these:
(Peters started to count the coffins with his fingers.)
One, two, three, four, five, six,

356

Seven, eight, nine, ten, eleven...
Twenty-nine, thirty, and even more –
Even more, and much more,
Because many were beyond recovery.
Never a pleasant duty,
And never our God's wish.

With innocence we set out on our journey.
Now see how they waylaid the journey
Our entire project of life in mourning
For injury, delay, stagnancy and death.
At injury they wished we were never healed.
At delay they wished us a total grounding.
At stagnancy, they wished us a total retrogression.
 At sorrows, they wish us tears unending.
At death, they wished we were never revived.
But now, we sorrow and tear no more
For our God is good. Amen. Amen?"

"A-y-men!"

"Therefore, we now see that for us His creation,
It is another idea different from their expectation –
The era suddenly turning from that of exploitation
To a time of seeing for the blind,
Of hearing for the deaf,
And of freedom from the brotherly shackles.
It is a day of reaping for some,
A day of paying for some,
One of witnessing for some,
And one of learning for all.
Why shouldn't we thank God –?
Our God that is good. Amen. Amen?"

Johnson was not going to give the gathering a chance to respond. He pushed himself out to lead a favourite hymn of his late father, a song that he made popular with his congregation when he was alive and leading the church, and one that swiftly went with what the Rev. Father had just sermonised. The crowd readily joined him:

"He is good, our God – Amen.
He is good, our God – Amen.
He loves us, our God – Amen.
Do you love Him, our God? – Amen.
Obey Him, our God – Amen.
He is good, our God – Amen.
He is good, our God – Amen."

Hearty, seraphim-ic, and wildly Pentecostal, it was. Johnson re-introduced repeatedly the lines and choruses of the song, each time turning to different directions – the coffins, the crowds, the temporary pulpits, and the sky where he believed God sits forever on His throne. Each time too, the crowd responded louder with physical body movements that dwarfed outright dancing.

At the peak of the ecstasy, he was on his way to his original position in the crowd when he noticed far back, someone waving and beckoning – frantically to him. He saw it was Ral Ralgrub, and wondered why, after being lucky enough not to have been arrested by the mob he still remained in their midst. He was sure Ralgrub was waving to him to come and save his soul with a passage out of the entrapment. Soon, with no notice at all from the crowd, and a very faint one from his mother who he walked pass, he went to the beckoner, and subsequently disappeared with him – still unnoticed.

"A-y-men. Do you mean amen?" Din Peters took over again.

"A-a-y-men!"
"Wish amen?"

"A-a-y-y-men!!"

"In that case, from this very hour, two things we must do, to stop forever, this type of tragedy.

"The first is that we must be careful that we don't rejoice like the toad. It was a normally walking animal with two long and beautiful legs – until one day when uncontrolled rejoicing got it so drunk to the point of daring the poles to a jump, and had its legs broken. And the final result for the toad as all of you could clearly see? Limping on broken limbs for the rest of its life! We must pray it does not come to that for us. Amen. Amen?"

"A-y-men!"

"The second and more important is that today, if we should total up the number of 'amens' that had been said by every mouth within the last couple of hours alone, it would run into several thousands. Unfortunately, they were all bare ones, and will remain as worthless as mere noise, unless they are protected.

"In other words, it's never enough to say 'amen'. You must not be fools who just leave their 'amen' unprotected.

"An unprotected amen turns into bitter curses and woes. Our 'amen' here today will be unprotected and will turn into curses and woes if we allow the likes of Retfil and Tolp to run any system here again. It will be unprotected if we ever allow the likes of their staff, children, friends and guards who supported and protected them up to here today, to move near the system. It will be unprotected if we adopt their art of thievery. It will be unprotected if we adopt their way of violence.

"It will be unprotected and there will be woes if we should part from the way of the Torah and other Scriptures and go on to idolize any transporter, be it Inina or Adamu.

"It will be unprotected if we do not recognise the caring roles of transporters like Inina and Adamu, the fair practices of officers like Tserra, Stern and Jonas, the bravery and endurance of the likes of Heron, Tonga, and Yob, the skills and heartbreak of the likes of Olga and Johnson, and the inconsolable pains of the Titoloujou and the Dorman households."

Lais, in her pains, instantly felt proud at the mention of her family. When she turned round to pass on the delightful look to her only living son, she realised he wasn't with her, and was nowhere to be seen.

But where was Johnson? She vividly remembered him leading the songs, and remembered faintly seeing him thereafter going past her with a smile that betrayed nothing. She looked at the direction he went but saw nothing. Where is Johnson?

"Our amen will be unprotected," the Rev. Father went on, "and we will be idiots if we should leave the drawing, interpretation and mending of the highway code to the transporters alone; and it will be unprotected if we don't support our own code.

"It will be unprotected if we allow fear or cohesion to reduce us to a generation of the blind, the deaf, the dumb and the lame. It will be unprotected if we feel too unimportant to play a role in any of our systems.

"It will be woe and a curse unto us if we choose to remain mass and single idiots – idiots too unintelligent to break off the brotherly shackles on our wrists and ankles."

Mass idiots, Lais knew it was impossible for her to be as an individual; and a single idiot she was certainly not prepared to be either. She must find her living son! And so she disappeared, zigzagging her way in the direction she thought she faintly saw him go – round the growths, round the ready-dug graves, and ending at the one awaiting Tonga's body. There she was confronted by the ugly spectacle – a body, Johnson's, in it! The dumpers did not have the time to cover him as they fled when they saw her approaching. He was bleeding but breathing.

CI Tserra heard a scream. Quietly and without disturbing the very end of the open service, he took two of his men with him and went in its direction. They found Lais besides a thoroughly beaten up, wounded and half buried Johnson, inside the grave meant for Tonga.

"Oh my God," screamed Tserra, "who did this?"

"Ralgrub and his thugs," answered Lais, weeping. "They fled when I appeared. Ralgrub promised to definitely come back and have his own revenge on the people. He promised to return! To return and avenge! To come and treat Johnson the way his father and brother were treated!" She pointed to the direction they went.

"Can we chase them?" one of the officers asked CI Tserra. "Can we now before they would escape?"

"No, not this moment," Tserra affirmed. "But we shall later – certainly.

"What we don't need now is diversion and distraction.

"Let's tighten up first on what we have in our hands.

"Get Johnson and Lais out of the grave please, and fast."

Tserra knew that saving Johnson was the only way of knowing the current extent of carelessness and omission on the side of the people. It would also expose the extent of resistance they could still expect from the transporters. So, the three officers carried out the rescue operation with all the vigour it deserved and brought back Johnson to the congregation – just in time to hear the last part of the sermon before the bodies would be buried.

"And lastly, my dear family," Father Peters called, openly holding down his tears and preventing them from taking over his message at that point, "as we take them away and lay our beloved ones to rest, may our present and future actions – not inactions – let their sacrificed souls rest in peace.

"Think about it, your only passage through life. May you never again be mass and single idiots."

THE END

About THE MASQUERADE

When Jacquensica challenges the male controlled Mask Culture of her kingdom, Ila, she instantly lands herself in hot water. Then, two tourists, Victor and Kazuggi, take the risk and rescue her to Glasgow only for both men to become guilty of high treason and Satanism. Ultimately, Glasgow decides to return her with her troubles to Ila, a decision that starts a woman-led all-out war involving three continents!

However, none of these ever sways Jacquensica away from looking for an answer to what it must take to challenge for a definitive cure, her people's highly corrupted culture that has dominated three whole generations. Surely, it will require more than intrigues, more than a bloody war...more than the Carnival dances of the masquerade!

ISBN 978-0-9571140-0-5

About the Author

Remi Shitu was born in Nigeria. He studied Textile Technology and Design in Leicester (UK), and Industrial Engineering in Pordenone (Italy). As his working experiences took him round Africa and Europe, he could see many great stories begging to be written. He took the challenge with *Brotherly Shackles*. *The Masquerade* is his second. He lives with his family in the UK.